Lost in the Storm

Ladies of Oberlin, Book 2

By

Tamera Lynn Kraft

Mt Zion Ridge Press LLC
http://www.mtzionridgepress.com

ISBN 13: 978-1-949564-62-4

Published in the United States of America
Publication Date: August 1, 2019

Managing Editors: Tamera Lynn Kraft and Michelle L. Levigne
Editor: Jennifer Kraft
Cover Artist: Tamera Lynn Kraft

Red Sky Over America, Book 1
Lost in the Storm, Book 2
The Aftermath, Book 3 (Coming Soon)

Other Books By Tamera Lynn Kraft

Resurrection of Hope
Alice's Notions
Soldiers Heart, From the Lake to the River Anthology
A Christmas Promise
Forks in the Road (Coming Soon)

The Story Continues

You can read more about the stories surrounding this novel.

Forks in the Road (coming soon) tells the story of Jed Jackson and his orphaned brothers.

Red Sky Over America, ***Ladies of Oberlin Book 1*** tells the story of Lavena's friend and college roommate, America Leighton.

Soldier's Heart (free as an eBook only on the Mt Zion Ridge Press website) is the story of Noah Andrews, a sergeant from the Ohio Seventh, after he returns home. It is also included in **From the Lake to the River: Buckeye Christian Fiction Authors 2019 Anthology**.

The Aftermath, due to release in 2020, continues the story of Nate and Betsy Teagan and Cage and Lavena.

I hope you enjoy all of them.

Dedication and Acknowledgment

I dedicate this novel to my daughter, Veronica Harris, who loves the Lord with all her heart. Her career as a Christian mental health counselor is a calling from God, but her love for God and her love for her family are the most important things in her life. I am very proud of the woman she has become.

I would like to acknowledge the brave men of the Ohio Seventh Regiment during the US Civil War, also known as the Rooster Regiment. As I was researching this regiment, I was amazed at what I found. This regiment earned the title, "most heroic Union regiment of the Civil War." I paid honor to some of the real men in this regiment by having them in my novel, including Colonel William Creighton, Lieutenant-Colonel Orin J. Crane, Major Dr. Jason Patella, Lieutenant John Regan, and some of the generals in Chattanooga at the time, including General Ulysses S. Grant. Colonel Creighton and Lieutenant-Colonel Crane died at the Battle of Ringgold Gap on November 27th, 1863.

Chapter One

September 18th, 1863, Cleveland, Ohio

Lavena Falcon, mouth drawn in a thin line, marched down Prospect Avenue with as much bluster as a Lake Erie squall. This time, she wouldn't back down.

She shielded her eyes from the bright sun and avoided plummeting into two women who chatted in front of the corner grocery. Yellow leaves crunched under her feet as she made a dash for the East Cleveland streetcar. She stepped up just before it rattled down the track.

The wooden benches were filled to capacity, so she grabbed hold of a strap hanging from the roof above them. An older chap with balding gray hair stood and offered his seat, but she shook her head, and the man sat back down. She wasn't about to take a seat from an elderly gentleman only because of her gender.

The car jerked, and Lavena strengthened her hold to keep from toppling. Her boss, Brian O'Brady, would have her resignation if he ever sent her to report on another Ladies Aide Society Meeting again. She sighed. Of course, she would never quit the only large newspaper that would hire a woman, but it was tempting.

She stepped off the streetcar and blew across Superior Avenue with a gust of yellow leaves falling from the green ash trees lining the street. Reaching the brick newspaper building where she worked, she pushed through the door.

The office bustled with activity. Because *The Cleveland Leader* had morning and evening penny editions, the newsroom never slept. Men with their sleeves rolled up sat at rows of desks writing out copy for typesetters and paid no attention to the roar of the steam-powered double cylinder rotary printing presses in the back. Suit jackets slung over their chairs, and cigar smoke circled their heads.

No matter how much she wanted to confront her boss the moment she returned, she had a story to write, and in the newspaper business, getting stories in on time were more important than any personal consideration. She'd never failed to do that yet, and she didn't intend to now.

The only thing more important to her than getting a story in on time was reporting the truth in a way that enriched society without destroying people needlessly. She'd always strived to accomplish both goals.

She removed her bonnet and let her dark brown braid fall over her shoulder then stepped over to the box stove in the corner of the room and started boiling a pot of water for bohea tea, a strong blend of black tea leaves.

Sitting at the desk nearest to the stove, she dipped her pen in a bottle of ink. She blew out a breath to calm her anger and wrote about the noble women who knitted socks and harvested fruit for soldiers far away from home and hearth. Their simple deed would help the Ohio Seventh Volunteer Regiment get through the cold winter.

She blotted the paper, marched to the office on the right, and knocked on the oak door. An indistinguishable grumble came from the other side which she took to mean she should enter. Pulling up her four-feet-eleven, ninety-pound frame, she squared her shoulders for battle and thrust through.

Brian O'Brady sat at a desk with papers stacked in uneven piles competing over which could get highest without falling. The stack on the far-right corner in front held the lead.

O'Brady, managing editor second only to Mr. Edwin Cowles himself, had reddish brown hair and whiskers as unkempt as his desk. Lavena suspected the cigar sticking out of his mouth was permanently attached.

He grunted. "Do you have the story?"

She handed him the paper and waited for him to read it.

O'Brady chomped on his cigar. "This will do fine. By tomorrow, every lady in Cleveland will be knitting socks for the troops."

Lavena set her hands flat on the desk and glared into her editor's eyes. "It's the last time."

Mr. O'Brady met her glower. "Miss Falcon, you'll write whatever story I assign you or you'll be reporting on the next dog show at Public Square."

She crossed her arms but didn't falter her gaze.

"I don't know what you're fussing about. You wanted to report on the war. This is a war story."

"Knitting socks?" Lavena sputtered. "A war story?"

"They're knitting them for the soldiers."

"I don't know how they have enough time to finish any. They're too busy trying to marry me off to their cousins, nephews, and sons too cowardly or sickly to enlist."

O'Brady chortled.

Lavena hoped a blush wouldn't show through her olive complexion. "Are you laughing at me?"

"No… no, All those busy bodies at the Ladies Aide Society met their match in you, lass."

She allowed a smile to cross her lips. Somehow, he had a way of getting past her defenses. "Any news yet?"

O'Brady took the cigar out of his mouth. A small piece of tobacco, reluctant to leave, clung to his lower lip. "What do you want from me? I told you we need a man for this job."

She pointed her finger at his chest and shook it. "I deserve this assignment. I got you the interview with the men accused of the Oberlin Wellington slave rescue, didn't I?"

A few days after Lavena had graduated from Oberlin College, slave catchers from Kentucky apprehended a fugitive slave in Oberlin, Ohio and took him to nearby Wellington to catch the train to Maysville, Kentucky. Half the town followed them, and a group of men forcibly took the captive away from his abductors. Many were arrested under the Fugitive Slave Act in what became the national news story of 1858. Her reporting garnered support for the Oberlin Twenty and gained their eventual release.

"Your friends helped you there, lass." The tobacco dropped off O'Brady's mouth and landed on her story. "You were lucky Teagan and Woods were the husbands of your college roommates at Oberlin, or you never would have been able to get those exclusive interviews. Besides, Woods was never charged."

She groaned. "Only because he and his wife left for China to become missionaries before the warrants were issued. That article was great reporting, and you know it. It influenced half the city of Cleveland to support the Oberlin Twenty's cause and rally against the Fugitive Slave Law."

"I know. You landed this job because of it, but you're still a woman." O'Brady flicked the stray piece of tobacco off the paper onto the floor.

Laying her hands flat on the desk, she leaned in. "What about the story on Copeland and the other men who tied in with John Brown?"

John Brown, an abolitionist from Ohio, raided Harper's Ferry, Virginia in 1859 to start an uprising among slaves. His raid failed, and he was captured and hung.

"Another fine piece of work, I grant you, but the only reason you got an interview with Copeland before he hung was because he attended college with you too." O'Brady flashed her a grin. "Part of your value is your associations with rebel rousers such as yourself."

The wind escaping her lungs, Lavena slumped into the spindle-back wooden chair. "What do I have to do to get the war correspondent job?"

"Nothing. I'm not going to send a lady in harm's way with a regiment of soldiers. It wouldn't be decent."

"There are other women in the camp." She hated this. She had come in her demanding the job, and now she sounded like a scolded child.

He grunted. "Wash women and nurses, not ladies." Grabbing the arms of her chair, he delivered a sober expression. "You're the best reporter I have and the only female reporter in the history of *The Leader*. If you were a man, you'd have my job by now. Why is reporting on the war so important to you?"

Lavena let out a gusty sigh. "These men aren't just battling for the

Union to stay together, they're fighting for freedom from the tyranny of slavery-- even if President Lincoln won't admit it. Once coloreds are given their freedom and seen as equals, men will see the good judgement in granting voting rights to women. These are causes I've strived for all my life. If I weren't a lady, I'd enlist. Let me at least document their story."

"Oh lass, what can I say?" He went to his desk chair and slunk into it. "I know your passion for the cause, but you'll never be a man, and that's what's needed for the correspondent position. The man we choose will be announced next week at the press meeting."

Lavena's eyes burned. She blinked, stood, and walked to the door as gracefully as she could muster. "I need to get back to work."

*****

Rapidan River, Virginia

Captain Macajah "Cage" Jones' heart pounded in beat with the drums as Union soldiers herded two prisoners across the saturated field to stand in front of wooden coffins. They staggered as their feet made sucking noises in the mud.

The lads were young, maybe eighteen, but Cage doubted it. One boy, a towhead, didn't even have peach fuzz on his face. They were thin, one tall, the other short. They had families, maybe a mother whose heart would break when she heard of their fate. Even sadder if they'd joined up young because they were orphans with nobody to grieve their loss.

Cage's thoughts flickered to Lieutenant Nathaniel Teagan, and a shiver went through him. If Union soldiers captured Nate, this might be his fate.

The drums halted.

General Slocum, perched on his gray horse, read the order of execution. His stoic expression implied the command could have been about anything from supplies arriving to an unexpected mail call. He handed the order to the sergeant-at-arms without a glance toward the prisoners. With a smack to his stallion's rump, he galloped off the field away from this unpleasant business.

The guards tied blindfolds over the deserters' eyes and directed them to sit on their caskets. One corporal, a thin man with a bushy mustache, squeezed the youngest boy's shoulder and whispered in his ear. The boy tilted his chin and squared his shoulders.

The corporal nodded to the guards, and they took their places in a V-shape to the right and left of the condemned.

The sound of the sergeant-at-arms' baritone voice rose over the prattle of raindrops.

"Ready…"

The execution squad loaded their muskets.

Cage fixed his eyes on the dogwood trees lining the swelling river and the moisture dripping from them, anything to divert his attention from the twisted mouths of the boys waiting to die. Two raindrops hit the ground and echoed as loud as the drums had been. Or was it the beat of his heart keeping time with them?

"Aim..."

The men leveled the muskets toward the prisoners and pulled back the hammers.

The leaves on one of the trees had died and turned red.

Two more drops thumped. Cage clenched his jaw and blinked twice.

"Fire."

Gunshots exploded with flashes and clouds of smoke.

The taller boy's body spun, twitched, and plunged to the ground.

The younger one pulled off his blindfold, revealing the fear in his eyes, and causing his blond hair to stick up in odd places.

The first-row firing squad had missed him, perhaps on purpose. If Cage had been part of the squad, he would have aimed for the older boy.

"Second squad."

The men moved aside, and the second row loaded and aimed their weapons.

A whimper escaped the boy's lips. He climbed over his coffin and ran toward the dogwood trees.

"Fire."

The gunshots blasted.

A wail pierced Cage's ears. The boy's body lurched, and his legs buckled under him. Blood gushed from his arm.

"Reload."

Both squads reloaded and marched toward the boy.

"Fire at will."

The boy's blue eyes widened as he staggered to his feet. His voice rasped. "Please no please no please no please." He ran a few steps into a pile of wet leaves then quivered against the dead dogwood.

Executioners closed in, pulled back their hammers, and pointed rifles in the boy's face and chest.

Cage forced his eyes to stay fixed on the scene no matter how hard his stomach threatened to empty its contents. His men had to watch, so he would too.

Guns boomed, and the boy's blood mixed with crimson leaves and brown mud. Drums hammered. Executioners marched off the field in beat with the dirge.

Cage strode to his tent without a word while guards tossed the bodies into coffins and nailed them shut. The injustice of it choked him.

Two scared boys dead in a Virginia field. He'd done worse, and they gave him a medal.

Chapter Two

The door opened briskly.

Betsy Teagan, Lavena's roommate, stood motionless in the doorway with her sky-blue, satin, hoop dress covered in sludge and her fashionable ivory lace boots with two-inch heels caked in mud and dried leaves. Her blond curls matted around her face, and her feathered plume set askew on the side of her head.

Lavena sprang from her chair. "What happened to you?"

Betsy tried to wipe the mud off her skirt but only managed to spread it. "I landed in a puddle in the middle of Public Square." She swiped a curl from her face leaving a smear of dirt on her cheek. "I didn't look where I was going and tripped over a tree root."

Lavena tried to hold back a chuckle, but it insisted on being released.

"Please, don't tease. This is important." Betsy pulled a handkerchief out of her pocket and wiped off the mud and a stray tear running down her cheek before planting herself in a straight-back chair propped against the wall.

Lavena poured a cup of tea. As tempted as she was to use this opportunity to show Betsy how cumbersome her fine attire was, the look on her roommate's face showed this had to be about more than falling in the mud.

Kneeling by the chair, she placed Betsy's hand in hers. "What's wrong?"

"I received a letter from Nate's commanding officer." She gazed at the mud on her dress and tried to straighten out her skirt. When she spoke again, it was barely a whisper. "Nate's been missing for over a month."

"Oh, Bets." Lavena swallowed the ache in the back of her throat. "I'm sorry."

"You don't understand." Betsy's hands trembled. "They say he deserted."

Lavena stood as a chill traveled up her spine. Nate, a coward? She wanted to say something to comfort her friend but couldn't think of a word to utter. She would have never thought it of him. She let out a sigh. Hadn't she learned long ago men can't be trusted?

"I don't believe it." Betsy's chin quivered. "He risked his life and our marriage too many times to forsake the cause now."

Lavena handed her the tea. "Why would they say he'd deserted if it wasn't true? It's like I've tol…" She stopped short. Even though she'd warned Betsy many times not to depend on any man with her future, not even someone as seemingly honorable as Nate, this wasn't the time to remind her of that.

"I don't know why they think he would do something like that. My husband bleeds blue, and a letter from his captain isn't going to convince me otherwise." Betsy gazed at the nectar swirling in her cup. "I need to find out what happened."

"How can you do that? It's not like you can travel there alone during wartime. Besides, what if he's…" Lavena drew her hand to her mouth.

The teacup rattled. "He's not dead. If he were, I'd feel it." Betsy set the tea down spilling a little on the desk and tried to wipe the droplets with her soiled, embroidered handkerchief. All she managed to do was wipe mud on the desk. "I need your help."

Lavena took out her own plain white handkerchief and wiped up the mess then handed it to Betsy. "What can I do?"

Betsy wiped her face and blew her nose. "I tried to book passage on a train to Chattanooga. His family's plantation is close to there, but nobody will sell me a ticket."

"I'm not surprised. The trains are being used to move troops." Lavena said. "Besides, it's too dangerous for you to travel alone in the middle of a war, let alone to a city under siege by Confederate troops."

"You could get a train ticket." Betsy's blue eyes lit up for the first time since she walked into the newsroom. "If you get that job, you could find out what happened."

"The assignment's going to another reporter." Lavena swallowed some tea to keep from showing the heaviness of disappointment sweeping over her. "Even if I could change my boss's mind, I'd be with the Ohio Seventh, and last I heard, they're in Virginia, not Tennessee."

"Maybe you could talk to Nate's commanding officer and some of his fellow soldiers, see what they know. Please, Lavena, you're my only hope."

"Let me see the letter."

Betsy handed it to her.

Lavena read it until her gaze landed on a familiar name. "You didn't tell me Nate's commanding officer was Captain Macajah Jones."

"So."

"The Cage Jones? The hero of Cedar Mountain?" If the reports could be believed, Captain Jones was too good to be true. She'd do whatever she had to for a chance to interview him.

Betsy raised her eyebrow. "What are you planning?"

"Wait here." Lavena pushed the door open and stormed into Brian O'Brady's office.

O'Brady glanced up and groaned. "Lass, you're going to be the death of me yet. What's so urgent you couldn't knock?"

She crossed her arms and gazed at him a moment until she was sure she had his full attention. "If you choose me, I'll get you the story of a lifetime."

"The story of a lifetime? Seems I've heard promises like that before." Her boss ran his hand through his reddish hair. "All right. What's this story of a lifetime only you can get?"

"Do you remember meeting my friend, Mrs. Teagan?"

"Yes, of course. She's staying with you until her husband returns from the war. What does she have to do with this?"

"She received a letter from her husband's commanding officer. Seems Lieutenant Teagan has deserted. She doesn't believe it and wants me to travel there to find out what really happened."

"This newspaper is committed to reporting about the brave men who are fighting for the honor of their country, not some coward who—"

"That's not the story." Lavena allowed the corners of her mouth to turn up. "The officer who wrote the letter is Captain Macajah Jones from the Ohio Seventh Volunteer Infantry Regiment."

O'Brady's cigar dropped out of his mouth.

Lavena chuckled. "My associations, as you call them, have come through again. I guarantee you an interview and a story you'll never match with another reporter. And while I'm there, I'll report on the progress of the Ohio Seventh."

"Anyone I send could give me updates." O'Brady scrambled to retrieve his cigar. "If you can get an interview Captain Jones, I might even get the boss to allow me to send a lady into war."

"I'll get the story. Before I'm done, he'll tell me everything." She'd find out if the man was really a hero.

"Think what you're saying, lass. The captain has never granted an interview to anyone. The last reporter who tried got a punch in the mouth and was kicked out of camp. What makes you think he won't do the same with you?"

"As you said, I am a lady."

"That you are, lass. That you are." O'Brady relit his cigar. "I know I'll live to regret this, but I'll talk to Mr. Cowles. I can't give you the job without his approval."

"Is he in his office?"

O'Brady raised an eyebrow as the hint of a grin reached his eyes. "Mighty quick to feed me to the lions, aren't you, lass?"

Lavena couldn't hide the smirk spreading across her face.

"All right. I'll ask him now." O'Brady marched to his office door and opened it. "In the meantime, get back to work. You have two stories assigned to you that still need written. If you think you're going to leave me in the lurch while you go gallivanting off to war, you'd better think again."

Lavena kissed his cheek. "Thank you."

O'Brady turned red. "Nice as that was, Cowles might not say yes. You're still a woman."

"He won't miss a chance for this interview to be published in his paper, even if I am the wrong gender."

O'Brady took off in the direction of the publisher's office as she made her way back to the newsroom.

She spotted Betsy sipping tea at her desk and let out a groan. She would follow the truth wherever it led even if it would devastate her friend. Nate had risked his life more than once rescuing slaves before the war, but men wore honor like women wore hats, easily put on or removed as the situation warranted. Apparently, he was no different.

She sat beside Betsy. "Mr. O'Brady is talking to the editor now."

"Promise me…" Betsy's voice cracked. "Promise you'll do your best to find Nate."

"There's no guarantee Mr. Cowles will even agree to this."

Betsy wiped a tear from the corner of her eye.

"I'll do my best." Lavena touched her arm wanting to soften the blow of what she was going to say. "If Nate is guilty and I find him, he'll most likely face the firing squad. Maybe we should let this be."

Betsy blinked. "You'll see. This is all some kind of a misunderstanding." She rose from her chair and set the teacup on Lavena's desk. "I'm a mess." She blinked back the tears. "I must go home to bathe and change."

Lavena escorted her to the door. "I'll be there as soon as I can."

The door clanged shut behind Betsy. Lavena tried to concentrate on a story she was writing, but she couldn't help catching an occasional glance toward Mr. Cowles' door. Five minutes passed, and she hadn't written a word. She dipped her pen in ink, set it on the page, and sighed. She wasn't going to get any work done until she heard their decision.

O'Brady came out of Mr. Cowles' office and motioned for Lavena to follow him. He closed the door behind her and slunk into his chair, his furrowed brow and bulging Adam's apple telling her everything she needed to know.

She pressed her lips together, determined not to display her disappointment. "So, he said no then."

He gouged at the back of his neck. "He said yes. Congratulations, Miss Falcon. If you want the spot, you're our new war correspondent."

Her stomach fluttered, and she resisted the urge to cheer. "Thank you. I'll do a good job for you."

"Hold up now, lass. You can refuse the position."

She slipped into her seat. "Why would I want to do that?"

He leaned back in his chair causing it to squeak. "There are conditions."

"What conditions?"

"First condition." He held up his pointer finger and locked eyes with her. "You'll be under the protection of the Ohio Seventh Regiment and Colonel Creighton. Give me your word you'll follow his directives for your protection and the safety of his men."

"You know I'm not good at following orders."

"I know better than anyone, but I'm still waiting for your promise."

Lavena tapped her fingers on the arms of her chair. "Fine, you have my word." Why didn't O'Brady just come out with it? She'd never known him to be so evasive. "What else?"

"This is a temporary post. You'll leave the beginning of October and only have one month to prove yourself."

"One month?" Her mouth gaped open.

O'Brady chomped hard on his cigar and held up a second finger. "Not only do you need to send me weekly stories by mail or telegraph whenever you have the chance," he set the cigar on the edge of a highest pile of papers and allowed the ashes to flick onto the floor, "you have to get that interview. We need to hear the story of heroism and honor from the captain himself, something that will cause our lady readers to swoon and the men to enlist, or something just as sensational in his own words."

"Of course." A nudging doubt caused her stomach to tighten. "That's why he's dispatching me there, but why would Mr. Cowles bother with the expense of sending me for only one month?"

He stood. "Because if you don't get the interview by November first, Mr. Cowles says there are plenty of men reporters who can take your place."

She expected as much. "So, if I don't get the story, you'll cart me back here on the next train." Being a woman, she had to get twice the results of any reporter on the paper. "I understand. If I fail, I'll be reporting on ladies' social events for the foreseeable future. At least it's a chance."

"No." O'Brady walked around the desk knocking the butt of his cigar on the floor along with some of the papers. He ignored them. "If you get us an interview with Captain Macajah Jones, this post becomes permanent. If you don't, you won't have to worry about writing any stories for this newspaper ever again. You cotton my meaning, lass?"

Her face flushed. "Are you saying if I don't get this story, I'm sacked?"

O'Brady cleared his throat.

"That's not fair. I've done a good job here. Why would he discharge me?"

"It's politics." O'Brady chewed off the end of another cigar and lit it. "This paper has always stood for equality of women and Negros, but Cowles believes a moderate approach is the best way to change things. The way you're spouting off in your news copy makes his advertisers nervous. This is an easy way to get rid of the problem."

Her ribcage felt like it had been gripped by one of those confounded corsets she refused to wear. "I can't believe it." She stood. "Knowing this is the only newspaper in Northeast Ohio that dares to hire a woman, he plans to give me an impossible task so he can boot me out the door?"

"I'm afraid so." He stood, picked up the scattered papers on the floor, and piled them on the corner of the desk. His hand rested on one pile. "You don't have to do it." He turned toward her. "Refuse his offer, and you can keep your job. I'll make sure you get the best assignments here in Cleveland. By the time I'm done, Mr. Cowles won't dare let you go."

It was a tempting offer. Lavena took pride in doing her part to influence her community through her stories. As much as she wanted this assignment, it wasn't worth losing her career and the chance to make a real difference.

She set a hand on the corner of O'Brady's desk to steady herself. "How long do I have to decide?"

"We make an announcement in one week. I'll need to know by then."

Lavena had graduated at the top of her class at Oberlin College, but that didn't matter. If she was dismissed, the only job she would be able to get as a woman with a degree was as a schoolmarm or governess, and she doubted anyone would hire her. Her radical views would keep most parents from allowing her to teach their children.

Nor would she resort to becoming a telegraph operator. Two skills she'd learned to prepare for a career in journalism were shorthand and Morse code, but the idea of setting at a table tapping out messages for other people all day made her a bit ill. Not that they'd hire a woman anyway.

Maybe it was foolish to push the boundaries further than she already had. "I'll let you know by then."

Chapter Three

Lavena stood outside her apartment on the second floor above Superior Textile and Tailor, a company that made wool uniforms for soldiers. It had been a long day, and she wanted nothing more than to eat the dinner Betsy would have waiting for her and sink into her warm bed.

She wasn't ready for a conversation about why she wasn't taking the job she'd dreamed of for so long. Letting out a sigh, she opened the door and slipped through.

Betsy had cleaned up and changed into a blue, satin, hoop dress with pink roses embroidered into it and was concentrating on a pot cooking over the potbelly stove in the corner of the room. She didn't look up.

Lavena sank into a rocker by the window and leaned back her head. The banging of the looms and roaring of the sewing machines emerged through the floor competing with her thunderous thoughts. As much as she had wanted this assignment, her stomach knotted like a seaman's rope.

If she took this post, her career as a reporter would hinge on getting an interview with Captain Macajah Jones. Mr. O'Brady had made that clear. No other reporter had been able to pry more than two words out of the captain. The knots tightened. To make matters worse, she would only have one month to accomplish it.

No story, no job.

She'd gone over it a thousand times. This might be the chance of a lifetime, but she couldn't accept. If she agreed to it and failed, how would she support herself?

Nobody would hire her as a teacher after some of the articles she'd written on women's equality. She hated the idea of scratching out a living as a wash woman or a maid, but she wasn't about to crawl back to New York for her maiden aunt to support her. Marrying some man who didn't have the gumption to enlist and fight for his country so she could be provided for was out of the question. She'd starve first.

She'd heard of some women pretending to be men and enlisting, but she would never do such a thing. She couldn't abide lying.

That left the nursing corp, but she became nauseous at the site of blood. Besides, nursing wasn't considered a reputable profession, and she might never be able to report the news again if she did.

Maybe that was reason enough not to go to the battlefield. Journalism was more than a way to make a living. It was a calling from God every bit as strong as her best friend America Woods' call to the mission field.

She missed America at times like these. She could use her friend's insight about now. Two days after William and America's wedding, the couple left on a train bound for New York. From there, they boarded a ship bound for China. Last she'd heard, they'd opened an orphanage and a church in Ningpo.

Lavena willed her breathing to slow to a steady rhythm. She wanted to be a part of the Ohio Seventh and write this story more than she'd ever wanted anything. She'd read of the heroism of Captain Macajah Jones. Hearing his saga gave her hope there were heroes in this world, men she could trust.

Hadn't Mr. O'Brady and Father Finney, president of Oberlin College proved there were decent men in the world? What about those fighting honorably on battlefields all over the country? Not every man was like her father.

She let out a sigh. Nate's desertion had brought back all the pain, the betrayal. She'd do anything to spare her friend the torment she'd gone through.

"Supper's on," Betsy said.

Lavena grabbed plates from the cupboard across from the stove, set the small wooden table in the middle of the room, and shook away her romantic notions of honor. Captain Jones would be no different than the others. He was probably avoiding reporters for a nefarious reason.

If he wasn't the man everyone thought him to be, she'd find out. She'd expose him as the hypocrite he was.

Another reason not to take this assignment.

It was an unusually warm day for late September, and they'd left the small window on the back wall open. The aroma of fresh bread traveled from the bakery across the street. Betsy dished out stew, cut some bread they'd bought there the day before, and sat at the table across from Lavena.

They blessed the meal, and Lavena brought a spoon full of stew to her lips.

"So, what happened?" Betsy asked. "What did Mr. O'Brady say? Did you get the job? Where are you headed? We need to sew you a new dress for the trip."

Lavena set her spoon down without eating anything. "I didn't exactly get the assignment."

"I'm so sorry. I know how much you were hoping for this."

"I didn't not get it either."

Betsy tilted her head. "Only you could get the job and not get it at the same time."

Lavena snorted. "I am remarkable." As they ate, she told Betsy what happened.

"One month. That certainly doesn't give you much time. When do you leave?"

"Give me a chance to have my tea first." Lavena poured water into the copper kettle and set it on the box stove to boil. Reaching for two teacups and saucers with yellow daffodils painted on them, she set them on the sideboard by the table.

Different tins sat on the shelf about waist high in the large wooden cupboard. Lavena chose the green tea, a soothing blend from Twinings of London, and spooned the leaves into the pot.

Most of her leaves came from a tea room on Superior Avenue close to the newspaper office. Twinings was her favorite brand, but she was running low. Because of the war shortages, she had to settle for local blends.

She loved her tea as much as Betsy loved fine clothes. Sipping good tea was almost a prayer where God held her in his arms and promised everything would be all right. Only this time, a cup of tea wouldn't fix anything.

Like her, most Oberlin College graduates didn't use sugar, salt, coffee, or tobacco believing these products to be unhealthy and therefore ungodly. Some didn't even drink tea, but Lavena believed that was taking the austere lifestyle too far since she was sure tea was the nectar God created.

When the kettle sputtered, she poured hot water into the teapot and turned over the three-minute hourglass on the counter to time the steeping. When the sand ran through, she poured it through a strainer into the cups and sat on the bench across from Betsy.

She wrapped her hands around the cup. "I'm not accepting the job."

Betsy lifted a single eyebrow and glared at Lavena as if she'd suddenly grown another head. "You've talked about this every day for the last three months. Of course, you're accepting the job."

"Haven't you heard a word I've said?" Lavena flustered. "If I do this, I'll be discharged from the newspaper. How will we live without income?"

Betsy poured some tea in her saucer to cool. "You'll find a way to get that interview. Even if you don't, we have Nate's army income."

Now it was Lavena's turn to raise an eyebrow. "Do you really think they're going to continue to pay him when he's deserted?"

Betsy's mouth formed a perfect o. "I hadn't thought of that." She took a sip of tea. "Something will turn up. After all, we are accomplished women. There aren't many female college graduates."

"As long as I don't take this assignment, we don't have to worry about it. I'll still have my job at the newspaper, and Mr. O'Brady has promised me better stories. No more Cleveland Ladies Society meetings or dog shows if I stay."

"I suppose there's nothing you can do about Nate then." Betsy stood and looked out the open window.

Lavena took a sip of tea, relieved Betsy was being sensible about this. "I wish I could help, but it's impossible."

"I'll volunteer to become a nurse for the Union Army in Tennessee. There was an advertisement in the newspaper looking for applicants. Since I worked for a doctor when I was at Oberlin College, I'm sure they accept me."

"Betsy, you can't." Lavena stood. "Being a nurse in wartime is different than working for a small-town doctor. You don't know what it's like out there."

"Doesn't matter. My mind is made up." Betsy dabbed her eyes with her handkerchief.

Lavena let out a snort. "And how do you plan to get there? It's a long way to walk."

"I'm sure they'll provide transportation to Chattanooga. If they don't, I'll buy a rig and drive down there on my own."

Lavena's mouth gaped open. "You're going to drive a horse and buggy clear to Tennessee in the middle of a war? Have you lost your senses?"

Betsy shrugged. "I have to do something."

"You need to face facts." Lavena placed a hand on Betsy's shoulder. She hated to be so direct, but in this case, it was a kindness. "You can't do anything to save your husband now."

Betsy's eyes narrowed, but she spoke in a calm manner that shook Lavena more than if she'd yelled or sobbed. "I don't care what Captain Jones, or the US Army, or you say. Nate didn't desert, and he didn't betray his country. He would have died first. If you won't help me, I'll do what I have to do to prove it."

Lavena let out a sigh. "Why are you so sure?"

"I know my husband." Betsy pressed her lips together. "His causes were always more important to him than I was. He never really wanted to settle down. I honestly don't know why he married me. He was too busy fighting for a better nation without me instead of starting a family with me."

"Nate adored you, but he wanted a land where freedom and opportunity are available to all men regardless of their color." Lavena poured some tea in her saucer to cool. She didn't want to admit it, but there was a ring of truth in what Betsy said. It didn't make sense for him to desert.

Betsy sipped her tea. "Did you know he almost got entangled with John Brown and the Harper Ferry Raid?"

Lavena gasped. She did hear rumors Nate was involved somehow, but she never believed them. "What happened?"

"Mr. Brown contacted him when he was in jail for the Oberlin Wellington rescue, but Nate didn't go through with it. I thought he changed his mind because of me, but I had nothing to do with it. A month later, he took off to Tennessee to rescue slaves. When he finally did come back, he promised he would stay put."

"You could have gone with him."

"I wanted to. I begged him to let me come along, but he wouldn't hear of it. He said I was too delicate for a dangerous mission like this." Betsy lifted her pinkie as she took a sip of tea. "I'm stronger than he thinks I am."

"Then you should have carried on with your life instead of waiting for him. You could have gone to medical school and became a doctor."

Betsy's shoulders heaved.

Lavena saw she was upsetting her friend and tried to soften her tone. "I know you were angry, but I thought you'd resolved things. When he enlisted, you went to the train station to see him off."

"That's not why I was there. I told him, if he left me, not to bother coming home." A sob came from Betsy's lips. "You know Nate. He said this had nothing to do with his love for me, and I succumbed to his charms-- again. After the train pulled out and his allure wore off, I decided to show him I meant what I said."

Lavena set her cup down. "What did you do?"

"He wrote letters, but I ignored them." Betsy picked up her teacup to take a sip but pulled it back before it reached her lips. "A few months ago, I wrote to him and told him if I received any more letters, I'd burn them."

"Oh Bets."

Her teacup rattled. "When I received the post saying he deserted, I knew it wasn't true. If he had any doubts about what he was doing, he wouldn't have risked his marriage."

Lavena stood and looked out the window trying to think of a way to help. Smoke billowed from the restaurant chimney like Indian smoke signals but didn't provide any answers. "Maybe your husband isn't the man you thought he was. After hearing about his desertion, I wonder if he really did rescue slaves in Tennessee. Maybe he reunited with his family and was too ashamed to admit he'd changed his mind."

"No! He wouldn't." Betsy set her cup on the table. "His father disowned him, and he hated him for it. If he did desert, it had nothing to do with that. It's because of what I wrote." Her eyes watered, and she dabbed them with her pink handkerchief. "It's all my fault. Oh, Lavena, if they catch him... What am I going to do?"

"If he took the cowardly way out, that's because of his own shortcomings, not yours."

Betsy blew her nose and stared at her hands. Then she gazed at Lavena, the resolve evident in her eyes. "Looks like he's not the only one. You were set on becoming a war correspondent, and you're shrinking back because you might lose your precious job."

"That's not fair. It's not the same thing at all."

"I don't know." Betsy gave a half-grin, "It sounds like Nate's not the only one taking the cowardly way out. I guess those grand words about being a part of it all were just words."

Lavena's cheeks burned. "Fiddlesticks." She'd never thought of herself as a coward. The awareness of it made her nauseous.

"All my life, people have treated me like a delicate flower as if I can't do anything on my own. That's why I went to Oberlin College, to prove I had the fortitude to do something important, but you and Nate treat me the same way. Just because I wear fine clothes and want to be a wife and a mother doesn't mean I can't rise to the occasion. You may be too afraid to go down there and find out what's going on, but I'm not."

Was it possible she'd misjudged Betsy? Her confidence in her husband made her stronger than Lavena ever thought she could be. Betsy, like Lavena, knew what it was like to have her heart crushed by a man, but she still had the courage to trust him.

Lavena pressed her lips together. She'd never backed down from a challenge before. She needed to get this story from Captain Jones and to find out what happened to Nate no matter what the cost. Hopefully what she found wouldn't crush her friend. "I'm taking the job."

Chapter Four

September 30

Lavena stepped into the hallway outside her apartment. Mr. O'Brady had tried to convince her to change her mind, telling her, she didn't have to prove anything to him, but she needed to do this, not only to succeed at her career and advance equality for women, but to find out the truth for Betsy.

He'd finally given his blessing and announced the assignment in the newsroom. The anger and frustration of the men who were being considered for the assignment choked the air out of the room, but after a few tense moments, they'd congratulated her.

Mr. O'Brady spent the rest of the day giving her instructions and warning her once again she only had until the beginning of November to get that interview, as if she needed reminded. The Ohio Seventh had been ordered to join Grant's troops in Chattanooga. She would catch up with their train in Columbus on October first. She would obey all orders given to her by Union officers, and she wouldn't get in the way during any skirmishes.

He had ended the lecture with a warning she would answer to him if she got herself wounded or killed. She thought about asking how she would answer to him if she were killed, but she'd held her tongue.

When Betsy had found out where Lavena was headed, she'd been thrilled. Lavena would end up only a few miles from the Teagan Plantation where Nate's family lived. Betsy was sure it was an answer to prayer. Lavena wished she could agree.

Wearing a pink hoop-skirt dress and a wide-brimmed hat with matching pink ribbons, Betsy waited for her by the stairwell holding an embroidered pink-flowered handkerchief in one hand and some letters in the other.

Lavena clutched her carpetbag, feeling more nervous than she had the first day she attended Oberlin College. She normally considered herself a confident woman, but this venture made her knees weaken.

What if she found out Nate had deserted? Betsy would be devastated. Lavena had to admit she would be just as distraught if she didn't get the interview with Captain Jones. Her journalism career was too important to her to throw away on a fool's errand.

Mr. O'Brady had told her the Seventh regiment would provide a tent and food rations but not much else, so she'd packed a couple of camp dresses, a blanket, and the supplies she needed.

She also brought the blue and green flowered Turkish bloomer outfit she'd made in college. It included bloomer trousers gathered at the ankles with a ruffle for modesty and a day dress covering it to the knees. It was practical, and she believed one day, women all over the country would be wearing trousers.

Lavena had packed away her bloomers when she became a reporter. People tended to be uncomfortable when she wore them, and she needed them to relax when she interviewed them. On the battlefield, she was sure she could make use of them again.

She'd also packed three containers of her favorite tea leaves, a tin cup, a small cookpot, and a small copper teapot. She may have been going to war, but she wouldn't go without her tea. It could be the only comfort she had.

"This is it." She turned around so Betsy could inspect her.

Even if she was traveling to the battle lines in time of war and should wear her usual austere clothing, train travel was exciting and called for something more festive. She wore her Sunday best for the journey, a dark green wool day dress with moderately spacious sleeves, a jeweled neckline with white piping, and a skirt whose width wasn't too cumbersome. Her brown wool tweed coat completed the look and would provide the warmth she needed as winter months approached.

She even wore her hair in a bun wrapped in a snood instead of braiding it like she normally did. She was pleased with the way it turned out. Ladylike, but practical.

"I don't know." Betsy tapped a knuckle against her mouth. "You look lovely, but I still think you should wear my blue velvet frock."

"If I wore dresses as full as yours, the enemy wouldn't have a chance. All I'd have to do is prance around in the field, and your skirts would plow down more Johnny Rebs than a hundred cannons."

Betsy's eyes watered.

A lump formed in Lavena's throat. When would she ever learn to hold her tongue? "Besides, I'm too small to wear your dresses, and we didn't have time to take it in for me."

Betsy nodded and dabbed her eyes. "Before you go, I have two letters for you."

"Two?" Lavena's Aunt Martha wrote her weekly. A heaviness gripped her chest. She could only think of one other person who would write. She wasn't ready to read any letters from him.

Betsy handed her an envelope. "This one's for you."

Lavena read her aunt's return address in the corner and let out a sigh of relief.

"The other is for Nate." Betsy gave her the letter. It was folded and had his name written on the outside of the paper. "I don't mind if you read it, but if you find him, give it to him. Let him know I love him. I'll always love him."

"I'll find out what I can, but I doubt I'll be delivering any letters."

"His family's plantation is near Chattanooga. You might find him there."

"It's unlikely unless he plans to join the enemy."

Betsy handed her another folded paper. "I've written directions to the Teagan Plantation."

Lavena gaped at her. "You expect me to go traipsing through enemy territory to find a deserter on Confederate land?"

Betsy shrugged. "You're a newspaper reporter. I thought you'd follow a story no matter where it leads."

"You expect too much. Besides, if I find him, it could mean his apprehension and execution."

Betsy waved her hand. "You won't turn him in. Just give him the letter. Then write me, and I'll join him."

"What?" Lavena could hardly believe what she was hearing. "You'll join him on his father's Confederate plantation? That's treason. Are you crazy?"

"He's my husband. I'll do what I have to, but you'll see. This is all a misunderstanding."

"I might not even find him there."

"In the meantime, I'll apply to join a nursing corp for Tennessee. They'll find me some transportation there."

This misguided loyalty her friend felt toward her husband would crush her. Lavena let out a sigh. She knew what it was like to have her heart crushed by dishonorable men.

*****

Captain Cage listened to the chugging to the train's wheels barreling through the wooded hillsides of West Virginia. His leg cramped, and since he didn't have room to stretch it out sitting wedged among forty of his men, he stood and leaned against the wall.

His stomach rumbled. They'd stopped to eat dinner, but even the smell of food threatened to make him sick.

Even here, carnage followed the men of the Ohio Seventh Regiment. As they trundled into Grafton, a sergeant known as Santa jumped off the train and slipped before it had rolled to a stop.

They left the man behind to have his leg amputated.

Colonel William Creighton, his young commanding officer, stepped through the crowded car as Cage and his soldiers, stood, saluted, and squeezed to the sides to make room for him.

The colonel stopped in front of Captain Cage, stood at attention, and returned the salute. "At ease. Step outside with me for a moment, Captain."

Cage relaxed his shoulders and followed the colonel onto the platform between his car and the officer's car. The platform rattled under his feet, and he kept a hand gripped on the railing.

He hadn't been sleeping well, never did on a train. Hopefully the colonel would require a duty that would cause him to collapse into exhaustion and dreamless sleep - one where he didn't hear the screams.

"At the last stop, we received a telegram." Creighton wiped the back of his neck with his hand. "This order comes from General Archibald Reese himself, Captain. I expect you to obey it."

Cage tensed. "I'll do anything required of me, Sir. You know that."

"A man named Falcon is boarding the train tomorrow." The colonel glared at Cage. "I'm assigning him to your company. You'll give him every courtesy."

Cage tugged on his right ear, the one with the scar that trekked across his right cheek to his chin. The scar itched at times. It itched now.

Creighton's green eyes remained fixed. "Mr. Falcon knows Lieutenant Teagan's wife and is interested in finding out more about the desertion."

"I'm still concerned about your plan, Sir. Too many things could go wrong."

"You've already made your reservations known," Colonel Creighton said. "I expect you to be discreet and to obey orders."

"Yes, Sir."

The colonel squared his shoulders making his thin frame look more imposing. "Falcon's a journalist with *The Cleveland Leader*."

The muscle beneath Cage's scar twitched. "I won't do it."

Colonel Creighton marched close enough for his breath to warm Cage's freshly shaven face causing it to itch even more. "You have no choice. Falcon's publisher is a friend of General Grant."

Cage jutted his square chin. "No, Sir."

"Captain, this is a direct order. You will tell this reporter everything about the incident, every detail."

Cage shook his head.

Creighton put his hand on Cage's shoulder. "You can't beg off this time." He stepped back. "Unless you want to spend the rest of the war in the stockade."

"You can't mean that."

"General Grant's orders... and mine."

Cage feared the coronel could hear the hammering in his chest. He snapped to attention, saluted. "Yes, Sir."

The colonel returned the salute.

It was the first time Captain Macajah Jones ever considered disobeying a direct order.

Chapter Five

October 1, 1863, Columbus, Ohio

Lavena ate breakfast at the lean-to dining room attached to Union Station in Columbus. She took a sip of what the cook called tea then moved the cup away. She was tempted to tell him how to make a decent cup, but she refrained.

She opened the letter from Aunt Martha and began reading. The first page caught her up on the news in New York City. Dr. Mary Walker, a personal friend of her aunt's, had been appointed as an army surgeon with the Ohio 52nd. Aunt Martha considered this a victory for the cause of women's rights.

As soon as she had a chance, Lavena would write to Betsy and let her know about Dr. Walker. Betsy would be excited to hear it. At one time, her friend had considered becoming a doctor, but then she met Nate. Why an intelligent women would give up everything for a man was beyond her?

Not that Lavena was against marriage. If a man would allow his wife to maintain a career and not be subservient to him, she would even consider it. She doubted she'd ever find a man like that.

She read on. Aunt Martha expressed her hope Lavena would also further the cause by becoming the first woman war correspondent.

I couldn't be prouder of you if you were my own daughter. Not only have you overcome adversity, but you have thrived showing that you are every bit as capable as any man.

A warmth spread through her that dissipated the chill in the early morning air. Her aunt's praise meant more to her than she could express.

She glanced out the window where yellow and red burst on the horizon as the sun rose. She would write her aunt as soon as possible and let her know that she did indeed become the first woman war correspondent in history even though most people would never know.

Mr. Cowles insisted she continue to use the byline, Lee Falcon. He didn't mind hiring a woman or espousing himself a champion for women's suffrage, but he wouldn't risk losing any advertisers or subscribers by openly admitting to it. She read on.

I'm also proud of the way you have held on to your faith through these trying times. I only have one request. It's time to forgive your father. This bitterness you have toward him is affecting your life in ways you don't realize. Our cause, equality, and the vote for women should not be born out of hatred or distrust for men, rather out of a compassion for all humankind made in the image of a loving God.

Why did her aunt keep pressing this? She would never forgive her father for what he did. How could she?

A train whistle blasted, and Lavena tucked the letter into her wooden lap-desk. She stepped onto the wooden walkway, treading carefully to make sure each footstep landed on the planks resting on the mud path.

The deluge of rain had finally subsided in the middle of the night but not before saturating the ground. After attaining safe passage, she entered the depot. It was a large wooden barn structure, open on both sides, with train tracks running through it.

The whistle blew again, and wheels clacked as the train pulled into the station. Brakes screeched and puffs of steam escaped its smokestack. Before it came to a complete stop, a man wearing the insignia of a pistol and sword on each shoulder and a rooster badge on his chest jumped off. It had to be an officer from the Ohio Seventh. They were known as the rooster regiment. A twinge of excitement rumbled through her. Maybe he was the hero of Cedar Mountain.

The captain wasn't tall, maybe five-foot eight, thinner than most men, but broad shouldered and muscular. She'd rarely seen a man depicting the virility and confidence he did.

The man looked around then stepped outside. A moment later, he returned. He must have missed the walking plank with his right foot. Mud caked on his boot and halfway up his leg.

Lavena suppressed a grin and cleared her throat. "Excuse me, Captain. I'm supposed to meet someone here."

"So am I." He stared at her for a moment and wrinkled his forehead. "Maybe he missed the train."

She reached out her hand to shake his. "I'm Miss Lavena Falcon, also known as Lee Falcon. I'm the reporter for *The Cleveland Leader*."

"No. It can't be." The man took a step toward her but made no attempt to shake her extended hand. "They sent a woman to interview me?"

She rubbed her hand against her skirt. "You're Captain Macajah Jones?"

He gazed at her with his hands on his hips until the silence became uncomfortable. His square chin showed a number of faded scars. The most pronounced one extended across his chin to his right cheek and earlobe.

The scars must have been from the fire when he tried to save a woman and her children. Lavena was anxious to hear the story from his own lips. She couldn't help gawking.

Captain Jones' Adam's apple bulged. "I've been ordered to escort you on board and to give you every courtesy."

The marks on his face blended with his strong features and intense hazel eyes, and instead of the disfigurement making him ugly, it gave him a certain rugged attraction, especially since she knew what caused those wounds.

The hero of the Battle of Cedar Mountain. He certainly looked the part.

The captain cleared his throat. "Is there a problem?"

Heat rose to Lavena's face. "What... I mean... No problem."

"You were staring." Captain Jones grabbed hold of his earlobe, the one with the scar.

Lavena tried to speak, but for the first time in her life, she couldn't think of what to say. She wasn't one to be flustered easily, but standing in the presence of a man like Captain Macajah Jones... "It's an honor to meet you."

"I'm at your disposal, Miss Falcon." This time he extended his hand.

She gave him a firm handshake. "Thank you, Captain Jones." Her face flushed when she realized she'd held on a moment too long.

"Please call me Captain Cage. Everybody does. The train's leaving soon." He grabbed Lavena's carpetbag and marched toward the next-to-last car. "We need to get you on board."

"Captain Cage," Lavena blurted out.

He spun back. "Yes, Miss Falcon."

"I have some socks for you."

The captain raised his eyebrow and one corner of his mouth. "Socks, for me?"

"What I mean is the Cleveland Ladies Aide Society knitted socks for the Ohio Seventh Regiment, and they donated apples and pears." She pointed to the wall of crates lined up against the side of the depot. "They're over there."

He rubbed his chin and gazed at the boxes. "Well this is a surprise." He climbed a step onto the train and bellowed inside with a deep bass tone. "Frank, Jake, Amon, Coby, get these crates loaded up in the baggage car."

"We'll get right on it, Captain Cage," a young voice rang out. Four men jumped off the train and headed to the boxes.

"Thank you for the supplies," Cage said. "I'll talk to my lieutenant about distributing them at our next stop. I'd appreciate it if you would help."

"Of course." Lavena tilted her head. "Whatever I can do."

Cage marched toward the train without waiting for her to catch up and called over his shoulder. "Let's go."

She hurried up the metal steps onto the train followed him through a crowded passenger car with men in blue uniforms sprawled on the floor. Most of the soldiers looked too young to fight. The uniforms, faded and stained, proved otherwise.

The men stood, parted to allow a walkway, and tipped their hats as Lavena struggled to keep up with the captain. He led her outside onto a metal walkway and into the last car, a small one reserved for officers. On cushioned benches sat half a dozen company captains, a quartermaster, two doctors, a lieutenant-colonel, and a regimental colonel.

An impressive group.

When they noticed her, the officers jumped from their seats in one accord as if pinecones had magically appeared beneath them. The lieutenant-colonel, a large muscular man with a bushy mustache who looked like he could single-handedly win the war, raised his eyebrow.

The open mouths of the others indicated they would have imagined anything from a mountain lion to a lizard before they'd believe a woman could be the reporter they expected.

The regimental commander, Colonel William Creighton, surprised her the most. This was the man who had been wounded twice yet still inspired and led what many considered the most heroic regiment in the Union Army, yet he looked like a dapper socialite, thin and handsome, with a mustache and sandy blond hair. Considering he was only twenty-six years old, the same age as her, she assumed he would be more intimidating like his lieutenant-colonel or Captain Cage.

Lavena's heart pounded loudly as the men approached her. This was always the hardest moment, convincing them she belonged there even if she was a woman, and not alienating them in the process. She breathed deeply to keep her nerves under control.

Cage stood at attention and saluted. "Colonel Creighton, Lieutenant-Colonel Crane, may I present Miss Lavena Falcon. I'll leave it to the rest of you gentlemen to introduce yourselves."

"There must be some mistake." Crane took a step back. "You're a woman."

Lavena had learned charm often worked better than bluster in these situations. She allowed her most amiable smile to cross her face. "It's so nice of you to notice, Colonel Crane."

"But..." Crane stammered. "They sent us a woman."

"What a pleasant surprise." Colonel Creighton's green eyes twinkled as he fascinated Lavena with a grin of his own. "When I worked at *The Cleveland Herald* before the war, I heard rumors *The Leader* had hired a woman reporter. I never really believed it until now."

Lavena shrugged. "My newspaper doesn't publicize my gender. I use the name, Lee, for my byline. Were you a reporter?"

"No," Creighton said. "I was a printer when the war broke out and I was mustered into service. I've always had a great respect for reporters though. My wife, who I adore, thinks I should pursue becoming one when the war is over."

The respect Lavena had for the colonel increased. In spite of his charismatic ways, he found a way to casually let her know he was happily married. Not that she'd be interested in him or any other man, but it was the honorable thing to do for a man whose very essence probably captivated more than one woman in the past.

Creighton tilted his head toward the back. "We've set you up in the back of the car and have provided two benches so you can interview soldiers."

Lavena followed the men to where a rectangular rubberized tent had been hung to hide the benches from prying eyes. A coal stove was in the corner. Perfect. She could brew some tea.

"We hung the tent," Colonel Creighton said, "so you could have privacy while interviewing the men. We didn't realize you would need it for… other considerations."

Crane kneaded the back of his neck. Lavena couldn't decide if he were aghast about her being a woman or if he always had an unpleasant disposition. Either way, he could be a problem.

"We've assigned you to Captain Cage's company," Colonel Creighton said. "You'll stay with them when we aren't on the train. Lieutenant-Colonel Crane set up interviews with each of the officers sitting in this car. Of course, anyone else you wish to interview will be at your disposal." He glanced toward Cage. "Isn't that right, Captain?"

The captain looked like he'd been sucking on a lemon. "Yes, Sir."

Lavena ignored Cage and his obvious displeasure. "Thank you, Colonel Creighton."

The colonel placed his arm on his stomach and bowed. "I'm at your service, Ma'am." He returned to his seat with his lieutenant-colonel frantically whispering in his ear.

Cage set her carpet bag down next to her seat and shuffled his feet. For a man with such a commanding presence, he looked unsure of what to do or say. The train jerked and began moving.

"Captain," she said. "Why don't we start the interview with you first?"

"It'll keep." He turned away. "I must get back to my men." He marched out as if being chased by a Confederate regiment.

Chapter Six

Sergeant Paul Garrett stood at attention and saluted Cage, holding it until Cage let out a sigh and returned the salute. Sergeant Garrett, a square-faced man with an unusually large nose, was a banker before the war, and his faithfulness and attention to detail made him invaluable, but sometimes his constant devotion to duty could make him a bit annoying.

Like now.

All Cage wanted to do was find a place to sit where he could sort his thoughts about having a woman reporter interview him, but Garrett's vigilance determined to interrupt his plans.

"At ease."

Even at ease, Sergeant Garrett looked ready for anything.

"Yes Sergeant. What is it?"

"It's a problem with one of the men, Sir."

"Which one?"

"Private Amon Smith."

Cage had a fondness for the young private and suspected where this was going. "What about him?"

"He's been hanging around Private Willard too much lately." Sergeant Garrett insisted calling the men by their rank and last name even though Cage had set the tone for a first name basis. "Before we left Virginia, I caught Private Willard with alcohol on his breath and ordered him bucked and gagged. Private Smith wasn't drinking as far as I could tell, but he was with Private Willard. I'm concerned Private Willard will lead him down the wrong path."

"I'm certain of it." Cage rubbed his hand across his cheek. "I'll talk to the boy, but I can't order him to choose different friends."

"Yes, Sir. I'm sure you'll know what to do."

Cage didn't have the sergeant's confidence in how much he could influence the young man, but he had to try. "If that's all, send Lieutenant Jed in here."

"You mean Lieutenant Jackson?"

Cage blew out a breath. "Yes, Sergeant."

"Yes, Sir." Garrett saluted and held it until he returned the salute then headed toward the next car.

Cage stepped over men's legs and hands making his way to the edge of the car. A few of the soldiers parted to give him room. He eased down the wall and closed his eyes. The stench of body odor and sweat from so many being in these closed quarters assaulted his nose, but he'd become used to it.

As the train jolted around the curve, bodies pressed in on him. Cage ignored the bustle about him but couldn't block out his own pressing thoughts. Miss Lavena Falcon was not what he expected.

Lieutenant Jedidiah Jackson, Cage's second-in-command since Nate left and unofficial regimental chaplain, plopped down beside him and delivered a piercing stare Cage was sure could see right through every secret he tried to conceal.

"You wanted to see me?" Jed asked.

"The reporter they sent to interview me made it aboard."

Jed wiped a hand over his mouth to hide he was enjoying this way too much. "You're not going to hit this one, are you?"

The last man who tried to interview Cage was an annoying rodent who'd paid to send another man in his place when he was drafted. The weasel wouldn't take no for an answer, and Cage had resorted to violence. It was worth the extra guard duty to put that man in his place.

"Not this time," Cage said. "They sent a member of the fairer sex."

"A woman reporter?"

Cage pressed his lips together and nodded.

"Imagine that." Jed chuckled. "Someone you can't physically assault. This should be fun." He raised an eyebrow. "You're not going to bully her, are you? I would hate to see you make her cry."

Cage gave his lieutenant a caustic look that normally caused Sergeant Garrett to stammer, but it never worked on Jed. "The lady is a reporter for a major newspaper in one of the largest seaport cities in the North. I doubt she carries tears in her arsenal."

"Will you do the interview then?

"I have no choice. The publisher is a friend of General Grant's. I've been ordered to cooperate."

"Then you'll tell her the truth." Jed wiped an ash brown wisp from his forehead and directed his glower that would put Old Testament prophets to shame.

Cage was sure Jed practiced the look in a mirror he'd hidden. He couldn't hold the gaze. "I don't know what you mean. I not in the habit of telling lies."

"Captain, even if you won't tell that lady reporter why you act like a twister is raging through your insides, you can trust me."

The scar on Cage's earlobe itched.

Jed let out a sigh. "So, if you're not seeking spiritual guidance, why did you call for me?"

"The lady brought knitted socks and fruit for the troops. Help her distribute them when we stop in Indiana."

"I'll take care of it."

"One more thing," Cage said. "Miss Falcon is friends with Nathaniel

Teagan's wife. She may inquire about him."

Jed raised an eyebrow. "So, you're going to have to try to skirt around more than one truth."

Skirt was a good word for it. Cage had never met a lady reporter before. Weren't women who did men's jobs supposed to be somewhat ugly, maybe tall and hefty, somebody who didn't attract the attention of men? That didn't describe this lady at all. She seemed more like a force of nature, graceful but with an inner strength hinting of danger. Her small frame and delicate features didn't match the confidence she exuded. Her Mediterranean complexion, dark foreboding eyes, and raven hair somehow managed to contain the power of her presence.

Cage felt the same inner thrill and warning he'd experienced looking into the storm spawning a twister that destroyed his neighbors crops and home when he was a boy. Like then, he couldn't seem to look away.

Chapter Seven

October 2nd

Lavena kept an eye open for a glimpse of Captain Cage as she handed a pair of socks and a piece of fruit to each soldier in line at the Centerville, Indiana station. She hadn't seen the captain since she boarded the train the day before and suspected he was avoiding her.

Cage didn't even make an appearance that morning when the ladies of the town sang patriotic songs to the soldiers in the center square on Main Street and invited many of them home for breakfast.

"Ma'am?" A young private with red hair and freckles interrupted her thoughts. "Are you all right?"

Lavena blushed realizing she'd been twisting socks in her hands instead of passing them out. "I'm sorry. My mind was elsewhere." She handed him socks and an apple.

"Thank you, Ma'am."

Lieutenant Jackson approached Lavena. "How is the distribution going?"

"Almost done," Lavena said. "When will Captain Cage be by?"

"He won't. Captain Cage never takes supplies meant for his men."

Lavena could feel her limbs tightening. "He could at least be here while they're being passed out."

"He left me in charge of that."

"Lieutenant, I boarded the train yesterday, and I haven't seen the captain since." She shot the junior officer a glare. "He's supposed to give me an interview. Where is he?"

Lieutenant Jackson cleared his throat. "He borrowed a horse from the livery and rode to Indianapolis. He'll meet up with us there."

Her voice rose. "Why did he do that?"

The private in the front of the line stepped back, his face turning red.

"Miss Falcon." Jackson shoved socks and a pear into the hands of the stunned soldier and jerked his head in a manner that said, "Get out of here." He lowered his voice. "May I remind you you're a guest of the United States Army? Captain Cage answers to his superior officers, not to you."

"Maybe not," Lavena sought to control her tone, "but if he thinks he can dodge me, I'll go to Colonel Creighton and see what he has to say about it."

Lieutenant Jackson let out a sigh. "Colonel Creighton sent Captain

Cage to Indianapolis. He's making arrangements for the troops to eat lunch there."

Heat flushed Lavena's face. "So, he's not trying to avoid me?"

One corner of the lieutenant's mouth turned up. "He doesn't want to be interviewed, but he did find a legitimate reason to leave. If you want to get Captain Cage to tell you the story of how he earned his medal, you have a task in front of you as great as winning this war."

Lavena pulled out another crate and put all the force her small frame allowed into prying off the lid. Lieutenant Jackson may have been telling her the truth, but she couldn't let a stubborn captain ruin her career no matter how formidable he was. She'd be the victor in this battle of wills. She had to be.

She finished handing out the socks and fruit to another half dozen soldier, then headed to the train. A throat cleared behind her, and she turned around.

Lieutenant Jackson shrugged. "May I have a moment of your time, Miss Falcon?"

Her shoulders tensed. "Lieutenant Jackson, if you are planning to berate me on my lack of military discipline--"

The chaplain chuckled and held up his hands. "No, Ma'am. I wanted to thank you for bringing the men the socks and fruit and for helping to pass out them out."

Lavena's face grew warm. "Forgive my outburst. I seem to be doing that a lot lately."

"That's all right. You can call me Chaplain Jed or Preacher. That's what the men call me."

"Chaplain Jed. You may call me be my first name as well."

Thank you, Miss Lavena." The chaplain gazed at her as if he were trying to figure out what to say. "Is something wrong, Ma'am?"

"What do you mean?"

He shrugged. "You don't seem the type to be easily riled, yet you've admitted to a number of outbursts of late. If there's anything you'd like to talk about, I'm a good listener."

Lavena pressed her lips together. "I have been preoccupied lately, but those are my concerns. I wouldn't want to bother you with them."

"I am a man of the cloth." Jed gave her a half smile. "At least I will be after this war is over. I was studying theology at Oberlin College and was finishing up my last semester when the war broke out and I enlisted."

"I graduated from Oberlin as well."

"Ah, I see. That explains a lot."

Lavena tilted her head and glared at him.

Jed smiled. "An accomplished and intelligent woman with a career usually reserved for men? That's rare, but it seems most Oberlin lady alumni either embark on a career or become the wives of missionaries or ministers."

She felt her shoulders relax. There wasn't any of the condemnation she expected in his tone, more admiration. "One of my dearest friends at Oberlin married a missionary. She and her husband are in China now, but I think she would argue the point of being a missionary's wife. She is a missionary in her own right."

"Of course. I meant no offense."

Perhaps it would be acceptable to confide some of what she was struggling with. This chaplain seemed a good choice. ""I'm concerned about my friend, Mrs. Betsy Teagan. This business with her husband deserting doesn't make sense."

Jed rubbed the back of his neck. "I don't have any answers for you there, but I am praying for them both. Surely that isn't the reason you're so frantic about interviewing my captain. What else is bothering you?"

She laid her hand over her chest. "You're very astute. Have you ever considered being a reporter?"

He let out a slight laugh. "Heavens, no."

She couldn't help but smile. Jed had such an easy way about him. "I've assured my newspaper I'd interview Captain Cage by November First."

Jed's brow furrowed. "The due date is almost a month away, but you're fretting as if your job depended on it."

She let out a sigh. "It does. If I don't interview Captain Cage in time, my job is in jeopardy, but I'm at a loss. The man is determined to avoid me."

"May I make a suggestion?"

"Please do," Lavena said.

"Don't come at him with a frontal attack. Outflank him by not asking questions. Give him time to get to know you a little. He needs to trust you before he'll share the details of his heroism."

"I only have a month."

"True, but it might not take that long. He has reason to distrust reporters. They've built him up as a larger-than-life hero who is single-handedly winning the war. Many times, they reported things he never said. Give him time to realize you'll be ethical and fair, and he'll come around."

"That may be good advice, but I'm not sure I'll be able to carry through with it. I'm not the patient sort."

Jed placed a hand over his mouth, but he didn't manage to hide the grin covering his face. "I hadn't noticed."

She let out a snort.

"I can think of no wiser course of action," Jed said. "Every reporter who tried to interview him has come in with cannons bursting. The captain is a private man. He's not happy with the attention he's been getting."

Lavena nodded. She assumed Cage was trying to hide something. It didn't occur to her he might be avoiding the fanfare of having his story printed in every newspaper in the country.

She would try the chaplain's way for now, but she only had twenty-eight days left.

*****

Captain Cage ate a few bites of stew. He hated throwing it away after the women of Indianapolis so graciously cooked it for him and his men, but his stomach stirred whenever he ate anything more than hardtack, broth, or bread.

The townspeople had set up tables and benches to feed the men on the lawn at Governor's Circle. Cage had waited until most of his men ate so he could eat his lunch in peace. He'd had enough of crowds on the train.

His hopes for a quiet meal disintegrated when Miss Falcon came toward him with a bowl of stew in one hand and a cup of tea in the other. If only she were a man so he could dispatch her in no time. Instead, he nodded as she sat across from him.

Miss Falcon slid a cup toward him. "Drink this."

"I'm not much of a tea drinker." Cage pushed the cup back. "Coffee's my beverage of choice."

"You should start." The corners of Miss Falcon's mouth turned up. "It'll help settle your stomach."

Cage's eyes narrowed. "How'd you know?"

"Most men eat twice their share when they get a chance." She slid the teacup closer to him. "You don't even eat as much as I do, and you're thin. I'm assuming you weighed more when you joined the army than you do now since your uniform hangs on you. All soldiers lose weight, but your uniform is looser than most."

He shrugged as the knot in his stomach tightened. "I can see why you make a good reporter, Miss Falcon."

"You can call me Lavena. Since I'm assigned to your charge, we should be on a first name basis."

"Miss Lavena."

"Drink your tea. It's a hyson and ginger blend, a mild green tea. It will help."

Cage drank a gulp. "My mother used tea to cure various ailments."

"Does she live in Cleveland?"

"No, my parents lived in Lorain." He drank another sip of tea. "They died of influenza."

Lavena offered an understanding nod. "When did they pass?"

He rubbed his scar. This conversation was getting too personal. He hadn't intended to reveal anything about himself to her. Now he was telling her his life history. "It was five years ago. Best forgotten."

"Still, it's difficult to lose family."

Heat flushed his face. His father would have been crushed if he'd known what Cage had done. He needed to change the subject before this went any further. He pointed to the tea. "It's good. Did the ladies in town provide you with this?"

"Goodness, no," Lavena said. "I carry my own tea leaves with me. I would never use tea I don't know about. You wouldn't believe what some people make it out of."

Cage repressed a smile. "Is that so?" He took another sip.

Lavena tilted her head. "I guess I do have a penchant for the beverage."

The churning in his stomach was subsiding. The aroma from the stew awakened his hunger. He took another sip then ate a bite of stew. It tasted rich and full of flavor. No nausea or heartburn. He took another bite, then another.

"It's working, isn't it?"

"It seems to be." With each bite, the hunger grew closer to being satisfied. He finished off the first meal he enjoyed in over a year. His stomach felt full and satisfied, but he didn't dare relax in the presence of this woman who could get him to reveal things about himself just by serving him a cup of tea.

He hated to think what would happen when Lavena's real agenda surfaced – the dreaded interview.

She finished her stew. "I'm glad you enjoyed the tea. I'm sure we'll meet again soon." Standing, she strolled to the train without saying another word.

Cage's jaw dropped. He didn't believe he could be more surprised than he was when they sent a woman reporter to interview him but curing his stomach with tea and then leaving without asking one question had done it.

Chapter Eight

Lavena sat on a park bench near the train station totally pleased with herself. The captain's reaction showed her tempered approach was working. It would only be a matter of time before he told her everything she wanted to know.

Time was not something she had an abundance of, but she could wait a bit longer.

Jed sat beside her. "How did it go, Miss Lavena?"

"I believe I left him completely confounded."

Jed laughed. "I would have loved to have seen that."

She let out a snort. "It was a sight to behold."

"All you have to do now is keep it up until he's ready to talk."

"Perhaps." She stared at the hands folded in her lap. "What if he won't yield before the time is up?"

Jed shrugged. "By then, maybe the frontal attack will work, but either way, you will have gained his trust."

"I hope so."

"The train leaves soon," Jed said. "Colonel Creighton has asked me to inform you all the senior officers are ready whenever you wish to interview them."

Lavena sighed. "Not all."

"Point taken," Jed said. "Shall I escort you to the train?"

"I would like that," she said, a little surprised she meant it. The chaplain was easy to be around. She could see them becoming good friends over the coming months. "Why don't you tell me a bit more about yourself?"

"Is this part of the interview?"

"Maybe." She let out a small grin. "I really would like to hear your story."

A sadness came over his face. "I'm just a poor farm boy. There's nothing special about me."

"Surely you can at least tell me where you're from."

"Lawrence, Kansas."

Lavena gasped. "I'm so sorry. Any family there?"

"I'm the oldest. I have a father, a mother, and five brothers there." His Adams' Apple bulged. "Four brothers. One was killed at Manasseh."

"Then the rest are safe? You've received word?"

"I've written letters, but the mail is so slow. The newspapers say Quantrill's raiders killed over 200, but I don't know if he hit their farm. It's been over a month, and I've heard nothing." Jed kneaded the back of his neck. "The hardest part is not knowing."

A lump in her throat threatened to choke her. The raiders weren't part of the Confederate Army, and the brutality of it outraged even the most passionate Secessionists.

She wished she could say something to comfort or reassure him. She touched his arm. "I'm so dreadfully sorry."

"Everyone's sorry." He stopped and tilted his head toward the train. "If you don't mind, Miss Lavena, I have some matters to attend to." He didn't wait for her to comment. He turned and walked away, shoulders slumped.

So much sorrow since the war began.

She climbed aboard the train and made her way to the officer's car. As soon as she entered, every officer to a man popped up like one of those jack-in-the-box toys children played with.

She let out a heavy sigh. "Gentlemen, please. As I told you before, there's no need to stand every time I enter the room."

Colonel Creighton smiled. "It's a difficult habit to break, Ma'am. I've asked Lieutenant-Colonel Orrin Crane to offer you an interview first."

"Let's get this over with." Crane marched behind the curtain, stood until she sank into her seat, then took a seat across from her. Even sitting, he seemed to be standing, his posture erect and stiff. "Miss Falcon, before we start, I think you should know I don't believe it is proper for a lady to have a career or to travel without a male escort."

"Understood." She stifled her annoyance and pulled paper, ink, and pen out of her lap-desk. It appeared Captain Cage wasn't the only one irritated by her presence.

The whistle blew, and the train jerked forward. She began the questions. After his initial declaration of disapproval, she had to admit Crane was polite and forthcoming. He was born in New York, grew up in Connecticut, and moved to Ohio as a young man where he worked as a carpenter building ships. He entered the army as a private but was promoted through the ranks quickly and learned everything he knew about warfare from his closest friend, Colonel Creighton. He'd been wounded once but not seriously.

He did have one bit of information to add about Captain Cage. Colonel Creighton had been wounded at Cedar Mountain, so Crane commanded the regiment when Captain Cage displayed his heroism.

"I was the one who recommended him for the Congressional Medal of Honor," Crane said. "President Lincoln himself signed the order. The whole regiment was proud one of our own received the highest award of the land."

Next, she interviewed the quartermaster, Lieutenant John Regan and learned about the shortage of supplies. After assuring her how much the soldiers appreciated the ladies knitting them socks and sending fruit, he went on a tirade about how slowly the mail moved.

Chaplain Jed had shared that concern as well. She couldn't imagine the anguish he felt waiting for a post letting him know if his family was alive or dead.

She made a mental note to send a reply to Aunt Martha at next stop when she sent her stories to Mr. O'Brady. Her aunt, the only mother she'd ever known, would be worried if she hadn't heard from her without knowing why.

She'd also promised Betsy she'd write as soon as she could, and she wanted to tell her about Dr. Walker. Hopefully her roommate had dismissed the idea of becoming an Army nurse. She'd be better served to apply at Western Reserve Cleveland Medical College to become a doctor instead of pinning away for Nate. In rural areas where doctors were scarce, even women doctors made a decent living.

After Lieutenant Regan excused himself, she interviewed a couple captains from other companies, but she didn't learn anything that Crane hadn't already told her.

The saddest parts of those interviews consisted of the stories about the men who had died. The Ohio Seventh had over thirteen hundred recruits when the war began. Now they were down to a little over four hundred able-bodied men. Some had been killed in battle, some by disease. The rest had been wounded too badly to return to duty or were captured and placed in Confederate prisons. Only a few had left the service for other reasons.

She looked up from her notes as Colonel William Creighton entered.

"I'm ready for my interview." He sat across from her.

She couldn't help but smile. His pleasant demeanor was infectious. "Thank you, Colonel. Why don't you tell me a little about your life before the war?"

He was completely forthcoming. Born in Pittsburg, Pennsylvania, he moved to Cleveland as a young man and entered the service as a lieutenant-colonel, He was promoted to regimental commander when Colonel Tyler became the brigadier general. Creighton married Eleanor shortly before he left and hadn't seen his bride since. He missed her terribly.

Now that the background information was collected, Lavena pushed forward with the interview. "I understand the Ohio Seventh is called the rooster regiment. Are you the one who started the habit of crowing as you enter battle?"

Creighton diverted his eyes. "No, General Tyler came up with that. It seems to inspire the men."

"Could you tell me a little about Cedar Mountain?"

He wiped his hands on his trousers. "There's not much you don't already know. We lost a number of men, many of them from the heat, but I don't remember much. I was shot shortly after Stonewall Jackson came riding in with his rebel army. It took me a month to recover and rejoin my regiment. Crane could probably tell you more than I could."

"Yes, he did. Thank you, Colonel Creighton."

Every interview had been helpful, but the officers' accounts wouldn't keep Mr. O'Brady satisfied for long. She needed the real story in Captain Cage's own words. It would be difficult not to press the illusive captain when the calendar moved so swiftly. She'd give it another week or two, but then she'd get that interview no matter what Jed said.

She looked out the small window in her curtained area. It was already getting dark. "Fiddlesticks." Too late to question anyone else tonight. Better to call it a day, finish reading her aunt's letter, and write the stories from the interviews she'd already done.

She placed her teakettle on the stove and pulled the letter out of her desk.

Your father is in poor health, and I fear he might not be long upon this Earth. I know you don't believe this, but he is a repentant man. If you hold onto this grudge, you'll regret it for the rest of your life.

Lavena swallowed hard. Her father didn't regret any of what he'd done. Despite his contrite confession to the police or his lengthy prison sentence, maybe all he regretted was getting caught.

Still, it disturbed her to know he was ill. He'd been a good father before all of this happened. One reason what he'd done hit her so hard was because he was her hero in every way. And even though she hadn't seen him in years, she couldn't imagine a world without him in it.

After writing letters to Betsy and Mr. O'Brady, she penned a note telling Aunt Martha about her new assignment, her impressions of Captain Macajah Jones, and where to send further letters, but she didn't write anything about her father. She didn't know what to say.

She couldn't forgive him. Not after how he had betrayed her trust.

Chapter Nine

October 3rd

The next day, Cage leaned against the wall and scanned the sea of faces packed in the car. He had made a decision to give Private Amon Smith a firm talking to. Hopefully the gangly, freckled young man, who looked like he belonged behind a plow instead of in uniform, would listen.

He found Amon and pulled him aside. "We need to talk."

"Sure, Captain."

"Over here." Cage led Amon to the outside platform, out of earshot of the other soldiers. He didn't want to embarrass the young man. He crossed his arms and glared at the private without saying anything, hoping it would intimidate him enough to take heed.

Amon shifted from one foot to the other. "What did you want to talk to me about, Captain?" He spoke in a loud voice to be heard over the chugging of the train.

Cage waited a moment longer while he mulled over what words to use. "Private Amon, you're a good soldier, but some things have been brought to my attention concerning you. I would hate for you to go down the wrong path."

Amon's normally ruddy face turned redder than the leaves on the maple trees the train passed. "I wouldn't do that, Sir."

"You will if you keep company with no accounts like Private Coby Willard."

The train jerked, and Amon grabbed hold of the rail. "Coby's not that bad."

Cage kept his eyes fixed on Amon looking for some sign he was getting through. "Find some new friends, or you'll end up following him into trouble."

Amon's clutch on the rail tightened. "I had other friends, Sir." He swiped his fingers through his hair. "They're all dead."

"I know, Son." Cage placed his hand on Amon's shoulder and squeezed. "But I'm telling you now, I'll do what's needed to keep you on the straight and narrow."

Amon stared at his feet. "Are you ordering me to stay away from Coby, Sir?"

Cage reluctantly removed his hand. "No, I don't have the authority to do that, but Cody's been drinking and visiting the women outside the camp. One of these days, I'll catch him in the act, and if you're with him, I won't hesitate to have you bucked and gagged too."

None of the men liked being hogtied and humiliated, but it was the most common way to deal with misconduct, and it was effective except for in hardcore cases like Coby. He hoped it wouldn't come to that. "This is the only warning you'll get."

Amon squared his shoulders and stood at attention. "Yes, Sir."

Cage delivered a final penetrating glower toward Amon. No change in his demeanor. The boy was embarrassed but not repentant. "That's all."

The private saluted and half ran inside the train car to get away from the scolding.

Cage rubbed his ear and gazed out into the landscape. If there was an answer in the trees passing by, he couldn't find it.

Jed sauntered out to the platform and stood beside him. "Think your talk helped?"

Cage shook his head. "It looks like he'll have to learn the hard way."

Jed didn't say anything more. He just stood with Cage, offering support by his presence alone.

*****

That night Cage couldn't sleep. It wasn't only fretting about Amon that kept him awake. He hadn't slept since that woman reporter arrived. He'd tried to avoid her, but she was there at every turn. What made it worse was she was being so nice about it. Since they ate lunch together in Indiana, she made a point of greeting him pleasantly every time they'd disembarked to eat or when he was called to the officers' car, but she hadn't even brought up the subject of an interview.

It unnerved him in a way that never had when she was trying too hard. She unnerved him.

Maybe I should get it over with. As tempting as that was, he wouldn't.

A sliver of light made its way into the car through the window in the door, and the train came to a stop. They'd reached Nashville. He wiped his eyes and stretched.

Jed sat sleeping in a sitting up position against the train wall. How did he manage it? He seemed to have no trouble sleeping, even under duress. He had enough reason to keep him awake fretting about his family. Instead he slouched against the wall with his chin in his chest and a soft snore coming out of him. It had been over a year since Cage slept like that. He stood and nudged Jed with the tip of his boot.

The young lieutenant rubbed his eyes and groaned. "It can't be morning already."

"We just pulled into Nashville. You have four hours to get the company fed before we move out. It being Sunday, I figured you could preach at them after breakfast."

Jed pulled himself to his feet. "I was thinking of entitling my message, the truth shall set you free."

If Cage hadn't respected Jed so much, he would have punched him in the mouth like one of those weasel reporters. Instead he delivered a scorching glower. It had no effect except to cause a smirk to cross Jed's face.

"You going to invite Miss Falcon to the service, or are you still sidestepping her?"

Cage groaned. "You can ask her if you want."

"You can't avoid her forever. She's a fine Christian woman. You should give her a chance."

Cage's scar twitched. "You're going too far, Lieutenant Jackson. Stand down."

Jed stood at attention, his lips pinched tight, with a slight grin in the corners, and saluted. "Yes, Sir, Captain Jones."

Cage returned the salute half-heartedly. "When you've assembled the men, let me know."

"Yes, Sir."

"Jed." Cage cleared his throat. "I'll invite the lady." As he made his way to officers' car, he caught Jed's chuckle behind him.

Chapter Ten

Lavena finished braiding her hair and tied a ribbon on the end when a knock sounded on the wall outside her curtain. She pulled it aside.

Cage stood there with an absurd look on his face, like a little boy being forced to talk to an adult he didn't know. "Good morning, Miss Falcon."

"Captain." She couldn't keep the caustic tone out of her voice no matter how hard she tried. Lieutenant Jed's plan to wait until Cage let down his defenses didn't seem to be working at all. The captain had avoided her at every turn. "Lavena, remember?"

"Miss Lavena." He offered her a sheepish grin. "I owe you an apology. It's been four days since you joined us, and I haven't given you the opportunity to interview me. I assume you've finished interviewing the senior officers on the train."

"All except for Major Patella... and you." She decided to push a bit. "I understand you have duties other than me, but..." Stuffing down her irritation, she delivered the most charming smile she could manage. "Do you finally have a moment in your busy schedule to give me some time? Or am I too much of a bother?"

Cage stroked his chin. "Bother might not be the right word, but there is a war on. I don't have time to devote to every reporter who waltzes into camp wanting to do a story."

"Every reporter?" Lavena sputtered. "From what I've heard you don't talk to any of them, but you sure have time to toss them out on their ears."

A low chuckle escaped his lips. "Perhaps, but if I treated you like that, I'd surely be lynched by my men. They don't have a chance to visit with a beautiful young lady too often."

She flushed. He was using his charm to disarm her. Despite her best intentions, it was working.

"Could we start over?"

"I suppose," she said. "Perhaps we could talk now."

"I'm afraid not."

She let out a gusty sigh. "Too busy again, Captain?"

He held up his hands as if surrendering. "We only have a short time to get the men fed. I promise to answer all your questions when we get to Chattanooga."

"And when will that be?" They'd made good time so far, but could she afford a delay?

"We should be there within a few days." He cleared his throat. "Until then, you could interview some of my men about the events at Cedar

Mountain. I know they'd be delighted to talk to you."

"Unlike you."

One side of Cage's mouth turned up.

"I'll have to settle for that." Lavena couldn't help the grin spreading across her face. "For now." She could afford to wait a little longer. After all, she did have until the end of the month, and she had other interviews to do. "I warn you, Captain, I don't give up easily."

"In the meantime," he offered his arm, "may I escort you to breakfast and to the church meeting afterwards."

She placed her arm in his, and heat rose to her cheeks. She enjoyed being so close to him, and it scared her. Captain Macajah Jones seemed to have a way of tearing down her defenses.

During breakfast, he chatted about the weather, the quality of Army rations, how much he depended on Lieutenant Jed and Sergeant Garrett, and how much he respected Colonel Creighton, but he avoided talking about himself.

Everything within her wanted to press him, but she didn't. Jed was right. It was better to wait for Cage to have the time to realize he could trust her, at least for now.

Before long, they'd made their way to the field where Jed preached. Almost every man in the regiment was there sitting on the ground or on tent flaps waiting for him to begin.

Impressive. She hadn't realized that many soldiers would be eager to attend church services. She'd mention that when she did an article about the chaplaincy.

Cage lay a tent flap on the ground in the back and helped her to sit before lowering himself beside her.

Two soldiers stood in front beside Jed. One had a trumpet and began to play. The other sang in a clear tenor voice, and all the soldiers joined in. Cage's bass voice booming beside her.

What a Friend we have in Jesus, all our sins and griefs to bear!
What a privilege to carry everything to God in prayer!
O what peace we often forfeit, O what needless pain we bear,
All because we do not carry everything to God in prayer.

Cage's voice cracked while singing the last two lines of the first verse. Lavena turned toward him, but he had turned away and stopped singing. It took him halfway through the second verse before he recovered his voice.

What was it about a man worshipping God that was so attractive? She looked around the campground. Every man on the grounds sang with the same devotion. Somehow, they didn't have the same allure.

Lord, I want Cage to trust me. Why can't I trust him?

She already knew the answer. She wanted to let go of her unforgiveness, to rid herself of this needless pain. Only God could give her the strength she needed to set aside the offense she'd carried so long. She lifted her eyes to Heaven, a prayer forming in her heart. *Help me to forgive my father.*

After two more hymns, Chaplin Jed began preaching. He had a way about him when he preached. Most preachers these days felt the louder their voice, the stronger the point they made.

She suspected they were trying to emulate Father Charles Finney, the fiery evangelist and president of Oberlin College, but with Father Finney, it was a natural part of who he was. Some of the other preachers who imitated the style just sounded angry.

Chaplin Jed was different. His words came across as passionate and anointed as Father Finney's but in a peaceful way. Always soft spoken when out of the pulpit, he seemed to have that same calm style of preaching, luring the congregation in.

This time, the congregation was a group of soldiers who'd seen their share of death and destruction, but they listened intently to every word. In spite of her intentions, the message worked its way into her soul as well, a message on forgiveness and trust.

Jed was a remarkable man with a strong anointing on him. He was a couple of years younger than her, and his sandy brown hair strewn in his eyes made him younger still, but he had a maturity about him that didn't match his youth.

In a way, he seemed every bit as formidable as Captain Cage, especially when he was in the pulpit, but he was so different from the captain in personality and temperament.

Captain Cage was a good man too.

Why was she even thinking this way? She'd only known him a little over a week, and she wasn't ever going to marry. Doing so would mean she'd have to put her career as a journalist aside. The whole idea was preposterous.

At a church service in her freshman year at college, Father Finney preached a sermon about seeking out truth in love. After the way journalists had destroyed her and her family with half-truths and innuendos just to get a story, she knew this was her calling, every bit as important as matrimony and motherhood. She wouldn't give it up for any man.

She had to stop these romantic notions about Cage, but she needed that interview, and that meant being with him and charming him until he opened up to her and revealed his secrets.

After church, the captain asked Lavena to join him at the hotel restaurant for lunch.

She diverted her gaze from his deep hazel eyes. "Does this mean you'll consent to the interview now?"

"You'd make a great general, Miss Lavena. You never give up."

She grinned. "I've been told it's my most endearing trait."

He lifted an eyebrow. "By who? Your editor?"

"How did you guess?"

A deep chuckle came from within him. She'd never heard him laugh before. It was a pleasant sound. "I've promised you an interview when we get to Chattanooga, and I'll deliver, but not yet."

If Lavena couldn't interview him about Cedar Mountain, she wasn't sure she wanted any more casual conversation with him. She already knew all she wanted to know about the weather and the food, and being around him stirred feelings she didn't want to have.

"The hotel is only a few blocks from the train depot," Cage said holding out his arm. "It has a nice view of the Cumberland River."

She pressed her lips together, the skillful preaching of Chaplain Jed Jackson still playing in the corners of her mind.

"Come now," he said. "Surely, you don't want to wait in line with all the other soldiers for lukewarm rations."

That was the last bit of convincing she needed. She took his arm. "Lead on."

A warmth she didn't want flowed through her.

They found a seat in the restaurant. As they waited for their meals to be served, she tried to make casual conversation that didn't have anything to do with the weather. She told him about her interviews with the officers.

He grunted a few times and asked a couple of questions.

The conversation came to a lull. She searched her brain for a subject other than his heroism - and found it. "Do you mind if I ask a question that has nothing to do with your military service?"

A young girl set their plates in front of them.

Cage nodded.

When he had a bite of eggs halfway to his mouth, she spoke again. "Betsy Teagan is my roommate. She doesn't believe her husband would desert."

He dropped his fork.

Lavena grimaced. She'd approached another touchy subject, but she trudged on. She took out her tea canister and sprinkled some green leaves in the two cups of hot water she'd ordered. She pushed one cup toward him. "I tried to convince her to accept what had happened, but... Could you give me any insight to help her understand why he would do something like that?"

He wiped his hand across his scar. He did that or tugged on his ear every time she brought up something that made him uncomfortable. A useful tool to keep in mind when she interviewed him.

"Lieutenant Nathanial Teagan was a good soldier and courageous in battle. When I got these burns," he pointed the scars his face, "he pulled me out of the house and saved my life."

A glowing tribute to a deserter, but why would he defend Nate? "I read your letter to Betsy. You were emphatic that he deserted. Is there any doubt?"

"I meant what I wrote." He rubbed his cheek.

So, there was more to the story. "You must have an idea why he deserted?"

His hand travelled up the scar on his face to his ear. "It bothered him more than he thought it would."

She tilted her head. "What bothered him?"

"Killing Southerners."

"Why would it?" Heat flushed her face. "He hasn't spoken to his family for years. He doesn't owe them any allegiance. They owned slaves and treated them shamefully. His father even disowned him for being a slave rescuer."

"I can see your passionate about abolition."

"As every Christian should be. That's why this war is so important. I know President Lincoln says the preservation of the Union is of utmost importance, but slavery must end. Otherwise all this killing and sorrow is for nothing."

"When I enlisted, I believed that too. I joined up for abolition and freedom from slavery as well as for the preservation of our nation, but most of the boys we're fighting against have never owned a slave in their lives and neither have their kin. They're fighting for their states and their homes."

"Fiddlesticks. The generals and leaders of this rebellion own plenty of slaves. They're manipulating these boys into doing their bidding."

"Perhaps so, but can war change people's hearts?" He forsook his ear and took a sip of tea. "I just don't know anymore."

She placed her hand on his. "Even if their hearts aren't changed, the law has to be. These captive men, women, and children have no recourse."

"Of course, you're right. We must do what we can." He glanced at her hand on his and smiled.

Her face grew warm, and she pulled it away. "Is there any more you can tell me about Nate?"

Cage cleared his throat. "He talked about his family often. Being put in the position of killing men who might have been his neighbors, his brother, or even his own father vexed him."

Lavena pressed her lips together. "Are you saying, he changed sides? That he's turned his back on everything he believed to become a traitor and a rebel? His wife needs to know the truth."

"Not wanting to kill rebels doesn't make him a traitor." He grabbed hold of his ear again. "There is one other thing..."

She let out her breath slowly to calm her ire. "Anything you could tell me."

"His wife." Cage pushed his plate away with both hands even though he hadn't eaten more than a bite of eggs and half a piece of toast then rubbed his face. "He never stopped talking about her. He sent her a letter every chance he got, but I don't remember him getting mail from home the entire time I served with him. Then, a few months ago, a post arrived for him. Nate acted different after that. He didn't even show up for drills. When I came back to the tent we'd shared, it had been ransacked. He sat in the middle of the mess, holding the letter, sobbing."

Lavena had always suspected Nate loved Betsy more than he showed. Maybe she had misjudged him, believing he was a coward when his real crime might be a broken heart. She touched Cage's hand again without thinking, noticed what she had done, and then pulled it away and wrapped both hands around her teacup. "Are you saying he left because of Betsy?"

"I can't say why he deserted, but I've never seen Nate like that before. He'd faced some of the fiercest battles of the war with a stoic boldness, but when I found him that day, he seemed more like a scared little boy. He wouldn't show me the letter."

"Betsy told me she wrote some horrible things to him, things she didn't mean." Lavena stared at the tea in her cup. "She wrote it was over between them and for him to stop sending her letters, that she'd burn them if he did."

"This explains a lot." Cage steepled his fingers together. "A part of him died that day. Even though he never touched the stuff before, he became strongly acquainted with whiskey."

Lavena gasped. "Nate drank alcohol? He was a part of the Oberlin Prohibition Society in college. He said strong drink had never touched his lips, and it never would."

"I had to punish him for getting drunk more than once."

Lavena pulled her friend's letter from her handbag. "Betsy gave me this for her husband. She wants him to know she still loves him."

"May I read it?"

She hesitated for a moment. "Betsy said I could read it, so I suppose it would be all right since you have such a close friendship with Nate." She handed it to Cage.

He read through the letter several times, almost like he was trying to memorize it, then folded it back up and handed it to her. "How does she think you're going to get it to him under the circumstances?"

"I've tried to reason with her. I advised her to forget about her husband and get on with her life. I even warned if we did find him, he'd be shot, but she won't hear of it. She's hoping for a miracle."

"That's what it will take." Cage grabbed his abused ear again. His earlobe should have been down to his shoulder as often as he tugged on it.

"I don't know where he is now, but I suspect he's on his way home. I just don't know if it's home to Tennessee or to his wife in Ohio."

She let it drop. She wasn't about to tell the captain of the decision she'd made. He'd try to stop her, but she needed to know the truth.

When she arrived in Chattanooga, she would find a way to visit the Teagan Plantation. If Nate was there, it would prove he was a traitor. If not, there was still hope.

Chapter Eleven

Lieutenant Nathaniel Teagan glanced toward the setting sun. He'd need to make camp soon, but the field he was standing in was too visible. Everything depended on him not being found by enemy soldiers scouting the area.

He worked his jaw. Which enemy? At this point, both the Union and the Confederacy would consider him an enemy. A deserter in a Union army uniform. When he'd stopped at one farm in North Carolina to steal some food, he'd almost taken some civilian clothes off the clothesline, but he'd heard the door from the house open and left without them.

Just as well. Any man out here alone, civilian or soldier, would raise suspicion.

He had to find a place to spend the night. There were caves near here, and he was sure he could find a secluded place before dark. If the cave was deep enough, he might even be able to risk a fire to warm himself. He hadn't dared light a fire since he got to Tennessee.

Rustling from deep within the woods. He paused to listen. Too loud to be an animal. It grew louder. He squinted his eyes to see the movement in the trees. Shadows of men coming this way. He dropped to the ground. They drew closer. Soldiers.

He frantically gazed the area for a place to hide and found it. Staying low, he made his way to the sycamore tree and squeezed into the hollow nook of the massive trunk. It was barely big enough, even as thin as he was, but he managed to pull in his haversack and blanket. He couldn't leave them out in the field to be discovered.

Dried leaves scattered in the hole and around the ground in front of him shielding the damp, cold earth. At least there was that. He tried to cover himself with the blanket, but he couldn't move enough to adjust it around himself. The haversack rested uncomfortably between his left leg and the wall of the tree.

Hopefully he wouldn't have to stay in this cramped position for long. Likely, they'd decide to keep going past this area and find someplace more secluded.

He let out short breaths.

More rustling.

A bullfrog croaked. Footsteps grew louder.

His heart beat faster.

He couldn't peek out to see if the men marching toward him were Confederate or Union. Not worth the risk. It would mean trouble either way.

If they wore gray, they'd capture him and place him in a prison camp. He'd heard about those places from another soldier who had spent some time in one before he escaped. Rat infested, rancid food to eat, beatings.

He might be better off with the Union Army. All they wanted to do was shoot him.

The temptation to have a look was almost too strong to resist. Voices.

"The general doesn't know what he's talking about." The first one sounded young and had a Tennessee accent. Tennessee meant Confederate. "There's nobody out here. Let's go back to camp."

Three Confederate privates came into view. They stopped twenty feet away from the sycamore. Probably a few more than that if they were a scouting party. If one of them glanced his way, there was no way they'd miss spotting him.

"I'm not going back until I've checked every inch of these woods." A tall soldier took off his cap and combed his hand through his matted hair. "You know what he's like. If we don't finish our mission, we'll wish all we lost was a meal and a good night's sleep."

"I guess." A corporal, a stocky man with a beard, came into Nate's line of site. "This is as good a spot as any to set up camp for the night."

Nate shivered. Why did they have to make camp here? It was too open. Why didn't they hide their position from the enemy? When he went on scouting missions, he used more stealth.

He craned his neck. From the little he could glimpse, they were all around. There was no way to escape without being seen.

No. No. No! They had to move on. He couldn't make it in the hollow of this tree all night. He was already losing feeling in his left leg.

The soldiers took their time building a fire then sat around it. So, five of them, the tall private, the corporal, a boy about sixteen, a man who looked like he'd had too many meals, and an older man. He couldn't see any more.

The opening of the tree faced west. The sun was low in the sky, but it still cast too much light. There was no way he could risk trying to make a run for it. They'd see him, and they'd hear him.

He tried to get comfortable without moving too much or making any noise. The dried leaves under him crunched, and he froze. The soldiers didn't look up from what they were doing. He let out a breath. They didn't hear, but he didn't dare try to move anymore. He rolled his shoulders and tried to pull the haversack up a little to give himself a little more room. It was wedged tight. It was going to be a long night.

The corporal stretched and leaned against another tree not more than six inches from Nate. "Jeff, why don't you take first watch? I'll have someone relieve you at sunset."

"Sure thing," the tall soldier said.

Nate uttered a rarely used curse word under his breath. If they hadn't posted a sentry, he might have snuck away after they'd fallen asleep or at least been able to stretch his legs.

Still an hour until sunset, and at any moment, they could turn toward the tree where he'd be in full view of them. Only a quarter moon tonight, so there was that, but the watch fire would provide plenty of light. Even after the sun went down, there was little doubt if they looked his way, they'd see him.

The early stages of dusk set in, and the soldiers sat around the fire talking, making jokes and eating beef jerky. A rumble sounded in his stomach, but there was no way he'd be able to pull any rations out of his sack the way it was wedged without making too much noise.

His shin cramped, and he barely managed not to fling his leg out and screech in pain. He placed his fist in his mouth and bit on it to keep from crying out. The spasm traveled to his calf, and he rubbed his leg as hard as he could. The guard marched back and forth near the opening of the tree until Nate almost wanted to announce his presence and surrender.

Almost.

Finally, the muscle started relaxing. He leaned back and thought about the letter in his pocket. The way he was wedged in, he couldn't pull it out to read it, but the words were seared in his mind. The words piercing his heart had the same impact as when he had first opened the envelope.

Betsy had been angry with him for leaving her, but he never thought she'd end what they had together. He'd never wanted anyone but her. A lifetime with her.

He hadn't wanted to leave her alone so many times, but his calling to free the captives kept getting in the way. His allegiance to the abolitionist cause had been an alluring mistress drawing him away from the woman he loved.

The last glimmering light of sunset disappeared below the horizon.

The heavy guard stretched his arms over his head and wandered over to where the tall man stood guard. "Get some sleep." The tall man sauntered to the fire and climbed into his bedroll. The other men joined him, and soon Nate heard their soft snores.

He hadn't been able to turn his back on everything he believed just to be with his wife. He had to act when John Price, an escaped slave, was accosted from Oberlin two days after their wedding.

It had cost him his freedom for months as he had sat in the Cuyahoga County jail charged with violating the Fugitive Slave Act, but Betsy had come to see him every day, had assured him she was proud of him. They'd talked about the future they would have together as soon as this was resolved.

The soldier who ate too much paced with his musket on his shoulder. Ten steps toward the fire. Ten steps passing in front of the tree. Every time he changed direction away from the hollowed-out spot.

Shortly after Nate had been released, John Brown had contacted him about his scheme at Harper's Ferry. Betsy had been angry at him for being so quick to desert her again. She didn't trust Mr. Brown and believed he would lead Nate into danger.

A couple of weeks later, when Nate realized Betsy was right, he returned home. And she'd forgiven him. She always forgave him.

Ten steps to the fire. Ten steps back. Always turning the other way.

He still remembered the look of betrayal in Betsy's eyes when he'd been asked to go to Tennessee to rescue slaves and had refused to take her along.

"I've had enough," she'd said. "You need to show as much devotion to our marriage and our lives together as you do to rescuing slaves you've never met." Then she'd sobbed.

His insides had quivered, and he had almost decided to stay or to take her with him. Almost.

"I won't wait much longer." It had been the last thing he heard as he rode off.

The corporal stopped, coughed, took a gulp from his canteen.

Nate held his breath. He could use a drink about now, preferably not water.

The guard marched toward the fire.

Nate had returned a year later relieved Betsy had taken him back. He'd secured employment at *The Cleveland Leader* as a typesetter, and life had been good even with the two miscarriages. It would only be a matter of time before Betsy had the family she'd always dreamed of, the family they both wanted.

Back toward the tree.

When war broke out and he had enlisted, she'd been livid, but he thought she'd come around like she had every other time. Until he read her letter.

The corporal moved in Nate's direction and gazed at the hollow spot where he hid.

The fire burned bright. Too bright. Nate's heart raced.

"You in there," the guard shouted and pointed his musket. "Come out and don't do anything stupid."

The other soldiers startled from their sleep, grabbed their rifles, and jumped to their feet. All weapons pointed at Nate scrunched in the hollow of the sycamore tree.

He squeezed out of the tree trunk leaving his sack and blanket behind and tried to stand, but his leg spasmed, and he collapsed to the ground face first. When he looked up, the tall man pointed a musket in his face.

"Get on your feet, Yankee," the corporal said.

Nate rubbed his calf and stood. "Leg cramp." He raised his hands.

The young soldier wiped his hand over his face. "What should we do with him?"

"We could shoot him," the tall man said. "Give him Tarleton's Quarter?"

He swallowed. They weren't going to kill him when he was offering no resistance, were they?

"That's what these Yankees deserve." The older man with rotten teeth spit in Nate's face.

The muscles in his arms clenched, and his hands drew into fists, but he made no attempt to wipe the spittle away.

"We're not going to shoot him," the corporal said, "unless you want to explain why the officer we captured is dead, especially since he might have information on troop movements."

Rotten teeth man backed up a step.

"Jeff." The corporal turned to the tall man. "Tie him up. In the morning, you and Ben can take him to General Bragg while the rest of us see if any of his friends are around.

The tall man removed Nate's Army revolver and tied him to the sycamore tree. They hadn't searched him. He let up a prayer of thanks for their incompetence.

It was only slightly more comfortable than being in the tree. At least they didn't tie his feet. It felt good to stretch his legs to work out the cramp.

The corporal turned to the sixteen-year-old. "You're on guard duty. Wake up Harry to take over in a few hours."

The boy nodded.

The other men slipped into their bedrolls.

Nate glanced back at the tree. "Could I at least have my blanket?"

The young private grabbed the blanket and jerked it out of the hollow and threw it over Nate. Then he began to march in front of the tree, back and forth, back and forth. After about a half hour he sat against a rock next to the campfire and leaned back against it.

Stretching his hand, Nate squinted his eyes closed enough so he could still see a little, steadied his breathing so the guard would think he was asleep, and tried to reach in his pocket. At least with the blanket over him, the private didn't notice. Nate got his finger inside the opening but couldn't dig down far enough.

The boy's eyes drooped.

Nate wiggled to get to his pocketknife.

The young guard's eyes closed, opened, closed again.

Nate reached again barely touching the knife. It took him three tries to grab hold of it.

The soldier's chin rested on his chest, and he let out a soft snore.

Nate went to work cutting the ropes as quietly as he could.

Chapter Twelve

Major Jason Patella, the company surgeon, had given Lavena a thorough interview about medical care during the war. She decided to quote him in her story and meticulously wrote his words to make sure she didn't forget them.

"The largest threat the soldiers face isn't combat injuries but disease. The soldiers who survive injury during battles are more likely to die of infection than their wounds."

This doctor certainly was impressive. Although only thirty years old, he had studied medicine at Cleveland Medical College. His gray eyes and sober look gave the impression of a serious-minded man, the kind of doctor she would want in an emergency.

The other officers had given interesting accounts, and she'd already sent Mr. O'Brady her stories about them, but this interview might convince him and Mr. Cowles to allow her to stay with this assignment even if the illusive ear tugging captain didn't give her his story in time.

If any army surgeon could answer the last question she intended to ask, he could.

She cleared her throat. "Doctor Patella, why are surgeons so quick to amputate limbs? Is it because they don't have the time to bother with trying to save them?"

"Not at all." Doctor Patella offered a slight grin. "I'm not surprised by the question. I've read the newspaper accounts calling us names like sawbones."

"Then what is the reason for so many amputations?"

"Our goal is to save lives." Doctor Patella folded his hands in his lap. "There's so much we don't know about infection, but we have made some observations. When a man's injured limb is amputated within the first twenty-four hours, he has a good chance to survive. When amputation is not carried out in a timely manner or an untrained doctor tries to avoid it, the man is twice as likely to die of infection."

"I had no idea the danger of waiting was that high."

The doctor steepled his fingers to his mouth. "Most people don't. I hope you'll report that in your article."

"I certainly will." She shook his hand. "Thank you for a most informative session."

Doctor Patella nodded his head and moved back to his seat.

Another stirring interview to add to what she had sent her boss. These stories were some of the best reporting she'd ever done. It had to be enough.

She glanced out the window. The sun had already set. She could barely see the backdrop of majestic mountains larger than any she'd ever seen, mountains larger than the fortress she'd placed around her heart. How could one stubborn captain start a crack in the wall in such a short time?

Cage had made it clear he didn't want to tell his side until they reached Chattanooga. Maybe if she were honest with him and told him how her career was at risk, he would allow the interview sooner.

Her heart pounded. No! She wouldn't depend on a man to save her career. The last time she trusted a man that much, it almost destroyed her.

Now Nate Teagan would crush Betsy with his treason and duplicity. She let out a sigh. She would see for herself if he'd returned to his family farm. If she found Nate there, it would prove what she suspected all along.

It was safer to keep that fortification around her heart.

They'd already left Nashville. If Cage was true to his word about granting the interview when they got to Chattanooga, she'd be able to mail the story in time, but it didn't hurt to send as many riveting stories as she could just in case. Even though the moon was little more than a sliver, her lantern and the light from the wood stove shone brightly She still had time for one more interview tonight.

She lit a candle and made her way through the officer's car. The men popped up out of their seats, but she ignored them. As she reached the outside platform between the cars, the train roared around a corner, and she grabbed hold of the railing until the jerking calmed.

Catching her breath, she stepped inside the first car for the enlisted men. The candle cast a dim light in the room. A rumble of noise and a stench of body odor rose from the disheveled soldiers sitting and lying on the floor of the car. Nobody looked up to see she had entered.

They hadn't gone to sleep yet. Good. She doubted Cage would look favorably on her waking them.

She bellowed her announcement so all could hear. "Men, may I have your attention."

The men in one accord stopped talking, jerked their heads toward her, and sat a bit straighter. At least they didn't try to all stand and cause mass confusion.

"Your captain graciously gave me permission to interview you about Cedar Mountain. I'll mention anyone I quote by name." She rubbed her hands together. "This is your chance to get your names in *The Cleveland Leader*, maybe even in *Harper's Weekly*."

Sergeant Garrett stood. "Captain Jones, Sir, are you going to permit this?"

Cage held up his hand. "Hold on, Ma'am. Sergeant Garrett is right. I said you could interview my men, but you're making this a spectacle worthy of a state fair."

Lavena crossed her arms and fixed her gaze on the captain. "Why don't you let them decide if they want their name out there?"

Cage's jaw clenched. "Isn't it a little late for an interview?"

"Fiddlesticks. The sun goes down early this time of year. It's only eight-o-clock."

He pulled out his pocket watch and scowled.

"I wouldn't do anything to disrupt the regiment or the men." She struggled to keep a smirk off her face. "So, if you'll just give me a complete interview now..."

His words sounded like a low growl. "I warn you, you're pushing this too far."

She was thankful she was a woman. If his glower was any indication, only her gender saved her.

Cage rubbed the scar on his cheek. "Fine. You can interview any man who agrees to it, but you'll follow my rules."

Sergeant Garrett's face turned red, and he stormed to the far corner of the car. He tripped over one soldier who didn't get out of the way in time and fell on his face. He stood, brushed himself off, and reached his destination, then leaned against the wall and crossed his arms. His glare darted between the captain and Lavena.

He wasn't the only one. The car full of men ignored the sergeant's tumble and fixed their widened eyes on the confrontation between her and Cage. They obviously weren't used to someone getting the upper hand with him.

Lavena tried to soften the tension by delivering her most charming smile. "That depends. What rules would those be?"

Cage held up a finger. "Interview them one at a time in the officer's car. I won't have this getting out of hand."

"Agreed."

He held up a second finger. "You can only interview one tonight. The sun has been down for hours, and my men need their rest."

"Anymore rules," Lavena said.

He folded his arms and glared at her, then let out grunt. "I'll let you know."

Lavena turned to the sergeant. "Sergeant Garrett, would you like to go first?"

"No, Ma'am." Garrett looked like he couldn't decide whether to salute her or push her off the train. "No offense, Ma'am, but I don't hold to women trying to do men's jobs. My wife is a lady, and you wouldn't see her gallivanting off with soldiers. It's not right. If you want to help the Union cause, you belong at home tending to your house or knitting socks for the troops."

It wasn't the first time Lavena had encountered that attitude, but it still caused heat to travel up her back.

"Sergeant Garrett," Cage stood and bellowed. "This lady is here by direct orders from Colonel Creighton. You will treat her with respect."

"Yes, Sir." This time, the sergeant did salute.

Cage made a sweeping gesture with his hand toward Lavena that she wasn't sure she appreciated. "Carry on."

One young private jumped to his feet. "Can I go first?" He was all legs and arms and looked like the kind of boy who would help an elderly lady with her groceries and shrug it off when she pinched his cheeks. "I was one of 'um."

Lavena turned toward the private. "One of who?"

"Why Ma'am," the boy said, "one of the men Captain Cage saved that day."

Cage slumped against the car wall and nodded.

She ignored the captain's sour disposition. "Private, what's your name?"

"Private Amon Smith." He removed his hat.

Lavena tilted her head toward the next car. "Shall we?"

Amon grinned and started toward the door. "Yes, Ma'am."

As he made his way through the crowd, many of the men slapped him on the back and encouraged him. "Way to go." "Make us proud."

They stepped into the next car, and the officers all stood. Amon halted his stride and saluted. The men returned his salute.

"Please, gentlemen," Lavena said. "Be seated."

The officers reluctantly found their seats.

Amon followed Lavena into the corner. He glanced back at the officers, now in their seats. He stayed standing at attention.

Lavena closed the curtain to ease his anxiety. "Please have a seat, Private Smith."

He sat. "You can call me Amon. Only Sergeant Garrett calls me Private Smith.

She nodded and sat across from him. "Private Amon, how old are you?

"Nineteen, Ma'am. I was just short of my seventeenth birthday when I joined up."

She opened her lap-desk and pulled out her ink bottle and pen and some paper. After closing the box and getting everything situated on the wooden surface, she dipped her pen, and wrote down Amon's name and age. She transcribed his words using the new Pittman Shorthand Method she'd taught herself in college. It came in handy at times like these when she wanted to record every word. "First tell me a little about yourself."

"Well, my ma and me live on a farm in LaGrange Township, not too far from Oberlin."

"What about your father?"

Amon glanced down. "When I was a baby, he fell off his horse and broke his neck." He shrugged his shoulders. "There's just the two of us."

"I'm sorry." Lavena reached out to touch Amon's arm, but drew back. He may have looked like only a boy, but he'd fought in his share of battles. Amon was a soldier. She cleared her throat. "It must have been hard on your mother."

"It would have been a lot harder if our neighbors, Mr. and Mrs. Brown, hadn't stepped in to help. Mr. Brown taught me all I needed to know about farming… and about being a man."

"Sounds like Mr. Brown's a good person."

"He is."

Lavena worked at keeping any sarcasm out of her voice. "So, what qualities does a man have according to Mr. Brown?"

"You know, the usual stuff."

Lavena leaned forward in her seat. "Enlighten me."

Amon tilted his head. "A man works hard to support his family, tries to always do the right thing, and is God-fearing. If he does do something wrong, he acknowledges the corn and takes his licking."

Lavena wrote down every word. She'd never heard a better description. She glanced up. "Do you think your captain is that kind of man?"

"If he's not, there's no man alive who is."

A warmth went through her, but she tamped it down. That's what she thought about her father. He'd fooled everyone, especially her. When the truth came out, he only confessed his wrongdoing because he had no choice. "So, tell me a little more. Is there a girl you're courting back home?"

"Sure is." Amon blushed. "Emma is the prettiest girl in Lorain County, and she's Mr. Brown's daughter which means as soon as I marry her, I'm really going to be a part of the Brown family. He gave his blessing, and I asked her before I left. He wants me to wait 'til after the war to tie the knot."

"Congratulations." Lavena wrote some notes. "So how does Mr. Brown say you should treat a woman, your wife?"

"I don't cotton what you mean, Ma'am." Amon ran his hands across the freckles on his face. "A man treats every lady he meets with courtesy and respect, and he treats every woman like a lady."

Lavena's face heated. Not every man. Not Warren Adder. As soon as he found out what her father had done, he scorned her like she was Biblically unclean.

"I still can't believe she said yes," Amon said. "I miss her an awful lot. It gets lonely. I've made a few good friends, but they were killed. It's hard to watch men you serve with… Well, you know."

Yes, she knew what it was like to lose someone you love. "Tell me a little bit more about Captain Cage."

"He's hard on us when needed, but he cares about his men. He doesn't want us to get hurt or in trouble. It's not just the soldiering either. He wants us to do right."

Captain Cage sometimes he seemed too good to be true, but if he had a chink in his armor, she'd find it. "How does your captain manage that?"

"We have church services almost every Sunday with Lieutenant Jed even though he not an official Army chaplain. The regiment's chaplain resigned about a year ago, so Captain Cage talked to Colonel Creighton about making him kind of an unofficial chaplain. Some of the men even have Bible Studies with Preacher when we're in camp. I've gone a few times."

Lavena wrote a few notes to follow up on Lieutenant Jed. "The lack of official army chaplains is a story my newspaper frequently reports. How does Captain Cage handle alcohol in the camp?"

Amon pulled on his collar. "Colonel Creighton's issued an order that soldiers in the Ohio Seventh aren't allowed to drink anything stronger than lemonade even when off duty. Some of the captains don't like it and ignore the command, but not Captain Cage. He's told us many times he won't tolerate drinking. He won't even let the sutlers bring in liquor or tobacco of any kind, and when a soldier's caught imbibing… well, a friend of mine's been bucked and gagged three times for it. Sergeant Garrett warned him that the next time he'd hang him by his thumbs."

Lavena dipped her pen in the ink bottle. "Sounds like severe punishments."

"At least they're not allowed to flog us anymore although I've heard some officers in other regiments still do."

"So, what do the soldiers think of these punishments meted out by the captain."

"Some of the men don't like it, but they respect Captain Cage, so they don't squawk too much."

"Have you ever been on the receiving end of Captain Cage's punishments?"

Amon's ears turned red. "No, Ma'am, but he has given me one of his talks."

"One of his talks?"

"You know, like a pa would give his son if he's up to no good. Not something I'd like to have happen again."

Lavena suppressed a grin.

"The captain's even harder on us if we're caught doing something wrong with the women who pitch their tents outside of camp."

"You mean soiled doves?"

Amon blushed. "Like I said, he cares about us. Anytime we have a problem, even if we're in trouble, we can go to him."

"You said some of the men don't like Captain Cage's firmness. Anyone in particular?"

"Private Coby Willard. He's the one who got caught drinking." Amon shrugged. "Don't get me wrong, Coby's a lot of fun, and he's about the only friend I have left, but he's kind of on the rough side. He likes to drink, and gamble, and visit the women, so yeah, he blows up about it sometimes."

Lavena jotted Coby Willard's name down so she could seek him out later. "If you don't mind me saying, Private Willard doesn't sound like the type of friend your ma or Mr. Brown would approve of, let alone your girl."

"You sound like Captain Cage." Amon's Adam's apple bulged. "You're not going to put in the article anything I said about Coby, are you?"

"No, of course not," Lavena said, "but he sounds like trouble."

"You don't know what it's like. The boredom and loneliness really get to me sometimes, and well, Coby makes things fun. Anyway, I'm not going to stop being his friend. I've lost too many as it is."

Lavena decided to drop the subject until she could talk to Coby and gauge what kind of man he really was. "Why don't you tell me everything you remember about the day Captain Cage saved your life?"

Despite her best efforts, a nudging hope, deep inside her, had taken root. The captain might be the hero he seemed to be.

Chapter Thirteen

Amon cleared his throat and tried to remember every detail. He didn't want to let the pretty journalist down by forgetting something important.

"It was over a year ago near as I can figure. It was August. We were ordered to march to Cedar Mountain. It was so hot and muggy, the sweat poured off us. And that sun beat down on us harder than any Johnny Reb.

"Some men got overcome by it. My friend Sam was so pale he looked like one of them appaloosa horses. He even got the red dots on his face that those horses have." Amon paused as the grief he'd tried to ignore swept over him. "He collapsed by an old elm tree and rolled down the hillside. I climbed down after him to see if I could help, but when I got down there, he wasn't breathing. He'd up and died."

He wiped his hands on his trousers. He wasn't sure he'd be able to tell this after all. "Sam and me, we grew up together. We joined up the same day, and he was going to stand up for me when I married Emma."

Miss Falcon gazed at Amon like she really cared about Sam even though he didn't die in battle and wasn't a hero or anything. "What was his last name? I'll add him to my story."

"His mama would like that. Last name was Gardner."

Miss Falcon dipped her pen. "Go on."

"The heat wearied me, and it was hard to breathe. We hiked on a trail near the river. It took seven hours to march six miles. We kept having to stop and rest. Every time, I'd drink my fill and get some more water out of the Rapidan River. I'd even pour some water over my head and wet my bandana so I could wear it around my neck. I reckon I drank more water that day than I did in my whole entire life, but it didn't help much. It was just plain hot.

"When we finally got to the mountain, about suppertime, we heard the muskets and cannon fire. I remember pondering how the mountain looked almost blue with all the dark green cedar and pine trees.

"Later on, I wrote Emma a letter about it. She's never seen a mountain. Before the war, I never had either. They're so pretty you just want to gawk at them, but to tell the truth, after marching up so many hills and stepping over my friends who were sprawled out dead on them, I'm not sure I ever want to see another one. After the war, I don't even want to leave LaGrange."

Amon paused to collect himself. He was grateful Miss Falcon didn't ask him any more questions. She just waited. Finding words was harder than he thought it would be, almost like going through it all over again.

Maybe that's why Captain Cage got so mad when someone wanted to interview him.

He swallowed the lump in his throat and continued. "Anyway, we took off after the enemy, and at first, we were doing good. It looked like we would break through the lines. I could see the Ohio Seventh navy blue banner with the eagle advancing ahead, and it made me proud.

"Then everything went wrong. General Stonewall Jackson and his brigade come riding toward us like something out of the book of Revelations. He waved his sword, scabbard and all, and yelled to his men to rally around him. It was fierce.

"It troubled me when Colonel Creighton was hit. I was glad he didn't die, but it was hard to think that a great man like that could be wounded. Lieutenant-Colonel Crane took over command and urged us onward.

"I wanted to run, but I just kept fighting. Smoke from the guns and canyons mixed with the musty air and pine and choked me." He shut his eyes, but he couldn't shut out the sounds or the smells. "What I remember most was the smell of blood.

"Another friend of mine, Jimmy Hudson, fought beside me. He got a little ahead of me when a cannonball hit. He dropped like a tree. Blood covered his chest, and I wanted to stop, but I jumped over him and kept marching into the fray. It was like that 'til dusk.

"The sun started going down and left a red glow over the mountain ...like it was grieving too... grieving over the blood shed there. The bugle call ordering retreat sounded, and we skedaddled out of there. We were done." He rubbed his hand over his face to hold back the emotions.

Miss Falcon's eyes watered, and she dabbed them with her handkerchief. "Take a moment. You can go on when you're ready."

Amon's eyes burned, but he shut them tight to hold the tears back. He drew in deep breaths and tried to swallow, but his mouth was so dry he couldn't manage it. It took a couple of minutes to collect himself enough to continue. "I'm ready. Where was I?"

Miss Falcon looked at her notes. "The bugle call ordering retreat sounded, and we skedaddled out of there. We were done."

He let out a gasp. She'd written down every word he said. He didn't think anyone could write that fast, not even his school teacher back home. "General Branch came riding up and made a speech urging us to attack again, and Captain Cage led the way with a rooster call."

His voice cracked. "Sam and Jimmy weren't the only friends I lost that day."

Miss Falcon paused. "Take your time."

He cleared his throat and adjusted himself on the seat. "We ran as fast as we could. There were about ten men with me, but they were bearing down on us. We split up hoping to lose them. I followed Sergeant Garrett over a ridge. That's when we were captured. Rebels waited over that hill with their muskets pointed at us. I don't mind telling you, I was a bit scared."

Amon wiped the sweat off his brow. "You don't have to write about that, do you?"

Miss Falcon stopped taking notes and looked up. "About what?"

Heat rushed up to his face. "You know, the part where I was scared."

She smiled and crossed something out. "Your secret is safe with me."

"Thanks, Ma'am. I wouldn't want Emma to read the story and think I was cowardly or something."

"You don't need to worry about that. This story will show you as the brave young man you are. Why don't you tell me what happened after you were captured?"

"I don't know why they didn't shoot," Amon said, remembering how he thought he was going to die. "Maybe because we threw down our guns. We were out of ammunition anyway. No point of resisting.

"The enemy soldiers told us to march, and we did, for how long I don't know, but it was a lot easier since the sun set. Even though it was still hot and muggy, it wasn't stifling like before. There was even a breeze.

"Even with the full moon and the lanterns they were carrying, we could only see about ten feet in front of us. It's funny. I heard a lot of sounds on that walk I didn't hear before. An owl hooted, and a wolf howled, so I didn't think anything about the rustling in the bushes. I thought it was an animal, maybe a deer or a possum. Everybody did.

"The sound of a gunshot blasted through the woods, and one of the soldiers guarding us was shot. We all scrambled and hit the ground. Nobody knew who was out there or where the shots came from. Then another blast felled another rebel. When bullets hit the third Johnny Reb, they all started running away.

"Me and my friends just lay there dumbfounded. If the look on my face was the same as my friends, then my mouth was opened wide enough to catch a cannonball. That's when Captain Cage, with only Lieutenant Nate by his side, marched into the clearing. We were glad to see them, I can tell you.

"After the surprise wore off, we figured out Sergeant Garrett and Corporal Jake weren't with us. The rebels still had them."

Miss Falcon stopped writing. "Do you mean Jake Edwards?"

Amon nodded.

"I don't understand. I've met both of these men."

"They showed up in camp a few days later," Amon said. "Corporal Jake told Captain Cage how Sergeant Garrett attacked their armed captors even though he was unarmed and how, if it wasn't for him, they never would have escaped. You should have Sergeant Garrett tell you about it. It's some story."

Miss Falcon gave a little snort. "I'm not sure your sergeant wants to give me an interview, but maybe I can get the story from your corporal. Anyway, what happened after your captain rescued you?"

"I don't know the rest firsthand, just what I heard. To me, it didn't matter. Captain Cage was a hero just for going after his men and getting us out of enemy hands. He ordered us back to camp, and he and Lieutenant Nate hightailed after the rebels."

Miss Falcon tapped her pencil on her chin. "You sound like you still have a great deal of respect for the lieutenant even though he deserted."

"I don't know much about that. I only know he and Captain Cage saved us that day. From what I hear, he saved the captain's life too. That should count for something."

"And you know nothing about the fire?" Miss Falcon asked.

"I don't, but you could ask Coby how the captain came upon that house and tried to save the woman and her children."

"How would Private Coby if the captain ordered you back to camp?" she asked.

He took off after Captain Cage after he was ordered not to. He never was one for following orders."

*****

"Private Amon." Captain Cage's booming voice startled Lavena.

Amon stood at attention.

Cage focused on the private without once glancing toward her. "We're stopping in Tullahoma. Help the men stack arms."

"Yes, Sir."

Lavena stood and faced the captain. "Couldn't this wait a few minutes? I'm almost done with the interview."

"Miss Falcon." Cage said it in a dripping sweet sarcastic voice. "We've been ordered to prepare for an attack, but I'll get word to the rebels they need to wait because you're doing an interview. I'm sure they'll oblige."

Heat rose to Lavena's face. "I'm sorry. I didn't know."

Cage crossed his arms. "When your newspaper appointed you as a correspondent, didn't they give you any instruction about the rules of war?"

She pressed her lips together. "I said I'm sorry. It won't happen again."

The captain turned and marched to the door of the train car.

Private Amon shrugged. "He's really a good man," he said, "if you're not a reporter."

"Private." Cage's voice bellowed.

Private Amon rushed to catch up with his captain.

Lavena plopped onto the bench. Even the war was conspiring against her getting this story.

Chapter Fourteen

Amon rolled a cannonball into place then stretched his back. The gurgling of the Duck River waterfall, crickets, a bullfrog, and the shuffling feet of men preparing for battle interrupted the quiet night. Clouds obscured the moon, but even in the gloom that settled over them, the line of soldiers stacking artillery functioned as a team used to working together.

Private Coby Willard straggled behind Amon. "I hear tell you talked to that pretty reporter." Coby was a stocky man, five years older and two inches shorter, with a smirk that seemed permanently attached to his face.

"Yeah, we talked." Amon picked up a cannon ball in each arm. "Come on, Coby. Help me with these or it's gonna take all night."

Coby scooped a cannonball in one arm and followed Amon. "So, you gonna talk to her again?"

"Probably." Amon stacked his balls next to the cannon.

"I sure would like to spark that filly." Coby dropped his ball, and it rolled away from the others. "Women like that will usually do anything to catch the attention of a man."

"Women like what?" Amon stacked two more cannonballs.

"You know, old maids. She must be near on twenty-five and doesn't have a husband yet. Probably why she has a job. She can't find no man to support her."

"Miss Falcon's not like that. She's real nice."

Coby chuckled. "I bet she is." He rubbed his hands together. "Maybe she'll interview me."

Amon rolled his eyes and grabbed two more balls.

"You're just jealous cause you ain't never been with a woman like that."

"Coby, I told you, I'm betrothed."

"Don't mean nothing if she don't know what you're up to."

"Anyway, you'll get your chance." Amon set the cannonballs on the pile, careful to make sure they didn't roll. "I told Miss Falcon how you followed Captain Cage after he rescued us. She wants to know what happened when he came onto the burning house."

"Is that so?" Coby sat on the ground next the cannon. "Maybe she'll get more of a story than she planned. There's a lot I could tell about that day, things I've kept to myself."

"There you go again, pretending you know something we don't."

Coby chuckled the way he always did when he talked about that day.

"Hey, you joining us for the poker game when we set up camp?"

Amon knew he shouldn't, especially after the warning Captain Cage gave him. The last time he played, he lost a month's pay, money he should've saved for his and Emma's future. He removed his hat and ran his hand through his hair. The captain hadn't punished anyone for gambling yet, just drinking and being with the women, and it would be nice to win some back this time. It wasn't like he was going to drink even if the other men did. "Sure, sounds like fun."

"Private Willard, Private Smith." Sergeant Garrett's voice boomed from behind. "Get those balls stacked. Now!"

"Yes, Sergeant." Amon grabbed two more cannonballs and delivered a glower to his friend.

Coby smirked and slowly rose to his feet. He was a lot of fun, but when he was around, Amon always seemed to get in trouble.

*****

Nate came to a decision. As soon as he had a chance, he would sharpen his pocketknife. It had taken hours, and he still hadn't cut through the ropes even with the guard sleeping on duty.

The young private coughed.

Nate stopped and waited.

The boy's coughing turned fierce and woke him up.

Nate closed his eyes.

The boy stood and meandered to where the men were sleeping.

Nate held his breath and pulled a little on the ropes. They wouldn't give way. He continued to cut.

The boy shook the man with rotten teeth. "Harry, it's your turn."

Harry stood, stretched, and filled the air with obscenities, and the boy settled into his bedroll by the fire. Harry paced, but he never bothered looking Nate's way. Nate kept a watch on him, ready to stop at any moment, while continuing to move his knife back and forth.

The ropes loosened. He tugged on them. A ripping and then a crack sounded through the night air. He cringed, held his hands under the blanket, and glanced toward Harry. The man didn't even look his way. Was it possible he hadn't heard over the sound of the crickets.

Nate thought about making a run for it. No, Harry would hear that. Nate would never make it to the trees before the shooting started. Better to wait a little longer.

Harry rolled a cigarette, lit it. While smoking he walked toward Nate. Nate kept his chin on his chest and his eyes open only enough to see slight movements. Harry threw the cigarette on the ground, sauntered toward the nearby elm tree, and leaned against it.

Nate waited..

Harry's eyes drooped. Jerking himself, he stretched and paced a few times.

Back and forth.

Back and forth.

The man didn't sit or lean against anything, nothing that might lull him into sleep. If only he'd lean against something and rest his eyes.

Back and forth.

Nate didn't know what time it was, but he suspected he'd taken too long with the ropes. It would be daylight in a couple of hours. If he didn't get away by then, he wouldn't have another chance. He had to risk a run for it.

Harry walked toward some blackberry bushes, turned his back to Nate, relieved himself.

Now was his chance. Heart racing, Nate inched off the blanket, stood, and took one footstep at a time, careful not to crunch the leaves blanketing the ground.

He was almost to the woods when a stick cracked under his foot.

Harry shouted. "Hey, stop."

Nate ran.

A musket fired, and a whistling sound passed by his ear barely missing him. Shouts grew louder. They were all awake now.

He rushed to the forest and ran into it. No trail guided him, and he did his best to avoid trees and bushes in his path. Another shot fired. He could hear them charging in to pursue him. He looked back.

They were gaining. He turned his eyes back toward the path, and a branch smacked him in the face. Stopping for a moment, he drew his hand to his face, dazed. Another shot. He ran as fast as his legs could carry him and almost tripped over a large rock, but he managed to jump it instead.

As dark as it was, it was hard to tell if he was going the right way, but any direction taking him away from those guns would do.

From behind, yelling, rustling, more gun fire. He loped through the trees. The mountainous region provided all kinds of caves and crevices, and he knew this area of the country better than his pursuers. He'd grown up not far from here.

If he could find some place to hide, he doubted they'd find him even with the torches they brought. The shadows would shield him. He darted behind a massive oak and squinted to gaze through the darkness.

The gunshots stopped. The rustling noises moved in another direction. He sagged against the oak and closed his eyes. He'd lost them for now, but they'd find him again. There had to be something around here.

He squinted and peered through the darkness looking for any variation. There it was, a hint of an outline a few feet ahead. He knelt on his hands and knees to keep from being seen. He had to go slow to keep the sound of rustling down. He concentrated on one movement at a time. Finally, he reached the crevice, an opening twice the size of the hollow sycamore, and squeezed into it.

His heart raced. Holding his breath, he listened.

Crunching noises drew close by. Either the soldiers had seen or heard his movement, or a wild animal was sniffing around for prey. He hoped for the wild animal.

The rustling grew louder, and a deer ran off into the woods. Nate let out the breath he was holding and listened. The voices drifted further away. He was safe.

He settled in the best he could. He had to leave his haversack and gun back at the campsite. That meant no canteen of water, no hardtack, and no compass to find his way. If a wild animal did cross his path, no weapon for protection. He wished he'd at least been able to grab his blanket on the way out. There would be no fire tonight. He shivered and blew his breath into his cupped hands.

Lord, please don't let it rain. He leaned back and allowed his eyes to close.

His sleep was fitful, and he woke as soon as the sun crested the mountains. Coming out of his hiding place, he stretched and surveyed the area. Now that there was daylight, he recognized the shape of the mountains and terrain. He was closer to his destination than he thought.

Three more days, and he'd be home, and in as much danger as he'd been as a Confederate prisoner or as a Union deserter.

Chapter Fifteen

October 11, 1863, Garrison Creek, Tennessee

Cage stood in the middle of camp, arms crossed and feet planted in the mud, and waited for Sergeant Garrett's answer.

Ping of mallets on metal rails sounded in the distance where the men repaired the track.

The sergeant stood at attention with jaw set toe-to-toe with Cage. No answer.

Ping, ping, ping.

Cage's scar itched from a week's worth of whiskers after spending days trying to catch up with a company of Johnny Rebs, most of the time in the rain.

Despite their best efforts, they'd arrived at the Garrison Creek Bridge too late. It had burned to the ground. They'd finally made camp near the river to repair the bridge and tracks the rebels had blown up, a task that would delay them for at least a week or two more.

Colonel Creighton had not been happy about the delay or the embarrassing way the rebs had made fools of the regiment, and he made no secret about it when he dressed down the company captains.

Cage couldn't help but feel he'd let the colonel and his men down. Even worse, if they didn't make it to Chattanooga in time, the plans Colonel Creighton and he had made in secret would come to naught.

To further aggravate the situation, his sergeant chose now to challenge him. The orders Cage gave were unusual, but he expected them to be carried out.

Ping, ping, ping. Another minute went by.

Garrett broke eye contact and let out a sigh. "When do you want me to do it, Sir?" The Sir had a sarcastic edge.

"Do it now. I'll keep her busy."

The sergeant looked like he'd sucked on a lemon. "Permission to speak freely, Sir."

Cage raised an eyebrow. "Granted."

"This isn't right even if it is that nosy lady reporter. If my wife or the bank I worked for ever knew I stooped this low… It's just not right."

"You don't need to know the reasons, Sergeant. I can assure you this has a military purpose behind it. You have your orders. She had it in her handbag earlier but check her lap-desk as well. It could be anywhere. Be thorough in your search."

Sergeant Garrett looked like he was about to say something else, but he didn't. Instead, he followed Cage to Lavena's tent.

Storm clouds threatened another deluge as Cage ambled toward her tent. "Lavena. Lavena." No answer. "Miss Falcon." He nodded to Sergeant Garrett.

All he needed to do now was find Lavena and distract her from going to her tent. He chuckled to himself. It shouldn't be difficult since she was always looking for him.

His respect for her had risen over the last few days. Even though she was told she could stay with the train, Lavena had joined the Ohio Seventh in marching from Garrison Creek, to Shelbysville, Bell Buckle, Wartrace, and back to where they started with little food or sleep.

She did her part collecting wood for the fire, cooking soup for the men, and helping in a hundred other ways, tasks not required of her as a reporter and guest of the regiment.

There weren't many civilian men who would have been able to keep up with them, let alone a woman.

Why did she have to be a reporter? If she'd been a nurse, or a laundry woman, or even a doctor, he would have considered pursuing a courtship with her.

Unlike most men, he didn't mind her having a career. He admired her for it, but gazing into her dark brown eyes made him want to reveal every secret he kept hidden, and that scared him.

He needed to find a way to keep his distance, even if he had no choose but to seek her out now. He had to keep her distracted while Garrett searched her tent.

The cold air blew a pile of orange and yellow leaves toward the watch fires guarding rows of dirty white linen tents propped up with sticks where the men had made camp.

A few men held their hands over the fires trying to fend off the chill caused by this incessant rain. In this weather, it was the most likely place to find Lavena. Cage walked toward them.

He stopped at every fire, but she was nowhere in sight. He headed to the other side of the embankment, near Duck River, and found her.

She was sitting on a felled tree staring at the rapid stream. When the train had stopped in Garrison Creek, she had changed into Turkish bloomers and men's work boots while the men unloaded cannon balls. She was still wearing them.

Her handbag and lap-desk both with her.

"Blast." He rubbed his cheek.

He'd assumed she would leave them in her tent. If she hadn't hid the letter somewhere else, he'd have to find another way. He did memorize most of it, but there was nothing better than having the paper in hand to prove what he said was true.

He watched her from behind a tree at the top of the hill instead of going to her straight away.

Normally he didn't approve of women wearing trousers even if they were bloomers. Many women at Oberlin had adopted this style with wide pantaloons gathered at the ankles and a short dress covering them to the knees. He had to admit they were more practical than long dresses in situations like this.

Butterflies had decided to take up square dancing in his stomach. Nobody would mistake her for a man no matter what she wore. Even in bloomers, she managed to look feminine.

She didn't wear her long dark hair in a bun or curls adorned with fancy hats. She wore a gray bonnet, and a single, silky braid issued from it and fell over her right shoulder. Simple, practical, but attractive.

Lavena took off her mud-caked boots, revealing her bare foot and slender ankle.

His breath caught in his throat. Perhaps too attractive.

She had chosen a good place for privacy. None of the men would see her unless they climbed the hill. Leaning down, she rubbed one of her feet.

Normally, he would have turned and headed the other way, this seemed too intimate, but he had a job to do, keeping her occupied so she wouldn't catch Garrett searching her tent.

Cage couldn't help a twinge of guilt going through him. He was sure if he asked her for the letter, she would give it to him. He shook his head.

No, there would be questions he couldn't answer. If Garrett didn't find it, he'd figure out a way to separate her from her handbag. He had to carry this through.

He strolled to her. "Ma'am, how are you doing?"

Lavena glanced up and smiled. She pulled the ruffles on the end of her bloomers over her ankles and rubbed her other foot. "I don't think I've ever been so hungry, tired, or sore in my whole life. How do you manage this all the time?"

Cage rolled his shoulders. "I have to admit when I first joined up, the constant drills and marching really got to me. I am glad we're staying put for a few days while the men repair the tracks."

"I'll never get used to it."

Cage sat beside her. "You did well."

"Thank you." She put her boots back on her feet, straightened her posture, and gazed at Cage until it became a bit uncomfortable. "Do you mind if I ask you a few questions?"

He snorted. "You never give up."

Lavena blushed. "Like you and your men, I have a job to do. I know you agreed to my interview in Chattanooga, but it seems we'll be stuck here for at least another week. Could you relent?"

Butterflies in Cage's stomach had stopped dancing and now were having a wrestling match. She was a remarkable woman. Under different circumstances, he would have gladly used the interview as an excuse to spend more time with her. He wouldn't lie to her, but he couldn't tell the whole truth either.

Did he dare allow this to continue? "I'll make an arrangement with you."

Lavena raised her eyebrow. "What kind of arrangement?"

"If you answer my questions, I'll answer yours."

"What questions?" There was a catch in her voice.

"About you."

She stood, took two steps back, and stared at the water like a skittish bird afraid of being captured. "I'm not the one being interviewed."

He offered her a lopsided grin. "Ah, but you haven't been able to get anything out of me. For each question you answer, I'll agree to answer one of yours. Isn't it worth giving up some information for my cooperation?"

Lavena wrapped her arms around herself. Until now, Cage would have described her as a gale force--bold and unstoppable--but now the wind had dispelled, and she was as reticent as the sun on a cloudy day.

She pressed her lips together and extended her hand. "Agreed."

Cage shook it, holding on a bit longer than needed, and motioned for her to sit. "Why don't you tell me about your childhood?"

Her gaze darted to the river. "There's nothing to tell."

"You promised."

She glanced up at the storm clouds gathering in the west. "What do you want to know?"

He placed a hand on hers, and tingles traveled up his arm. He liked the feeling. "How about telling me where you were born, if your parents are still living, and how many brothers and sisters you have? That's all for now."

Lavena pulled her hand away and unbraided and braided the last few weaves of her hair, then retied her ribbon. When she did speak, her faint New York accent grew thick. "I was born in New York City. I was an only child. My mother died in childbirth. My father and his spinster sister, Aunt Martha, raised me. That's all there is to tell."

"Now that wasn't so bad, was it?"

Lavena eyes widened as if she'd revealed a secret worse than Cage's. She pulled paper out of the wooden lap-desk with her and dipped her pen in a small bottle of ink. "You asked three questions, not one. So now it's your turn, and I want plenty of details. Tell me about your life before the war."

Cage let out a breath. An easy question. "I was born in Wellington, Ohio. My father pastored a small church. Never married. I graduated from Oberlin College a few years back, but I never settled on a career. I tried preaching, but I wasn't called, and it showed. I couldn't make a go of being a lawyer. I owned a general store for a time, but nothing seemed to last. I finally ended up teaching school. I did meet a lot of people and made some friends. When the war broke out, I joined up, and they voted me captain of this company."

Lavena wrote down some notes. "What are your plans for after the war?"

"I plan to be a lawman. During this conflict, I realized I'm good at protecting my men and keeping them from trouble, and I do better than most in a crisis. I believe God is calling me to that in civilian life."

Lavena nodded, wrote some more notes.

"I gave you the details you asked for. Now it's my turn." Cage veered the conversation away from Lavena's family, sensing it was something she didn't want to talk about. "It's unusual for a lady to take up a profession, let alone journalism. How did it come about?"

Lavena smoothed out her skirt. "My aunt encouraged me to be an independent professional woman." Her shoulders relaxed. "She was involved in rights for women and people of color and was a part of the convention at Seneca Falls."

Cage had heard of the Seneca Falls Convention in New York State where the woman's rights movement was born fifteen years earlier. "So, you're a suffragette. That's not a surprise considering your chosen career."

Lavena tilted her head and smiled. "I believe in total equality under the law regardless of race and gender, including the vote."

Cage decided not to mention he spoke in churches and to social gatherings about equality for slaves and for women before the war. She would think he was being insincere to impress her, and he didn't want her to stop talking about herself. She was a fascinating woman. "Isn't that a radical view considering the current opinion?"

"I suppose, but it's only a matter of time before society accepts it is the only fair way to conduct matters of humanity. Some churches are even beginning to understand it is not contrary to the Word of God and are ordaining women. Of course, full equality may not happen in my lifetime."

"You still didn't answer my question. Why journalism?"

Lavena shrugged. "In college, I heard Father Finney preach a sermon about the importance of the truth, and I knew then what I wanted to do. You could say I'm called to it. I graduated from Oberlin a few days before the Oberlin-Wellington Rescue, and that gave me my opportunity."

Cage wiped his hand over his mouth remembering that night. "I was there. I believe half of Oberlin followed the slave catchers to Wellington. I never managed to get close enough to the hotel to help with the rescue."

She nodded. "Some of my close friends' husbands were involved, and I realized, through the written word, I could sway opinions by reporting what really happened. So, after trying three other newspapers, I marched into *The Cleveland Leader Newspaper* with the story and interviews of some of the men involved, and Brian O'Brady, the managing editor, hired me on the spot." She dipped her pen in the ink bottle. "How many battles have you fought in?"

"I've lost count. The Ohio Seventh's been in more than most." The scar on Cage's ear itched. He didn't like to talk about this, but he wasn't about to go back on his agreement. "Our first battle was the Battle of Knives and Forks in West Virginia in August of '61. The rebs beat us bad. Over a hundred of our men were wounded and nearly ninety were taken prisoner. Captain John Dyer, a friend of mine from Company D, was killed. It tested our mettle."

"In your very first battle? I'm so sorry. That must have shaken the men."

"It made us more determined. When we fought in the Kanawha Valley, we drove the rebs away. After that, Shenandoah Valley, Bull Run, Antietam, and Chancellorsville. We lost most of them, and some good men, but we were victorious in the last battle we fought, Gettysburg. Only one man killed, but the loss of every soldier is important."

Lavena pressed her lips together. "You left out Cedar Mountain."

"Yes, I did." Cage rubbed the right side of his face and tried to think of a way to divert her to another topic.

"So why are you headed to Chattanooga?"

Cage grinned. "That's two questions."

She smirked.

"All right, but you have to answer two of mine. We're headed there to help General Grant break the Confederate stronghold on Lookout Mountain and Missionary Ridge, so General Sherman can rally the troops to march south to Atlanta."

She wrote down a few notes.

"Next question." He leaned closer and gazed into her stormy eyes. "Why are you so passionate about reporting the truth?"

Her lips pressed together. A deep sigh came from somewhere inside, and she slumped against the felled tree. "My father was a politician at Tammany Hall. He worked for the good of the common man, and to me, he was larger than life, a hero who spent his life helping others. With my aunt's encouragement to pursue a career for the betterment of society, I even considered following in his footsteps and going into politics."

"There must be more to the story. For a woman who seeks the truth, why are you being evasive?"

Lavena bit her lip. "He wasn't the man he pretended to be."

Cage placed his hand over hers. "What happened?"

Thunder rumbled in the distance.

Lavena pulled her hand away. "Captain, that's three questions." She placed her supplies in her portable desk, latched it, and stood. "Maybe we should end the interview for today. A storm is brewing, and I don't want to be caught up in it." She darted up the embankment toward the tents.

A light drizzle began to fall. Cage stroked his chin. This was a new development. Lavena was now the one avoiding his questions. At least he wouldn't have to answer about Cedar Mountain - for now.

He made his way back to his tent where he would meet Sergeant Garrett. By the time he got there, rain came down in sheets soaking into his uniform, but Garrett wasn't there. The sergeant surely had enough time by now. If Lavena caught him searching her tent, Cage didn't even want to think how she would react. Where was the man?

The sergeant marched toward him. Finally. "It's not there." He didn't even bother to salute before tramping off.

Cage rubbed the scar on his cheek. As dangerous as it was, he needed to spend more time with Lavena. He needed to get his hands on that letter.

Chapter Sixteen

October 12, 1863

Well after sunrise, Nate lay on his belly on the crest of a hill and watched for movement. After the incident with the Confederate scouting party, he had little difficulty getting here. He knew this area so well.

Smoke drifted from the brick chimney of the large white colonial house and circled above. The paint was peeling, and the shrubbery needed trimmed, but someone had to be there.

He'd been lying on the cold ground for hours, but there had been no movement. He took a chance and sat up to stretch his arms and legs. A shiver went through him. The grass he'd been lying in was wet from the morning dew, leaving a large spot on the front of his uniform. Couldn't be helped. It would dry when the sun rose higher.

It would be nice to sit in front of a warm hearth. The last time he did that was with Betsy the night before he left. His insides twisted. He tried to ignore the memory. Failed.

He stood to survey the fields and stretched his back to get the crick out of it. The land looked bare, but he expected that. The crops would already have been harvested by now, but even this time of year, slaves plowed over the ground preparing it for winter, but they were nowhere in sight.

The barn needed a fresh coat of paint. There weren't any animals around. No pigs feeding from the trough or wallowing in the mud, and no horses or cows standing in the corral. If there were any, they'd probably wandered away through the places where the fence had been torn down. It sorely needed repaired.

The slaves must have taken off. That was the only explanation. She wouldn't have freed them no matter how bad off she was. Nate swiped at the back of his neck. Maybe she sold them. He shook his head.

She might have sold some, but she'd at least keep one or two around. Cooking and doing the farm chores herself was beneath her.

He'd been on this hill for hours, and the rooster hadn't even crowed. No one came out to collect eggs or milk the cow. Maybe the chickens and cows were gone too. If the war got too close, she might have gone to visit her sister and taken her slaves with her. If she'd done that, what would he do now? All his plans depended on reaching her first.

A raccoon scurried through the field. A squirrel climbed a nearby elm tree to deposit the nut it had in its mouth. Somewhere in the distance, a frog croaked, but no farm animals emerged. Not even the dog or the barn cat.

He couldn't wait any longer. He started down the hill. He'd check inside the barn first. The front door opened with a bang, and he scurried for cover on the ground behind the elm. He landed in a puddle and clapped his hand over his mouth to keep from groaning out loud. He peeked around the tree.

A woman in her fifties, carrying a Henry rifle, trudged toward the barn with a basket looped over her arm. His mother.

She was thinner than he remembered, and she wore a wool gray day dress, not the satin and velvet finery she used to wear.

Nate swallowed the lump in his throat. He couldn't believe his eyes. She was doing the farm chores.

Her husband, father, and grandfather were plantation owners with slave labor. She'd never done menial labor in her entire life. She wouldn't even know which end of the cow to milk.

Rising to his feet, he brushed off the wet leaves and marched down the hill toward the barn. He stopped at the door and peered inside, but she didn't see him. She was too focused on her task.

His mother held the basket with one hand and collected eggs from a handful of chickens with the other. She'd set the Henry rifle on a hay bale beside her where it would be easy to grab if needed.

She'd always been a beauty. Growing up, even his friends would sometimes make remarks about it. The attire she usually wore reminded him of how Queen Victoria might dress. She had been the queen of this plantation, but now she looked more like a poor dirt-farmer's wife. Her salt and pepper hair knotted in a bun on top of her head. The curls and combs usually adorning it nowhere in sight. She didn't even wear a hat or a bonnet. A strand of gray fell onto her face.

"Mama." His voice was thick.

She dropped the basket, reached for the rifle, and pointed it at him.

"It's me. Nate."

"I know who you are." She raised the rifle a little higher. "They haven't driven me crazy yet."

His jaw twitched. "I've come home."

"I can see that." She pinched her lips together and glowered at him in the way she'd normally reserved for the slaves. "I see you're wearing Yankee blue, the uniform of the men who stole our horses and crops and butchered our pigs."

Pain lodged in the back of his throat. "Mama."

"The ones who stole our people and gave them guns to fight against us." She cocked the hammer.

"Please, Mama." His voice sounded like a whispered croak.

"The same enemy who didn't leave us anything except a few chickens."

Nate raised his hands, praying she wouldn't decide to shoot. "I'm still your son."

"They killed Zach." Her lip quivered. "My son's dead."

The news of his younger brother's death hit him in the gut, and he tottered back a step. He hadn't seen Zach since he was twelve, a gangly kid who came running after him the night he left, begging him not to go.

His brother had to be nineteen by now. Nate tried, but he couldn't picture him as a grown man. Dead? How many other Confederate boys joined up for the glory of the South to end up the same way.

He moved a step toward her.

"Stay back, or I'll pull the trigger, so help me."

He halted. "I'm not a Union soldier anymore. I deserted."

Her brow furrowed. "So how does your Yankee wife feel about that?"

A sob escaped Nate's lips. "She left me."

She blinked and lowered the gun slightly.

He took another step. "Please, Mama."

Her lower lip quivered, and she released the hammer.

Nate fell to his knees. "I want to come home."

After setting her Henry rifle on the ground, she ran to him. He sobbed on her shoulder as he used to years ago.

When he was her son.

Chapter Seventeen

After glancing at the rain beating down, Lavena considered waiting to carry out the tasks she'd planned until it slowed down a bit. No matter how tempting it was to wait, best to get on with it. It had rained all night, and it didn't show signs of stopping, but she needed to mail out the stories she'd written and the letters to Aunt Martha and Betsy while she had a chance.

Colonel Creighton had told her that Wartrace was only a mile up the road from the camp where they'd set up near Garrison Fork Bridge. She couldn't believe her good fortune. Not only was it occupied by the Union Army, it had a post office and a telegraph. She didn't want to use the army telegraph when she didn't have to. No need to give Lieutenant-Colonel Crane something else to complain about.

After she mailed the stories, she would contact Mr. O'Brady to let him know of her progress. With the articles she was sending, she was sure he would give her more time if she needed it.

Even with the downpour, the tent Lavena stayed in was comfortable compared to what the soldiers had to endure. Colonel Creighton had ordered the quartermaster to provide her with an officer's tent, two large rubberized flaps, a cot, and a chair. She used one of the flaps as a floor for the tent.

She'd kept dry, but she didn't envy the men who had to stand in the elements while guarding rebel prisoners or sleep in the mud with two small tent flaps half the size of hers propped up with sticks draped over them.

Lavena looked outside. The dark clouds and torrents of rain gave her pause, but she had a job to do. She tied a bonnet to her head, stuffed the stories in an inner pocket in her jacket, and draped one of the rubberized flaps around her head and shoulders to keep her dry. She stepped outside and bumped into Chaplain Jed, also draped in a flap.

She invited him into the tent.

"Ma'am." He nodded a greeting toward her. "I was planning a trip to Wartrace and wondered if you'd like to accompany me."

"Yes, thank you. I was headed there to post my stories for the paper. I've amassed quite a number of them." She pressed her lips together. "I also need to stop by the telegraph office if you don't mind."

"That's where I'm headed." Jed motioned for her to take his arm, and they headed toward town. "I heard about the heated discussion you had with Lieutenant-Colonel Crane about the army telegraph. I thought

Colonel Creighton gave you access to it."

She stepped aside to avoid a large puddle. "He did. I've already telegraphed my editor about the attack on the bridge and railroad track at Garrison Creek and other pertinent information I've gained from interviewing senior officers, but I think it wise to find other means whenever I can."

"I also plan to send a telegram. I've decided not to wait for word on my family any longer."

"Oh, I pray you hear good news."

"Me too," Jed said.

They didn't say any more the rest of the way there. The chaplain seemed too lost in his thoughts to offer idle conversation, and she didn't know what to say. So many men and boys died in the Kansas raid, the chances of Jed's family being untouched by the tragedy was unlikely.

Her troubles were insignificant in comparison to his. All she had to worry about was getting Captain Cage's story in time while trying to avoid telling him any more about her life. If she'd been in a better mood, she would have chuckled at the irony.

She couldn't wait until they arrived in Chattanooga to interview the captain. The regiment wouldn't be able to go any further until the soldiers fixed the train tracks and bridge the enemy destroyed. They would be camped here for weeks, and time was running out.

She considered Cage's question to her. *What happened?* Closing her eyes, she remembering the scandal of the decade as if it had happened yesterday.

*****

Father had asked her to dine with him at Charlie's, their favorite restaurant on the pier. She'd assumed it was a luncheon to celebrate her seventeenth birthday. Every year since she could remember, he'd invited her and Aunt Martha to Charlie's for her birthday, but that was only the start of her birthday week.

The day after her birthday, the two of them would go camping and hunting in upstate New York. He'd taught her how to quietly track animals, how to start a fire, and everything she needed to know about living off the land.

She once asked if he took her on those trips because he didn't have a son. He'd let a grin cross his features. "I don't know what your gender has to do with it. I enjoy your company." That had made her so happy.

When she'd arrived at the restaurant, he hadn't seemed his usual cheerful self. His normally twinkling brown eyes had a haze clouding them. His shoulder hunched as if a quarry had deposited heavy stones on them. She barely recognized him.

A dread tightened around her chest. This wasn't a celebration. Something was wrong. She sat across from him. Maybe something happened to Aunt Martha.

Lavena took his hand. "Father, what's wrong?"

He let out a snort as if the question was preposterous. "I prayed you'd never know what I've done, but..." He wiped his hand over his face. "The Bible is right when it says, 'Be sure your sin will find you out'. I was a fool for thinking I could get away with it."

"You're scaring me." Her stomach churned. "Did something happen to Aunt Martha?"

His chin quivered. "Honey, I would have done anything to spare you this, but the city prosecutor has issued a warrant for my arrest."

Her mouth gaped open. "What? Why? This has to be a mistake. Have you talked to Esquire Johnson? Or Mayor Westervelt? I'm sure the mayor will have something to say about this. After all, you are his biggest supporter."

He stared at his coffee cup but didn't answer.

"Say something."

"I thought about going out West to escape, but I couldn't take you away from your aunt or your fiancé. We'd be on the dodge the rest of our lives, and I won't leave without you. At least you'll have Warren by your side. He's a fine man with a good reputation. If anyone can keep you out of this scandal, he can."

The people around her became a blur. Her thoughts jumbled. This had to be a mistake. "Why do they want to arrest you? You haven't done anything wrong."

His voice thickened, and he lifted his gaze toward her. "I've decided to surrender myself to the authorities and confess everything before they come after me." His shoulders relaxed as if making the decision had lifted some of the weight from them.

"Confess what?" The back of her throat ached, and she swallowed at the sour taste in her mouth.

Father let out a gusty sigh. "I'm not the hero you think I am."

"No."

"I didn't start out that way. Lavena, I want you to believe me. I went into politics to make a better life for the common man." He let out a snort. "Since I'm being honest, it wasn't the only reason. I wanted to make my mark in the world, to be important."

She took a few shallow breaths trying to get air in her lungs. She tried to catch hold of the words he was saying, but a fog enveloped her.

"It started small. A bribe to look the other way. A small compromise to further my career. Before I knew it, I was so deep in, I couldn't get out. A reporter made it his job to expose the corruption. The whole story will be in *The Sun Newspaper* tomorrow morning. He's turned over the proof to the district attorney. They have all they need to put me in prison for the rest of my life."

She pulled her hand away.

He reached toward her but pulled back at the last moment. "Everyone in the city will know what I've done, and I'm afraid they'll draw you into it. I'm guilty of all of it. I deserve whatever they decide to do to me, but I'm sorry my crimes will cause you so much grief."

She stood and covered her ears, not wanting to hear any more. It couldn't be true. Her father had never missed a church service, and he'd helped so many people. He wasn't corrupt. He couldn't be. She stumbled through the restaurant, bumping into tables on her way out and pushed through the door.

Her father's voice trailed behind. "Lavena, wait."

She ran away from him as fast as she could.

*****

The thought of seeing him again had made her sick to her stomach. She hadn't visited him in jail, nor did she come to the trial. She couldn't. She had torn up the letters he sent her without reading them.

He'd done as he promised by going directly to the prosecutor and making a full confession, but nothing he could say would ever change things between them, not after what he'd done.

The scandal did follow her. Reporters did everything they could to expose her father, but that wasn't enough for them. Their lies about how she must have known and kept quiet filled the front page. Camping outside her house, they plummeted her with their accusations every time she dared show herself in public.

Friends shunned her. Women she'd known all her life turned the other direction when they saw her. She was no longer considered worthy to attend gatherings in polite society.

Her fiancé did nothing to help. When Warren heard of the scandal, he couldn't wait break off the engagement. He was afraid she would ruin his chances for being elected.

Aunt Martha had quietly arranged for her to leave the city and attend Oberlin College. From that time, her main pursuit had been advancing her career and becoming an independent woman. She would never allow herself to be in a position where she needed a man to support her.

Her aunt had urged her to see or write to her father, but the pain was too great. She wouldn't risk being betrayed again.

Her thoughts raced to all the times she'd hurt those around her by refusing to break down the fortress around her heart.

Lord, I don't want to be like this.

Now, a decent man, a man she could trust with her heart, wanted to know everything about her. Maybe she should tell Cage the truth. It wasn't like it was a secret. It had been in all the newspapers, the scandal of the decade.

And truth always had a way of coming to the surface.

A sadness washed through her. That fortress would stay in place a little longer. She couldn't deny her attraction to Cage, but when he learned the whole story, it would be over before any type of affection could start.

More reason not to allow any attraction to bloom between them.

Chapter Eighteen

They'd reached the telegraph office and pushed inside. Lavena was so grateful to be out of the storm she wanted to shout, "hallelujah." Chaplain Jed and she removed the covers from over them and allowed the water to drip off.

The telegraph operator, a thin, older man with a clean-shaven face, raised an eyebrow at them. "Did you have to bring the rain in here? You Yankees don't got the sense God gave a mule. Ain't bad enough you gotta take over the town. Now you got to come in and drip water all over my clean floor."

"I'm sorry as I can be," Chaplain Jed said. "If you get me a mop from the back, I'll clean this mess up."

The telegraph operator waved him off. "No need. It'll dry soon enough. Now what can I do for you?"

"We each have a couple of telegrams we'd like sent."

"You got Confederate money or greenbacks?"

"Greenbacks," Jed said. "I hope that's all right."

The telegraph operator nodded. "The Confederate money ain't worth the paper it's printed on. I'm not taking it as currency anymore. All them Reb soldiers want to do is send out telegrams without paying for them anyway. They got some idea I'm working for free."

Lavena couldn't help but grin. The man couldn't seem to decide which side he was on. He was probably more for himself than any cause.

"Well," the telegraph operator grabbed a pad and pen and passed it to Jed. "I don't have all day."

Jed scratched down what he wanted to say and pulled out a greenback. "I'll wait for the reply. This should be enough for hers too."

Heat flushed Lavena's face. "Chaplain, no. I'll pay for my own."

"Nonsense. I insist."

"No." She pressed her lips together. "I think you mistook my intentions coming to town with you. I have no interest in romance, and I will not be beholden to a man, any man. I will pay my own way."

The muscle in Jed's jaw twitched. "I assure you, Ma'am, I have no designs on you and no desire for a courtship. We're in the middle of a war in case you hadn't notice. I meant the gesture as a thank you for accompanying me on this difficult errand." He looked at his feet. "I didn't want to be alone when I heard the news."

Lavena flushed. "I'm so sorry." When would she learn to just accept an offer of kindness without looking for an ulterior motive? "I just thought..."

Jed's jaw jutted. "You thought I would come here to find out the fate of my family but be so overcome by your charms, I would try to buy your affections for the price of a telegram. Believe me, the price would be too high."

"I said I was sorry." Heat rush up her back. "Perhaps it would be better if I left. I could send my telegram later."

"Please don't go." Jed swiped his hand through his hair. "You aren't the only one with a temper. I've been so worried, I didn't think how my offer would sound. Of course, you misunderstood."

She smiled to let him know all was forgiven. "I'll stay, but I'll pay for my own telegram."

He nodded. "Perhaps that would be best."

She wrote out the message to her boss in as few words as she could. She gave him a list of articles to expect in the mail. One of the best was about the ordeals the men suffered. Most civilians could only guess at what they endured.

She also reminded her boss about the article she'd already sent him, based on her interview with Major Patella. The doctor gave her great insight on the challenges army doctors faced. That story alone was worth her keeping her job.

Handing the message to the clerk, she said, "I'll also wait for the reply."

They sat on the bench against the wall as the telegraph offer tapped out their messages in a series of dots and dashes.

"I'm worried about my two youngest brothers the most," Jed said. "Caleb is only ten years old, and Joshua is only two years older. It would devastate them if something happened to Pa."

"So young," Lavena said. "At least you know your mother is all right. From what I heard, Quantrill didn't attack women."

"Yes, there's some comfort there."

The telegraph began making a series of taps, and the operator grabbed a pen and paper to record them. Jed and Lavena stood and rushed to the counter.

"Probably not for either of you," the operator said. "Too soon."

Lavena's shoulders slumped. She turned to Jed. "Would you accompany me to the post office? It would give us something to do while we're waiting."

"Wait," the operator said. "I have a reply for the lady." He tapped a few times and finished writing the message. He handed it to her.

Lavena's hand shook as she stared at the paper. O'Brady had sent a two word response.

Timeline stands.

*****

Captain Cage headed to Lavena's tent. Nobody was around. He had suggested Jed see if Lavena would accompany him to town, and it looked as if she'd agreed. As much as he needed her out of the way, he was also gratified Jed wouldn't be alone. It was likely some of his family was dead, and nobody should hear news like that alone.

He glanced around to make sure nobody was looking and darted into her tent. Perusing the space, he saw everything he expected. He peered under the cot where she kept her carpet bag and lap-desk. He opened the lap-desk first. Paper, pen, ink, and the story she'd started on Private Amon Smith.

He sat on the nearby chair and read it. It had scratch marks and notations, probably not the draft she was sending to the paper, but it was a great story. He nodded his approval even though she wasn't there to see it.

She had captured the horror of war, boredom, and grief these young men faced, yet there was more on these pages. She'd also managed to convey the hope and heroism behind the cause. He'd never read any news article more compelling. If he were willing to share what happened at Cedar Mountain, he could think of no better reporter to record the events.

He swiped at the scar on his face. How was he going to do this interview? He wouldn't lie to her no matter how much he was tempted. He cared for her too much.

The realization startled him. They were in the middle of a war, not exactly the time for a courtship, but there it was. A deep fondness for her was growing inside of him, and he didn't know what to do about it. Once he told her what he'd done, it would be over.

He wanted to have the courage to take whatever came of it even if everyone in the country would know what he'd done. The secret had been weighing hard on him, and he longed to be free from it. Better to get it out in the open, but now, how could he? How could he admit the whole truth and lose her respect?

Time to worry about that later. For now, he had a job to do. He searched through the paper in the lap-desk. There was a letter from a woman name Martha Falcon, probably a relative. She'd mentioned a maiden aunt.

He considered reading it to find out more about Lavena, but he wouldn't do that. He wasn't in her tent to snoop. He was only after the letter Mrs. Teagan wrote to her husband.

Finding nothing more in the lap-desk, he replaced everything as he found it. He grabbed the carpet bag and hesitated. If searching her lap-desk was an invasion of privacy, going through her unmentionables would even be worse. He remembered ordering Sergeant Garrett to do the same thing, and his face flushed. He'd always said he wouldn't order his men to do something he wouldn't.

Setting his jaw for the task at hand, he searched her belongings while trying to ignore the garments he was rummaging through. Skirts, bodices, her bloomers, chemise, petticoats. Drawers.

Heat traveled to his face and fingers, and he dropped them to the ground. He wiped a hand over his mouth and finished searching. Nothing but clothes and tins of tea. She must have kept the letter in her handbag and taken it with her.

He let out a groan, folded the clothing, and placed it in the carpetbag in the same order he removed it. There was nothing more he could do here. He draped a cover around his head and headed to town. He'd suggested Jed have Lavena accompany him to the telegraph office, but if things went as he expected, Jed would need him to lend his support.

When he got to town, he found them still waiting at the telegraph office. Both sat on the bench in stoic silence.

Cage sat beside Jed. "No word yet?"

Jed shook his head. "We've been to the post office and the general store, but when we got back, nothing."

"The general store?"

Lavena blushed. "I wanted to see if they had any decent tea I could purchase. They don't."

Cage covered his mouth to hide the grin spreading across it. "I'll wait with you."

The clerk stepped up to the counter. "That's right. Why don't you invite all the Yankee soldiers around here to wait around in this tiny office? You could have a sewing bee. That will drum up business. I'm sure all the fine Southerners in this town will want to come in here and send telegrams with you..." Tapping sounded on the telegraph caused the man to stop his tirade and rush to the desk.

Jed stood and walked over the counter, his brow furrowed. Cage and Lavena stood stepped to his side. Lavena put a hand on Jed's shoulder and shook her head slightly.

"It's not for you," the man called out as he wrote out the message.

Jed's shoulders sagged, and they all made their way back to the bench. The clerk finished writing out the message and scurried to the door. "I'll be out for delivery. You need to skedaddle while I'm gone. I won't have you using my telegraph trying to get military secrets."

Cage started to say something, but Lavena grabbed hold of his arm.

"I have something to tell you." She tilted her head toward the door.

He motioned them to head outside. At least the rain had stopped for a while. The sun was a welcome sight after two days of this constant deluge.

After they exited, he held a finger to his lips. Lavena and Jed nodded to show their understanding, and they waited until the clerk locked the door and walked a few yards up the street.

"All right, what is it?" Cage said.

"The message was for a man named Thomas Becker," Lavena said.

Cage wiped his hand over his mouth. "How did you know that?"

Lavena grinned. "I know Morse Code."

Cage's mouth gaped open. She always managed to impress him in some new way. "So, did you catch what it was about?"

"Sure did. It was from someone named General Hardee. He told Mr. Becker about the bridge and train tracks being destroyed."

Cage whistled. "General Hardee is Confederate. When we get back to camp, I'll report this to Colonel Creighton."

"Good idea," Jed said. "Why don't we get something to eat while we're waiting?"

"The Chockley Inn and Tavern's up the road," Lavena said. "We could go there?"

Cage shook his head. "We're in the South, and Wartrace has been used as Confederate headquarters more than once. This isn't a good place to waltz around, buying tea at the general store, making conversation with the locals, and eating at the local inn. Sending a telegram is one thing, but ..."

Jed's jaw twitched. "It's my fault, Captain. My mind was elsewhere. I didn't think."

"We're in occupied territory," Lavena said. "Everyone seems to accept things the way they are, and we need to eat. What's wrong with going to lunch at the tavern? It's not like they're going to shoot us in the back or poison us."

Cage placed his hands on his hips. "They might. They're still getting telegrams from Confederate generals. Who knows what they'd do. Each one of these good people could be informing soldiers nearby or storing supplies like gunpowder in their storm shelters." He rubbed the scar across his cheek.

Lavena's featured softened. "Is that what caused the fire that burned you? A gunpowder explosion?"

Cage nodded, a blanket of guilt covering him. "We'll go back to camp to eat. After I report your information to the colonel, Lieutenant Jed and I will come back to see if there's an answer to the telegram."

"I may be a woman, but I can take care of myself. I don't need your protection, and I refuse to be sheltered at the camp. Jed might need me."

Cage's stomach hardened. What was going on between them? "I assure you I am well able to keep him company." He glanced at his friend. "Lieutenant Jed doesn't need a woman to hold his hand. Perhaps you could coddle one of the privates you've insisted on interviewing."

Lavena's mouth twisted in an unflattering way. She spun around and headed back to camp without another word.

"Why did you do that?" Jed delivered his preacher glare. "She was just trying to help." He ran to catch up with her.

Cage's stomach churned. He doubted he would be eating any time soon.

Chapter Nineteen

Lavena couldn't remember a time she'd been angrier. She thought she and Cage had made peace with each other, and he had to ruin it with his accusations. Coddling. She'd never coddled a man in her life.

Jed caught up with her. "I'm sorry. He's under a lot of stress."

She kept walking at a steady pace. There was no way she would share her past with that man. Somehow, she'd get the interview while sidestepping his questions. She'd have to spend a couple of days thinking of how to approach him, but she'd figure out a way. "You shouldn't apologize for your captain. You wouldn't want to coddle him."

Jed stopped, stared for a moment, then let out a snort followed by a large belly laugh.

Lavena couldn't help it. The thought of anyone coddling Captain Cage was ridiculous. She slowed her pace and let out a giggle.

Jed struggled to contain himself. He finally managed to stifle the snickers and rushed to catch up with her. "I didn't know you knew how to laugh. You're always so serious."

Lavena shrugged. "These are serious times. I'm surprised you have any merriment when you're waiting for word about your family."

Jed's face dropped, and she regretted saying anything. "The joy of the Lord is my strength. He sustains me." He offered his arm. "Would you care to dine with me today, Miss Falcon? It would be as friends only." He gave a halfhearted shrug. "Afterwards, we could take a stroll back to the telegraph office."

Lavena placed her arm in his. "I'd be delighted, Lieutenant Jackson. What will we be having for lunch today?"

"I thought we could dine at the Garrison Creek encampment. I hear they have a very tasty dry tack and rabbit stew and beef jerky for dessert."

Lavena let out an unladylike snort. "Sounds delicious. And to think Captain Cage will miss such a magnificent fare."

"Not to mention your tea," Jed said. "It's a whole site better than the essence of coffee the US Army serves. We can stop by your tent and get it."

"I brought some bohea tea leaves with me."

"Have you now?" He said.

She grinned and lifted an eyebrow. "I never go anywhere without my tea."

Jed's smile slipped. "My mother likes tea."

"Does she?"

He nodded, but didn't say anymore as they walked slowly back to camp.

After they made it back and placed a pot of water over the cook fire, Lavena decided to do something to get his mind off his family.

"Chaplain Jed, while we're eating, I wondered if I could interview you about the way you're providing spiritual comfort to the men."

"Just Jed is fine. I don't mind being interviewed, but you don't have your pen and paper with you."

"My tent is in the next row. It would only take a moment to fetch my lap-desk."

Jed nodded, and she hurried to her tent. Pulling her lap-desk from under her cot, she caught a glimpse at her aunt's letter. Strange. She was certain she'd tucked it away in her desk. Perhaps it fell out.

Opening her carpetbag, she stuck it in beside her undergarments and hurried to Jed's tent. The water was already boiling, so she made them both a cup of tea while they ate some beef jerky.

After they were done eating and the tea was poured, she set up her inkwell and pen. "Okay, Jed." She wrote his name and rank and the date on the top of her paper. "I'm ready."

Jed wrapped his hands around the cup. "I don't see why you want to interview me."

"Fiddlesticks," Lavena said. "Your story might help the US Army see the importance of chaplains."

He raised an eyebrow. "In that case, what do you want to know?"

"How do you prepare the men to face battle?"

"There isn't really anything I can do. It's something they have to decide in their own hearts."

"You must help them in some way."

Jed shrugged. "I pray with them. I help them spiritually by having Sunday services, and I teach the Word and disciple them at midweek Bible studies when possible." He took a sip of tea. "That's about all I can do other than giving them godly counsel when they seek it."

She drank a gulp. The warm liquid coated her dry throat. "Amon told me about a couple of his best friends who died."

Jed nodded. "A number of men have lost friends." A sadness cast over his face. He gazed at her a moment before he said more. "You understand I won't tell you about anything said to me in private."

"Of course." Lavena dipped her pen in ink and made some notes. She hated to ask the next question, but it was important to the story. "Have you been able to pray with any of the men as they passed?"

Jed tugged at his collar. "A few."

She took a sip of tea to give him a moment. "I imagine that was a great comfort."

"I hope so. God is the only comfort they can rely on out here."

"What do you think of the Union Army's chaplain program?"

"I'm not the one to tell the army what to do." Jed gulped some tea. "I only know that most regiments don't have official chaplains even though the men request them. That's why those with any theological or ministry background, like me, are generally appointed as unofficial chaplains for their regiments."

"Who appointed you?"

"The Seventh started out with a chaplain, but he resigned over a year ago, so I requested the extra duty. Captain Cage went to Colonel Creighton with the request, and he agreed to it. Colonel Creighton and Lieutenant-Colonel Crane both come from strong Christian families and are in favor of an army chaplaincy."

"Doesn't that put a hardship on you since you still have your military duties?"

"Yes, being both soldier and chaplain is a lot of work. Cage didn't want to put that heavy burden on me, but I insisted. Until recently Lieutenant Nate Teagan took on some of my load."

Lavena bit her lower lip. "You mean before he deserted and became a traitor."

Jed raised an eyebrow. "He might not be the scoundrel you're portraying him as. Either way, it's not our place to judge. The Lord requires us to love our enemies and forgive those who despitefully use us."

The hair on the back of her neck irritated her, and she swiped at it. Sometimes that wasn't easy, especially when those who despitefully used her were the same ones she thought loved her. "So how are you managing since Nate is no longer in camp?"

"Sergeant Garrett has helped by taking some of my responsibility on himself. Maybe you should interview him. He knows more about what goes on with the men of this company than Captain Cage or I do."

Lavena let out a huff. "I'd like to, but he doesn't believe ladies should be journalists. He let me know very clearly he will not let me interview him, and I'm to…" she stood at attention and used a scratchy deep voice, 'Stay out of my way, and don't cause a ruckus, or I'll forget you're a woman and ...'" Heat flushed her face. "I can't say the rest."

Jed chuckled. "You don't have to. Sergeant Garrett is rather opinionated about doing things by the book. He takes his responsibility very seriously."

"I've noticed."

"He does his duty exceptionally well, and he's helped me with the workload."

She swallowed a sip of tea. "Betsy Teagan, Nate's wife, is a close friend of mine. Is there anything you can say that would bring comfort to her after what her husband has done?"

Jed head cocked to one side. "Am I still being interviewed for your newspaper?"

She set down her pen. "I'm asking this for her benefit only."

He nodded and set his teacup down. "I can't say much. The only thing I can offer Mrs. Teagan is she should pray for her husband. He needs it."

"Because he needs salvation before he's caught and executed?"

Jed kneaded the back of his neck. "Miss Falcon, we need to change the subject, or I'll have to end this interview."

She nodded. Better to leave it be for now, but when the time was right, she needed to find out what the chaplain knew about Nate. She took a sip of tea then put away her pen and paper. It was time to go back to town to find out about the reply to the telegram anyway.

Chapter Twenty

Nate lay in the rope bed he slept in as a boy and stared at the ceiling. Rain hit the roof and thunder crashed, another dreary day. He hadn't slept much. His mother hadn't said a harsh word to him when he was growing up. He would have never expected her to point a gun at him. If she was that angry, how would his father react when he arrived in a few days?

It was late. He should have gotten up hours ago, but after a month of sleeping on the ground, it felt good to lie in a real bed. He pulled the log cabin quilt his mother had made over his head.

His mother loved to quilt and embroider. She used to have quilting bees for all the ladies in Hamilton County, at least the married ladies accepted in society. Free blacks and white women married to dirt poor farmers were never invited. Nor were the ladies with scandal attached to their names.

Betsy would like his mother. She also had a penchant for fine gowns and enjoyed embroidery and quilting. Maybe that's what attracted him originally. She reminded him of his mother.

A lump formed in his throat. There was no point brooding about his wife. His causes kept her from the life she wanted. She wanted a husband who would stay home and build a decent life for them as they raised a large family. He had ruined any chance of being that man.

At least, if his father decided to shoot him and she became a widow, she'd be free to marry a man worthy of her.

He groaned, stretched, and meandered to the washstand where the porcelain pitcher and bowl painted with pink roses sat. Splashing water on his face didn't help him feel any more awake.

Opening the top drawer of the walnut dresser, he pulled out the clothes his mother had provided, wool patched trousers a couple of inches too short and a plaid flannel shirt that had seen better days. Slave clothes. The night before, she had burned the Union uniform, said she didn't want it around.

He'd almost stopped her, but he kept sight on why he was there and resisted the temptation. A sick feeling had come over him as he watched the wool cloth catch on fire, but as proud as he was of his Union Blues, it was for the best. He didn't want to be dressed in his uniform when his father came home.

The last time he'd seen the man was after he'd helped five slaves escape. He couldn't erase the look of anger and hurt Father's eyes.

Nate had tried to explain, to tell him he couldn't be a party to slavery anymore.

A vein in Father's forehead had pulsed. "You betray me and steal my people from me, and you accuse me of sinning?" He'd grabbed hold of Nate's collar. "Get out of my house."

Nate's stomach churned. He wanted to see his father again, but at the same time, he dreaded the encounter.

He finished dressing and sauntered through the halls to find his mother. The parlor where she usually sat in front of the fireplace doing her embroidery was empty. The fireplace lay dormant and cold. No cinders or ash dirtied the bottom. Dust covered the pine tables and oil lamps. Even the blue and green flowered sofa needed a rug beater applied to it.

He searched for her in her bedroom and the dining room. The bedroom had been used, but the dining room was in the same condition as the parlor.

He entered the music room expecting to see the grand piano in its place of prominence. It was there, covered in a layer of dust, but the room had been emptied of everything else. No violins or cellos. No furniture of any kind. Even the painting of mother and father when they were first married had been removed.

This room used to be his mother's favorite place. She insisted her sons learn to play instruments. Now there was nothing left. He sat on the piano bench and pecked out his favorite hymn, *And Can It Be That I Should Gain*. The notes clanged, jarring him inside. "Amazing love! How can it be, That Thou, my God, should die for me?"

The song didn't set right in him anymore. His parents had disowned him, and Betsy had rejected him. He didn't blame any of them. He could see what he'd become. How could God love him?

His stomach growled, and he shuffled down the hall to rummage through the kitchen for something to eat.

His mother stood over the fireplace with a faded, stained apron tied around her waist. Not bothering to look his way or acknowledge him, she cracked some eggs over a cast-iron skillet and set them on the grate.

A coldness overtook him, and he let out an audible gasp without meaning to. In the entire time he was growing up, he never saw her cook.

He stuffed down the shock. "Good morning, Mama." He kissed her cheek and sat on the bench next to the oak table.

"Morning's half gone."

"I overslept."

She poured him a cup of coffee from the pot sitting on a grate over the coals. Striding to the counter, she cut a slice of bread and dished up some eggs from the skillet.

He bit into bread dryer than his hardtack rations. The eggs would have been easier to eat with a spoon as runny as they were. "How about some bacon?"

"We don't have any." Mama turned to face him, a scowl crossing her features. "Your Yankee friends butchered the pigs and took all the meat in the smokehouse. And don't bother asking for milk or butter. They stole our cows too."

"I didn't know things were so bad."

"You probably would have done the same. You're one of them."

He stared at his plate. "Not anymore."

She tilted her head. "Eat your breakfast. It's all you're getting until supper."

After sopping up the eggs with the dry bread, he took a bite. They were hardly digestible, but he'd had worse since joining the army.

Mama dished out a plate and sat beside him. She picked at her food then set her fork down and let out a sob.

A chill went through him. Things had to be worse than he'd figured. She'd always said a lady doesn't parade her emotions. She hadn't even shed a tear when three of his younger brothers and his baby sister had died of typhoid fever. Nate wrapped his arms around her while she cried for the first time since he could remember.

His chest tightened. He did regret what he'd done to his family, but he regretted what he was about to do more.

Chapter Twenty-One

Cage was by his cook fire in front of the tent he and Jed shared. At least it wasn't raining today. The sun had even made a reappearance. He tried to swallow down some essence of coffee.

After the argument he'd had with Lavena, he'd planned to meet Jed back in town, but he'd never got there. When he'd relayed the information about General Hardee to Colonel Creighton, the colonel wanted him to find Mr. Becker and bring him to camp, by force if necessary. Turned out Becker was really Captain Becker, a Confederate officer left in Wartrace to spy on the invading Union troops.

That had taken the rest of the day.

Jed had guard duty the night before and was still asleep. Cage hadn't even heard if there'd been a reply to his telegram.

He couldn't believe how jealous he was when he saw his friend and Lavena cozying up to each other in town. He owed them both an apology. Now he realized how foolish he'd been. He was the one who insisted Jed escort her to town so he could have someone with him when he received news about his family.

That didn't work out well. After Cage blew up at Lavena, she probably didn't bother going back to town. Jed most likely was alone when he heard.

Cage groaned. How did that reporter get under his skin so quickly? All he knew was he needed to see more of her, and the only way to do that was to give her the interview she wanted.

He couldn't tell her all of it, or he'd lose her respect, and lying didn't set well with him. Somehow, he had to figure out a way to tell her what everyone knew about the account and leave out the rest.

His mother would have said his intent was to deceive, so it was still a lie. Maybe it was, but he'd lived with this lie so long, how could he come clean now and risk losing a woman he was starting to love?

Love. That was the truth. He was falling in love with her, and he didn't want to lose her.

A relationship is based on truth and forgiveness. Another of his mother's famous sayings. Only there would be no relationship. When Lavena found out the truth, there would be no forgiveness.

Jed wandered out of the tent and sat beside him. He poured himself a cup of essence of coffee and watched the men working near the creek, saying nothing.

"Did you get a reply from the telegram?" Cage tried to make it sound casual, but the words caught in his throat.

"No, not yet." Jed glanced toward him. "Would you like to go with me to town today, or do you have more subterfuge with Miss Lavena planned?"

Cage rubbed his ear. "We need that letter."

"No, we don't. You know what's in it. Isn't that enough?"

"It doesn't matter. She keeps it with her in that handbag of hers, and I'm not about to abduct her to get it." Cage poured out his coffee. It had soured in his stomach.

A cup of Lavena's tea would settle his gut, but he wasn't sure he wanted to face her yet. "We might as well get going. I don't have any duties keeping me at camp today anyway."

They walked to town in silence. There was nothing to be said until Jed learned what happened to his family.

When they reached the telegraph office and went inside, the clerk jumped up and grabbed a piece of paper off his desk. "I got it fifteen minutes after you left," he said. "I wondered if you'd make it back here today."

Jed's hand trembled as he reached for the folded paper. He stared at it without opening it.

"Would you like me to read it first?" Cage offered.

"No, but let's go outside." He jerked his head toward the telegraph operator.

Cage understood. Better to open it without some weasel watching. They left the office.

Jed sat on the wooden bench next to the office and unfolded the telegram. His hand moved to his throat and loosened his collar. He leaned his head back against the building and squeezed his eyes tight.

Cage swallowed. He'd never seen his friend so overwhelmed. They couldn't all be dead. "What is it? What happened?"

Jed stood, paced a few times, and sank into the bench. A stifled sob came from his throat as he handed the telegraph to Cage.

Cage read it.

Jed Jackson. Father, 2 brothers killed by Quantrill. Stop. Mother died from snakebite after trying to stop them. Stop. Raiders pushed her. Stop. Joshua and Caleb only survivors. Stop. Heartfelt condolences. Stop. Letter should reach you soon. Reverend Fowler.

He reached out a hand to touch Jed's arms, then drew it back.

Jed's voice quaked. "I need to go to them. I have to get back there."

"I meet with Colonel Creighton later today. I'm sure under the circumstances, something can be arranged."

Jed nodded. "I need some time alone."

Cage swiped his hand across the back of his neck. "I can't leave you like this."

"Please." His voice grew thick. "I need to pray." He stood and meandered away, shoulders slumped.

*****

Lavena paced in front of her tent. She tried everything she could to get her mind off of her problems, but somehow, she couldn't. Even what Jed was going through didn't distract her.

The day before, she had waited with him at the telegraph office most of the afternoon. The clerk ordered them out of the office at closing time. Jed looked so forlorn when they left. Maybe she should have gone to his tent and offered to accompany him into town this morning.

No, he shared a tent with Captain Cage, and she didn't want to run into him after the way he acted, but she would have to see him eventually. Only a little over two weeks left, and Mr. O'Brady had made it clear there would be no reprieve if she didn't get the interview before the end of the month. Not that she'd ever missed turning a story in on time in her life, but this one had to be finished by the due date. Her livelihood depended on it.

She didn't want to be near Cage, let alone answer questions about her life. Betsy had been right. She was the coward.

Trying to distract herself, she sat on the chair in front of the tent and opened her lap-desk. She wrote the account of the officers she'd interviewed. She'd wait to write the story of Amon Smith on how Captain Macajah Jones rescued him and four other men during the battle of Cedar Mountain until she was able to finish the interview with the young private. Maybe that story would change Mr. Cowles mind and give her more time.

No, she was deceiving herself. She didn't have a prayer of changing his mind.

She felt a presence standing over her. Glancing up, she saw Cage. She pressed her lips together and stood. "What are you doing here in my tent?"

A sheepish look came over Cage's face. "I called out your name. You must have been preoccupied. About yesterday..."

Lavena crossed her arms. "I don't want to hear about yesterday. You've been avoiding this interview for far too long, and I've had enough of it."

"I'm sorry for the way I acted, but I have some news."

She turned away. "What news?"

"I went into town with Jed this morning. He received a telegram about his family."

Her heart dropped to her stomach. She turned back toward him. "And."

"His father, mother, and two older brothers were killed. Only the two youngest were left alive."

All the anger seeped out of her. "How is he?"

"Distraught."

She reached for her jacket and headed to the door then glanced back. "You can come with me if you like."

"He said he wants to be alone."

Lavena paused for a moment. "When storms crash in and destroy everything you love, all you want to do is get away from everybody and curl up in a ball alone, but that's not what's best. He needs our love and support more than ever."

"It sounds like you have experience with those kinds of storms."

She ignored the comment and the question it implied. "Where is he?"

"I don't know," Cage said. "Maybe in our tent. Maybe still in town."

She put on her jacket and stepped outside. She turned toward Cage. "Are you coming?"

He took a few brisk steps to catch up.

She wiped her face with her handkerchief and tried to calm her racing heartbeat. "Jed is more important than this story, but this thing between us isn't over. After we do what we can to comfort him, I expect that interview from you."

*****

They hadn't said anything to each other on the way to Cage and Jed's tent. What was there to say? Lavena's harsh words lodged in his gut, twisted his insides. After the way he acted, he was surprised she asked him to come along in her search to console Jed.

Lavena was so different than other women he'd known. When she waited with Jed all day yesterday, her compassion had shone through.

The whole idea of being jealous of her and Jed was preposterous. Even if he was attracted to her, they were in the middle of a war. It wasn't the time for long buggy rides or church dances.

This war was the only reason he'd met her. She wanted his story of what happened at Cedar Mountain, and she was determined to get it. It would be easy to tell her what she wanted to hear, what everyone believed. Her estimation of him would rise, and he'd have a chance of courting her.

Why did Nate have to lie? Cage would have told the truth if he'd been able, but when he finally came out of it, he'd already been given a medal. The heroic story of his magnificent rescue had been in every newspaper in the country, and he'd been hailed a hero.

He assumed if he'd avoid reporters and didn't talk about it, everything would die down. He was wrong. The reports of how he had dispatched everyone wanting an interview had only made the accounts grow larger until no man could ever live up to their image of him. His anger toward reporters had been seen as humility when it was really cowardice.

Then she stepped into his life. A part of him wanted to tell her everything, but if he did, she would recoil from him. He wouldn't blame her.

He needed to talk to someone about this, and Nate was the only one who knew the truth. If Jed hadn't received such devastating news, Cage would confide in him, but that would have to wait, at least for a few days.

As they reached the tent, Jed sat outside on a stool in front of a small fire he'd made. He didn't bother to look up even though Cage knew he'd seen them.

Lavena rushed to him. He stood, and she wrapped her arms around him. "I'm so sorry."

Jed sobbed on her shoulder.

Two feelings rushed over Cage at the same time, each vying to be at the forefront. The first, an overwhelming jealousy, embarrassed him. Jed was grieving his family, and all he could think of was what it would be like to have Lavena embrace him like that.

The other emotion could only be described as shock, or maybe sorrow. Jed was the bravest soldier Cage had ever known. He always handled himself with decorum. He never worried and always seemed to have a quiet courage inside that guided him. Cage had never seen him cry.

Jed pulled back, blew his nose, and wiped his face with his sleeve. "I'm sorry for that. I... I don't know what came over me."

Lavena ignored what he said. "I came as soon as I heard. Is there anything we can do?"

"Yes, there is." Jed gave a pointed look toward Cage. "I need you to have that talk to Colonel Creighton for me now. I have to get home to be with my brothers. I'm the only family they have left."

Cage nodded. "I'll do what I can."

As much as he didn't want to leave Jed alone, or with Lavena, he turned and made his way to the colonel's tent. He'd do everything he could to help Jed get mustered out of the army.

When he reached the tent and looked inside, half a dozen men were meeting inside, including General Geary and all of the top commanders. They looked up at him. He'd definitely interrupted something.

He cleared his throat. "Excuse me. I'll come back."

Colonel Creighton stepped to him and slapped him on the back. "Captain Cage, just who I wanted to see. We're having the prisoners we caught transferred to Murfreesboro. You'll lead the party escorting them. Take Jed and as few men as you think you need to handle them."

All Cage could think of was how angry Lavena would be if he left without an explanation. She would believe he did this to avoid the interview for another week. "When do we leave?"

"Immediately," the colonel said. "It's vital we get those men to a secure location so we can leave as soon as the track is finished."

"Yes Sir." Then no time to let her know. "Could I speak with you first? It's important."

Creighton nodded and stepped outside. When they walked far enough away not to be heard, he said, "What is it?"

"Jed, I mean Lieutenant Jackson has received bad news from home."

"Is that what you brought me out here for, because his sweetheart back home wrote she was giving him the mitten?"

"No, Sir. Of course not. Lieutenant Jackson's family lives in Lawrence, Kansas."

Creighton swiped at the back of his neck. "I'm sorry. Sometimes this war gets the better of me. What happened?"

"His father, mother, and two older brothers were killed."

The colonel let out a gusty sigh. "I thought Quantrill didn't murder women."

Cage clenched his jaw. "From what I understand, his mother tried to stop the raiders. They pushed her, and she was bitten by a rattler. In my way of thinking, they might as well have killed her."

"Yes, yes." Creighton walked a few steps away. His back was turned to Cage. "I can give him a few days leave to help him get through this. Did anyone survive?"

"That's the thing, Sir." Cage moved closer to him. "Two younger brothers survived. They're ten and twelve years old. He's the only family they have left."

"I see." Creighton's shoulders slumped, and he turned to face Cage. "He's asked to be mustered out?"

"Yes Sir."

"Under the circumstances, of course I'll grant his request, but he's going to have to wait. Once we get to Chattanooga, I'll let him go as soon as I can find transportation, but that might take a few weeks."

"Thank you, Sir," Cage said, relieved the colonel understood. "Would it be all right for him to use the telegraph to get word to them he's coming?"

"I'll arrange it. Tell him to stop by before you leave for Murfreesboro."

Cage saluted. It would be difficult for Jed to wait, but this was the best they could do.

Chapter Twenty-Two

October 16th

Nate tried to avoid the mud as he carried a basket out to the barn, but after a week of rain, it was impossible There was no way to avoid getting it caked onto his boots. His army boots. His mother didn't have shoes that fit him, so she hadn't gotten rid of them.

He glanced up at the sky. Even with all the rain they'd had over the last couple of weeks, it felt good, warm. The sun would dry up the mud in no time. He missed the mild weather in this part of the country. In Northern Ohio, he'd even seen snow by this time of year. They rarely had a warm day like this in October.

Before slipping into the barn, he paused. Orange and red leaves hung from the elm and sycamore trees on the hillside where the empty huts stood. No matter how much cruelty toward slaves took place on this plantation, as a child, he'd been happy here.

A man marched over the crest and strode toward the house. His father. Nate scurried behind the barn door and watched through the planks. Father's full beard and brown hair had turned gray in places. He looked strong like Nate remembered. His double-breasted Confederate uniform had three gold stars arranged horizontally on the collar.

Nate had been informed by General Grant his father was an officer under General Bragg, but a colonel? That made it harder and easier. Attached to his father's belt was a sheathed sword and a holstered revolver. Hopefully he'd leave it holstered.

His stomach knotted as it had years ago when, as a boy who had gone fishing with a friend when he should have been in school, he'd waited for his father to meet him in this very barn.

Not a pleasant memory.

He dared another look. Father slipped into the house.

Nate walked over to the hens and reached for an egg. No matter what happened, at least that was one chore his mother wouldn't have to do. When the job was finished, he grabbed the basket and headed toward the house.

He squared his shoulders and stepped into the kitchen. No sign of them. He set the basket on the sideboard, beads of sweat forming on his forehead.

They weren't in the abandoned parlor where his mother had loved to entertain using the household slaves to cook and serve at parties. He checked the bedrooms and his father's office. No sign of anyone.

Where were they? He wiped his brow with his sleeve. He'd been prepared for the confrontation when he stepped into the house. Delaying it only made it worse.

Maybe they were outside. He pushed through the front door onto the porch. His parents stood about a hundred feet from the house, huddled together deep in conversation, his father towering over his mother. At six foot, he was taller than most men, taller than Nate.

Planting himself on the swing, Nate watched, hoping he could see something to convince him he'd be taken back as a prodigal son. He wasn't going to approach them. Better to let them come to him after they'd decided a course of action.

Father glared up at him and crossed his arms. Mama grabbed hold of Father's arm and continued entreating him, but he was having none of it. He turned away from her and headed to where Nate was sitting. The furrowed brow and narrow eyes reminded Nate of their last conversation.

When his father told him to get out.

Nate stood and walked toward him.

Father drew his volcanic revolver and aimed. "So. You're back."

Heat rushed to Nate's face. He raised his hands. "Yes, Sir."

"Why?"

"I couldn't do it anymore." Nate's knees felt like they would buckle. "I couldn't kill Southerners who might have been my friends and neighbors – and family."

"Why'd you come back here?"

"This is my home." He couldn't hide the hitch in his voice. "Where else could I go?"

"How about to that Yankee wife of yours?"

"It's over. I'm home no matter what happens to me."

Father's face turned red. "No, you're not."

"Sir?"

"This isn't your home anymore." Father cocked the hammer. "Now, why are you here? Were you sent to spy on us?"

"Father, please." Nate stepped back. "I was wrong." He took another step back and bumped into a spicebush next to the porch. "I'm sorry."

"You're sorry?" Father lowered the pistol and grabbed Nate by the shirt. "You have a lot to answer for." He pushed him against the porch railing. "Sorry does begin to take care of it."

Nate resisted the urge to react, to shove his father away. "Yes, Sir."

Father raised his revolver. "You're my prisoner."

"If that's what you want." A lump formed in Nate's throat. "I'm here to do whatever it takes to make things right."

The set of his father's jaw and blaze in his gray eyes reminded Nate of the time his father caught an escaped slave. The young black man was never the same after the beating.

"Make things right?" The muscle in Father's neck throbbed. "Make things right? After you betrayed Tennessee and joined up to become a bluebelly? I can't see how you're going to make up for it – unless you plan on letting us execute you for treason."

Nate's mouth went dry.

"Then there's the matter of you stealing my people from me, your own father. You deserve the same whipping I'd give a runaway for that alone." He tightened his grip on Nate's shirt. "Tell me, just how do you plan to make things right?"

Nate paused. He'd known this wouldn't be easy, but his father's rage shocked him. "I was hoping I could join the Army of Tennessee." He swallowed back the terror lodging in his throat. He had no choice but to go through with it now. "I'll accept whatever you say. If you want me arrested, maybe that's what I deserve."

Father uncocked the gun. "I'll take you to General Bragg and let him decide, but he's going to demand to know about troop movements and such. If you're lying, he'll treat like any other traitor or spy and hang you on the end of a rope."

Mama gasped.

The muscle in Nate's jaw twitched. "I'll tell him everything I know."

"You'd do that? You'd betray your Union friends?"

"I already have. If they find me, I'll face a firing squad. I'll do whatever I have to for Tennessee." Nate's voice cracked. "And for you."

Father's Adam's apple bulged as he holstered the revolver. "I needed to be sure. Welcome home, son." He held out his arms.

As Nate hugged his father, the lump in his throat threatened to choke him. Becoming a traitor was harder than he thought.

*****

Lavena headed to Cage's tent with rain pouring down on her again. Her boots sloshed in the mud, and she could barely see the path, but she didn't care. She'd been to their tent numerous times over the past couple of days, and they were never there. She hadn't seen either of them at the railroad tracks or anywhere else.

It was obvious Cage was avoiding her, and she wasn't going to be put off any longer. She'd even tell him about her sordid past if that's the only way she could get him to answer some questions.

After he promised to come to her tent after meeting with the colonel and make things right two days ago and didn't show up, she no longer had any illusions he returned any of her affection for him. It wouldn't make any difference if he thought less of her when he learned about her father as long as she got her story.

She'd never wanted anything but a career in journalism anyway. The illusive captain kept her unbalanced for a time, but she had come to her senses. She would get that interview before the day was out. That's what she came here for, and she was determined to see it through.

When she made her way to Cage and Jed's tent, she knocked on the post holding it up and cleared her throat. "Captain Cage."

No answer.

"Captain?" She peeked into the flap.

Nobody was there. Again.

If he wasn't at the tent at this time of night, there was only one other place he could be. Guard duty. When she headed toward where the prisoners were being guarded, she didn't bother to hold her jacket over her head. She'd become so drenched by now that her coat was as wet as she was.

Nobody was there, no guards or prisoners. Nobody.

Her heart raced a bit. What had happened to them?

If they'd escaped... She headed to Colonel Creighton's tent as fast as she could in the dark. She stepped in a puddle but didn't bother slowing down. When she reached the colonel's tent, she knocked.

Colonel Creighton opened the flap. "Miss Falcon, do come in. You look like you were caught in that downpour. Is there anything I can do for you?"

Lavena stepped inside the tent. She couldn't help but be embarrassed at the puddle around her feet. She'd brought the wetness inside. "Colonel Creighton, I'm sorry to bother you this time of night, but I was looking for Captain Cage. I thought he might be on guard duty, but he wasn't there. In fact, none of the prisoners are there either. Or any guards."

The colonel chuckled. "Is that why you were out in this weather?"

Lavena pressed her lips together to keep from saying something she'd regret. "Could you confide in me where they are?

"Of course," Colonel Creighton said. "It's not exactly a military secret. I ordered Captain Cage, Lieutenant Jed and half a dozen of his men to escort the prisoners to Murfreesboro to hand them over to the Provost Marshall. We can't very well take them clear to Chattanooga with us."

Relief flooded Lavena, then a sense of dread prickled at her. She only had two weeks left. He probably volunteered for this assignment to avoid her. "How long will they be gone?"

"About a week."

A week. She let out a slow breath. She still had time. Not much but a little.

When the captain came back into the camp, she'd let him know what she thought of his little excursion. She would give him no peace until he told her his story, every last bit of it, including what he was obviously trying to keep hidden.

Chapter Twenty-Three

October 19th

Nate sat across the kitchen table from his father. It had been four days since his father had gotten home, and he didn't seem to be in any hurry to get back to camp. They'd talked through a lot of what happened in the past and had both made peace with each other, but now it was time for the next step.

It was time to join the Confederate Army. He couldn't think of a way to bring up the subject. He ate a bite of eggs.

Father leaned on his elbows and tapped his fingers on the table. "I'm glad you're home, Son."

"Me too." Nate took a sip of water.

"We can't put it off forever." Father leaned back and wiped the corners of his mouth with his napkin. "It's time. We're headed to Missionary Ridge in the morning."

Nate gave a somber nod. He was a little scared, but now that the day was finally arriving, he also felt a bit relieved. This is what he had come here for.

"It won't be easy. General Bragg's a hard man."

Nate set the cup down. "I've heard."

Father readjusted in his chair. "He's not going to let you come waltzing into a Confederate camp without an armed guard even if you are my son."

"I'm willing to do whatever it takes."

"What about spending the rest of the war in a prison camp?" Father leaned back, lips pressed in a thin line. "Because that might just be what he'll require."

Nate had known the risk when he started this journey, but it was worth it. "I can tell him things. That might help convince him I want to change sides." He took another sip of water.

"What kind of things?"

"The Ohio Seventh along with the whole Twelfth Army Corp is headed this way as we speak. They're due to arrive any day now. I hear Sherman's troops are on their way too." Nate swallowed some more water.

"That might be enough to convince him." Father stroked his beard. "But are you sure you want to do this? You served alongside those men."

Nate cleared his throat. "I'll do what I have to." Another gulp of water.

"We'll go see him tomorrow."

Nate emptied the glass. The faces of the men he served with flicked through his mind, men he'd called his friends. "Father…"

"If you're not ready, you can hide out here for another week," Father's brow furrowed, "but you need to resolve which side you're on."

Nate filled up his glass with more water but decided not to drink it. His gut sloshed and churned until he thought he might be sick. This was what he came here to do. He had no other choice.

"I'm ready."

*****

Lavena had finished her breakfast of hardtack and was washing it down with a cup of Bohea tea. At least, it hadn't rained in the last couple of days. The sun had dried up most of the ground.

Clangs from the railroad tracks were growing louder and more enthusiastic. She imagined the men were enjoying this sunny day. It was time for her to get to work as well. She could at least get some more interviews while she was waiting for Cage to return.

She set the cup down and headed toward the tracks. Surely there were men in Cage's company who wouldn't mind taking a respite to answer her questions.

When she arrived, Sergeant Garrett blew a whistle. "Good news, Company C. Colonel Crane's orders. Each company is to have a day because of the good job you men are doing, and he's starting with us."

The men cheered. A couple of them threw their hats in the air. Lavena almost wanted to join in. This fit into her plans to interview the men perfectly.

"Make sure you're back at fourteen hundred hours," Garrett bellowed, and the men promised they would be.

Lavena walked up to one of the youngest looking soldiers and introduced herself.

"I know who you are, Miss Falcon," the boy with buck teeth said. "You're that lady reporter."

"That's right. Would you like to be interviewed?"

"I sure would," he said. "The other boys at the orphanage would be tickled to see my name in the newspaper."

Lavena directed him to a nearby tree stump. They sat, and she pulled paper and ink out of her lap-desk. "Name and age, Private."

"Name's Ben Sawyer. I'm fifteen years old."

"When did you enlist?" Lavena asked, trying to keep the surprise out of her voice. The Ohio Seventh was mustered into service over two years ago for a three-year term.

"I enlisted right after I turned thirteen. I'm an orphan, so I didn't need my folks' permission or anything."

Lavena wrote the information down in long hand to give her time to keep her emotions under control. She hated the practice of turning orphans out on their own at such a young age. She even wrote an article about it once. What was even worse was that the US Army insisted on accepting these boys into service and treating them as if they were grown men.

She looked up at him and smiled. "So, tell me about some of the battles you've been in."

He told her how he killed ten men in the Battle of Kernstown and about how Captain Cage had rescued him at Cedar Mountain, but he didn't add anything new.

She remembered what Amon said about Private Coby Willard. "Do you know if Private Willard followed Captain Cage after you were rescued?"

"No, and I don't care to know. Coby's no good. He makes it his mission to get out of work, and he's always in the back of the line during a battle. I don't know why Amon would want to be his friend." Ben leaned closer to her and lower his voice. "I even hear he has a poker game going on where there's drinking and all kinds of carousing."

"Is that so?" Lavena asked. "What about Private Amon? What kind of man is he?"

"I really like him. When I first enlisted, all the rest of the men treated me like I was the kid brother they didn't want around. Amon was different. He acted like I was one of them. I don't know why he doesn't see Coby for who he really is."

Lavena didn't know either, but when she talked with Amon, she was going to find out.

After she finished up the interview with Ben, she managed to get Corporal Jake Edwards to sit down with her for a while. Corporal Jake seemed to have a quiet assurance that was rare among young men, like he didn't need to prove anything.

She asked about his life before the war. He was a twenty-five-year-old farmer from outside of LaGrange. He had a wife and two children, age four and two. The two-year-old was born after he joined up, so he'd never seen his son. He loved his wife and missed his family.

He also gave her a harrowing account of all the battles the Ohio Seventh had fought including an interesting frontline perspective on Gettysburg. He was promoted shortly after Gettysburg.

"Corporal, could you tell me more about Cedar Mountain?"

Jake glanced down. "What do you want to know?"

"I understand when Captain Cage came to the rescue of his men, you and Sergeant Garrett were captured."

"Yeah." His hands clasped in his lap. "It's not something I like to talk about."

"I understand, but could you tell me how you escaped?"

"Well, Ma'am, if it weren't for Sergeant Garrett, I'd be serving out the war in a Confederate prison right now."

"What did he do?"

"When the shooting started, five rebel soldiers grabbed hold of the sergeant and me and marched us out of there. I tried to shout to the others, but one of them put a hand over my mouth while another one pointed a musket at my head. I was plum scared.

"I hate to admit it, but it was more fearsome than the battle. I don't know why. I guess I prepared myself for getting wounded or shot, but I never figured on going to one of them Confederate prisons. One of the men, Corporal Simon, ended up in one of them prisons for a time before he got out on a prisoner exchange. He told us how bad it was.

"Anyway, we were hiding in the woods until the others took off. Then they made us march. I expect they were taking us back to their camp."

Corporal Jake rubbed his hand against his neck. "I guess their camp was a mite distance 'cause we didn't make it the first day. They made camp and tied us to a tree. Sergeant Garrett had a knife of something on him and cut through his ropes. Then he started on mine."

The muscle in Jake's jaw twitched. "I suppose you want to hear all of it."

Lavena stopped writing and looked up. "Private Jake, this story isn't vital to what I'm writing about. You can tell me what happened or not, but I can promise you, if you need to talk about it, I'll only print the parts you want."

Jake rubbed his hands against his legs. "I do want what Sergeant Garrett did for me to be in your story, but how I acted... Well, I'm not too proud of it, and I'd just as soon not have you write about that."

"Corporal, I give you my word."

"In that case, I'll tell it." Jake's Adam's apple bulged. "I don't know what happened except maybe the fear got the better of me. I've been in every battle the Ohio Seventh fought, and I've seen men die. I even reckoned I'd be one of them when the bullets were blasting all around me and I had to keep charging on, but when Sergeant Garrett started cutting my ropes, I panicked. I told him to leave me alone. I didn't want to die."

Lavena swallowed hard. "Sergeant Garrett wouldn't leave?" It was rare for a man to be honest about his faults instead of pretending to be something he's not. She respected that.

"No, he shushed me, but I wouldn't stop going on about it. I guess the commotion I made woke up our captors. He punched the first man that started toward us and grabbed his rifle. Before the others knew what happened, he shot one of them and bayonetted another one. He grabbed the second one's musket and fired at the third. All this time, the other two were loading. He knocked them off their feet without even breathing hard."

The corporal's voice cracked. "I didn't do a thing to help. I was just sitting there on the ground watching him fight those men with my jaw stuck on my chest. He grabbed hold of my arm and pulled me to my feet.

"That's when I came to my senses. I grabbed one of the muskets and followed him back to where the Seventh was camped. The rebs didn't come after us. I guess they figured we weren't worth getting any more of them killed over. Probably stayed back to take care of their wounded."

Jake hunched over until his shoulders almost rested on his knees. "I never told anyone what happened except for the part where the sergeant gave them a good whipping. Neither did Sergeant Garrett. I don't know why I told you."

"I'll keep my word, Corporal." Lavena set her notes on the seat next to her. "This had to be eating away at you. That's probably why you told me."

"Maybe," Jake said. "It's a hard thing to admit you're a coward."

"You're not a coward, Corporal." Lavena let out a sigh while she tried to figure out how to help the man who'd shown so much bravery, not only in battle, but by telling her the truth. "Maybe you should confess this to someone else. Lieutenant Jed would keep your secret, and I'm sure he'd know how to help."

Jake nodded his head. "I'll do that, Ma'am. And I want to thank you for not writing about me being a…" He cleared his throat. "About what happened."

He ambled away without another word or backward glance.

Lavena wandered to her tent and fished out some of the dried tack rations the army had provided for lunch and fixed herself a cup of tea.

War caused so much heartache. Jake, a man who had run into a barrage of bullets in more than one battle, felt himself a coward because he had one weak moment. Most men would have lied about it and pretended to be a hero. The corporal was an honest man, and that took more courage than being on the battlefield.

When the tea was finished, she dipped her hardtack to moisten what she'd described in her story as eating sawdust pressed together and shaped in a cracker.

Sergeant Garrett surprised her. That man was the epitome of stubbornness about things being done according to military regulations and about a woman knowing her place, but when Jake cowered, he not only saved his life but kept quiet about Jake's shortcoming. There was more to that man than she'd observed.

Chapter Twenty-Four

Amon sat in front of his tent sipping essence of coffee, the instant coffee the army provided, and leaned over the small cook fire barely warming him. As the hot liquid slid down his throat, he wrapped his hands around the tin cup.

When the sergeant had announced the day off, he had cheered. Between chasing enemy troops, and fixing the railroad, he was done in. Now, he wished he was back to working on the rails. Better than sitting around doing nothing.

He should get some rest, maybe write a letter to Emma, but a few days off playing cards with Coby and some of the others would be a welcome diversion. When they were pounding in railroad ties, Coby had complained the most even though he'd done the least work. Still, he was fun to hang out with after the work was done.

Amon needed to be more careful this time. The last time he'd played, he'd lost his whole week's paycheck. He still hadn't figured out how to tell Emma. If he won big this time, she wouldn't need to know anything about it.

While he was working the tracks, he'd noticed sutlers, the merchants who followed the troops everywhere they went, setting up a robber's row outside of camp where they sold cards, whisky, and anything else that might line their pockets with hard-earned greenbacks from soldiers.

They weren't the only ones who showed up outside of camp. The ladies pitched their tents and offered free lemonade and back rubs to anyone who would enter their web. For a price, they offered more.

Since Coby hadn't shown up, it wasn't hard to figure that's where he'd be headed. Amon had said no to those kind of excursions often enough that Coby hadn't bothered to ask this time. Probably a good thing. The temptation to go with his friend might have been too strong to resist, this time.

Amon let out a sigh and threw out the rest of his so-called coffee. Since he'd joined the army, he was either so bored that watching his toenails grow was the best part of his day or he was cold, wet, hot, tired and just plain miserable from marching, drilling, guarding, and laying train tracks. Or drained from fighting another battle.

Or dazed from watching his friends die.

With so much devastation around him, what harm did it do to have a little amusement?

Like playing baseball or listening to the band play.

The band wouldn't be playing in this weather, and it was too wet to play baseball. If only Coby had invited him to play poker with the guys. Any adventure that didn't involve getting killed was a good thing.

Whenever Amon went into battle, he always threw out his deck of cards. If something happened, his ma or Mr. Brown wouldn't find them in his personal belongings. It would break Emma's heart to hear what he was up to. That's why he was careful. He could always pick up another deck after the battle.

Nobody at home would ever know he'd been gambling.

Coby strode toward him with a grin on his face, and Amon couldn't help the sigh of relief that went through. Things were about to get exciting.

"Whiskey sutlers showed up outside of camp. It's time you got your first taste of liquor." Coby slapped Amon on the back.

Amon's pulse raced in anticipation, but at the same time, a warning pulsated inside his gut. "I'll play some poker, but I don't want to drink."

"Oh, come on, Amon. A little whiskey's not going to hurt you. We're meeting some men from another company later for some cards, and I offered to bring some jugs."

Amon's stomach squeezed tighter than the tourniquet Major Patella used on his arm when a bayonet sliced him during the Battle of Antietam. "What if Captain Cage catches us?"

Coby spit a wad of tobacco into the fire. "The high and mighty Captain Cage has no right to tell us what to do on our time off."

"You know he won't abide drinking or…" Amon blushed. "Visiting the ladies."

"He's not going to catch us." Coby's jaw clenched. "He's not even in camp. Someday you need to grow up and become a man. Or are you going to be a yellow dog all your life?"

Heat rushed through Amon. He grabbed Coby's collar. "You take that back. I'm not scared."

Coby pushed Amon away. "Prove it."

"It's not right," Amon said more to remind himself than Coby. "Emma would never marry me if she found out I hang out drinking and gambling away our money."

"And how's Emma gonna know unless you tell her? She didn't find out about the poker, did she?"

"I guess not." Amon stammered. He knew he should refuse, but a part of him wanted to get out of this cold tent, sitting in the mud, watching leaves change color.

Remembering.

"I might as well go along. It's better than sitting in this tent with nothing to do."

Coby grinned wide like Amon's barn cat used to when it caught a mouse. "I'll make a man out of you yet."

"I'm only playing poker." That's what he told Coby, but he had already begun to wonder what it would be like to become drunk enough to set aside the memories of the blood drenched battlefields littered with the bodies of his dead friends. He stood and followed Coby to robber's row.

Coby was right. Emma would never know.

*****

Cage filled his canteen in Garrison Creek.

The sun began to recede to the west. Delivering the prisoners had been an easy job, and they were headed back to camp.

"Sergeant Noah," Cage called out. Sergeant Noah Andrews was a man he'd brought along from Company G. Since he wasn't taking his entire company, the colonel suggested he take Noah along so Sergeant Garrett could remain at camp to supervise the men.

"Yes Sir." The sergeant saluted.

"Time to make camp."

The sergeant gave the order and arranged the men, and Captain Cage dumped his pack on the ground and stretched his shoulders.

Soon, the camp was set up for the night, and watchfires burned brightly.

Cage sat by the fire closest to his tent and warmed his hands. The first thing he would do when he got back to camp was find Lavena. He had to explain he hadn't made this trip to avoid her.

It was time he told her the truth about Cedar Mountain. This had gone on long enough.

Jed plopped down next to Cage. "How are you doing?"

Cage glanced up. "Shouldn't I be asking you that question?"

"Once a chaplain, always a chaplain. Besides, I need to get my mind off what I can't do anything about."

Cage warmed his hands over the fire.

Jed placed a hand on his shoulder. "Isn't it time you tell someone about whatever is bothering you?"

Cage gave Jed a sideways glare. "You?"

"Either me or that woman reporter you're so fond of," Jed said.

"What makes you think I'm fond of her?"

"I'm not blind."

Cage swallowed the lump in his throat. "You're right."

"So out with it."

Cage pulled on his ear and tried to find the words. "Most of what happened at Cedar Mountain was just like the newspapers say. Nate and I rescued the men, and then we chased after the enemy soldiers. They split up. Nate went after one group. I went after the others."

He stood and tucked his hands in his pockets. An owl hooted from somewhere nearby. "I chased the rebels to the farmhouse. They ran inside."

Jed pulled some hardtack out of his knapsack and took a bite. "Is that when they started the fire?"

"No!" Cage swiped at the scar on his face. He couldn't wipe it away no matter how hard he tried. "I didn't know they escaped out the back door. I thought if…" His voice cracked. "I figured I'd smoke them out.

Jed gasped. "You started the fire."

Cage's legs wobbled. He slunk to the ground next to where Jed was sitting. Head lowered, he kept his eyes focused on Jed. "It spread so fast, the house engulfed with flames within minutes. That's when I heard the screams." His voice cracked. "I tried to rush in the front door to rescue them, but I couldn't make it through the flames. I could feel the heat scorching my face. I tried to get to them."

"Oh, Cage."

Cage's heart raced even though it felt good to finally tell it. "The next thing I knew, Nate was pulling me out."

"Why did you lie about it?"

"I didn't." He paused for a moment. "I was in the army hospital, not even conscious for weeks. Nate told them what happened and left out that I started the fire. He thought I was going to die, so there wasn't any point in bringing that up. When I came to, they'd already given me a medal. They told me it wasn't my fault that family died. I did all I could."

Cage cupped his hand over his mouth, overwhelmed with the horror of what he'd done. "Two young girls and a baby boy burned to death along with their mother. I wanted to tell the truth, but I couldn't." It was an excuse, and he knew it. "I'm not a hero. I killed them."

"So, you kept quiet," Jed said.

An overwhelming urge to escape, to get away from what he'd done swept over Cage. He stood and ran toward the creek, his boots making sloshing noises in the mud. He couldn't face the loathing in Jed's gaze and see the repulsion in his own heart.

Jed chased after him and grabbed his arm. "Stop. Stop running."

Cage stopped but wouldn't turn around. He watched the water surging up the bank from all the rain and wished it would swallow him up.

"Look at me, Cage."

He turned toward Jed and slowly raised his eyes. Instead of the disgust he expected, Jed's features offered compassion.

"Have you asked God to forgive you?"

"I hadn't prayed since it happened." Cage glanced at his feet. "How could I? I murdered a mother and three young children and kept quiet while they gave me a medal for it."

"Don't you think it's time you get things right with God?"

Cage's voice caught in his throat. "There are consequences to what I've done."

"Are you afraid of being thrown in the stockade or losing your medal?"

Cage leaned against an elm tree as his stomach threatened to empty its contents. "I wish I'd never seen that medal. Any punishment the army hands out would be worth getting this off my chest, but how can I face my men again after they've found out I'm not the hero they think I am? The worst part is as soon as I tell Lavena, I'll lose her."

"I didn't realize it was that serious between you?"

"It is on my part. I'm in love with her. I didn't plan for it to happen, but..."

"Does she feel the same way?"

"I don't know. I think so. I haven't talked to her about it. How could I with this hanging over my head?"

"You have to tell her the truth. God will give you the strength you need." Jed's gaze grew more intense than any Old Testament prophet. "Before you even think about confessing to her or the commander, you need to make things right with God and trust Him with whatever happens."

Cage nodded his head.

"You know what to do. I'll leave you to it." Jed stood and walked into his tent.

Cage gazed at the stars. The clouds had finally blown away. It was the first time he'd prayed in over a year. Before it happened, he talked to God about everything. His men didn't notice he'd stopped. They still considered him a godly man they could turn to.

Another deception.

He dropped to his knees on the muddy ground. "God, forgive me."

Chapter Twenty-Five

October 20

Amon startled out of a deep sleep and peeked through half-open eyes at Coby hovering over him in their cramped tent.

"So how did it feel taking your first step to becoming a man?"

Amon pulled his wool blanket over his head to block out the daylight and groaned. The bright light gave him a headache, and his stomach was flipping like the flapjacks his ma used to cook in her cast iron skillet. "Just leave me alone."

"Hung over huh?" Coby smirked. "It'll go away in a few hours, but you got to admit, it was fun."

Amon didn't want to admit anything. The worst part is he didn't remember all of it, but what he did recollect through the haze were some ladies hanging on Coby and some of the other men. He was almost afraid to ask. "Did I do anything with those women last night?"

"You don't remember?"

Amon shook his head.

"You're not quite a grown man yet, Amon, my friend." Coby slapped him on the back causing his head to pound. "Maybe next time."

He considered wiping that smirk off Coby's face with a punch to the jaw. He needed to get away. He stumbled out of the tent and bumped into the branches holding it up. He struggled to untangle himself and only managed to knock the flaps into the mud. A wave of nausea assaulted his stomach, and he ran a few steps toward the bushes before he retched.

"Don't worry." Coby came up behind him and placed a hand on his shoulder. "The first time is always the worst. It will get better." Coby's face turned white. "I gotta go."

Amon glanced up. Miss Falcon tread toward him. He wished he were dead.

*****

It didn't take a reporter to figure out what Amon had been doing the night before. He reeked of alcohol. Lavena waited a moment while he emptied his stomach behind a bush. Her intention had been to finish interviewing him about Cedar Mountain, but seeing his drunken state, she decided to talk to him about Private Coby instead.

"Private Amon, I wonder if we could continue the interview where we left off?"

The young soldier pressed his lips together and wiped his mouth with his sleeve. "Now's not a good time."

Lavena felt sorry for the young private, but letting him sleep it off wasn't what was best for him. Facing the full effects of a night of strong drink might discourage him from doing it again. "Only a couple more questions."

Amon nodded.

"I'd rather interview you at my tent. I have a fire going with water for tea heating over it."

He paused. "I don't feel so good. Maybe later."

She crossed her arms. "Perhaps I should let Sergeant Garrett know you're ill. I'm sure he wouldn't mind stopping by your tent."

"No need." His Adam's apple bulged. "Lead on." He followed her to a with as much enthusiasm as he would have if he were on latrine duty.

Once they got to his tent, she poured two cups of ginger hibiscus tea. It would help him with his nausea. She handed a cup to Amon before reaching into her lap-desk for her pen, bottle of ink, and paper. "You already told me how Captain Cage saved you from Confederate soldiers who had captured you and the others. You also said that Captain Cage and Lieutenant Nate ordered you back to camp and chased after the men alone and that Private Coby Willard followed them against orders."

The private drank a sip. "That's right."

"Is there anything you'd like to add to your account?"

He shrugged. "Not that I can recollect."

Lavena pressed her lips together. "Then I have only one more question. Why did you decide to get drunk with Private Coby after your captain warned you not to?"

Amon's eyes grew wider. "Do you have to put that in the story?"

"No." She sipped some tea. "I don't, but I'd like to understand why you'd do such a thing when you have a good Christian girl waiting at home."

Amon looked at the cup in his hands. "I've never had whiskey touch my lips before last night, but Coby kept going on about what I was missing. I wanted to find out for myself."

Lavena leaned back. "So, did you learn your lesson? Are you going drinking again?"

He raised his hand as if he were making an oath."Never again, I promise."

She wished she could believe him, but the deviance in his eyes proved he would go right back to it as soon as the hangover wore off. "Drink has ruined a lot of men. I wouldn't want to see you going down a path that could destroy your life."

"I told you I'm not going to drink again." Amon stood and set the cup on the floor. "Are we done?"

Lavena nodded. She wanted to say more, but Amon would have to learn the hard way.

Chapter Twenty-Six

October 21

Lieutenant Nate Teagan stood in a cabin on Missionary Ridge facing Confederate General Braxton Bragg and his father, Colonel Daniel Teagan. His hands were tied behind his back, and a sergeant who looked like he could win a battle single-handedly pointed a rifle at him.

His father had apologized when General Bragg ordered him treated as an enemy prisoner but said it was necessary if he wanted to earn the general's trust.

Bragg looked much as Nate expected. He was tall, thin, and had a military bearing of confidence. What struck Nate the most was the man's eyes. They had a depth of hardness about them that made him nervous.

The recently built log cabin where the general had his headquarters had two rooms. The door to the back room was closed, probably sleeping quarters. Although sparsely furnished, the main room had a desk, four chairs, and a box stove to heat the place.

Nate appreciated being inside where it was warm, but he had been interrogated since early morning, and it was almost noon. He was hungry and tired.

He tried to answer their questions honestly without giving away something that would hurt the Union war effort. His responses could mean the difference between joining the Confederate Army as a soldier or being shot as a spy.

Leaning his weight on one leg, he quietly asked, "Could I make a trip to the outhouse and maybe get a bite to eat?"

General Bragg glared at him as if he'd suggested they crown Abraham Lincoln supreme ruler of the world.

"I've told you everything I know to the best of my ability." He shifted his weight to the other leg. "And I'm willing to do anything else that's asked of me. A short respite is all I'm asking."

"I'll go with you." His father turned to General Bragg. "With your permission, Sir."

Bragg nodded. "Meet me back here in thirty minutes."

Father motioned to the door, and Nate started toward it.

"One thing," Bragg said.

Nate halted and faced the general.

"If you're not a little more forthcoming at our next session, I'll fit a noose around your neck myself."

Nate swallowed. He'd stalled as long as he could. He had to give the information he'd been holding back, or everything would fall apart.

His father fixed him lunch, and he devoured the coosh, cooked beef fried with bacon grease and cornmeal, as his father watched in silence. His hunger surprised him. He expected the churning of his stomach to kill his appetite. Instead, he ate like a man who hadn't had eaten in days.

An autumn breeze whipped through, blowing the flaps of a sea of tents lined up on the hill in rows. Thin grayback soldiers huddled in front of small fires they'd built to stay warm. From the looks of the soldiers, this might be his last decent meal.

Nate finished the last piece of beef and downed his coffee. His father's stoic expression gave him indigestion. Did he believe him? Or did he think his son should be hung as a spy?

"Why now," Father said. "After everything that's happened why change sides now? If you want my help, I need to understand."

Nate set his down his tin plate and furrowed his brow as he tried to think of an answer that would satisfy. "Do you remember Mr. Price, that teacher who had it in for me? I must have been about twelve years old at the time."

Father snorted. "I remember you leading the other boys in a mutiny against him."

"You really tanned my hide." Nate wiped his mouth with his sleeve. "At the time, I thought you were unfair, but no matter how vindictive he was toward me, I should have obeyed him."

Father pressed his lips together. "What does that have to do with this?"

"Mr. Price wanted to expel me, but you stood up for me. Even though I was wrong in what I did, you told him if he laid a hand on me again, he'd be the one getting the beating."

"Yeah." Father stroked his chin. "He left a month later, and the town blamed me for having to get a new teacher midterm."

Nate swallowed a gulp of coffee. "Anyway, I asked you why, after what I'd done, you would come to my defense against Mr. Price. Do you remember what you said?"

"No, I don't."

"You said I was your son, and family meant more to you than any rules I'd broken." Nate swallowed another sip hoping it would settle his stomach. He'd eaten too much and too quickly considering what he needed to do. "I'd forgotten that when I rebelled against you and stole your slaves. Slavery is wrong. I'll believe that until my dying day, but I might have found a way of being an abolitionist without betraying my family. Being right was all I cared about."

Nate rubbed his hand over his stomach. "When I married Betsy, I did the same thing to her. I would take off for months at a time to go off stealing slaves to set them free. I didn't consider her feelings."

"Is that why it's over between the two of you?"

"Yes." He let out a sigh. "It's my fault. If just once, I'd put her first, she would have stayed with me."

A cannon fired from halfway down the ridge and smoke rose until it created a cloud in the sky. Nate paused until gunfire from the valley below answered the blast.

"When she wrote and ended it, I finally realized what I'd done, both to her and to you. I can't win her back, but I thought maybe if I came here and turned myself in to you, I might be able to repair some of the damage I caused."

"Do you still believe slavery is wrong?"

Nate's Adam's apple bulged. "Yes, I do, but my family is more important than my opinions. As far as holding the Union together, I enlisted to end slavery, but it seems to me the South is fighting for freedom too. I'm not sure what's right anymore."

Father wiped his brow with his bandana. "If I hadn't blown up at you like I did, we could have worked it out."

"It wouldn't have made a difference." Nate stared at his empty plate. "It took losing Betsy to make me realize what I'd done."

Father placed his hand on Nate's shoulder. "Be careful with General Bragg. Don't cross him."

"I'll be mindful," Nate said.

"Son, I'll help you however I can." Father pulled the ropes out. "For now, we need to do things his way."

Nate burped up a bit of bile and placed his hands behind his back. Then Father led him to Bragg's headquarters.

Bragg paced in front of Nate a few times then faced him. "You better tell me everything, boy. I'm running out of patience."

Nate nodded. He had stalled long enough. It was time to tell the general everything he wanted to hear, troop movements, strategies, everything. He rattled it all off, point by point, holding nothing back.

The clerk, a clean-shaven major with bifocals and slicked back hair, wrote down every word Nate said. Bragg glared at him with his arms crossed the whole time.

When he finished relaying the information, Nate stood at attention. The general's brow furrowed causing Nate's chest to tighten. He wondered if he'd said enough, and at the same time, he felt guilty for saying too much.

"Untie him," Bragg said.

Father patted Nate on the back and untied the ropes.

The general rested his hand on the grip of his sword. "Are you ready to change sides, Lieutenant Teagan?"

Sweat beaded Nate's forehead. "I'd like to join up and fight for

Southern independence, if you'll let me."

"You'll have to renounce your allegiance to the United States of America," General Bragg said. "That means if Union troops catch you, you can expect a rope instead of a firing squad."

Heaviness swept over Nate until he didn't know how he remained standing. "Sir, I'm a deserter. The United States is bent on killing me no matter what I do." He placed his hand over his midsection, not quite on his heart. "I no longer hold any allegiance to the United States of America, a nation that wants me to turn on my family and my home. I pledge my allegiance to the sovereign state of Tennessee and to the Confederacy."

At that moment, it wouldn't have surprised him if lightning had struck him and left everyone else in the room unscathed. It was as if he'd just blasphemed God. Everything within him wanted to take back what he'd said, but he couldn't.

"Welcome to the Confederate Army of Tennessee. You'll be under your father's command as my messenger to my commanders. It's not the safest job, but you'll keep your rank as lieutenant." General Bragg shook Nate's hand then folded his arms over his chest again. "If what you've told me doesn't pan out, or if I find you falsifying information or impeding the war effort in any way, you'll wish all I did was hang you."

"Yes, Sir, General Bragg." Nate grinned as big as his face would allow, masking the guilt stirring inside. He wasn't sure he'd be able to live with what he'd done, but there was no other way.

Chapter Twenty-Seven

October 24

Cage arrived at camp with Jed and the other men late into the evening and drifted toward his tent. Delivering the prisoners had taken longer than he expected. The Provost Marshal had been short on men to guard the prisoners and required their help until his men arrived.

The bright moon and watchfires lit up the tents in the field. The only soldiers who hadn't retired for the night were the guards, and the scene almost looked peaceful.

Jed stepped beside him. "A respite from the carnage of war."

Cage glanced over toward him. "Are you adding poet to your many jobs?"

Jed chuckled. "I don't think Walt Whitman has anything to worry about. So, what are your plans?"

An owl hooted. Cage dreaded telling everyone what he'd done, but he wanted to get it over with. Ever since the night he'd confessed his sin to Jed and to God, an urgency to get it out into the open stirred inside him. "Lavena must be furious at me for leaving without telling her why."

"Once you explain, she'll understand."

Cage rubbed his hand across his scar. "Of course. I'll talk to her tomorrow after church." He gazed into the distance. "For the best anyway. War is never a good time to pursue a courtship. I'll tell her straight away and end whatever this thing between us is before it gets too far."

Jed placed a hand on his shoulder, but he didn't say anything.

Leaves rustled in the distance, but it was too dark to see who it was. "Someone's out there." Cage marched to the old willow tree at the edge of the field with Jed close behind. It was probably a squirrel, but he needed to be sure.

They dashed toward the noise. A young man in blue stood at the edge of camp. Cage and Jed took a few more strides.

It was Amon. The private doubled over while holding onto the tree and threw up. He wiped his mouth with his sleeve.

"He looks ill," Jed said, stating the obvious.

Concern gripped Cage as they approached him. If Amon was sick, it would spread throughout the company. Disease had killed more soldiers in their regiment than the battles they faced. "Private Amon, are you all right?"

Amon staggered as he tried to stand at attention. "Yesssssir, I'm fine."

Cage's jaw clenched. Stepping closer, he sniffed. The stench of liquor permeated the air around Amon and confirmed his suspicion. How many times had he warned the young man? For him to go off and get drunk the first time Cage left camp for a few days was direct defiance.

Jed set his hand on Cage's arm. A warning to keep him from losing his temper. Cage nodded to him, and he let go.

Amon's footing wavered, and he stumbled into Cage.

He pushed him away. "You've been drinking."

Sweat beaded Amon's forehead. "Yesssir."

"With Coby Willard?"

Amon looked down. "I'm not gonna tell you who was with me."

"I expected more of you." Cage delivered a glower he hoped would drive his point home.

Amon tried to stand at attention, but instead, he turned away and retched. After wiping his mouth, he staggered, and leaned against the tree to steady himself.

Cage pressed his lips together. Even though it was the first time he'd caught Amon drinking, he wanted to make sure the young soldier considered the consequences before he decided to do it again. "I warned you what would happen."

"No excuses, Sir." The words came out slurred.

At least the boy was owning up to it.

Jed stepped toward Amon. "Captain, perhaps it would be better to take care of this in the morning. Private Amon might be ready to listen after he sobers up a bit."

Cage nodded. "Private, I'll decide your punishment then, and trust me, it will be memorable."

"Yes, Sir." He tried to salute but almost lost his balance and leaned against the tree instead.

"Until then, sleep this off."

Amon stumbled to his tent.

Cage punched the tree. An intense pain gripped him. He groaned and tried to shake it off.

"What good did that do?" Jed asked.

Cage gripped his hand and let out a gusty sigh.

Jed's brow furrowed. "Looks like Whisky sutlers have set up outside camp while we were gone."

"I need to take care of this right away. I won't have alcohol destroying my soldiers." Cage said.

"What about Lavena?"

Cage rubbed his scar. "I'll have to wait to let Lavena interview me. I need to focus on this for the time being. It can't be helped."

Jed delivered his preacher gaze. "The longer you wait, the harder this will be."

Cage knew he was right but taking care of his men came first.

*****

October 25

Amon woke with a groan. His head hurt. He didn't remember much of the night before, but he did have a faint recollection of Captain Cage and Chaplain Jed standing over him. Hopefully he'd been dreaming. He let out a groan. It was more like a nightmare. No, he'd been awake, he was sure of it.

He stepped out of his tent. Another rainy day. At least, it was Sunday. He wouldn't have to lay rails. He growled. There was no way he could manage going to the church service today. His head hurt too much and facing the chaplain after last night would only make it hurt worse.

Coby squeezed out of the tent and patted him on the shoulder. "We sure saw the elephant, last night."

"It feels like the elephant is standing on my head. How do you do it?"

"Do what?" Coby asked.

Amon wiped his hand over his face. "I like the way drinking makes me feel while I'm doing it, but the morning after..." He swiped his hand across the back of his neck.

"You'll get used to it. The more often you drink, the better you'll feel afterwards."

"I don't know," Amon said. "I'm not sure this is worth it. Besides, Captain Cage and Chaplain Jed saw me last night. I'm in a lot of trouble."

Coby scowled. "You didn't tell him about me or the other guys, did you?"

"I wouldn't do that, but I hate the idea of being punished when I'm played out like this. The captain is probably planning to have me bucked and gagged."

"It's not that..." Coby looked past him. "Gotta go." He darted off through the deluge into the woods.

Amon glanced back. Captain Cage strode toward him. *Oh, no.* So, that's why Coby took off. The coward.

His stomach churned, and he turned and retched even though there was nothing left in his stomach. He wiped his mouth with his sleeve and stood at attention. Rain drizzled off his cap. When the captain finally made his way to him, he saluted.

Captain Cage delivered a stony glare without returning his salute or saying a word. With every second, Amon's head pounded harder and his salute became harder to hold.

The captain finally returned the salute. "At ease. I see you're well enough to be on your feet."

Amon looked at the ground beside him. "I threw up."

"I see that." Captain Cage rubbed his ear. "Meet Sergeant Garrett in the field after reveille. I've already ordered you bucked and gagged until sundown."

Amon wanted to protest, but there was no use trying to get out of it. The captain wasn't about to change his mind. "Yes, Sir."

"Was it worth it, Private?"

Amon's Adam's apple bulged, but he didn't answer. Why couldn't the captain leave him alone? He was trying to cope with all this death the best way he could. What harm did it do to drink a little whiskey and forget when he wasn't on duty?

"You may think you can play with sin, Private Amon, but if you continue down this path, you'll end up lost in the storm that's destroyed many men. Think of what your family would say if they knew what you were up to."

Heat rushed to Amon's face. "They won't find out."

The captain lifted his hand as if he might place it on Amon's shoulder, but he pulled back. "Then I guess there's nothing more for me to say. Maybe the buck and gag will teach you to think twice next time."

He watched Captain Cage march away, the downpour soaking his uniform and drawers. Captain Cage was trying to help, but he didn't care. The pain and grief had rooted itself so deeply within, Amon would do anything to have a respite from it even if it meant moving further into the storm.

*****

A few men gathered on the field in the center of the camp. The rain had let up, but dark clouds still threatened the sky. Captain Cage stood beside his lieutenant as Sergeant Garrett gave the order to buck and gag Private Amon Smith.

Being bucked and gagged was a tough punishment, but it was the most commonly used discipline for enlisted men. Some of the harsher captains would hang the men from their thumbs, make them strip and wear a barrel, or the worst of all – ride the horse, a punishment consisting of straddling a narrow piece of wood high enough so the soldier's feet couldn't touch the ground. Fifty-pound weights would be tied to each of his legs.

After riding the horse, a man wouldn't be fit to return to duty for days and might never be able to father children.

Captain Cage only used the thumb and barrel punishments in extreme cases. He'd never ordered a soldier to ride the horse, and he never would.

It was unpleasant to be bucked and gagged, but it did no long-term harm. The men suffered more from the embarrassment than from the sore muscles that resulted afterwards. In most cases, it was effective.

Amon sat on the drenched ground with his knees bent. Two young corporals who assisted Sergeant Garrett placed a stick under Amon's knees and tied his hands to the stick.

The cool air and mud did everything to make sure this experience was thoroughly miserable. So far, the private seemed to be handling it well. He hadn't made excuses or tried to get out of it, and he was prompt for the punishment.

Corporal Jake Edwards tied a gag around Amon's mouth. Corporal Simon Waller hung a sign over his neck that read *Drunkard*. They took their positions on either side of the private.

Sergeant Garrett marched over to Captain Cage and saluted. "Punishment carried out, Sir."

The scar on Cage's face itched. As bad as he felt about Amon going through this on a dreary cold day, he wasn't about to show any mercy for the boy's sake.

Most regiments weren't as strict as the Ohio Seventh when it came to drinking. They would punish their men only if they were drinking on duty and wouldn't do anything if the men visited soiled doves or spent their paycheck gambling. Some officers even participated with the men.

Early on, the first commander the regiment, Colonel Tyler, had decided it would be best for the men to prohibit fornication and alcohol use altogether. Captain Cage agreed with the policy. He'd seen the damage these sins had done in other regiments.

He needed to get to the bottom of this and soon. Throwing out the sutlers would only go so far. The men who wanted to drink would find them closer to town where he had no authority to shut them down.

What he needed to do was somehow stop the man who was leading the others down this path. He needed to set a trap for Private Coby Willard and end this.

Jed tilted his head toward the field where the wretched private sat. "Do you think you got through to him?"

"I don't know," Cage said. "I hope so."

"I was planning to have a church service in the field. I expect the rain to stop soon, and I told the men to meet me here in half an hour."

Cage couldn't help the smirk that came across his face. "Yes, I know."

"You still want me to have it here?"

Cage nodded. "It'll do Amon some good to be preached at while he's in that condition especially with the other men gathered around him."

Jed snorted. "I don't know if I like the men considering my preaching to be part of their punishment."

"What's your topic today?"

"Resisting temptation."

The captain rubbed his ear. He always tried to be fair by punishing any man caught drinking no matter who it was. Even though Nate was his best friend, Cage came down hard on him when he decided to drown his sorrows in liquor after Mrs. Teagan wrote him that letter. It wasn't difficult to do since Nate always presented himself for the consequences without ever being caught.

Nate had more integrity than any man Cage had ever known except for maybe Jed. He only remembered once when Nate lied, and that was to protect his captain. Now the man was branded a deserter and a coward, and Cage couldn't help him.

Cage gazed at Amon. His punishment would be worse when he confessed the truth to Lavena and Colonel Creighton, but he needed to do it as soon as possible. In a way, he envied the private.

Chapter Twenty-Eight

A drizzle sprinkled onto the field as Jed closed the church service in prayer. Lavena strode toward Captain Cage, her boots sloshing in the mud from the rain. He wouldn't put her off any longer. Even though she'd grown fond of him, she only had five days left until she lost everything she had worked so hard for. She wouldn't let a man ruin it for her.

When she reached him, his back was toward her, and he was staring at the poor private tied up in the middle of the field. "Captain Cage, may I have a word with you?"

Cage turned toward her, and his face lit up. "Yes, I'd like that. Could we maybe go somewhere less... wet?

She tried to hold on to her anger, but his response caused it to seep out of her despite her intentions. No matter how attractive he was, he wouldn't charm her out of an interview this time. "Where do you suggest?"

"My tent is closer," Cage said. "We could leave the tent flap open, so there wouldn't be any misunderstanding. Or I could ask Lieutenant Jed to join us."

She didn't expect him to be so cooperative. Her irritation eroded into the puddle on the field. "The open flap will be fine. Lead on."

Cage offered his arm. She hesitated a moment then looped her arm in his. It was a short walk, and they soon reached the tent. She pulled her jacket off, shook out the rain in the doorway, and stepped inside. The captain offered her a stool, and they both sat.

She hadn't brought her supplies since she hadn't expected to see him back in camp. She stood and headed toward the flap. "I left my lap-desk at my tent. I need to go and fetch it."

"No need," Cage said. "I'm not giving you that interview yet."

Anger swept over her again. "What do you mean you're not giving me the interview yet? Your colonel ordered you to give your account of Cedar Mountain. Do I need to go to him and let him know you're still evading me?"

Cage stood and lifted his hands in the air, palms toward her. "Please, give me a chance to explain. Afterwards, you can go to anyone you want."

She slowly lowered herself onto the bench. "I'm listening."

He let out a heavy sigh. "I'm sorry I took off like that without telling you. Colonel Creighton ordered I leave right away, and there wasn't time to let you know."

"That doesn't explain why you won't give me the interview now."

"No, it doesn't." He rubbed his scar, started to reach for his ear.

"That does it. Don't you dare start rubbing your ear again. I want answers."

Cage pulled his hand away. "I... I didn't realize... Do I rub my ear that much?"

Lavena couldn't help the chuckle escaping her lips. "Only when you don't want to answer my questions."

The red-faced captain looked at his hand, then at her, and placed his hands in his lap. "I'll try to keep my hands away from my ear."

"Let's start again. Go ahead and tell me why you won't let me interview you again."

"I can't help apologizing over and over, but I am sorry. Did you see Private Amon on the field today?"

She pressed her lips together. "I assume he was caught drinking."

His eyes grew wider. "How did you know?"

"A few days ago, he was suffering the ill effects of too much drink. It wasn't hard to surmise."

He reached for his ear, stopped, and placed his hand back in his lap. "Then last night wasn't the first time?"

"I'm afraid not."

He paced a few times and sat down. "I'm delaying the interview yet again because I need to devote my attention to taking care of this lack of discipline among my men. Ejecting the sutlers will help some, but I want to find the man corrupting the other soldiers. If I can catch him in the act, I have a chance of saving Amon and other young men from the drink."

She wanted to protest, but how could she when his mind was so preoccupied? "So, how do you plan to catch Private Coby?"

His jaw dropped. "How did you know?"

"As you say, I'm a good reporter. There's very little I miss."

Cage nodded. "When do you have to turn in this story?"

Now it was Lavena's turn to be surprised. She hadn't thought he cared about her missing her due date. "October thirty-first."

"I see. So less than a week."

"That's right, Captain Cage, and I intend to interview you before then."

The captain wiped his scar, realized what he was doing, and moved his hand back to his lap. "I'll answer all of your questions before the appointed time, but I need a few days to take care of this situation."

If she had been a ship, the wind would have emptied from her sails. She no longer had any anger or fight left in her. He'd agreed to being interviewed, and in time. "It seems I have little choice, but I need your word you won't let me down."

Cage stood. "I give you my word, but for now, I need to discuss my plan with the colonel and get his blessing."

Lavena nodded, then felt a euphoria sweep over her. For the first time in a long time, she felt safe, and she wanted to find a reason to stay. She flushed and looked outside. "I'd better be getting back to my tent."

They both stood and bumped into each other. He touched her arm to keep her from falling. A jolt went through her, and she became aware of his closeness.

A silly grin came over his face, and he backed up a step. "Sorry... I mean... well... I'll see you soon."

Her heart hammered inside her chest. She felt glued to the spot. "I guess I better go then. I pray you find a way to help Amon."

"Thank you." His Adam's apple bulged. "I'll let you know what happens."

"Yes, well, good-bye then."

"Good-bye." He gave her a slight wave.

She left and sauntered toward her warm dry tent. The rain had completely stopped now, and she gazed at a hawk spreading its wings and flying toward the mountains. A double rainbow spanning the sky. Her stomach fluttered.

What was wrong with her? She knew she was attracted to Cage, but had it turned into something more?

She arrived at her tent and started a small campfire. She filled her pot with water and set it on the grate over the fire. A cup of tea would be just the thing. She should feel chilled from all the rain, but a warmth came from inside her.

This was foolishness. After what happened with Warren, she'd never wanted to marry. She was content to be a spinster reporter. Why now? Why him?

Enough of this swooning. She needed to concentrate on her work.

After fixing a cup of bohea tea, she opened her desk and finished the stories she would send Mr. O'Brady in the morning. The story about Private Amon was ready to send. She left out his current trouble. If would do no good to expose his sins to the world. Reporting the truth was important, but unlike her colleagues, she preferred to temper it in grace. Better to pray for him and let God and Cage help him through this.

She took a large envelope from her lap-desk, placed the articles inside, and then addressed it. These stories were some of the best work she'd ever done, but it all came down to whether Captain Cage would keep his word in time. She knew from deep inside he would do as he promised.

She'd stopped believing there could be such good men, men of integrity. There were a few exceptions, of course, men like Father Finney and Mr. O'Brady. Now Captain Cage soared to the top of that list. Maybe it was time to tell him about her past and see what happened.

She placed her tea tin inside her carpetbag and came across Aunt Martha's letter she'd tossed in there. Her father had sinned greatly, there was no getting around that, but it was time to consider forgiving him.

She penned a letter to her aunt, writing about the men she'd met and about how her feelings for Cage had grown into something she wasn't sure she wanted.

Then she told her aunt she would be willing to receive a post from her father. She wasn't ready to build a relationship with him yet, but she was willing to hear what he had to say.

Since there were men of integrity like Cage in the world, then God could give her the strength and courage to forgive her father.

First, she needed to talk to Captain Cage. It was obvious to her there was a strong affection between them, but before it went any further, she needed to tell him about her past. If he was still interested, she needed to make sure he didn't have any objections to her pursuing her career. Journalism was her calling from God, and she'd never give it up.

A month ago, she never would have considered a courtship. A lot changed in such a short time.

She should be concentrating on the men she still wanted to interview, but she couldn't stop thinking about Cage and how he'd react when she told him.

It wasn't as if she hadn't told the sordid story before -- to her aunt and former fiancé the day her father was arrested and later to reporters, police officers, and lawyers. The scandal and gossip followed her everywhere she went.

When Warren broke off the engagement and reporters camped out on the front lawn, Aunt Martha asked the fiery evangelist, Charles Finney, for help. She had supported Father Finney's ministry for years and made a plea for Lavena to escape New York by studying at Oberlin College where Finney was president.

Lavena boarded a train headed for Ohio a few days later. It was the best decision she'd ever made. Father Finney was so supportive and understanding. He and his wife, Mother Elizabeth Finney, would invite her to dinner at their house where they would encourage her in the Word. Mother Finney would often invite her and the other female students to Bible studies she held on campus.

Her time at college gave her room to heal and an opportunity to get an education at a college that allowed women to earn a college degree. It became a foundation for her to start a career as an independent woman. She'd been able to start over.

The captain had a lot on his mind, but she couldn't wait any longer. As soon as he returned to his tent, she would be there to talk with him. If she wanted him to tell her everything, she needed to trust him with the truth about her past. She put on her cloak and walked back to his tent.

Chapter Twenty-Nine

Cage wiped the scar on his face. If he'd had any doubts about his love for Lavena, they were gone now. What was more, she seemed to feel the same way. That would change when he told her the truth, but he had too much to do to worry about that now.

He'd informed Colonel Creighton about his plans, then he found Sergeant Garrett. "Sergeant, I want you to give the men in our company the day off tomorrow."

"But Captain Cage," the sergeant stammered out, "Colonel Creighton wants the tracks finished as soon as possible. He wants us on our way by Wednesday."

"Be that as it may, give them the day off. Tell them it's a reward for working so hard while I was gone."

Garrett looked like he'd swallowed a lemon. "Yes, Sir." He saluted.

Cage knew the order would be carried out even if Garrett wasn't happy about. He headed back to his tent. He wasn't about to look for the whiskey sultlers today. He would take care of them tomorrow. Tonight, he would use them as bait.

When he reached his tent, he was surprised to see Lavena waiting outside. He strolled to her. "I thought you'd be willing to wait a few days for the interview."

"Yes, of course. I've come to you about another matter."

"There's something I want to talk to you about as well." Cage swallowed and sat facing her. He gazed into her eyes. Even if it wasn't a convenient time to tell her everything, he needed to know if she had the same fondness for him he had for her.

If she didn't feel the same way, he'd let her interview him now and be done with it. If there was a chance between them, he needed to wait until this business with his men was taken care of. One disaster at a time.

He touched her hand. "I must tell you, I have a deep affection for you. I didn't plan on it, but from the first moment I saw you in Columbus, you captivated me."

She looked away and blushed. "I admit, I feel a strong closeness with you as well. For someone avoiding me at all costs, you seem to have worked your way into my heart.

Cage chuckled. "So, where do we go from here? A courtship during wartime would be difficult."

Her shoulders slumped. "You won't want to court me when you've heard my past, but I believe in honesty no matter what the cost."

He took hold of her hand. "Honesty is important." He had to tell her no matter what else he had on his mind. He couldn't wait any longer. It would only hurt her more when the truth came out. "I also have something I need to tell you."

*****

Lavena pulled her hand away. "No, please. Let me get this out first." Now that she'd decided to reveal her past, she didn't know where to start.

The back of her throat ached, but she forced out the words. "My father is Luther Falcon, and he's in prison for bribery and exhortation."

Cage leaned in. His gaze held no disdain.

"I grew up believing my father was a hero, a champion for the poor and destitute of New York City. He had money, but he contributed a large portion of it to our church and to local Christian charities." She glanced down at her hands.

"Aunt Martha helped raised me. She wanted me to attend Oberlin College and go into politics. She thought I should continue the good work Father was doing and, at the same time, advance the causes of women's rights and abolition."

She pressed her lips together. "I had other plans though. I fell in love with a young man who was destined for greatness, a man my father was mentoring. He'd already become a councilman in the ward, and many considered him as a contender for the mayor's office. I assumed I could contribute to the cause by becoming Warren Adder's wife."

"Governor Adder from New York?"

Her face grew warm. "Yes."

"What happened?"

"My father was a great man in the city, well known for his causes to help the common man." Her hand trembled.

Cage set his hand over hers. "You don't have to say another word. It won't make any difference to me."

"Please let me finish." She eyes lowered to the ground. "A district attorney had investigated him and found out about the corruption. So, Father confessed everything to me. He was guilty of all of it. Then he turned himself in and acknowledged the corn."

Cage started to grab his ear, then swiped the back of his neck instead. "He told the truth?"

Lavena's gaze darted to a squirrel climbing a nearby tree. "Not until he had no choice. All of my life, he lied to me and to the people in his district. He pretended to be some hero when he was really a scoundrel. Owning up to the truth after he lied for years didn't make up for anything."

Cage's face turned ashen, obviously horrified about what she had told him. "Your father knew they'd found out about him before he was arrested. He could have escaped out west, or he could have tried to find a way to lie and get away with it." His voice thickened. "That has to count for something."

A tear slid down her cheek. "He said the same thing, that he wanted to make things right, but I didn't believe him."

He handed her his handkerchief. "What did your father say to you after he was arrested?"

She wiped the tear away. "I never saw him again. I couldn't. I didn't even go to the trial. The gossip followed me wherever I went. Ladies I didn't know would point at me and whisper. People I'd known all my life wouldn't speak to me. Newspaper reporters stood outside my door waiting for me to leave my house so they could pounce with their questions. I swore I'd never be that kind of reporter, preying on people who had done nothing wrong."

Her voice cracked. "The worst part is when I told my fiancée what happened. His pompous chest practically puffed out of his shirt when he broke off the engagement. He said he couldn't continue his association with me. Marrying me would ruin his aspirations for public service."

"That must have been horrible for you." Cage rubbed his scar. "You have nothing to be ashamed of. Warren Adder was a fool."

Tears welled up behind Lavena's eyelids. Cage knew everything, and he still cared. She wiped her face. "After my father was sentenced to twenty years at the New York Penitentiary, my aunt suggested I get away from the city and further my education at Oberlin. It took some time, but I came to realize that, even though my father betrayed my trust in him and Warren deserted me, God had not left me. I committed my life to championing for women and slaves who could not defend themselves and revealing truth wherever I find it. This is how I serve God and bring meaning what happened in my past."

"Your views on women's rights are strong."

She raised an eyebrow. If he wanted a meek little housewife, it was better she find out now, no matter how painful it would be to end this. "Does that offend you?"

Cage shrugged. "I admit I have spoken in churches and meetings both on abolition and on women's rights. I have no problem with a woman, even a married woman, pursuing a career if that's what she wants."

Every muscle in Lavena's body relaxed, and she realized how worried she'd been, apparently for no reason. "For a man to be an ardent supporter of women's rights is more unusual than it is for a woman to feel that way." She leaned in closer to him.

"I'm an ardent admirer of you." His lips parted.

"I haven't even considered courting anyone since it happened." Their faces moved closer, lips almost touching. "You really are a hero."

Cage pulled back, let go of her hand. "I'm not the hero you think I am. All men fail at times."

"You're nothing like most men." She still felt the warmth of his touch on her hand, but something had come between them, and she didn't understand why. "Most men hide their failings and pretend to be something they're not. Look at Nate Teagan. He went off on all those slave rescues, pretended to be a man of character, and ended up a coward and a traitor."

Cage pulled on his ear.

Had she misunderstood his intentions? Her face and ears felt like they were on fire. "Now that you know everything, I'm sure you'll want to withdraw your offer of a courtship."

"No, not at all." He pulled her toward him and kissed her on the forehead. "I love you" He pulled back, a sadness covering his features. "It's time I give you that interview. You to know everything."

She let out a soft sigh. "I love you too."

Colonel Crighton seemed to appear from nowhere. "Captain, we need to talk about this plan of yours." He nodded toward Lavena. "With your permission, Ma'am."

Her face warmed. How much had the colonel seen?

Cage pulled on his ear. "Sir, can this wait? I was about to give Miss Falcon her interview."

"You haven't done that yet?" Crighton crossed his arms. "I'm sure she can wait another day or two. By then the tracks will be finished, and we'll be on our way." He glanced toward Lavena. "You've waited this long. She can wait another couple of days.

"Of course," Lavena said. She turned toward Cage. "We still have time. You need to take care of your men first."

Cage took her hand and squeezed it. "We'll talk soon. I give my word." He held her gaze for a moment longer as if he wanted to say more, but he didn't.

As he and the colonel walked away, a warmth swept over her with a tinge of fear pressing in. She loved him, and he loved her, but something was wrong. She felt it in her soul.

*****

At sundown, Cage marched to the field where Amon was bucked and gagged. The private looked suitably miserable. "Corporal Jake, release him."

The corporal did as he was told.

"Private Amon, I hope this is the last time we have to have this discussion."

"Yes, Sir." Amon saluted, turned, and limped back toward his tent. If Cage's plan didn't work, maybe it was a good idea to pair him up with another soldier. Anyone would be better than Coby.

Cage grabbed some beef jerky from his tent. He wished he'd insisted on telling Lavena everything earlier. How could he keep his focus on the matter at hand when this was between them? It was too late now. He'd confess everything as soon as this business was over.

He headed to his lookout. A felled tree sat around fifty feet from where the sutlers had set up. Brush obscured anyone's view of him from where he sat, but he could see them clearly. He waited.

At least it was a full moon. Throughout the night, soldiers staggered in and out of tents, and the smell of alcohol assaulted the dank air, but none of them belonged to the Ohio Seventh, so he couldn't interfere.

Scantily dressed ladies hung on the men in uniform with motives of collecting their money to ward off the loneliness. Some of the men were officers, captains and majors from other regiments, the regiments that allowed this kind of behavior. The first and third brigades were stationed in Wartrace before they got there and had been helping them with the bridge and tracks.

No matter how much it disgusted him, Cage had no right to stop what was going on out here unless one of the men from his regiment was involved. Colonel Creighton had given him strict orders. He was only to confront the men of the Ohio Seventh.

It had been hours since he had stationed himself there. Maybe Coby hadn't taken the bait. He hated to think of another night out here.

He stood and paced to keep himself awake. Back and forth. Back and forth.

Another soldier staggered into camp with a woman on his arm, but he didn't stop at the peddler's. He'd obviously gotten his liquor before Cage had set up this lookout.

The private came closer. Coby Willard with a half-clothed woman.

Heat rushed to the back of Cage's neck. He had him this time. Coby was in camp, drunk, and with a prostitute. The man practically flaunted what he was doing.

"Private Coby Willard." Cage's voice bellowed even in his ears.

Coby stood at attention but swayed a little.

The girl kissed Coby on the cheek. "I gotta go, honey." She took off in the other direction.

Cage took a breath and let it out to calm himself. "You're drunk."

"Yes, Ssssir."

"And you brought that girl into camp."

Coby looked around and delivered his characteristic smirk. "What girl?"

Cage's jaw clenched. "I won't stand for this, Private. Report to Sergeant Garrett at dawn. You'll be hanging by your thumbs all day tomorrow. Then you'll be too busy with your extra duties and two weeks of guard duty to have time for gallivanting around like this again."

Private Coby's smirk slipped. "No, Ssssir."

Heat rose up Cage's back. "What did you say to me, Private Coby?"

"You're going to forget about this little incident, Sir, or you'll wish you did."

Cage gripped his rifle tighter. "Are you threatening me?"

"No, Sir." Coby's stance became steady. "I saw what happened in Cedar Mountain. Unless you act like this never happened, I might just tell that pretty little reporter or maybe even the colonel."

All the air left Cage lungs. He struggled to regain his voice. "You weasel." He grabbed Coby by the collar. "You didn't see anything."

"I saw you start the fire."

Cage let go, stepped back. "What... How... You're lying."

"I followed you to the house."

Cage struggled to catch his breath.

"I saw the Rebs run in, and I saw you start the fire to smoke them out."

No, he couldn't have seen. He would have said something before now.

Coby chuckled. "The look of shock on your face when the house blew up was something to behold, but when the woman and children screamed… I saw everything."

Cage backed up a couple of steps until he slumped against a maple tree. "Why didn't you say anything then."

"I was waiting for the right moment." Coby said. "When you ran in after them, I was hoping you'd burn up in there, but Lieutenant Nate ran in to save you."

An overwhelming dread came over Cage. "I'm planning to tell all it anyway." His voice cracked. "Your blackmail won't work."

Coby chuckled. "Sure, you are. You're not going to say anything about this, or I'll make sure the high and mighty Captain Macajah Jones ends up being exposed as the hypocrite you are."

He started toward Coby then stopped short. His chest felt like it was going to explode. He couldn't let Coby be the one to tell Lavena what he'd done.

"You can go, Private."

Chapter Thirty

October 28th

Lavena stood to the side of the tracks watching the crush of men in blue boarding the train to Alabama. They'd finally finished the bridge the day before. After all the rain they'd endured, they had to be happy to finally be on their way in a warm, dry train no matter how crowded it was or how much adversity waited at the end of the line.

When the train stopped again in Bridgeport, they would march to a camp outside of Chattanooga called Lookout Valley. A chill traveled up her back. These men, who had been in more major battles than any other Union regiment, were going to yet another battleground where General Grant determined to break General Bragg's Confederate stronghold surrounding the city.

Some of these young soldiers she'd come to know would die there.

A steady stream boarded, first high-ranking officers then enlisted men. Private Amon climbed aboard but kept his eyes down. He'd seemed to have found a sudden interest in his feet since he'd been bucked and gagged.

Corporal Jake and Private Coby followed him into the car. Coby stopped to leer at her in a way she didn't like. She knew how defeated Cage felt at not being able to catch the private in the act of drinking. She hadn't asked him about it. His melancholy mood told her everything she needed to know.

She let out a sigh. Even though Cage had promised her he'd tell her his story as soon as the train was boarded, she really needed interview Coby first. If he really followed the captain to that house, she wanted to know what more he had to add to the story. It would provide background and make a better article.

He probably hadn't gone anywhere near there but boasted about it to show off. It wasn't something she looked forward to, but if she was going to be the only lady war correspondent among a regiment of soldiers, she would have to get used to an occasional ogle. As long as it never turned into anything more.

Lieutenant-Colonel Crane arrived late and pushed his way in front of the men. He didn't acknowledge her presence making it clear he was still miffed they sent a woman, but he was a good officer, devoted to duty and to his men. And he did give her thorough updates to report to her paper as Colonel Creighton had ordered. His attitude toward career women didn't hinder his professionalism when it was important.

Sergeant Garrett waited with Cage and Jed until the men boarded. He was also devoted to his duty, but, unlike the lieutenant-colonel, he would not succumb to being interviewed by a woman. Last time she tried, he told her, "Women need to learn their place." The attitude wasn't unusual.

She needed to find a way to get Garrett to agree to relent. She wanted to report the story of his escape in his own words. Her readers would be interested, and it would make good copy. Maybe Jed or Cage would have some ideas about how to get him to cooperate.

The last of the enlisted men boarded.

Jed was about to step up when Lavena called out. "Lieutenant Jed."

He paused and turned.

"How are you holding up?"

His Adam's apple bulged. "It's difficult, but I have the Lord to see me through it, Ma'am. Thanks for asking."

"I'm praying for you and your brothers."

"I appreciate that." Jed stepped on board.

Cage reached for her arm. "May I escort you?"

She smiled. "I'd like that."

He helped her on to the train and through the path the soldiers made by standing and squeezing against each other.

They reached the officers car, and every officer stood.

"Gentlemen." Lavena decided to try one more time. "Now that we're on the train again, you don't have to stand every time I enter or come from behind my curtain. I wish you'd think of me as you would any other reporter."

Colonel Creighton chuckled. "That's going to be a bit difficult Ma'am."

Cage led her to the draped off quarters in the corner. He grinned. "I'm afraid I agree with the colonel."

A warmth flushed her face. "Thank you."

He rubbed his scar. "If you want to interview me now, I'm available."

The train jerked, and the clanking of the wheels signaled they were on their way.

"I would like that, but I need to talk to one of the other men first. Could we talk afterwards? I'll make us some tea."

Cage nodded, a somber expression crossing his features. "Yes... a... well... Yes, tea would be nice. I can wait another hour or two."

"Well then."

He moved closer, and she thought he might kiss her, but he pulled away and left.

Time to interview Private Coby Willard. She marched past officers, allowing them to get their daily exercise by jumping to their feet, and leaned against the doorframe of the next compartment. A low murmur of soldiers' conversations filled her ears. Sweat and body odor left a stench that hovered over them.

Coby sat on the far wall close to Amon. Rather than have the men all try to press against each other to make way for her, she decided to call out loud enough to be heard over the din. "Private Coby Willard."

He looked up. He was a little older than Amon, probably in his mid-twenties, medium height and weight, with a look about him like he'd seen the elephant and wasn't impressed.

"Could I interview you?"

He stood with a smirk traveling across his mouth.

Captain Cage sprang from the wall to her side with the agility of a mountain lion. "That's not a good idea."

"You said I could interview your men."

Cage's brow furrowed. "You can, but please may I give you my interview first? Then Coby can tell you whatever he has to add."

Coby made his way through the crowd. "I've got plenty to add, Sir." The sir had a sarcastic edge to it.

Lavena looked at Cage waiting for his cue. She didn't want to go against him in this. She trusted his judgement.

Coby chucked. "I could tell Miss Falcon what I know right here and now."

Cage delivered a pensive gaze toward the private. Coby matched the captain's stare with an innocent look of his own as if he couldn't imagine what the fuss was about. Finally, breaking eye contact, Cage nodded. "It appears I have no choice."

Coby rubbed his hands together. "This should be fun."

"All right then." Lavena walked toward the door. "Follow me."

Coby bowed to the men eliciting a cackle from a few of them and followed her to the officer's car.

Lavena didn't bother to offer him a cup of tea. She doubted tea was the man's beverage of choice.

She pulled out her pen and paper and set the ink bottle on the floor beside her. "Why don't you tell me a little about yourself?"

"I'm the youngest of thirteen children, was born in Lorain. My pa had a blacksmith shop near the lighthouse on the lake."

"How about your ma?"

"She died when I was little. I was mostly reared by my older sisters, at least 'til they started sparking and got married. After that, I pretty much was left on my own. I worked in my Pa's shop from the time I was ten. Pa didn't hold much for schooling."

"What do you think of army life?"

Coby snorted. "Not much. I'm tired of being told what to do, and we're always marching. It's either too hot or too cold or there's a thunderstorm, but it doesn't matter to the big bugs. No matter what the weather, we still keep marching. Things get really boring around here."

"Weren't you one of the men Captain Cage rescued?"

Coby let out a chuckle. "Yeah, the high and mighty Captain Cage rescued me." He emphasized the word, rescued.

"You don't seem to have as high of an opinion of him as the rest of the men."

He rolled his eyes. "Let's just say he's not the hero everyone makes him out to be."

She bit the inside of her cheek. "You obviously know something the rest of the men don't. Amon says you followed your captain when he chased down the Confederate soldiers. Why don't you tell me what happened?"

"No Ma'am." He crossed his arms. "I'm already on his bad side. If I were to tell you what he did, being bucked and gagged or hung by my thumbs would be the least of my problems. Maybe you ought to ask him what happened."

Lavena tried to hold back her ire. She set her lap-desk and pen down. "If you weren't going to answer my questions, why did you agree to this interview?"

Coby winked. "You ain't fooling me none. A pretty gal comes down here to be with us men?" He ran his fingers up Lavena's arm. "You're as lonely as the rest of us."

She pulled away, stood, and knocked over the ink bottle with the heel of her boot. "How dare you." After grabbing the bottle before too much ink spilled out, she tried to regain her composure. "This interview is at an end."

He chuckled. "Come on, you little tart. Your secret's safe with me." He stepped toward her, slid a finger down her cheek.

A shiver went through her, and she backed away, leaned against the window.

He placed a hand on the wall next to her. His fetid breath blew on her face as he leaned in.

She turned her head. "Get away from me!"

Colonel Creighton lifted the tarp. "Is there a problem, Ma'am?"

Coby stepped back.

Crane moved next to the colonel.

Coby saluted the officers and tipped his hat to her. "We'll meet again when we can have a little privacy."

The colonel looked at Crane and tilted his head toward Coby. Crane followed Coby as he meandered through the officer's car back to his company's car.

"Are you all right?" Colonel Creighton asked.

Lavena grabbed hold of the wrought iron on her seat. "I'll be fine." Her voice came out as barely a whisper.

Creighton's eyebrow raised.

"Really. I just need some time to myself."

The colonel furrowed his brow and nodded. "If you want to tell me what he said to get you so upset, let me know." He pulled the curtain closed.

Lavena slumped to her seat, wrapped her arms around herself, and tried to catch her breath.

She now knew what kind of man Coby Willard was.

And it terrified her.

Chapter Thirty-One

The train rumbled through the Appalachian Mountains. Coby had returned to the car, but Lavena wasn't with him. Instead, Lieutenant-Colonel Crane had escorted him back. Cage tried to convince himself he had nothing to worry about. Coby wouldn't tell Lavena anything. It would destroy his power over Cage.

It seemed odd. Cage expected Lavena to come back and request his presence for the interview. He'd rehearsed in his mind what he would say a dozen times, how he would tell the whole truth, but it had been hours, and she hadn't appeared.

His stomach roiled.

What if Coby told her what happened before he had a chance to make things right? Lavena would never forgive him for keeping it from her the way her father had. He should have gone to her tent and confessed everything the moment Coby threatened him. It was such a shock; he hadn't been thinking clearly.

He did have the authority to go into the officers' car to see what happened. Most captains rode in that car. Perhaps it was nothing. He rubbed his cheek. He had to know what happened. He stood.

Jed stretched his back. "What's wrong?"

"Nothing," Cage said.

The lieutenant furrowed his brow.

Cage motioned toward the door. After they stepped out on the platform between their car and the officer's car, he turned to Jed. "Coby knows everything."

Jed gasped. "How?"

"Doesn't matter. The other night when I caught him drinking, he threatened to tell before I have a chance."

"Is that why you didn't punish him?"

Cage nodded. "He might have told her anyway just to spite me."

"You're worrying too much. He wouldn't say anything as long as he has a hold on you, but this makes it even more imperative you confess the truth now."

"I know. I know." Cage rubbed his ear. "I don't want to lose her. I'm in love with her."

Jed placed his hand on Cage's shoulder. "Does she know?"

"Yes, we had a long talk a couple of days ago. I planned to tell her everything as soon as we got on the train, but she said she had another soldier to interview first. If I'd known it was Coby, I would have insisted."

"You can go to her now."

"Colonel Crane escorted Coby here. Why didn't he come back on his own?"

"I know one way to find out," Jed pushed him toward the officer's car door. "Go."

Cage entered the officer's car.

Lavena sat in her draped off corner with the flap half open staring out the window. Cage made his way past the other officers, closed the flap, and sat on the bench across from her. Her eyes glazed over, reminding him of dark clouds circling Lake Erie.

She knows. His chest tightened. *Coby told her.*

Lavena's voice quivered. "Captain, I need to talk with you." Her eyes fixed on the window. She was shaking.

Cage tried to remember how to breathe. "What's wrong? What did Coby tell you?"

"He said..." Her chin trembled. "He... he... he said I wasn't fooling him. That I was interviewing the men because I wanted..." She splayed her hand over her mouth. "He called me a little tart."

The hair on the back of Cage's neck stiffened.

A sob hiccupped from her. "He hemmed me in against the wall, touched my cheek. If Colonel Creighton hadn't walked in on us... I was so scared."

"Did you tell the colonel what happened?"

Lavena shook her head and looked at the ground. "I couldn't."

"Don't you fret." He placed his hand on hers. "I'll take care of it."

Her voice lowered to a whisper. "He said he'd be back when the other men weren't around." A tear rolled down her face, and she quickly wiped it away.

Cage changed seats to sit beside her. He placed his hand on hers.

She buried her face into his shoulder and cried.

He slid his arm around her slender shoulder and didn't move for a long time. Comforting her until she calmed down was more important than the anger raging inside him or the sin he needed to confess.

After a few moments, Lavena pulled back, wiped her eyes, and blew her nose. "I'm sorry. I didn't mean to display my emotions all over your uniform. Thank you for the use of your shoulder."

"Not at all." Cage's heartbeat pounded in his ears. Coby would pay for what he did. "Will you be all right while I take care of this?"

She blushed. "Of course. I'll be fine."

He marched through the offices' compartment into the car crammed with men, not caring who he stepped on. He reached Coby. With hands shaking, he grabbed hold of the collar on the private's shirt, pulled him to his feet, slammed him against the car wall.

Coby smirked. Rage pulsated through Cage's muscles.

Shouting and murmuring echoed in Cage's ears, but he ignored them as he spat out his anger. "If you ever bother her again, I'll kill you." He punched Coby in the stomach.

Jed's voice blasted from behind. "Garrett, get Colonel Crane."

Cage drew back his fist to punch Coby's jaw. Somebody grasped his arm. Jed yelled in his ear. "Cage! Stop it!"

Soldiers grabbed him and yanked him away.

Coby sunk to the floor, shook his head, and chuckled.

Cage struggled to jerk away from his captors. He'd wipe that smirk off Coby's face.

Jed grabbed Coby by the collar and pulled him to his feet. "You think this is funny."

Coby's Adam's apple bulged. "No, Sir."

"You keep it up." Jed jabbed a finger in the private's chest. "And I'll finish what he started."

A shout behind him. "Stand down!" It was Lieutenant-Colonel Crane.

Jed stepped back.

Time returned to normal speed. The men stood around Cage with mouths agape. He stopped struggling, and the soldiers surrounding him let go of his arms.

The lieutenant-colonel marched toward Cage and got in his face. "What's this all about?"

He felt Crane's warm breath. "Private Coby Willard accosted Miss Falcon."

Crane turned to Coby who'd slumped against the wall. "Is that right?"

"I just told her she was pretty, Sir." Coby brushed himself off. "And that she was probably lonely. I didn't hurt her."

Crane glared at Cage. "Did he hurt her?"

"I don't think so, but he scared her."

Lieutenant-Colonel Crane rubbed the back of his neck. "They shouldn't have sent a lady out here. One of the men was bound to upset her eventually."

Cage sputtered. "He threatened her."

Crane faced Coby. "Private Willard, until we get to the bottom of this, you are ordered to stay away from Miss Falcon. Is that clear?"

Coby stood at attention. "Yes, Sir."

Crane grabbed Cage's arm and led him through the gawking crowd into the officers' car. When they got there, Crane stopped to inform Colonel Creighton in whispered tones what happened, Cage stood at attention. He felt like a boy who had been ordered to the woodshed.

It didn't matter if Coby planned to tell what happened anymore. After what he did to Lavena, Cage would tell her everything himself as soon as possible.

When Crane pointed to the opposite end of the car where Lavena sat,

Cage followed him and Creighton there. He slacked his hip and leaned against the wall, worn out from the turmoil of emotions inside of him.

Lavena looked up at them with puffy eyes. She still had Cage's handkerchief in her hand.

"Miss Falcon," Lieutenant-Colonel Crane said. "Captain Cage has told me about the difficulties you've had. This is why women should not travel with soldiers at war time. A lady in your position should expect men to... well... be men. If you want to go back home, I'll find a way to provide transportation."

Cage held his breath. She wouldn't do that, would she?

A storm brewed in Lavena's dark eyes. She stood and planted her feet toe-to-toe with the lieutenant-colonel. The top of her head didn't even come to his chin, but as her jaw set and her shoulders squared, she seemed to grow almost to his height. "Lieutenant-Colonel Crane, I do not intend to go back home. I am here on an assignment approved by my publisher and General Ulysses S. Grant, and I can assure you that General Grant is well aware of my gender."

The muscle in Crane's jaw twitched.

"If you can't control your men, men being what they are..." Lavena jabbed a finger in the lieutenant-colonel's chest. "Then maybe I should write a story on you being unfit to command. I'm sure my publisher, Mr. Edwin Cowles, could make some suggestions in the newspaper to General Grant and to President Lincoln on how you can regain control... if you can."

Cage wanted to give her a round of applause, but he didn't dare. He was in enough trouble.

Colonel Creighton grinned so big his teeth took over his face. "Ma'am, I'm sure we can figure out a way to protect you. I'll be your defender while you ride with us on the train." He turned to Cage. "Captain, make sure Private Willard is severely punished."

Cage suppressed a smile. "I could have him executed at dawn."

Colonel Creighton cleared his throat. "Just hang him by his thumbs or have him wear the barrel when we reach camp. That should suffice."

"Yes, Sir." Cage saluted.

Lieutenant-Colonel Crane turned to Lavena. "Will that be satisfactory, Ma'am?"

"Yes, Colonel, it will." Lavena sat and turned toward the window showing by her actions that he was dismissed.

Crane shoulders slumped, and he became fascinated with the toes of his boots.

"We'll take our leave, Ma'am." Colonel Creighton gave a slight bow.

Lavena turned her head toward Creighton and nodded.

Cage lingered near Lavena's bench as the colonels made their way back to their seats. It wasn't many women who could get the better of

Lieutenant-Colonel Crane.

"Captain Cage." Creighton's voice bellowed.

Cage's face itched. "Yes, Sir." He tipped his cap to Lavena and darted to where Colonel Creighton and Lieutenant-Colonel Crane stood waiting. He saluted and stood at attention waiting for the dressing down he deserved.

Colonel Creighton returned the salute. "I understand why you did it, but assaulting an enlisted man is a serious offense, Captain."

"Yes, Sir."

He turned to Crane. "Under the circumstances, I'm not calling for a court martial, but I expect this man to be punished."

"When we get to Lookout Valley, Captain," Crane said, "assign yourself to nighttime guard duty for two weeks in addition to your regular duties."

"Yes, Sir." Cage let out the breath he was holding. He expected a harsher punishment like he'd received when he hit that reporter, but he wasn't sorry for what he did. A part of him wished Jed hadn't stopped him.

Once the truth came out, he'd get far worse, maybe hanging by his thumbs alongside Coby or spending the rest of the war in the guardhouse. He couldn't imagine the colonel would be pleased with him getting a medal under false pretenses and then having it come out in the newspapers. It would be an embarrassment to his men and to the regiment.

He glanced toward Lavena. Everything in him wanted to get this over with, but he needed to make sure everything was all right with his men first, and she needed some time before he thrust more turmoil upon her.

When he wandered to the other car, he scanned the faces of the men. They lowered their eyes when they saw him, but Coby wasn't anywhere in sight. He slumped beside Jed.

"I moved him," Jed said without looking up.

"What?"

"I ordered Coby to move to the next car. He can ride with Company B."

Cage let out a breath realizing how anxious he'd been at riding the rest of the trip with Coby in the same boxcar without being allowed to finish what he started. "Thanks."

"You're welcome."

Cage set his jaw and prepared for the sermon his junior officer no doubt would deliver.

"What happened?"

"Coby will be hung by his thumbs when we reach Chattanooga."

"And."

Cage rubbed his scar trying to stop the itching. It did no good. It was down deep where he couldn't reach. "I have two weeks night guard duty."

"You got off easy."

"I know, but I'm sure when it all comes out, my punishment will be more severe."

Jed waited until it became uncomfortable before he said more. "You must care for her a great deal. I've never seen you lose your temper like that. Except with reporters."

Cage lowered his eyes. "I'm going to lose her."

Jed slumped back. "Probably, but it's better if she hears it from you."

Cage stood.

"Where are you going?"

"Where do you think?" He headed to the officers' car. It was time to tell her the truth.

Chapter Thirty-Two

Cage marched through the officer's car, avoiding the looks he knew they were giving him. He swept the curtain aside and closed it behind him.

Lavena stood. "Cage?"

He leaned into her, brushed his lips across hers. She moved closer, and he kissed her, timidly at first, then with great passion.

He paused and pulled back. "I'll tell you everything you want to know." The pressure of her lips lingered sweetly on his mouth, but it would be the last kiss they ever had. He would lose her love before it had even started, but he couldn't live with this lie any longer.

Lavena gave him a quizzical look then pulled a notebook, pen, and bottle of ink out of her case. "I already have the background information on you. I'd like an account from you of how you saved your men."

He told her about how the rescue happened then stopped. He couldn't bring himself to continue.

"Thank you." Lavena wrote down some notes, then looked at him. "Now could you walk me through what happened next.

Cage released air through his mouth. "I chased after the enemy soldiers. Lieutenant Nate Teagan was with me, but the graybacks separated. I took one group, and Nate chased the rest." He paused, swallowed hard.

"And you caught up with them?"

"Yes, I saw them run into a two-story colonial farmhouse."

"Is that when they started the fire?" When he took too long to answer, she placed a hand on his arm. "I know this is hard. Take your time."

He gazed into Lavena dark eyes. Adder was a fool for so easily throwing away her love. "Yes, that's when the fire started, but the rebs got away. They took off out the back door. The flames overtook the house faster than I ever would have figured. They must have had gunpowder or ammo stored there. They sometimes do store supplies in homes of Southern civilians."

A smoky haze settled over the mountains outside the window resembling the fog he'd been in since it happened. He had been lost in the same storm he'd warned Amon about. "The next thing I remember was the screams. They pierced right through me. I looked up. A woman and a couple of children were beating on the second-story window trying to get it open. I ran through the front door, but something fell on me. I think a beam fell from the ceiling."

He rubbed his hand across his cheek. "My hair and shirt caught on fire. I tried to get up, but I couldn't. I've never felt such pain. It was like being held down in the fires of Hades."

Lavena's eyes glistened. "How did you escape?"

"I remember hearing Nate's voice, and someone grabbed my arms, but after that... When I woke up in the infirmary, my face and chest were wrapped in bandages, and I was in so much agony even the morphine couldn't touch it. I was released for duty a few weeks later, but it took months for my hair to grow back."

"What happened to the woman?"

"She and her children died." He grabbed his ear. "One was just a baby."

"Is there anything you'd like to add?"

The air escaped Cage's lungs, and he struggled to voice the words. "What do you mean?"

"I don't know." Lavena bit her bottom lip. "It seems like you're holding something back."

"Yes." *Please, Lord, give me the courage I need to do this.* "There is more to the story."

Lavena set the paper and pen down and took hold of his hands. "I know this is difficult. I already have enough from you for the story. You don't have to say any more if you don't want to."

Cage placed his hands in hers. It was time to step out of the tempest and into the light. "I started the fire."

******

The air sucked out of Lavena's lungs.

Shoulders slumped, his gaze remained fixed on her. "I was trying to smoke out the Confederate soldiers."

She tried to catch her breath.

"It was a small fire, just one torch through the window. There was an explosion. Within seconds the house filled with flames." His voice caught. "That's when I heard the screams."

There had to be a mistake. She pulled her hands away, stood, stepped back, bumped into the stove.

He folded his hands in his lap, and his voice remained calm, almost too calm. "I should have told the truth when I woke up in the army hospital, but they'd already given me that cursed medal. I thought if I didn't talk about it, everyone would forget. Then the newspapers picked up the story and portrayed me as some kind of great hero who was single-handedly winning the war."

She tried to choke out words, but they caught in her throat. "That's why you didn't want to do the interview, to hide your wrongdoing."

"Yes." His head lowered, but his eyes didn't. "I'm no hero."

Her throat ached. How could she have allowed this man to get close enough to rip her apart again? She wrapped her arms around herself. He was no different than her father, or Warren, or even her friend's traitorous husband.

She had to get away. She stumbled past the officers toward the platform outside.

Cage's voice sounded from behind. "Lavena, wait, please."

******

Cage prayed for Lavena as he headed after her. He couldn't leave her out there, alone on the outside platform, in the state she was in. He'd been a fool trying to hide the truth to save his reputation instead of bringing it out into the light. All he'd done in trying to protect himself was hurt the woman he loved.

He wouldn't evade it anymore. Pain ripped through his soul, but even now with this ache, he was relieved Lavena knew. As agonizing as it was standing in the light, at some point, he would tell his colonel and his men what he'd done to dishonor the regiment. The whole country would read about it as soon as Lavena's story was published, but he didn't care.

She held onto the railing, sobbing. He rushed to her but didn't know how to help. She turned, placed her head on his chest, and sobbed in his arms. His insides ached for her, and he wrapped his arms around her.

He didn't know how long they stood like that, but eventually, her shoulders stopped heaving with an occasional tremor going through her.

"I'm so sorry."

She drew back, a horrified look on her face. "Get away from me."

Cage stepped back.

"Leave me be." She wrapped her arms around herself and rocked.

"I can't leave you out here like this."

"I can't trust you. You're reprehensible."

Cage stepped toward her to console her, but she scooted away like a scared child, just inches from the edge of the platform.

The vision of a soldier falling off the train over a month ago flashed through his mind. He held up his hands to calm here. "I won't come any closer, but please don't move."

"What do you want from me?" She shuffled an inch closer to the edge. "Are you trying to make sure I don't write a story?"

His heart raced. If he went toward her, she'd move away from him. She'd fall. He took another step back, trying to keep his voice even. "Just come away from the edge. Please."

She looked down, gasped, then stepped closer and grabbed hold of the rail.

He let out the breath he was holding. "I want to make sure you're all right, that's all. I don't expect you to forgive me, and I'm not trying to stop you from reporting this. I've been living with this sin for a year now. I want it out in the open no matter the cost."

A sob escaped her. "I don't believe you."

"No reason you should, but I'm done trying to hide."

"Then leave me alone," she screamed.

"I can't do that." He pulled on his ear. "It's too dangerous out here. I'm staying on this platform until you're ready to move back inside."

Lavena edged further away from him. She was too close again, but this time she knew it. She held onto the rail and gazed at the river running beside the tracks.

Everything in him wanted to reach out and grab her, but if he did, she might slip. He prayed the train wouldn't jerk and make her lose her balance. "Please, I only want to make sure you're safe."

She moved only one step closer to him, but it was enough.

He moved to the door of the soldier's car and waited.

She didn't stir, just stared at the landscape for a long time. "How could you allow me to care for you when you knew this would happen?"

"I know it will take time, but if you'll let me," his voice thickened, "if there's any chance, I'll spend the rest of my life trying to make things right."

Lavena wiped the tears from her face. "How?"

"When we get to Chattanooga, I'll tell Colonel Creighton everything. If I'm not placed under arrest, I'll assemble my men and let them know what I did too." He cleared his throat. "I'm sure you'll take care of informing everyone else."

Lavena let a half grunt escape her. "By the time I'm done, there won't be a place you can go where this won't follow you. You can forget about a career as a lawman. You'll be lucky if you can get a job cleaning up horse manure from the streets of Cleveland."

"Fair enough."

"I thought you were different. You're worse than my father. And Nate. At least they never killed anyone."

Cage felt a knife plunge into his soul. "And I did. A mother and three children." He wished he had died in that fire. "There's nothing I can do to change that. I live with their screams every day."

"I have an article to write." She wiped her face and stepped back into the officer's car.

Cage stood outside a while longer. It was a bright clear day. Almost too bright. He couldn't go inside and face his men yet. After a time, he didn't know how long, Jed stepped out on the platform and stood beside him.

Cage wiped his hand across his scar. "It's done."

"Thank God. How did she react?"

"Horror, accusations, sobs. Apparently, the lady does have tears in her arsenal. She says she can't ever trust me again."

"Is she going to write the story?"

"Yes. I want her to." He was surprised he meant it. "I'm not hiding the truth anymore."

"So, what now?"

"Colonel Creighton is preoccupied about getting to Chattanooga after being delayed so long, but as soon as we get settled, I'm confessing everything to him. Then, whatever happens, happens."

"What about Lavena?"

"I love her," Cage said thickly. He cleared his throat. "I doubt she'll ever forgive me, but after this is all out in the open, I'll try somehow to make amends. At least, she'll get the article in on time, and she'll give them a better story than they ever thought possible. They'll probably give her a raise for this."

Jed leaned back. "I can't promise the next few months are going to be easy, but God will work everything out for the good now that you've surrendered this to Him."

Cage nodded. "I should have told her as soon as she'd come into camp." He swallowed at the lump in his throat. "I should have told Colonel Creighton as soon as I woke up from the fire."

"You can't live in regrets." Jed placed a hand on Cage's shoulder. "God has forgiven you. There are earthly consequences, but He'll walk you through them and give you the peace and joy you need to go on from here."

Nothing would ever be the same, but a peace swept over him he hadn't known for a long time. *Lord, is there some way of winning back Lavena's love?*

No, he didn't deserve her.

Chapter Thirty-Three

October 30th

Nate surveyed the landscape from Craven's House near the top of Lookout Mountain. Storm clouds were in the distance, but from here he still had a clear view of the city of Chattanooga and of the Tennessee River.

Union tents propped up all around the city as well as in the valleys below. Mountains surrounded the city on every side. If it weren't for the Confederate camps on Lookout Mountain and Missionary Ridge, Chattanooga would be lost forever to the Rebs.

General Bragg had been furious that the Union Army had surprised his troops at Brown's Ferry and had seized the Cracker Line at during the Battle of Wauhatchie. He'd planned to starve the Union troops out, but now they had control of the river and could bring troops and supplies into the city at will.

What Bragg didn't know was Nate was responsible for the command mix-up that made it possible. Because he'd been entrusted with delivering Bragg's messages, he was able to change the commander's message to General Oates just enough to make it possible.

Colonel Creighton would be pleased with how effective the plan to have him infiltrate Bragg's command had worked. By being entrusted with every message from Bragg to his men, he had information on every operation and could change orders anytime he wanted.

One of the reasons the colonel had chosen him was because he had become a master forger when he was rescuing slaves, making sure they had letters of transport and documents of freedom in the handwriting of their masters.

The other reason, of course, was because his father was under Bragg's command. They hadn't known Father had risen to the rank of colonel. Last they'd heard, he was still a major.

It had been so easy to get Father to trust him. Father did the rest to earn the general's trust. A part of him felt guilty for betraying his parents after they'd reunited for the first time in years, but it had to be done.

The mission was dangerous. Nate had to be careful not to change too many messages. The ones he did rewrite, he modified only a bit to confuse but not to completely alter the orders. That kept suspicion off of him. If he was caught, he would be hung, but without Betsy, life didn't matter. At least, he could further the cause.

This time, he had delivered the messages as written and was now searching for the right cave, some place hidden and easily accessible by him and by Union soldiers.

He had expected the Ohio Seventh to make it to Chattanooga Valley a couple of weeks ago, but he'd kept watch for them, and they hadn't arrived. He was sure they'd be here any day now.

While he was off on this mission, it was the perfect time to find a place for him to meet with Cage and Jed. He'd leave a coded message at the line about the meeting place and time. They'd find it when they finally got here.

There was a small hill in the distance that might work. He'd hidden escaped slaves there a few years ago. He climbed down the hill and headed toward it as stealthily as he could. Hopefully the weather would hold while he checked it out. If the cave was still there and not occupied, it would make the ideal meeting place.

******

Lavena read the article, then crumbled it up and threw it in the corner with the rest of the discarded stories. What was wrong with her? She knew the truth and had the most explosive story of the war, but she couldn't seem to put it onto paper.

Every time she tried, it either sounded revengeful or justified Cage's actions too much. She gave up for the moment and set a pot of water on the stove.

Even though it was still daytime, dark clouds swarmed around making it as dreary as her mood. Her throat ached from all the tears she'd shed since yesterday. She'd secluded herself behind her curtain and cried into a pillow so none of the officers would hear, but every time she'd wiped her face, blown her nose, and decided the tears were done, it would start up again. She hated herself for being so weak.

Hadn't she known better to allow herself to feel affection for a man? It was bound to end poorly.

She grabbed another piece of paper and started again. A knock sounded on the wall next to her curtain. "Just a moment." She took a wet cloth and wiped it over her face. All she needed was to allow one of the officers to catch her sobbing like a little girl. She pulled the curtain aside.

Chaplain Jed stood there. "May I come in?"

"This isn't a good time. I have a story to write."

Jed touched her arm. "I know what happened."

Thunder boomed in the distance.

"What do you mean?"

He kept his voice low, almost a whisper. "Captain Cage told me everything."

She let out a sigh, then motioned for him to have a seat. Before he did, he pulled the curtain back in place. She sat across from him and blinked several times to make sure the crying didn't start back up. "What did he tell you?"

He kept his voice low. "He confessed the truth to you and told you how he started the fire."

"So, you knew about it."

Jed nodded. "He's worried about you, but he didn't want to make things worse. He asked me to come make sure you're all right."

All right? How could she be all right when her heart was breaking into a million pieces? "You can tell the captain I'm fine, but I need to concentrate on my story. It will expose him as the fraud he is."

Just then, the heavens opened, and rain came down in sheets causing the car to be filled with a low rumbling sound. It was if the sky itself was reflecting her turmoil.

Jed placed his hand on hers. "I can see how distraught you are, and for good reason. Please let me help."

She pulled her hand away. "Would you like some tea?" She began making it. "I'm using chamomile this time. It's the perfect tea for times of crisis."

"Yes, that would be fine."

After allowing it to steep, she poured both of them a cup. "It was my fault. I should have known better than to allow myself to become close to the man I was writing about. Uncovering the truth should have been my primary focus."

"I see." Jed sipped some tea. "So, your feelings for him are as strong as his for you."

She sputtered. "You must be joking. I detest the man. As soon as this assignment is over, I never want to see him again."

"Mmm, hmm," was his only response.

She shivered and wrapped her blanket around her shoulders. "I only want write this story and save my job. Then I'll leave this wretched war behind. My editor was right. Women have no place in the battlefield."

Jed's eyebrow lifted slightly. "I didn't think you were the kind who would hide behind her skirts and run away."

"How dare you?" Lavena stood. "I've worked hard for this position, twice as hard as any man, and I came through with the story no other reporter could get."

"Then you should be happy," Jed said. "This story will bolster your reputation as a journalist for years to come. You'll probably have other newspapers trying to hire you. Your articles might even end up in *The Harpers Weekly*."

She slinked back into her seat. "This is all I ever wanted, but now..."

"May I see what you've written?"

She let out a grunt and pointed to the waste paper in the corner.

"Having a hard time writing it?"

"Yes, I'm having a hard time writing it. I'm so furious I could spit, but I don't want the whole world to know what he's done. Is that what you wanted to hear?"

Jed took another sip of tea. "He didn't have to tell you. He could have relayed only what everyone already knew. He told you the truth because he cares for you, and he couldn't keep this lie between you."

She leaned back in her bench, feeling totally drained. "Now, I know why he kept putting off the interview. He didn't want to let anyone know he'd killed women and children. The high and mighty Captain Macajah Jones, the hero of Cedar Mountain."

Lightening let up the sky, then a second later, a crash of thunder.

"That's not fair." Jed set his cup down. "He struggled with this, but he did tell you even though he knew it would cause a rift between you. He plans to confess it to the colonel and his men and accept the consequences."

A sinking feeling lodged in her stomach. "I know, but I have to write the truth. To leave anything out would be a deception, and I couldn't live with that."

"Neither could Cage." Jed took hold of Lavena's hand. "But perhaps he didn't tell the whole truth."

Heat rushed up Lavena's back. "You mean there's more?"

More thunder.

"Captain Cage should have confessed everything as soon as it happened, but he was in an untenable position." Jed gazed into her eyes until the silence between them became uncomfortable. "He woke up scarred and confused, burned while trying to save the woman and children he believes he killed, and everyone was already hailing him as a hero."

She glanced away. "He killed them when he started the fire. He should have admitted it."

"It's not that simple." He let go of her hand, stood, and gazed out the window at the torrent surrounding the landscape. "In the heat of war, Cage had no way of knowing the deaths his actions would cause. Is he more responsible than the Confederate soldiers storing gunpowder in a civilian house? He wanted to smoke them out, not start a fire, and he didn't know there was a woman and children in the house. The Confederate soldiers did, or maybe they didn't."

Lavena took a sip of tea to try to wash away the lump in her throat. "What do you mean? Of course, they did."

Jed turned toward her. "Perhaps it's the woman's fault. She allowed that gunpowder to be stored in her house knowing her children were there. Or maybe it was her husband who hid the gunpowder there without telling her. The truth is bad things happen in war. Women and children are killed without anyone meaning to hurt them. Brave men like

Captain Cage feel guilty about killing civilians when he had no intention of doing so. It's the nature of war."

She let out a sigh. "Perhaps you're right, but the moment he went along with the lie, he became culpable."

"He knows that," Jed said. "It took a lot of courage to come forward."

"Too little, too late." Just like when her father confessed.

"You want the truth, yet you're not willing to search beyond the obvious."

Lavena's shoulder sank. "What do you want from me? I was sent to report Captain Cage's story in his own words. I don't have time to delve into all the nuances of war. My job depends on turning that story in on time. I have to send a telegram as soon as the train stops that the story is on its way, or I'm done."

"Then I'll leave you to do the job you came here for." Jed stood, gave her a deep penetration look, then walked out.

Tears ran down Lavena's face, and this time she didn't try to stop them. The sound of the storm covered her sobs anyway.

She took another sip of tea, but her hand shook so much, she spilled a little on the front of her dress. She set the cup down and stared out the window at the dark billows.

Years ago, her life had almost been destroyed by overzealous reporters. They reported what her father did wrong, but they had no compassion in the way they told it. This article wouldn't only destroy Cage, it would hurt the reputation of every brave men of the Ohio Seventh.

She had to report what Cage had done no matter who it hurt. The clanking of the wheels slowed. She'd already lost her respect for Cage. The whistle blew. She couldn't lose her career too.

The train came to a stop. They had arrived in Bridgeport. It was time to send that telegram.

Chapter Thirty-Four

October 31st

The Ohio Seventh arrived at Lookout Valley late the night before, and Amon had barely pitched his tent before climbing into his bedroll. After marching all the way in a severe thunderstorm, and all he wanted was a good night's sleep.

He shook the grogginess from his mind and made his way out of the tent. The rain had stopped, and the sun was shining. He stretched, enjoying the warmth drying his clothes. Even the muddy ground was beginning to soak up the moisture.

They had been ordered to make camp today near Racoon Mountain. The accommodations were better, a large tent with a floor where five men could comfortably sleep.

He surveyed the area. Massive mountains overshadowing a valley with a river running along it. Tents and cannons surrounding the city.

He almost wished he could see what the rebs saw from Lookout Mountain. One of the men said, on a clear day, you could see five states from there. Wouldn't that be something? They wouldn't get to see that view until they defeated the Confederate Army stationed there.

Men would die on this hillside as they had on every other mountain he'd climbed. He might die here.

A cannonball blast from the top of Lookout Mountain, shaking the ground and making Amon's stomach tighten. Union soldiers returned fire, but the cannons were too far away on both sides to hit anything.

At least there were a lot of wagons and tents set up to sell wares to the soldiers, and since they were outside the city, Captain Cage wouldn't be able to chase them away. Some of them would have whiskey for sale. He'd have to check it out later. The fire was dying, and he poked it with a stick. He could use some strong drink.

Reveille sounded, and he rushed to the field where they'd been ordered to congregate. Coby was already there since Sergeant Garrett had dragged him out of his tent at dawn to tie his thumbs to a tree limb just tall enough so he would have to stay on his toes. He'd be there all day.

Normally Amon would have felt bad for him, but this time, Coby deserved it. He shouldn't have tried to force himself on that nice lady reporter.

The sergeant ordered the men to get in formation to do drills for hours. They had to gather on either side of where Coby was being punished, part of the humiliation.

Heat seared Amon's cheeks. That was the part about being bucked and gagged he'd hated the most. Everyone had gawked at him while Chaplain Jed preached about sin crouching at the door. If it meant a night full of whiskey helping him forget, he'd open the door wide for it.

Coby didn't look like he was enjoying his punishment any more than Amon had. A look of pure hate seared his face.

It didn't make sense. After what he'd done, Coby should have been embarrassed or ashamed. Instead, he showed deviance.

It left a sour taste in Amon's mouth. He shook his head. Captain Cage was right. He needed to choose his friends more wisely.

******

Lavena stood outside and watched the men drill. Normally it made her a bit queasy to see the harsh punishments inflicted on the soldiers. She had plenty of sympathy when Amon was bucked and gagged, but she wasn't sorry at all to see Coby being hung by his thumbs. If anyone deserved it, he did.

Jed saw her, nodded, and strode toward her. "Have you gotten settled in?"

"Yes, thank you. A cabin by the Tennessee River is a vast improvement, although I see the enlisted men are still in tents."

Jed chuckled. "Even so, their accommodations are vastly improved as well."

"True," she said. "How about you? Do you have your own cabin?"

"I'm sharing one with Captain Cage."

"Oh." Her heart skipped a beat, and she tried not to react, but by Jed's glance, she must have failed miserably.

"You won't be alone for long. There are some nurses coming in about a week. I'm sure they'll want you to house one or two of them."

Lavena nodded. "I'll look forward to it. I could interview them and find out what it's like being a nurse."

Jed chuckled. "Always working, aren't you?"

She shrugged.

He offered her his arm. "It's a nice day. Would you like to take a stroll with me?"

"I'd like that." She placed her arm in his, and they walked toward the river. There were so many men gathered in the valley between Lookout Mountain and Racoon Mountain that they constantly had to sidestep to miss them.

"What are your plans for today?" Jed asked.

"I need to collect information about the Battle of Watashe that took place here the other night. I figured I'd talk to General Geary about it since he was here for the battle. Then I'll stop by and ask Lieutenant-Colonel Crane if I can convey the information using their telegraph."

"I see. Anything else."

"I don't know," Lavena said. "I was hoping to stop by the Army Hospital and interview Dr. Mary Walker. It would be exciting talking to an Army surgeon who is a woman."

Jed stopped and faced her. "You're avoiding my question."

She smiled and walked on. "I answered every question you asked me."

He ran a couple of steps to catch up with her. "Stop please."

She halted her steps. They were on the shore of the river now. Some geese were swimming as if there hadn't been a battle on this very spot two days ago.

"All right. Since I have to say it, you have to let your boss know you are sending the story today. Did you write it yet?"

A sandhill crane squawked and flew overhead. She watched the graceful bird soar to the top of Lookout Mountain. What would it be like to soar like that? "No, I didn't."

His mouth gaped open. "Isn't your time limit today?"

"Yes... Yes, it is." A lump formed in her throat, and she walked on with Jed strolling beside her. "Actually, I have written it about fifty times, but I'm not satisfied, and I can't turn it in until I am."

"Why? What's the problem? Surely, it's not because Cage would be angry about it. He told you to write it."

"No, that's not it." She didn't know how to explain it because she didn't understand her reluctance. "Even if he were angry, I don't care. After what he did, I never want to see him again."

Jed raised that infuriating eyebrow of his. "It's war. Things like this happen. He certainly didn't mean for it to."

"He should have told the truth." Her words came out thick, and she hated her emotions for displaying themselves. She pulled out a handkerchief and wiped a stray tear off her face and blew her nose.

"Fair enough," Jed said. "What will you do?"

She stopped, turned away from him so he couldn't see her eyes watering up, and watched the ducks. "I have to telegraph Mr. O'Brady today. If for no other reason, to let him know about the battle two days ago."

He placed his hand on her arm. It was a gentle touch, not demanding. He was letting her know he was there for her.

"I'll tell him I interviewed Cage and got his side of the story, but writing the article will take a few weeks. By then, I should be able to figure out what to do."

Jed walked around her until he was facing her. "Do you think that will satisfy him?"

"Yes... No..." She pressed her lips together. "I don't know."

Jed set his hands on her shoulders. "Maybe I can help. What is stopping you from exposing a captain who set a house on fire, killed three people, then lied about it?"

Her chest felt so tight she was amazed she could still breathe. "I don't want to hurt him." It barely came out as a whisper.

"You still love him."

It was a statement, not a question, but she answered him anyway. "I don't want to, but I do. How can I allow the pain he's brought on himself to come from my hand?"

He pulled back and gazed at her intensely. "Is there a chance between the two of you?"

"No." She turned and began walking at a brisk pace. "I could never forgive him for this any more than I could forgive my father."

Jed kept up with her, matching his gait to hers. "Your father?"

Lavena stopped, realizing what she let blurt out. "That's a conversation for another day, Chaplain. I have a telegram to send." She headed toward General Geary's cabin.

Chapter Thirty-Five

Cage had spent most of the day inspecting the line. It was really just a fence, but it kept Union and Confederate troops separated. He wasn't sure if it had been there before the war or if one of the officers had ordered it built, but it served its purpose.

Separated might not be the right word. Troops on both sides would trade pipe tobacco and playing cards over the fence and would sometimes strike up conversations.

It was a strange war. Members of the same family on different sides. Men exchanging pleasantries one day and trying to kill each other the next.

He had been at this for hours with no luck, and tonight he would be assigned guard duty here. It would be a long night. He had to find it soon or he'd have no time to rest before he was due at his post.

A boulder sat against the fence post, and he thought he could make out something etched on it. He walked a little further, careful to not allow anyone to see him focused on the rock. He got to it, took a furtive look around to make sure nobody was nearby, and glanced down. It had an X etched into the wood, probably with a knife. This was it.

He kicked the rock aside, then dropped his canteen to give himself an excuse to reach down, grabbed the metal tube, and slipped it in his pocket.

Walking at a gentle pace, he cleared the area, then he hurried to the cabin where Colonel Creighton had set up his office.

Sergeant Noah Andrews from Company F stood guard. Cage strode toward him and saluted. "I need to see him. Is he in?"

"That lady reporter is in there now, Sir. Do you want me to announce your presence?"

He didn't want to bluster in carrying the tube. "No, I'll wait." Lavena would ask questions about it. He paced. Everything inside of him wanted to see her, to talk with her. No, he needed to wait. He paced a little more, stopped, and headed to the heavy pine door.

The door creaked open, and she slipped through, saw him, and tried to walk by without saying anything.

"Wait," he blurted out.

She stopped. "What! What could you possibly have to say to me?"

He motioned her to a nearby tree so Sergeant Noah couldn't overhear.

She leaned against the tree and crossed her arms, almost defying him speak.

He rubbed his ear, let go, then grabbed it again. Did it really matter if his ear pulling showed how distraught he was? "I'm telling Colonel Creighton everything. That's one of the reasons I'm here. I wanted to let you know."

"Why should I care?" Her chin quivered. "I got my story, didn't I? That's all that matters now."

"Well, yes, I..." Cage didn't know what to say. "I... I'm sorry."

She didn't answer but delivered a glare twice as deadly as any rebel cannon.

A profound sadness swept over him. He should have tried harder to resist the urge to try to talk to her. Of course, she'd reacted this way, and he didn't want to cause her any more pain.

He tipped his cap, turned, and sauntered back to the Colonel's cabin then knocked on the door.

Colonel Creighton opened it and motioned him in. "Good evening, Captain Cage."

When Cage entered and greeted the colonel, the heat from the stone fireplace on the back wall warmed his chilly face and fingers but did nothing to heal his heart. It was time to put aside his feelings and concentrate on the task ahead.

"Did you find it?" the colonel asked.

Cage held up the metal tube. "Yes, it was right where he said."

"Let's have a look at it."

Cage unscrewed the top and pulled out two papers. The first was written in code. The second looked like some sort of a map.

Creighton pulled out a piece of paper, set at his oversized oak desk in the middle of the room, and worked to decipher the message.

Cage stood at attention and waited.

The colonel finished and handed the translated message back. "Sit down, Captain."

Cage sat in one of two nearby shaker chairs and read it out loud. "Things going better than expected. I am General Braggs' messenger. Have been able to change some of his communications before I delivered them. Will meet you in the cave Friday, November sixth with the code for the Reb messages. Hope you arrive by then. If not, I'll be there every Friday until the battle. X marks spot on map."

The colonel let out a grand laugh. "Didn't I tell you we sent the right man?"

"Amazing," Cage said. "General Braggs' messenger? How did he ever pull that off?"

"Tomorrow, take a few men and scout out the area. I don't want any surprises when you go to meet him."

Cage swiped his hand over his scar. "Sir, you might want Jed to go alone on the scouting mission. I have guard duty, remember?"

"I forgot about that," the colonel said. "I'll rescind the order, but I'm only postponing it for now. I can't have my officers striking enlisted men without any consequences. I'll assign you that extra guard duty when the mission is over."

"Yes, Sir."

Colonel Creighton stepped over to the wood stove in the corner and poured two cups of coffee. "Lieutenant Teagan is a brave man. I'll see he gets a medal when this is over."

At the mention of a medal, Cage felt like a knife stabbed his heart. He rubbed his ear. Time to get this out before he lost his nerve. "Speaking of medals, Sir, there's something else I need to tell you concerning mine."

The colonel offered Cage the second cup.

Cage shook his head. "Thanks, Sir. I'm not thirsty."

Creighton sipped some coffee. "Does this have anything to do with that reporter?"

"In a way," Cage said. "I told her everything, and she's going to write the story."

"I'm glad that's over with." Colonel Creighton set the coffee on the table and placed both hands flat, leaning over one of the maps as if something on it distracted him. "I admire how well she's gotten on here. There aren't many ladies who could do this job."

"Sir." Cage stood and came to attention. He inhaled a large breath and released it. "I've been lying about the incident at Cedar Mountain."

The colonel leaned forward, and the muscle in his cheek twitched. "Go on." His words had a caustic edge to them.

"The Confederate soldiers didn't start the fire that killed the woman and her three children."

Creighton raised an eyebrow. "Who did?"

"I did, Sir." Cage's scar itched, but he resisted rubbing it. "I planned to smoke out the enemy. By the time I realized there were civilians in the house, it was too late."

A relief washed over Cage despite the scorching glare the colonel delivered. The truth was finally out. No more deception.

The colonel stood and paced. "Things like this happen in war." His voice stayed steady but there was a menacing tone to it. "But lying to your superior officers… that's another matter."

"No excuses, Sir."

"Does this lady reporter know everything?"

"Yes, Sir."

"You really put us in the middle of a scandal, Captain." Creighton hit the table with his fist causing a pile of papers on the edge to strew to the floor. He exhaled as if trying to regain his composure. "President Lincoln awarded the medal himself. You've disgraced the honor of your company, your regiment, and the entire Union Army, not to mention the integrity of being a Congressional Medal of Honor recipient."

Heat rose to Cage's face. His actions affected so many, his regiment, his men, Lavena. There was no way to undo the harm he'd caused.

"Did you even consider how this would dishonor the men bravely serving in the Seventh before you decide to blurt out everything to the press? You could have at least warned me first. Last I checked, I am your superior officer and the commander of this regiment."

"Yes, Sir." Cage couldn't think of anything else to say. There was nothing to say.

"General Geary and I will discuss this at length. Under most circumstances, I'd have you in irons." The colonel swiped the back of his neck then began pacing. He didn't say anymore for at least a couple of minutes.

Cage stayed at attention, knowing the colonel wasn't finished with him. He'd expected to be in trouble, but the realization he let the regiment, his men, down troubled him more.

He'd had learned a long time ago that he could never live up to what people expected. His father, a preacher in the small city of Kent, Ohio, had drilled into him that as the son of a preacher, he needed to be perfect.

His father had expected it, and every parishioner in his father's congregation had watched Cage to make sure he towed the line. He'd tried hard to keep that look of disappointment out of his father's eye, but no matter how hard he tried, it didn't work.

After high school, he'd studied theology at Oberlin College then became a pastor. When he'd realized he wasn't called and quit the ministry, Father's disappointment grew to something deeper, something that weakened his parents physically until they succumb to influenza and died.

Now, those weren't the only deaths on his conscience. He had killed that woman and her three children. He alone was guilty their murders.

He'd tried to be a soldier his men could look up to, a hero, a man of courage and integrity, but he'd dishonored them just as he'd disappointed his father. Worse yet, he'd devasted the woman he loved.

The verse from Romans 8:1 Jed had preached last Sunday whispered through his spirit.

There is therefore now no condemnation to them which are in Christ Jesus, who walk not after the flesh, but after the Spirit.

His father had rarely preached that verse, instead concentrating on what he had to do to earn God's favor.

Maybe that's why he'd kept quiet so long. There was nothing he could do to please God or his father, but he finally knew that was okay. He quietly exhaled. There were consequences, but he was forgiven, and the peace encompassing him was worth what he now faced.

Colonel Creighton stopped pacing and turned to face him, anger still evident on his face. "The information we need from Lieutenant Teagan and the impending battle are too essential to concern myself with your transgressions now. I'm hesitant to do without one of my captains. Until this battle is over, you'll stay at your post."

He hadn't expected that. "Yes, Sir."

The colonel stepped in front of Cage and poked a finger into his chest. "Know this. As soon as this is over, I'll have your hide."

"Yes, Sir." Whatever Creighton came up with would be fine with him. Until then, he'd do his duty and keep his men safe.

"Dismissed, Captain."

"Sir, there's something else."

Creighton spoke through gritted teeth, his tone low and threatening. "What more could there possibly be?"

"When I get back from meeting with Lieutenant Nate, I'd like permission to tell my company what I've done. I want them to hear it from me."

The colonel rubbed his chin but didn't divert his gaze. "Don't you think that might jeopardize your ability to lead?"

"One of the men already knows." Cage swallowed hard. He was done with duplicity. "He tried to blackmail me with the information to keep from getting punished for drinking and visiting the women outside camp."

The vein in the colonel's neck pulsed. "Not Private Coby Smith?"

Cage nodded. He thought he might be sick.

"Did you allow him to get away with it?"

"Yes, Sir."

"I see." The colonel glared at him with hard narrow eyes. "You've already compromised your command by allowing a private to coerce you. When we discuss what to do with you, Captain, rest assured, I'll address your dereliction of duty."

Cage didn't say anything.

"Do you think he'll tell the other men after what happened?"

"As long as he thinks he can continue to threaten me, he'll keep the secret."

"Try to keep this quiet at least until after the battle," Colonel Creighton said. "Let the private think he's got you over a barrel for now."

"Yes, Sir." He hated letting Coby continue to believe he had power over him, but he would follow orders. "What if he decides to share the information with the other men?"

Colonel Creighton let out a groan. "If that time comes, let me know first this time."

"Yes, Sir."

"One more thing," the colonel said. "Until this matter is dealt with, unless you are on assignment or off meeting with Lieutenant Teagan, in addition to your other duties, you will take one shift of guard duty every night along with your regular duties. See to it."

"Yes, Sir."

"Dismissed."

Captain Cage saluted and marched out of the tent. All things considered, that went better than he expected, and the extra guard duty would help him keep his mind off Lavena. He still wished he could tell his men and get it over with, but that was the least of his problems.

Chapter Thirty-Six

When suppertime came, Amon ate with a group of men from the Ohio Third Regiment camped nearby. He knew Coby's punishment would be up soon, and he didn't want to run into him. These men had been camped near Racoon Mountain since Bragg formed a siege of the city.

Amon gnawed off a piece of hardtack. "I sure wish we could go hunting. I'm tired of dried pork and hardtack."

Jack, a scrawny private with buck teeth, said, "If you'd been here as long as we have, you'd be happy to have it."

"What do you mean?"

"Didn't you hear about the battle a few days ago?" Sam, one the older men, asked.

"Yeah," Amon said. "What does that got to do with anything?"

"General Grant opened a cracker line into the city," Sam said. "Before that, we barely had enough to eat, and the rations were about to run out."

Amon couldn't help being relieved it happened before they got there. "How about the whisky supply?"

"Even before the battle, they've always had plenty of whiskey, cards, and women," Jack said, "but if you know what's good for you, you'll stay away from them."

Three other men nodded their agreement.

Heat rushed to Amon's face. "Isn't that for me to decide?"

"It's not worth the grief," Sam said. "Some of what they sell is pure rot gut, make you blind it will."

"And the women," Jack said, "let's just say a night with Venus will get you a year with Mercury."

"What's that supposed to mean?" Amon said.

Henry, a kid with freckles all over his face, let out a snort. "It means the soiled doves here are diseased."

"I don't do that." Amon flushed. "I'm betrothed. Just wanted some good red eye is all."

"I do know one place that's safe," Sam said.

Amon could already taste it. "Where?"

"A brothel downtown. I have guard duty tonight, but I can show you tomorrow."

"Sure, but I don't want to visit with the women."

"Wait," Sam said. "Aren't you with the Ohio Seventh? From what I heard, they come down hard for drinking even if you're off duty."

"Who said they're going to catch me," Amon said, but a nudging inside tried to persuade him this wasn't a good idea. Coby had convinced him to take his first drink, and he didn't want to end up like him.

Sam shrugged. "Whatever you say. We'll be here at sundown tomorrow. If you don't show up, we'll go on without you."

Amon nodded and headed back to his tent. None of his tent mates were there, so he lay down on his bedroll. No matter how much he knew he shouldn't meet up with them, he wanted a drink. More than one. He wanted enough to forget his dead friends.

Coby ambled inside, but Amon ignored him. After what happened with Miss Falcon, he didn't want anything to do with the man.

Coby patted him on the back. "How about a poker game tonight?"

Amon clenched his jaw. "Forget it."

"What's wrong with you?"

"You accosted a lady." His jaw clenched. "I told you Miss Falcon wasn't like the women outside of camp. You shouldn't have touched her." He pushed past Coby on his way outside. The sun was low in the sky.

Coby followed him out. "I didn't."

"If nothing happened, why did Lieutenant-Colonel Crane order you hung by your thumbs?"

Coby shrugged. "I didn't say nothing happened. I told Miss Falcon I got lonely. I asked if she was lonely too, and she went plum crazy. I admit I was making my play, but I didn't touch her, or disrespect her, or nothing. She just blew up. When Captain Cage heard her side of things, he let it fly." Coby expression turned dark. "I'll get back at both of them if it's the last thing I do."

Amon had the sensation of lice crawling on his skin. If he'd had any doubts, he now saw Coby for who he really was, and it disgusted him. "You leave Miss Falcon alone, or you'll answer to me."

"I didn't do anything. I swear." Coby placed his hand in the air. "You want me to put my hand on the Bible or something?"

Amon let out a sigh. Maybe Miss Falcon misunderstood Coby's intentions, but he doubted it.

"Come on," Coby said. "Don't you want to play poker tonight?"

"Not with you." Before Coby could say anymore, Amon took off toward the river.

He'd meet with the other soldiers tomorrow night. He'd do anything to some good whisky and a night of respite, even if it meant going to a brothel, but all he would do was drink.

He could already taste it wetting his lips. When he drank, he could forget the war.

Chapter Thirty-Seven

November 1st

Lavena looked forward to visiting the Army Hospital in Chattanooga to talk to Dr. Mary Walker, but the first thing she needed to do this morning was make sure she had a job. If she'd been let go, she wasn't sure what she would do.

She had wanted to go to Colonel Creighton's office to ask if he had any telegrams even before breakfast, but that wasn't a good idea. If he'd read a message from Mr O'Brady saying she no longer worked at the paper, it would be bad no matter what time it was, but she wasn't sure she was up to facing him on an empty stomach. But she had to know.

Drills were taking place now, so she headed there as fast as she could and knocked.

Colonel Creighton answered the door and smiled. A good sign. "Miss Falcon, two visits in two days. To what do I owe the pleasure?"

"I was wondering if your telegraph operator had received a message for me."

"Yes, as a matter of fact..." He went to his desk and started rummaging through papers. "This arrived shortly after you left, yesterday. I planned to have one of my men bring it by."

She tried to wait patiently, but her stomach did somersaults. She had gotten the interview everyone else couldn't get. That had to count for something.

He finished searching through the pile and pushed it away. "I know it's here somewhere." He drew in another stack of papers and grabbed the one on top. "Here it is." He held up a folded piece of paper with a look of triumph and handed it to her.

She paused. "You haven't read it..."

The colonel blushed. "I assure you, Miss Falcon, I would never do that unless it had a military objective. Telegrams are private."

"I'm sorry." She let out the breath she was holding. "Of course, you wouldn't. Thank you."

He nodded. She said her good-byes and ambled to the tree where she'd had her conversation, or lack of it, with Cage the day before.

Her hands shook as she unfolded it.

Take your time to write it, but telegram some details of Cage's story today, or you don't have a job. O'Brady

Today? The colonel said the message arrived yesterday. So that was it. She swiped at the tear running down her cheek.

What was she going to do? Even if she did telegram Mr. O'Brady and let him know she'd just received his message, she couldn't reveal the sordid details of the interview, and if she didn't reveal the part about the fire, it would be a deception, and she wouldn't lie. She had to write this story, but the thought of it made her sick to her stomach.

She couldn't send this information through a telegram. It would be on the front page of *The Cleveland Leader* by tomorrow without any explanation about his side of it.

If that happened, she wouldn't be any better than the journalists who destroyed her reputation in New York City. They painted her father as the biggest villain since Samuel Green, a murderer known as public enemy number one and executed in the 1820s.

Every friend deserted Father after the articles, and most of what was written was false or painted the crimes as worse than they were. They even implied she and her aunt knew what he was doing and kept his secret.

When she became a journalist, she promised herself she would always report the whole truth, not just one side, and she would never write a story out of spite.

Despite herself, she let out a sigh. She didn't know when it happened, but she'd already begun to forgive her father. She loved him and hated the way he'd been treated, and she regretted that she was responsible for a large part of his pain. What he'd done was wrong, but he didn't run from it. He confessed everything and accepted the consequences, no matter how severe.

Wasn't that what Cage was doing?

No, this was different. Her father wasn't responsible for any deaths.

Deep down, she'd always wanted someone who would love and accept her for who she was, but after what happened with Warren, she never believed that was possible. She gave up the fairytale of a man who would cherish and protect her, a man who would be there for her throughout life.

Cage changed all that. He did love her deeply: career, radical opinions, quirks, and all. But he turned out to be more flawed than Warren. If only he'd told her the truth earlier.

Would it have made a difference?

She'd find a way to write the story, but she wouldn't destroy him no matter what the cost to her career. So where did that leave her?

Colonel Creighton hadn't read the telegram. Nobody knew she didn't have a job anymore. She didn't know how long it would be before the newspaper contacted him or if they would. Could she still function as a journalist?

One thing was for sure. Until the colonel said differently, she wasn't going anywhere. She had a job to do, and she wasn't going to shirk her responsibility or her calling. If she no longer had a job, she'd send her stories to the *Harper's Weekly* and other large newspapers around the country and see what happened.

"Colonel, may I use the telegraph to reply?"

Colonel Creighton wiped a hand over his mouth. "Our telegraph officer has other duties as well. I'm afraid he won't be available until tomorrow."

"With your permission, I can send it. I know Morse Code."

"Of course." Colonel Creighton gestured toward the side room where the telegraph was.

She sat at the desk in the middle of the room and tapped out a telegram for O'Brady.

No details before story is written. Stop.

She closed the door and waited for a reply. She didn't have to wait long.

No longer employed at Cleveland Leader. Stop. Inform regimental commander. Stop. Find transportation home. Stop. Newspaper will reimburse. O'Brady

Wandering outside through the side door, she plopped down on the doorstep. What should she do now? What she sensed wasn't anger or distress. She felt numb. A heaviness swept over her like a heavy blanket.

Her world started folding in on her. First, Cage. Now, her career. *Lord, what do I do?*

Should she do what Mr. O'Brady said? Should she find a way home and give up on the most important stories she'd ever written and the interview no other reporter could get? She had at least ten articles she hadn't sent yet besides the one she hadn't written.

Somewhere inside a hope crept to the surface. She was called to be a reporter. Whether she worked at *The Cleveland Leader* or found other news sources to print her stories, she would write them.

She stood to her feet. Let Mr. Cowles and Mr. O'Brady do their own informing if they wanted. Until they sent another correspondent to relieve her and the colonel ordered her out of the camp, she would do what she came for. By then, maybe another newspaper would print what she had to say.

Setting her jaw, she headed to the Army Hospital in downtown Chattanooga to interview Dr. Mary Walker.

******

Lavena had received an extensive interview with Dr. Mary Walker and was pleased to find her wearing bloomers similar to hers. After the interview, she confided about her current difficulties.

Dr. Walker told her she was doing the right thing in staying the course when it came to her career. "Women have to remain bold in the face of discouragement. Do you mind if I say something on behalf of Captain Cage?"

Lavena nodded her head, even though she wasn't sure she wanted to hear what the doctor had to say.

"I'm married," Dr. Walker said. "My husband has neither been faithful nor has he accepted my career as being equal to his. I've filed for divorce."

Lavena considered what she said. "All the more reason to avoid romantic liaisons."

"Do you believe this captain when he says he will accept your journalism profession."

"Yes, I do." Lavena had no doubt of that.

"And despite the moral failing he tried to hide, did he confess it voluntarily?"

Lavena swallowed. "I had no idea what he had done. He offered it with no compulsion from me."

"Do you believe he would be true to his word and a faithful husband if he was given a chance?"

"I don't know." She chided herself for the lie. Of course, he would be faithful and devoted.

"I would do anything if Albert had been a faithful, honest man. Everyone has failures, but for a man like your captain, I would forgive him of a greater sin."

Lavena shook her head. She had been hurt too many times to even consider giving him another chance. Dr. Walker didn't understand what she'd gone through.

*****

The next morning, Lavena finished writing her articles from the accounts General Geary and General Grant had given her. She was thoroughly impressed by General Grant. He wasn't a tall man, but he exuded being in command. It's as if he knew who he was and didn't need to prove anything to anybody.

She sighed. Why did he have to remind her of Cage? She copied the stories she'd planned to send to *The Cleveland Leader*. After getting out more paper and dipping her pen in her inkwell, she wrote five copies of every story. She would post them this afternoon and send them to *The New York Tribune, The Chester County Times, The Philadelphia Inquirer, The Cleveland Plain Dealer,* and *Harper's Weekly*, keeping one copy for herself.

All five had established themselves as pro-Union. Hopefully at least one paper would buy them.

She needed to get them mailed as soon as possible, and she already had plans tomorrow. She didn't know how long it would be before another reporter showed up in camp and the colonel found out she was no longer employed, but she would finish this assignment before he did.

Amon had told her Cage and Jed would be outside of camp tomorrow on some secret mission. That gave her the time she needed to travel to Nate's family farm and see if he was there. Betsy was counting on her, and that was one assignment she'd finish before she was booted out on her ear.

Chapter Thirty-Eight

Friday, November 6th

Lavena followed the map Betsy had given her and found it lined the Tennessee River for a couple of miles before moving into the mountains.

Two Union soldiers strode ahead of her. She paused. They were too far away to make out their features or their rank, but she didn't want them to see her - or stop her.

They traveled out of view, and she slowed her pace to make sure they stayed that way. Occasionally she would catch sight of them and hide behind a tree or bush.

They headed out again.

She couldn't help but be curious who they were and why the two of them would be out here. Using the hunting skills she'd learned as a child, she managed to catch up with them without them hearing her.

Cage and Jed. She clapped her hand over her mouth.

They looked back, and she barely made it behind a bush in time.

So, Cage and Jed on their secret mission. Good. She'd follow them and see what they were up to. Although she'd never report military secrets before a battle, it would make a great story after the battle was over.

They headed out again, and she waited until they were almost out of sight before she rose from behind the bushes where she was hiding. She travelled off the path through the trees and trailed them.

*****

It had taken only a few hours for Nate to reach the small cave in a mountain near the Tennessee River. It was only three miles away, but the terrain was rough, and he had to make sure nobody followed him. Hopefully the Ohio Seventh had arrived and Cage found the missive.

While he waited, he took out the dispatch from the general and read it three or four times then sealed it in the small metal tube.

He wouldn't change the wording on this one, but he did plan to show it to Cage and Jed first. It was almost dusk, and they weren't here yet. If they didn't arrive soon, he'd have to explain why he was so late getting back. It would be difficult, but his information was too important to dismiss.

Rustling leaves signaled him someone was approaching. He stepped into the shadows. Hopefully it wasn't another soldier who wandered this way. Two men entered the cave.

He squinted, trying to make out their faces, then ran to them and gave them bear hugs. "It's sure good to see you again. I was beginning to wonder if you'd get here in time."

"We got a late start," Cage said.

*****

Careful to be quiet, Lavena drew closer and noticed the opening of a cave. It was almost dusk, and the way the opening of the cave curved around, she was able to stay out of sight as she entered. She squinted her eyes and recognized Nate even before she heard their voices.

This wasn't possible.

Cage and Jed were meeting with Nate, the deserter and traitor.

She leaned in to listen.

"So, did you find out anything?" Cage asked.

"I sure did." Nate grinned as he pulled out letters and gave them to Jed.

Jed flipped through them. "I don't believe it." He handed them to Cage.

Cage looked through them and whistled. "We knew you're resourceful, but this? You have every communication between General Bragg and his commanders as well as where all of his troops are stationed. This will be a goldmine for General Grant. How did you ever manage to become Bragg's messenger?"

Lavena put her hand over her mouth to keep from gasping out loud. Nate was a spy for the Union Army?

Nate leaned against the wall of the cave. "He trusts me because my father vouched for me, and he doesn't want to risk any more of his men for the job. The last three messengers were killed."

"With your acting ability, you should be on the stage," Cage said. "I never would've thought you could pull it off."

Jed placed a hand on Nate's shoulder. "Are you sure they believe you? This might be some sort of a trick."

"I'm sure," Nate said. "I did just what you told me. I fed them some true information they already had and held the part they didn't know back until they threatened to hang me. It worked. They believed every word."

"I'm still amazed," Cage said.

"It helps I'm expendable since everyone wants to kill me anyway."

"Still," Cage said. "For him to trust you with this kind of information..."

"It wasn't all me. My father wanted to believe me. He's a colonel and adjutant to the general, and he may be the only subordinate General Bragg trusts."

Lavena could barely believe what hearing. Betsy had been right. Nate hadn't deserted. He was risking his life for his country.

*****

"Are you all right with this?" Jed gave Nate that look of his like he could see right through him. He'd missed that. "It can't be easy betraying your father."

Nate cleared his throat. "I'm doing this for the cause."

"But he's your father," Jed said.

"Given the chance, he'd do the same to me. When he saw me for the first time in years, he pointed a rifle and threatened to shoot me."

"You expected that," Cage said. "After all, you are the enemy. He couldn't take any chances."

"I know." Nate ran his fingers through his hair. "It's harder than I thought. Is that what you want to hear? He regrets how we ended things before, and he's trying to make up for what happened before."

"He wants his son back," Jed said.

"Yeah, well, it's too late for that. When he finds out what I'm doing, it will be over for good just like with Betsy."

"We have a new reporter in camp," Cage said. "Miss Lavena Falcon."

"Lavena?" Nate chuckled. "My guess is you haven't punched her in the jaw or kicked her out of camp. You've met your match with her. Have you done the interview yet?"

"Yes, I told her and Colonel Creighton everything." Cage rubbed the scar on his cheek. "The problem is I'm in love with her, and now I've lost her forever."

"You told them about ..." Nate stopped short remembering Jed was there. "You know."

"Jed knows. I confided in him before I did the interview."

"How did Colonel Creighton react?"

"About as I expected." Cage pulled on his ear. "He said he'd have my hide, but he wants to wait until after the coming battle. If I get out of this without ending up in prison, I'll consider myself fortunate."

"I'm sorry, Cage. I shouldn't have lied, but I didn't think you'd survive. I didn't want to destroy your legacy."

"It's not your fault," Cage said. "I should have told the truth before now."

The conversation stopped, and Lavena inched closer to see what they were doing. They were leaning against the studying some papers, probably the messages Nate gave them. Nate slipped the paper back in his pouch. Maybe it was time to let her presence be known.

"I have some news for you from home," Cage said.

Nate raised an eyebrow. "What news could you possibly have for me?"

"Your wife gave a letter to Lavena," Cage said. "I ordered Sergeant Garrett to snatch it from her belongings while I kept her occupied, but she always kept it with her. I can tell you the gist of what it says."

Chapter Thirty-Nine

Heat traveled up Lavena's back. So, another deception. She stepped out of the shadows.

All three men simultaneously drew their guns and pointed them at her.

Startled, she raised her hands. "It's me, Lavena."

Cage's face turned red. "What are you doing here?"

They holstered their guns, and she lowered her hands. "I followed you." She turned to Nate and handed him the letter.

"Why did you follow us?" Cage obviously wasn't going to let this drop. "You had no right."

"And you had no right to have my things searched." Lavena took a deep breath and let it out slowly to calm herself. If you'd told the truth about needing the letter, I would have given it to you, but honesty isn't something that comes easily to you, is it?"

Cage's Adam's apple bulged, but he didn't say any more.

She turned to Nate. "Aren't you going to open it?"

He stroked his hand across the envelope and ran his finger across the words. *To Nate.* "It's Betsy's handwriting." He opened it. "My Dearest Nate, My darling, if you are reading this letter, I know Lavena has found out your whereabouts. I pray you're not a Union prisoner awaiting execution. I still can't believe you deserted. I'll never believe it.

"I didn't mean anything I said in my last letter. I was angry because it seemed like you cared more about your causes than you did about me or our life together, but I've come to realize that love isn't just a fairytale romance. It's a commitment to walk in love and forgiveness every day of our lives." His voice cracked.

He paused a moment before reading on. "Here's my decision. I choose to love you whether you're off chasing one of your causes, fighting in a war, or being shot for desertion. Nothing shall ever cause me to stop loving you. And no matter what you've done, I forgive you." He fell to the ground.

"May I?" Jed said.

Nate nodded but didn't look up. He handed him the letter.

Jed started reading where he'd left off. "I hope and pray we can have that happy family I've always dreamed of one day, but even if I never see you again, you will have all my love from this moment forward.

"All My Love, Betsy."

For a few minutes, nobody said anything. Nate's shoulders heaved occasionally, but he stifled the sobs. Finally, he wiped his face and stood. He gazed at the letter, reading it silently. He cleared his throat, but his voice caught. "Thank you. This means more than…" He couldn't say any more.

"Now that you've read it, you need to destroy it," Jed said. "If anyone finds that letter, they'll know where you got it. You'll be exposed as a spy."

Nate held the letter to his chest. "I can't."

"You have to," Cage said. "You have no choice."

"I'll hide it in a place they won't look, but I can't destroy Betsy's declaration of love. I won't."

Lavena placed her hand on Nate's arm. "Why don't I keep it for you until this business is over?"

Nate nodded and reluctantly handed her the letter.

Cage put his hand on Nate's shoulder. "You better get going. They'll know something's up if you take too much longer."

"Don't worry so much, Captain," Nate said, plastering on a grin that wasn't quite genuine. "I've made it this far, haven't I?"

Cage grunted.

"When do you want to meet again?" Jed asked.

"Next week. Same place and time. I should have more by then."

Cage stood at attention and saluted. "You've done better than anyone ever expected, Lieutenant Teagan."

Nate returned the salute. "Thank you, Captain."

"Don't take any unnecessary chances," Jed said. "We want you back in one piece."

"I won't, but…. if something does happen to me," Nate said, "would you make sure Betsy knows I'm not a traitor and that I love her?"

Lavena stepped toward him and hugged him. "Don't worry about that. I'll make sure she knows what you've done for your country and how much you love her."

They said their good-byes, and Nate skulked around the river bank. Dried leaves crunched as he made his way into a grove of trees and scampered out of sight. The last glimmer of sunlight disappeared behind the mountains.

Cage turned to Lavena. "You can't tell Mrs. Teagan any of this – or anyone else. Do you understand me?"

Lavena pressed her lips together and got close enough to his face to smell the jerky he'd eaten earlier. "She needs to know the truth. You shouldn't have written her that letter telling her Nate deserted." She couldn't help yelling.

"I followed orders." His voice rose. "If I hadn't written her, the men would have wondered why not. We had to make sure this rouse worked."

"You shouldn't have allowed him to do this." She pointed her finger at his chest. "He's going to end up getting killed."

"Maybe, but he'll save a lot of Union soldiers in the process. He's already delivered valuable information to us, and this is just the beginning." Cage wiped his hand over his face. "You didn't tell anyone about this?"

"I didn't know."

Jed got between them. "You won't have to worry about her telling anybody if you two don't stop shouting. Everyone within five miles will know."

Her face grew warm, and she lowered her voice. "I had a map from Betsy with the location of the Teagan Plantation. I had no idea I'd find you here."

"So, you're saying this is all a coincidence." Cage had lowered his voice, but his tone showed he didn't believe her.

"Yes, that's what I'm saying. Unlike you, I don't lie."

Jed crossed his arms. "I'm sure Lavena knows enough to keep our secret. She doesn't want Nate discovered any more than we do." He reached down and grabbed his bedroll. "It's late. Why don't we make camp? This cave looks like a good place."

Cage turned to Lavena, his jawline firm. "You'll stay with us tonight. That's an order." He acted as if she were one of his soldiers.

"I assure you I'm not planning to stay anywhere near you. I'll make my own camp." She started to leave, but he took hold of her hand.

"I can't let you leave to go traipsing off, maybe into the hands of the enemy."

She pulled her hand away. "I'm not that incompetent, Captain. I know how to make a campsite, and I followed you here without you ever noticing me."

"Please stay," Jed said.

Lavena hesitated, seeing the sense in it even though she didn't want to. "Fine."

They laid out their camping gear, and she lay down as far away from Cage as she could get and still remain in the cave. She didn't want him to see her conflicting emotions. One thing was for sure. She'd keep Nate's secret from everyone else, but as soon as they got back to camp, she would write Betsy telling her everything.

The mail was guarded well. Nobody else would read the letter, and Betsy wouldn't tell anyone. She deserved to know.

*****

This was the last time Amon would ever go drinking. It wasn't watching the tent spinning or the nausea just under the surface rising from his stomach that made him come to this decision.

If Sam hadn't told him he could get some good whiskey here, he never would have been here, in a place he didn't want to be.

He'd consumed a lot, more than he ever had before. That was the only explanation he had as to why he'd followed Sam and the others to the ladies' tent like a lamb being led to a den of wolves. He'd enough wits about him to assure them he only was here to drink, but not enough to run the other way.

A lady almost as old as his ma ushered them into the tent and had them sit on a couple of stools. She looked more like a schoolmarm with her hair tucked in a snood. She wore a camp dress every bit as modest as Miss Falcon's attire.

"Welcome to my home." She gave them each a glass of lemonade.

"I'm not here to do anything bad." Amon's speech slurred. "Just came with my friends."

"Of course," the lady said. "No need to do anything but sit here and relax. You can keep me company while your friends are occupied."

"I guess I could do that," Amon said, relieved she didn't try to convince him.

"Ladies." The older woman clapped her hands.

Four beautiful women entered the tent. They didn't look at all like school teachers. One girl, tall with blond ringlets, wore a red camp dress, but the buttons on the front of her bodice were all unbuttoned. She had some kind of lacy thing underneath, but Amon wondered why she bothered. It didn't cover much.

Sam kissed her, and they took off. Jack went with the second girl, and Henry followed the third girl out. That left him with the older lady and a girl who looked a lot like Emma. She had brown wavy hair, blue eyes, and a small nose that turned up, but Emma would never dress like that. This girl had on ladies' underthings and a corset but no dress.

His eyes followed her soft curves. He knew he should look away, but he'd never seen a woman wear so few clothes before. A surge of excitement swept through him.

Emma's lookalike used a wooden device to rub Amon's back. "I'm Amy."

"I'm not here for anything wrong," he stammered as she moved the wooden thing lower. Warning bugles were going off in his head, but he didn't want to move. It felt good. "I'm just waiting for my friend. I have a girl back home."

"I wouldn't want to get between you and your girl." She didn't stop rubbing. "You soldiers go through so much. Let me help you relax."

Amon's shoulders loosened as he leaned into the massage. His brain turned to fog. He couldn't think clearly.

The older lady wasn't in the tent anymore. He couldn't remember her leaving. He started to get up, but Amy placed her hands on his shoulders and kneaded them. Her hands caressed lower.

Before he knew what happened, he'd handed over three silver dollars and was sitting on the tick mattress with Amy, but all he could think about was Emma.

Emma smelled like soap not this nauseating lilac. He missed her so much. He dreamed of kissing Emma, holding her, loving her. He nuzzled his face in her hair as she unbuttoned his blue wool shirt and started to fondle his chest.

But this wasn't Emma. He tried to pull away, but something deep inside wanted this. "No! No, I can't."

Amy tugged his shirt off. "Sure you can, sweetie. You've already paid." She planted a kiss. "Just sit back and enjoy."

Heat coursed through him. He allowed her to draw him back to the mattress. He closed his eyes, and his lips parted. "Emma."

Amy whispered in his ear. "Let me help you forget about your girl back home."

"No!" He pushed her away and grabbed his shirt. She came toward him, and he staggered out of the tent.

Looking around to get his bearings, he slipped into his shirt, and made his way back to camp. He got there before dawn, but he didn't want to go into his tent. If Coby were there, he'd know. Not just about the drinking, but he'd notice Amon smelled of lilac.

He headed to the Tennessee River and dunked himself into the cold water. The effects of the drink and smell of lilac faded, but he couldn't wash away what he'd done.

If Emma found out his first kiss wasn't with her, she'd never forgive him. How could he have betrayed her like that?

Chapter Forty

The next morning, Lavena, Cage, and Jed left early so they could make it back to camp long before nightfall. For the first few of hours, nobody said anything.

Lavena was a bit relieved. She was so lost in her swirl of thoughts and emotions, she wasn't sure she could put more than two words together.

Nate was not only wasn't a deserter, but he was risking his life for the Union. She'd been shocked by the revelation. Betsy had believed in him, and he'd always shown himself to be an honorable man. Why was she so quick to condemn him when everything in his past pointed to the truth?

Then there was Cage. She'd heard enough of the conversation with him and Nate to know he'd told the truth about everything. Nate was the one who lied when Cage was too sick to protest.

He still started the fire. And he allowed the lie to continue, but he didn't have to tell her or the colonel the truth. Nobody would have known.

She wondered if her father would have eventually confessed if a reporter hadn't found out what he'd done. Probably not.

It was difficult having Cage so close, walking beside her. Everything inside wanted to reach out to him, let him know she understood, maybe even hold his hand, but she couldn't. How could he have kept quiet for so long?

She tripped over a root in the path. In an instant, Cage was there to steady her and keep her from falling. He wrapped his arms around her, and for a moment she let him. It felt good, right, for him to be so close.

No, she pulled away.

"We probably should stop here and have a bite of lunch," Jed said.

Cage wiped a hand across his scar. "Yes, I... we'll stop here."

Jed headed toward a wooded area. "I'll get some kindling so we can start a fire. You stay with Lavena."

"No," Cage said. "I'll go too."

"Captain, this is enemy territory. You can't leave her out here alone."

Heat travelled up her back. "I'm not helpless. My father and I used to go camping all the time when I was young. I made it this far on my own yesterday."

"Even so," Cage said. "It's not safe, but I'll get the firewood. Jed, you stay with her."

Jed crossed his arms and glared at them a moment before speaking. "I'll get the kindling. You two take some time to talk." He didn't wait for

Cage to argue the point. He headed for the woods.

Cage directed her to a felled log near the path. "Please sit."

She did, and he sat beside her. They didn't say anything for a few moments. She wasn't surprised when he grabbed his ear.

"I told Colonel Creighton everything about the... incident."

"Yes, I heard," she said. "He told you when this was over, he'd have your hide."

Cage blushed. "You heard everything then?"

"I spotted you entering the cave. I was going to announce my presence, but when I heard Nate's voice, I was so surprised, I didn't know what to do."

He paused. "Now that your story is coming out, the colonel will have to make an example of me. I expected it." He rubbed his cheek. "I deserve it."

"Yes, you do," she said, but she couldn't look at him. She kept her focus on a box turtle crossing the path ten feet away from them. "I didn't write the story yet." She hadn't intended to tell him that, but it was all so confusing. She wanted to talk to him about it. "I will write it, but I need to think about the best way to do it. I wouldn't want to cause harm to your regiment's reputation."

"I appreciate that," he said. "So, your newspaper is giving you the time you need?"

"No." A sob escaped her despite her best efforts to keep it in. "I sent them a telegram quitting my job."

He took her hands in his. "Oh, Lavena, I'm sorry. Maybe if I'd told the truth earlier. What will you do now?"

She gazed at their hands intertwined. As much as she wanted to pull away, she didn't. "Until the new correspondent shows up and I'm booted out of camp, I'll continue to do my job and sell my stories to other papers. What other choice do I have?"

"I don't want to be the cause of you losing your position at the paper. I already have enough regret. You should have written the story."

"I tried." She pulled her hands away.

Cage stood and turned away from her. "I need to say something, but I don't want to make things worse between us."

A heaviness overtook her. How could this be any worse? "Go on."

His shoulders quivered then squared. He faced her. "What I did was wrong. There's no denying that. I have a lot to answer for, and it will take time to get through all the repercussions of this, maybe I never will, but I'm ready to do whatever it takes."

Her voice cracked. "I know."

"The thing is I love you. I knew when we began to grow close, I needed to make things right. I couldn't pursue a courtship with you with this lie between us. In a way, my love for you gave me the courage to tell the truth."

Her eyes watered, and she blinked to clear them. "What do you want from me?"

"I know your father hurt you, and Warren betrayed you, but I'm not them. I was wrong, and I'll pay for my sins, but if you let me..." He wiped his hand over his face. "I want a chance to show you can trust me. I want a chance to prove my love to you."

"It isn't love that's the problem. I thought you were heroic, a man of integrity." She stood and walked a few steps away from him. She watched an eagle passing overhead, then turned toward him. "I love you. I don't want to. I can't help it, but I can't forget what happened, what you did."

Cage's posture slumped until he seemed almost shorter than Lavena. A profound sadness covered his features. "I guess this is good-bye then."

The tears flowed freely now. She wiped her face. "Yes, it is."

He strode toward her, took her in his arms. "I'm so sorry."

The hug was comforting, and she didn't try to stop it. She cried on his shoulder, then stepped back and did her best to contain her emotions. "After this journey is over, I don't ever want to see you again."

******

It was late in the afternoon before they'd arrived back in camp. As soon as she got to her cabin, she wrote a short letter telling Betsy she didn't have to worry. Nate wasn't a deserter. He still was loyal to the Union Army. She wanted to explain more, but she didn't think it wise. She added a postscript on the end of the note letting her friend know not to tell anyone and she'd explain more later.

She sealed the letter and headed to the quartermaster's office to mail it. The post office was on the other side of the river, about a mile away, and was where the quartermaster had set up shop. A large crowd had gathered outside, and more were coming from all directions.

She asked a group of soldiers what was going on.

"The mail wagon just arrived," a ruddy-faced private told her. "They're having mail call as soon as they get all the letters sorted."

This would work out great. If the mail wagon was here, the letter to Betsy would be sent right away along with all of the articles she'd mailed yesterday morning.

Jed had told her it had been months since they'd received any mail. She could tell by the excitement in the air, all of the men were happy it had finally arrived.

She squeezed through the men and knocked on the door.

A voice from inside. "Mail call in an hour. You'll have to wait."

She raised her voice so it could be heard through the door. "I want to send a letter."

A scrawny man with wire-rim glasses, dressed in a sack suit at least two sizes too big for him, poked his head out of the window. "There's some collection bags on the wagon. Put it in one of them."

Lavena headed to the wagon sitting on the right side of the building and placed the letter in one of the duffle bags on the back. All of them were already filled with mail.

She took her place among the crowd of men outside and waited. Maybe Aunt Martha or Betsy had written her a letter. She hoped so.

*****

"Mail call," the quartermaster yelled out. "Mail call!"

Amon's stomach fluttered as he ran to the field where the Ohio Seventh Regiment's mail would be delivered. He pressed through the crowd of soldiers trying to get as close as they could as if that guaranteed their names being called. There had to be a letter from Emma. It had been months since the last mail call.

The flutters turned to a hard knob when he remembered how he betrayed her. He hadn't decided yet if he would ever tell her what happened. He couldn't think of a good reason to do so. It would only hurt her.

The quartermaster called out names.

"Private Coby Willard."

Coby had already pushed his way to the front, so he reached up to grab the envelope and took off.

More names were called. "Corporal Jake Wilson. Sergeant Paul Garrett. Sergeant Noah Andrews."

Each man squeezed through to get his mail.

More names. Anxiety grew as Amon waited. Surely Emma would have written him by now. There was no order in the way the names were called, so all he could do was wait.

"Captain Macajah Jones. Major Jason Patella."

Each man squeezed his way through to get his mail. Before long, Amon had been pushed almost to the back of the crowd. The announcement had been made in the afternoon. Now, it was dusk. Amon's stomach rumbled, but he wasn't about to leave to get supper without his letter.

"Private Rufus Butler. Private Thomas Carl. Private George Clark. Lieutenant Jed Jackson. Miss Lavena Falcon."

The men stepped aside to let Miss Falcon get her mail.

Amon wiped the sweat off his forehead. It was a warm day for a change even though the sun was going down, not a cloud in the sky.

"Private Amon Smith."

"Here," Amon shouted as he shoved his way through over two hundred men still waiting.

The quartermaster handed him a stack of letters. He didn't go back to the tent. He didn't want to be near Coby while he read Emma's letters. Instead he found a willow tree and sat leaning against it.

He looked through them. Three were from his mother, one from Mr. Brown, and six from different townspeople and farmers he knew who sent letters regularly to the troops. Then, there were the letters from Emma, all ten of them. She must have written him every week.

He opened the posts from his neighbors first. He was touched by their encouraging words. Most of them said they were praying for him and they were proud of him. They wouldn't be if they knew how he been acting lately, but he appreciated them writing.

Mr. Brown's letter was next. He told about what was happening on the farm and in town. He also said he was praying.

I couldn't ask for a finer man to marry my daughter, but I'm concerned about your relationship with the Almighty. I hope you've turned to God through these difficulties in a way I've never seen before, but I have a deep burden for you I can't shake. I am praying for you.

Amon wiped his hand over his face. He never understood why Mr. Brown kept asking him about his faith. He had always gone to church, and he tried to live a good life. He was better than most of the boys in town.

A twinge of guilt swept over him. Maybe he hadn't done so good lately, but with all the death around, what did Mr. Brown expect?

Next Ma's letters. More prayers. She missed him. Mr. Brown helped her with the farm, and she was managing, but it would be better if her son were home.

I know in my heart you'll come home safe.

She didn't say how she knew. Maybe she just hoped he would.

He opened the first letter from Emma, and his hands trembled. She loved him; she prayed for him; she couldn't wait to be his wife.

Blinking, he read the second letter. She'd grown closer to God since he'd been away. In the next couple of letters, she talked a lot about a series of meetings with an evangelist and how it changed her life.

He read the fifth letter. *I know you're a good man and go to church, but there's so much more to the Christian life. I want you to know our Lord as I do now. I'm praying for you.*

His jaw clenched. She was beginning to sound like her father.

By the time he got to the sixth letter, his chest felt like a tree had fallen on him. Reading the eighth letter caused pain to the back of his throat.

He opened the last one. *I look forward to our wedding day when we share our first kiss.*

Crossing his arms around his knees, he curled up in a ball. If he could have become small enough to hide among the yellow leaves on the ground, he would have, but there was nowhere to hide from himself or from God.

Chapter Forty-One

Lavena sat in her cabin at the wooden table in the middle of the room and surveyed the envelopes. Three letters from her aunt but none from Betsy. Odd her friend wouldn't have written.

She read the first two letters. Not much to say. Aunt Martha wrote how proud she was for the success Lavena had achieved and that she'd received Lavena's first letter. She also wrote about how interesting Captain Cage sounded.

If she only knew.

The second letter contained more of the same. She reached for the third post. It had another envelope tucked in with it, but Lavena put it aside to read her aunt's final letter. She gave her warmest wishes for Lavena's courtship with Cage saying that she was glad her niece had found a decent man who would treat her as an equal.

Heat rushed through her body. Aunt Martha was responding to her last letter, the one she sent after they declared their mutual affection for each other but before the interview, the one she mailed before getting on the train to come here.

She needed to write and let her know there was no longer anything between them, nor would there ever be again. She read on.

I hope you don't intend to marry this young man until you make things right with your father. Until you allow God to place that forgiveness in you, you'll always expect perfection that your husband can never achieve. In order to love, you need to know how to forgive.

Forgive. Cage had pretended to be a hero and ended up a coward who hid the truth when it showed him in an unfavorable light. He killed a woman and her children. She didn't expect perfection, but that was too much to simply sweep under the rug.

She let out a sigh. Maybe she did want Cage to be perfect, the hero he'd pretended to be.

We can't expect God to forgive us until we forgive others. That's why I've included a letter from your father. He has consumption, and his health is failing. I insist you read his letter before it's too late. If you don't make peace with him before he dies, you'll regret it. Write to him before you write a reply to me.

Lavena's heart skipped a beat. *Consumption?* That was a death sentence. He might only have a few months left. She lightly touched her fingers across her father's letter and swiped at the tear running down her cheek.

It wasn't as if her father hadn't written her before. The first couple of years, he wrote every week. She never read or answered them. After a while, the frequency slowed, then they stopped.

Aunt Martha told her Father would wait until she was ready. Somehow the anger toward him had dissolved in the last month, an answer to her prayer. She now had a sadness and a longing for him she hadn't expected.

She opened the letter from her father.

My Dearest Lavena,

Your aunt said it was time to write to you. You don't know how many times I wanted to in the last few years, but I knew you needed time. I know this is overwhelming for you, so I'll keep it short. There are a few things I need to say. You're my daughter, and I love you. I have never lied to you about that.

I have sinned greatly. I don't deserve your forgiveness, but I'm asking for it. Even after eight years in prison, I'm only now beginning to see that God forgives, not because I deserve it, but because Christ shed his blood for my sin.

Even with this great cost, I'm glad everything is out in the light. God has been with me through all of this. I don't want to be the man I was before, pretending to be a good Christian while living as if I didn't believe in God and wouldn't be held accountable for my actions.

This prison has become my freedom. I no longer have the luxury of lying to myself or anyone else. That gives me the liberty to serve God as the broken man I am and to share God's love with other prisoners. Through all of this, I have joy and peace.

Your aunt gives me monthly reports about you, and I'm so proud of the woman you've become. I hope someday you'll come to the place where you can write to me. I'd love to hear from you.

If you're not ready yet, I understand. If you never write to me in this lifetime, I can accept that because I know we'll see each other again. I pray for you every day, not only for your protection and happiness, but that you will follow the Lord all the days of your life.

Your Loving Father

Lavena wiped the tears running down her cheeks and fell to her knees. She was the one who needed forgiveness for the bitterness she'd allowed to take root in her heart. She didn't know how long she stayed there on the floor crying out to God, but when she did get up, she wrote her father a letter telling him she forgave him and asking him to forgive her.

*****

Cage read the letter from his pastor back home. He had written him right after he'd told Jed about the fire. They weren't really that close, but he needed to know somebody back home was praying for him, and he had hoped his pastor would.

Rev. Henderson assured him he and his wife were praying and wrote a long letter encouraging him in the Lord.

It did encourage him. Even with the loss he was facing, God's peace rested on him in a way that amazed him. The pain and longing still ached inside of him, but it was overshadowed by God's love and forgiveness.

He tucked the letter away, splashed water on his face, and headed to the door. He had guard duty in an hour.

Jed stepped into the cabin, his face pale.

Cage stood, and a knot formed in his stomach. "You received the letter you were expecting from home."

Jed nodded. "Rev. Fowler found a couple to take in my brothers until I arrived."

"I'm sure you're relieved to hear that."

"Cage, they're missing. The couple gave false information. They don't know where Joshua and Caleb have gone."

He placed his hand on Jed's shoulder. "What do you want me to do to help?"

"I'm leaving in two days. Colonel Creighton said I could get a ride with the mail wagon. I know I'm leaving you in the lurch with a battle coming up, but..."

"Stop. You have to get home to find your brothers. They need you."

"Thanks," Jed said thickly.

Cage lowered his head and prayed out loud for Jed and his brothers. "Is there anything more I can do?"

"There is one thing. I have a lot to take care of before I leave. I wanted to talk to another chaplain about taking on the Ohio Seventh along with his regiment, and I need to meet with Sergeant Garrett about his extra duties. Besides, I hate good-byes. Could you tell the men and Lavena for me?"

Cage's chest tightened. He'd told Lavena he wouldn't trouble her again. "Of course, I will." He doubted she'd be happy about seeing him so soon, but he would do anything to make it easier for his friend.

"I'll write to let you know how I fare as soon as I get home."

Cage nodded, overwhelmed with compassion for his friend.

"Hang in there, Captain. God will work this all out for good."

"Yes, He will, for both of us."

Chapter Forty-Two

The next morning, Amon marched out drills for over an hour, but he couldn't keep his focus. The sun shone bright and warmed the valley giving them a reprieve from the rain, but it didn't stop the torrent inside of him.

It wasn't difficult to follow the drill orders. They'd been through them countless times. It gave him the time he needed to mull over what he'd done, and what he should do now.

Sergeant Garrett's voice boomed out orders. "Attention, Squad."

He resumed position. He may not have gone through with it, but there was no way around it. When he kissed that girl, he had been unfaithful to Emma.

"Shoulder Arms."

Bringing his Springfield rifle to his right shoulder, he positioned his right hand and dropped his left hand to his side. He would give anything for it not to have happened.

"Load."

Grasping the rifle in his left hand, he took hold of the cartridge box in his right. If only he'd listened when Captain Cage warned him about the dangers of strong drink.

"Handle Cartridge."

He grabbed a cartridge out of the box and placed it between his teeth. The captain had his best interest at heart. He knew that now, but it was too late.

"Tear Cartridge."

He tore the cartridge with his teeth and held it level with the muzzle. If he told Emma the truth, she would never marry him.

"Charge Cartridge."

Amon loaded the powder in the muzzle. He deserved her scorn, but he couldn't bear to think of it. The truth would only hurt her.

"Draw Rammer."

He drew the rammer from the musket. Starting his marriage with a lie about an act of infidelity gnawed on him.

"Ram Cartridge."

He pushed the rammer down the muzzle twice. It was a little more than his conscience could live with.

"Return Rammer."

Amon returned the rammer to its place on his musket. He couldn't even blame Coby this time, but he had learned his lesson. He would never go carousing or drinking again.

"Cast About."

He raised the musket. As soon as drills were over, he would talk to Lieutenant Jed about what he'd done.

"Prime."

Cocking the hammer to the safety position, he placed it back on his right shoulder. Even if the lieutenant told him to report himself to Captain Cage, he would do it.

"Ready."

It would be worth getting bucked and gagged to rid himself of this guilt.

"Aim."

"Fire."

Weapons exploded. His heart pounded.

"Dismissed."

He marched to the chaplain's cabin and knocked on the door. "Lieutenant, could we talk?"

Lieutenant Jed glanced toward him. "I'm sorry, Private Amon. I didn't see you there." His voice sounded heavy, like something was wrong.

Amon considered leaving. He felt awkward, as if he was interrupting something, but it wouldn't hurt to ask. "If you're busy, I could come back."

"Well... I... I have time now." Jed offered a half grin, but it didn't look like his heart was in it. "I wanted to talk with you too. Why don't we take a walk so we won't be disturbed?"

"Sounds good."

They ambled toward the edge of the Tennessee River. Amon shivered from the chill in the air and glanced toward the sky. Storm clouds were forming again.

"I noticed you were bucked and gagged for drinking a couple of weeks ago." Jed's tone was kind, not reproachful. "Do you want to talk about it?"

"Yes, Sir." The tightness in Amon's stomach unraveled. "I've done a lot I'm ashamed of lately."

Jed picked up a rock and skipped it over the river's surface. "So, when did you start drawing away from God?"

Amon pondered the question for a moment, trying to think of a time he knew the Lord like Jed and Emma talked about. "I'm not sure I ever was close to Him. I know my Ma loves Jesus. And Emma and Mr. Brown act like they're on speaking terms with the Almighty, but it's never been that way with me. I lived right and went to church. I guess I figured that was enough. Don't get me wrong. I do believe in God, but lately I haven't been acting like it."

"I've noticed."

Amon's knees wobbled as he sat on a tree stump near the river's edge.

"I've done worse than you know about."

Jed sat beside him but didn't say anything.

"I went drinking again, only this time with some men from another regiment."

"Go on."

Amon let out a breath. "Well, they took me to this tent with… well, with soiled doves. I was so drunk, I hardly knew where I was. The next thing I know, I paid for this girl, Amy was her name, and well… I cheated on Emma."

Amon expected Jed to look angry or shocked. Instead, he placed a hand on Amon's shoulder. "You had relations with her?"

"No. I kissed her, and I would have done more, but I came to my senses in time and skedaddled out of there like Johnny Reb was chasing me."

Jed didn't say anything.

"This thing shook me up." Amon's voice quivered. "To know I could stray that far and hurt the people I love the most. It seems like ever since my friends died at Cedar Mountain, it's... the captain said it best, it's like I'm lost in this storm. And well, I'm scared about not finding my way back, if that makes any sense. I don't know what to do."

"I do," Jed said. "You need to make things right with God. Trying to do the right things, going to church, and believing the Bible isn't enough. You need to be born again, to surrender your life to the one who created you and start living for Him."

"I can't go on the way I have." Amon wiped his hand across the back of his neck. "I need God."

"There's no time like the present." Jed reached out his hand.

Amon grasped it and prayed to the only one who could save him.

*****

November 9th, 15 days before the battle

Amon headed toward Captain Cage's tent. Since he'd prayed with Lieutenant Jed, things had been different. It was like when he carried a heavy pack into battle, then when he got back to camp, he would let go of the pack and let it fall to the ground. The load had been lifted.

Now he was following new orders for his life. The commands God issued weren't easy, but since he'd been in the army, he'd learned that most orders aren't. All he knew was he needed to obey and leave the rest to God.

He'd talked to the chaplain after he'd prayed about what God was telling him to do. He didn't want to make a mistake. Lieutenant Jed agreed he heard right.

The first order was to come clean, and he'd wanted to make sure he got the letters in the mail before chaplain left with the mail cart. He'd written a letter to Mr. Brown confessing everything he'd done since joining the army including that night with Amy and about his new commitment to God.

After writing a letter to Emma, he'd placed it in Mr. Brown's envelope. He should tell Emma about it first. It would be easier for her hearing from her father than in a letter. The letter to his ma was even harder to write, but he wanted her to hear what he'd done from himself and not somebody else. They might not forgive him, but that was in God's hands.

It had been a couple of days since Jed left, and he'd prayed for the courage to carry out the next step, confessing to Captain Cage that he'd been drinking and visiting a prostitute since they got to camp. Being bucked and gagged was not something he looked forward to. It was humiliating and uncomfortable, and caused his muscles to ache for days, but he was willing to do it to make a new start.

Facing the captain would be harder than the punishment. There was no man he respected more, not even Mr. Brown. Captain Cage deserved the title of hero.

Coby came alongside him. "You haven't talked to me since we arrived here, and that's pretty hard since we share a tent. You're avoiding me."

"Sure am," he said without looking away from his destination. "I visited Lieutenant Jed before he left and had a long talk with him." He turned and faced his former friend. "Coby, I got right with God."

"You've become one of them Bible thumpers?" Coby chuckled. "It won't last."

"Other men live godly lives, and I'm set on it too."

Coby snorted. "Men like who, other than that holier than thou chaplain I mean?"

"Captain Cage. I'm going there to tell him what I did."

Coby grabbed Amon's arm. "You can't."

"Don't fret," Amon said. "I'm only telling on myself. You're safe."

"So, you think the high and mighty Captain Macajah Jones is a godly man." Coby crossed his arms. "I think there's something you should know about your war hero."

Coby told him the truth about what he'd seen Captain Cage do, and Amon's heart sank.

Chapter Forty-Three

November 10th, 14 days before the battle

Lavena arose early and went for a walk along the Tennessee River. Jed had left a few days ago, and she wasn't sure how she felt about that. She didn't love him like she had Cage, but he'd been a good friend, and she needed that.

She had determined she wanted nothing more to do with Cage, but even though she'd made the decision, her emotions kept getting stirred up. It would be good to have someone to talk to about it, someone she could trust.

The sun crested over the mountains as Lavena sat on a rock near the river and watched a flock of geese swimming downstream. It hadn't rained in over a week, and the mud had dried up. She breathed in the crisp air. Most of the trees were now bare, but there was a whiff of pine and spruce. The perfect fall day if only she could enjoy it.

A buck stood near the water and stared at her for a moment before darting toward Raccoon Mountain. If she could only capture in words the serenity around her, so unlike the turmoil within.

The calmness of this scene would end once the battles for Lookout Mountain and Missionary Ridge started. She'd talked to General Grant, and he told her it could start any day now. She couldn't help but be a little relieved. He'd obviously not received word from her publisher that she was no longer working for them.

The new correspondent from *The Cleveland Leader* hadn't shown up, and any day now, everything she'd worked for could be taken away. Hopefully another newspaper would decide to publish her articles by then.

Lavena heard a twig snap from behind and turned to see what it was.

Private Coby stood there with his arms crossed. "Well, well, if it's not Miss Falcon, the lady reporter."

A chill went through her. She stood, backed up a step.

"What are you doing out here all alone?" That horrible smirk. "Looks like you need some company."

Her knees shook so much she wasn't sure they would hold her. She tried not to show her fear, but she wasn't sure she was succeeding. "I'm... I'm meeting your captain. He'll be here any minute."

"Is that so?" He moved toward her.

"Yes." She stepped back. Her gaze darted around. Behind her, the river. He was standing where the path narrowed on the way back to camp. Why did she have to choose such a secluded spot?

Coby chuckled and took a couple of steps toward her. "Then we better hurry, hadn't we?"

She backed up to the water's edge, afraid to take her eyes off him. Her heartbeat thrashed in her ears. "Don't come near me, or I'll scream." She glanced back. She didn't know how to swim, and the river was too deep for her to jump in. Everything closed in. She was trapped.

"You picked a nice spot." Coby took another step. "Away from camp, private, secluded. There's nobody around to hear you." He dashed toward her.

She tried to run past him, but he grabbed her, threw her on the ground, and climbed on top of her. A scream came from deep inside as she kicked and hit her fists against his chest.

A gunshot fired.

******

Cage and Sergeant Garrett had taken a walk to discuss the sergeant's new duties when he came upon them. Coby had her on the ground, and she was wrestling to get him off. Cage's heart raced, and he rushed toward them.

Her scream pierced his heart. Heat rushed through him, and he fired his Colt army revolver into the ground as a warning shot.

Coby stopped and jerked his head toward Cage.

Cage took aim. "Get away from her!"

Coby stood and raised his hands. A cold smile flashed across his face. "Just having a little fun, Captain."

Cage's neck corded, and he took a breath and exhaled it. "Lavena, are you all right?"

Sergeant Garrett pulled his gun. "I've got this, Captain. Go to her."

Cage rushed to her side, pulled her to her feet, and held her.

Her body trembled in his arms as she gasped for air. "I'm... I'm fine. He didn't..." Her voice sounded soft, hollow as if it were traveling through water.

Cage directed her to a nearby rock and helped her sit.

An ugly laugh emanated from Coby.

Cage released his hold on Lavena and lunged toward Coby grabbing him by the collar.

"Captain Jones," Sergeant Garrett said, a warning in his tone.

He pushed Coby against an oak tree and took a deep breath to calm himself. "I'm not going to hit him." He let go and backed up a step. "Private Coby, you're under arrest. Sergeant, take him to the stockade and file charges against him for assaulting a lady and attempted rape."

Coby's eyes narrowed. "You wouldn't dare." He rubbed his hand over his mouth. "I'll tell everyone what I know. I'll even tell your pretty little strumpet."

The rage Cage tried to stuff down flared again. He lifted his fists and took a step toward Coby.

Sergeant Garrett squeezed in between. "Captain Cage, this isn't right. He'll get what he deserves."

Cage nodded and forced his hands to lower and unclench.

"Think this over, Captain." When Cage didn't respond, Coby straightened his shirt and continued. "Lady, let me tell you what Captain Cage, the hero, did."

"She already knows." Rage dripped from his words. "I told her and Colonel Creighton everything. Sergeant Garrett, get him out of here before I do something I'll regret."

"I don't believe you." Coby started toward Lavena.

Sergeant Garrett cocked his revolver.

Coby halted. "He's a murderer. He set the fire that killed that woman and her children."

The sergeant's face wrinkled with the question he undoubtedly wanted to ask.

"I'll explain everything later, Sergeant," Cage said. "For now, get him locked up."

Sergeant Garrett grabbed Coby's arm. "Get moving."

Cage drew to Lavena's side. He almost touched her shoulder but brought his hand back to his side. "What are you doing out here?"

Lavena let out a sob. "I needed some time alone... to think. I didn't know he'd..." She wiped her face.

Cage grabbed hold of her elbow. "I'll escort you to your tent."

She nodded and let him guide her, but she didn't say anything until they reached her cabin. "Thank you, Captain. I'll be fine now."

"I can't leave you like this. You've had a shock. At least let me boil some water. You can have a cup of tea."

She tilted her head. "All right. The kettle already has water in it."

He set the kettle on the fireplace and rubbed where his scar itched. This was his fault. If he'd told the truth earlier, Coby wouldn't have thought he could get away with this.

An exhaustion worse than any he'd known on the battlefield swept over him. *Lord, please help me.* "I know things will never be right between us, but I'd do anything to take back the hurt I've caused."

Her chin quivered, and she turned away from him. "I can fix my own cup of tea. I'd like you to leave."

Cage nodded, rubbed his ear, and stepped outside.

The pain in his heart was more intense than his burns had ever been, but he ignored it. Lavena was in hurting too. Maybe the only way he could help her was to stay away. *Lord, I deserve this. Help her.*

He made his way back to his cabin and sunk into the chair by the fireplace. So tired from his daytime duties, nighttime guard duty, and all the heartache. His eyes closed. He missed Jed at times like this, when he needed wisdom and somebody to talk things out with.

Enough of this brooding. He moved to the table and wrote the orders to make sure Coby stayed locked up for the remainder of the war.

Now that Coby was arrested and Sergeant Garrett had heard his accusations, he needed to talk with Colonel Creighton about telling his men everything as soon as possible. No matter what the colonel said, he wouldn't wait any longer.

Private Amon Smith burst into the room. "Captain Cage, I need talk to you about something."

Cage stood. "About what, Private?"

"Did you set the fire that killed that woman and her children?"

Cage's heart dropped to his stomach. "Yes."

Amon drew closer until he was toe-to-toe with him. "I can't believe it. You tell me how I should live for God, and you do this?"

"I didn't intend to kill them." His voice sounded low, hollow, as if it barely came through his lips. "I was trying to smoke out enemy soldiers. Kegs of gunpowder were in the house. It exploded with flames before I could do anything. I tried to save them."

Amon twisted his mouth. "And you lied about it?"

The heaviness resting on Cage made his muscles so limp he wondered how he was still standing. Why did his men have to hear it like this? "It was weeks before I came around and found out I got that cursed medal. I didn't know what to do, so I stayed quiet."

"I planned to come here yesterday because I wanted to make a fresh start with God and confess to my drinking and carousing." Amon's rigid shoulders heaved. "Coby stopped me and told me what you'd done, what a hypocrite you are. I couldn't believe it. I stayed awake all night trying to figure it out. I was sure Coby was lying to get back at you, but now you tell me everything he said was true?"

Cage tried to place his hand on the private's shoulder, but Amon brushed it away. "Please don't let my sins keep you from God."

The private marched out of the tent without saying a word.

He let out an audible sigh. He should have insisted to Colonel Creighton that he needed to tell his men as soon as possible. He'd waited too long.

Despite the exhaustion, he headed to the colonel's cabin.

Chapter Forty-Four

November 11th, 13 days before the battle

Amon stood at attention. Drills were over, but Sergeant Garrett ordered the men to stay put until Captain Cage addressed them. Probably instructions for the upcoming battle.

He knew why Coby wasn't there. News had spread through the camp that he'd been arrested for accosting the newspaper lady. Amon's face flushed with shame as he thought about how Coby had led him around like a dog.

When Coby told him what the captain did, it shook him to the core. He never believed Captain Cage would let people think he was some kind of hero after what he'd done, but the captain had risked his life to save his men, to save Amon, and he had rushed into the burning house to save the woman and children he'd killed.

Amon didn't like it, but sometimes things like that happened during war. Why would Captain Cage lie about it though? That's the part that bothered him the most. It's not like the captain caused those civilians to die on purpose.

He had to admit that he'd strayed farther from God's commands than he ever thought possible. Didn't the man who saved his life and tried to help him deserve as much forgiveness as he'd received?

All men were sinners. All men needed God's grace.

Heaviness crept through his body causing his shoulder to hunch. If the captain really was sorry, he would have confessed everything. If he had, he wouldn't still be in command.

He shouldn't let the captain's shortcomings affect him like this, but they did.

Captain Cage marched onto the field.

Amon pulled himself to attention and ignored the stiffness in his neck. He hadn't slept much last night.

The captain cleared his throat. "Men, I've been honored to serve with you these past few years. You have shown yourself as honorable soldiers, men of fortitude and courage, but I haven't always lived up to being the leader you deserve." Captain Cage poured out the truth about Cedar Mountain, holding nothing back, as he relayed the events to the men.

There was a low murmur as soldiers whispering among themselves.

Private Harry Todd leaned toward Amon. "I can't believe he would do that."

Sergeant Garrett stepped forward. "You're at attention. The next soldier who says a word will be bucked and gagged."

Amon snapped back. He couldn't help but wonder if Captain Cage was about to tell them he'd been relieved of duty. Either way, the weight that had gripped his chest since he heard what his captain had done lifted, and he couldn't keep from displaying a slight grin.

Captain Cage rubbed the scar along his face. "You may have questions about this incident. I'm available to talk to any of you about it all day today. Tonight, I have guard duty. Colonel Creighton and General Geary will decide what happens to me after the upcoming battle, but for now, you're still under my command.

"You've been the best company any man could have." His voice cracked. "We have one more battle to fight. I'll do my best to get you through it safely. Dismissed."

*****

Cage looked around, trying to gauge how the men took the news. The soldiers didn't seem in any hurry to leave. They stood there, in a daze, as if they forgot how to move. Finally, they broke off in small groups muttering to themselves as they left the field.

Only Sergeant Garrett remained.

The sergeant headed straight toward him as fast as an incoming cannonball and saluted. "Permission to speak freely, Sir."

Cage returned his salute and braced for what was coming. "Go ahead, Sergeant." He'd worried about how Garrett would take the news the most, and the truth was he needed him to get the men through this, especially with both Jed and Nate gone. He didn't have another sergeant he could count on. The others had been killed in battle over the last couple of years.

"I'm going to request a transfer to another company." Sergeant Garrett practically spit the words toward him. "I will not serve under a man so dishonorable and cowardly in his conduct."

The scar on Cage's face itched. He'd expected this, but it still dropped on him like a barrage of enemy fire. "You're a bit premature, Sergeant. In a few weeks, I may no longer be in command of this company."

"I have no stomach for following you into battle."

"You have no choice." Cage pulled on his ear. "Permission to transfer is denied for now. I can't let you do anything to jeopardize the men's faith in me as we head into battle."

"I don't have to." Garrett scowled. "You've already done the damage."

Cage stood as erect and commanding as his guilty conscience would permit. If he allowed the sergeant to undermine his authority now, it could be dangerous for his men when the battle finally did start.

"My shortcomings aside, you will do your duty, Sergeant, or you'll end up in the stockade. Do I make myself clear?"

"Yes, Sir." Garrett's tone didn't inspire Cage to believe he'd won him over, but the man would follow orders. He always did.

Cage softened his tone. "After the battle, if I'm still alive and in command of this company, you'll have your transfer. In the meantime, the men need you more than ever."

"Yes, Sir." Garrett saluted and headed toward his tent.

Cage let out a sigh. He wished Jed or Nate were still here. He could use the support. He needed all the help he could get to keep his men safe.

*****

As Amon left the supply cabin, a flock of birds flew toward Lookout Mountain. He watched them for a time then headed to where other soldiers in his company stood warming themselves.

His company started with a hundred and thirty soldiers. Over two years later, forty-three men standing in a cluster around the fire were all that still were capable of fighting, the rest dead, wounded, or taken prisoner, Amon wondered if there would be anyone left when their three-year commitment ended in April.

He neared the fire. Corporal Jake was talking to the men. He drew closer.

"You're right. He should have owned up to it earlier," Corporal Jake said, "but Captain Cage is flesh and blood just like us."

"Yeah, but I looked up to him," said Private John Caroon. "When I think about that lady and her young'uns in that fire. Well, I got kids at home."

"Civilians get killed in war," Jake said. "We've been in this long enough to know that. He didn't mean for it to happen."

"He shouldn't have lied about it," a voice from the crowd called out.

"That's right," another voice said.

Murmuring passed through the group.

"Is there anyone here who hasn't had a weak moment they regretted?" Jake asked. "I have, but I kept my mouth shut cause I didn't want you men to know I acted cowardly. Well I'm admitting it now."

Jake wiped a hand across the back of his neck. "When I was taken prisoner of war with Sergeant Garrett, I panicked. If it wasn't for the sergeant, I might be dead right now. Is there one man here who has a right to throw stones at Captain Cage?"

Private John kicked at the dirt near his feet. A few of the others looked down.

"The captain's been good to us. He's led us heroically when some of us wanted to run the other way. When all this happened, he risked his life to save us from them Johnny Rebs. And he almost lost his life in that fire running in after that lady and her kids. I, for one, aim to stand behind Captain Cage until my dying breath. Who's with me?"

"I am." Amon took a step forward.

"Me too," Private Ben said.

A few others voiced their agreement, but John stood back, crossed his arms, and stared into the fire.

The men gazed at the private, and Amon figured whatever he said would decide the matter. John was older than most of the privates, around thirty years old, and his opinions influenced many of the company's younger soldiers.

John shrugged. "I don't like what the captain did, but I'm in too. We've always fought together. No reason to stop now."

Amon let out the breath he was holding. When the battle finally came, if they weren't fighting together, they didn't have a chance.

The muscle in his jaw twitched. Some of them would die anyway.

Chapter Forty-Five

November 15th, nine days before the battle

It was past midnight when Nate was called to General Bragg's office on Missionary Ridge. He'd gotten into camp only an hour ago and had immediately headed to bed, wanting nothing more than a good night's sleep. Instead, he had to hurriedly put on his uniform and head out into the cold.

He entered Bragg's cabin and saluted. "You asked to see me, Sir?"

"Yes, I did. I want to hear your assessment of the commanders' reactions when they read my message."

Nate raised an eyebrow. At this time of night? He didn't bother to say what he was thinking. Bragg was a hard man, and he'd woken others in the middle of the night for trivial duties.

He told the general they accepted the orders well, but some were complaining about where the cannons were placed and about the conditions. Since the cracker line broke, the Confederate soldiers were on half rations. He didn't bother to say that the Bragg's harsh punishments for any offence added to the complaints. He didn't want to be on the receiving end of the general's anger.

"Understandable. That will soon end."

A cryptic statement. Did he suspect something?

A commotion sounded outside. General Bragg went to see what was going on, and Nate followed him. Nate's father and other officers rushed from their tents.

Soldiers surrounded two men, one in civilian clothes and one in a Union uniform.

"What's going on here?" General Bragg bellowed.

The men parted until Nate had a clear view. One of the prisoners was Jed. He had a swollen jaw, and the scrawny civilian with him had a black eye. Heat shot up Nate's back. He took exhaled to calm himself. He didn't dare show his anger.

One of the Confederate soldiers, a big hulk of a man who looked like he could carry a tree trunk without breathing heavy, answered. "We caught up with these men driving a Union mail wagon. We got the wagon and the mail too."

"Good job, Captain Cooper." General Bragg said. "Throw them in the lock-up, and post a guard."

Nate gouged the back of his neck with his hands and took a step toward Jed. "I'll do it, Sir."

Jed shook his head, almost imperceptibly.

"No," General Bragg said. "Let Cooper take care of it. I need you to get some sleep. I'll have another message for you in a day or two."

General Bragg turned to his father. "Go through the mail. Report to me if you find anything important."

"Sir, it might take a week to get through it all," Father said.

"Do what you can."

The general walked back into his cabin.

Father walked over to Nate and squeezed his shoulder. "The Union officer has a rooster patch on his uniform. He's from the Ohio Seventh. Anyone you know?"

Thoughts raced through Nate's mind. If he said he didn't know them, his father would have misgivings, but he couldn't admit how close a friend Jed was. "I know him. Not well." Hopefully Jed hadn't mentioned what company he was from.

"This must be difficult for you," Father said. It would have been easier if his father wasn't trying to be so compassionate.

"It is," Nate said, "but I've made my choice." He tried to figure out what else he could say to get suspicion off himself. "If that lieutenant had taken me prisoner, he would have wasted no time getting me before a firing squad."

Father nodded. That seemed to satisfy him. "Get some sleep, Son."

"Yes, Sir." Nate saluted and wandered back to his tent in as easy a manner as he could muster. He had to figure out a way to get Jed out of here.

He didn't bother getting out of his uniform. Instead, he listened. If he waited until the early hours of the morning, shortly before sunrise when most of the soldiers and all of the officers would be asleep, he might be able to bluff his way past the guards to at least talk to Jed.

Maybe slip him a knife or a gun. He had to do something to help.

The night passed slowly. He paced then sat on his bedroll. Under normal circumstances he would have found it difficult to stay awake all night after a three-day assignment, but he was too worried about Jed to sleep.

He finally heard the birds singing their before dawn chorus. It was time. He stood and hid a knife in his boot. He'd considered a handgun, but all he had was his Colt Dragoon Pistol, and it would be too bulky. A knife would be easier to hide anyway. He headed to the place where Jed and the other man were kept prisoner.

There was no building or tent. Some men had put up a barbed wire fence with a gate in the shape of a square. Four soldiers stood outside guarding them. Fortunately, Captain Cooper wasn't one of them. Made sense. He would have assigned the men under his command so he could get a good night's sleep.

Jed and the scrawny balding man, who had to at least be fifty, were the only prisoners. They slept on the hard ground without even a blanket to keep them warm. He wiped a hand over his face.

Look confident. If this is going to work, you can't show any timidity.

He spoke with as much bluster as he could manage. "Guards, I need to talk to the prisoners, Colonel Teagan's orders."

All four men were privates, and none of them looked like they were about to question an officer's orders. They saluted, pulled the gate aside.

Nate entered. He suspected they would be watching closely, but he didn't look back to see. He kicked Jed's side. "You there. I have some questions for you."

Jed looked up, and his eyes widened, but he didn't say anything. He stood to his feet.

Nate lowered his voice so the guards wouldn't hear him, but he tried to gesture as if he were questioning an enemy soldier. "I'll get you out of here somehow."

"No, you won't." Jed whispered. "After everything we've done to get you here, don't you dare do anything to jeopardize your mission."

"I can't just leave you like this. Copper might not be the only soldier to decide to give you a beating."

"We'll be all right," Jed said. "When the battle starts, the rebs will be distracted. You'll be joining the Ohio Seventh, and you can take us with you when you go. Until then, we need to wait."

"I have a knife in my boot," Nate said. "I can at least leave you that."

Jed crossed his arms. "And who do you think they would suspect if they find it? Now get out of here before the guard changes or one of the officers wakes up and wonders why you're out here talking to me."

Nate's jaw clenched.

"Lieutenant, I outrank you by a week. That's an order."

He didn't like this, but Jed was right. "I won't leave this camp without you."

"I know," Jed said.

For now, there was nothing more he could do. He headed back to his tent.

Chapter Forty-Six

November 16th, eight days before the battle

Lavena was drinking the last of her tea when she heard a commotion outside. Surely the battle wouldn't start this time of day, would it? She set her cup down and stepped out to see what was going on.

A woman with blond hair, a huge hoop skirt, and a parasol appeared to be scolding one of the orderlies. If Lavena didn't know better, she would swear the lady was... "Betsy, what are you doing here?"

"Lavena!" Betsy gasped and threw her arms around Lavena almost dropping her parasol. "It's so good to see a friendly face. You can't imagine what I've been through trying to get here. We had to change trains in Columbus, Indianapolis, Louisville, then in Nashville, and again in Dalton. When we got to Bridgeport, Alabama, they didn't even have a driver to take us nurses to camp. They said the wagon was needed for medical supplies. We actually had to walk. Can you imagine? It took us two whole days to walk here. Just look at my boots." She held up her foot to show her mud encrusted shoes.

"What are you doing here?" Lavena knew she was repeating herself, but Betsy hadn't answered her question.

"I told you I was going to join up as an Army nurse. I've already checked in at the hospital."

"Fiddlesticks. You're going to be a nurse in that dress?"

"Of course not, but I wasn't going to wear that dreadful nurse's uniform to travel down here. Why don't you stop gawking and invite me in for some tea? I'll tell you everything."

Lavena invited her into the cabin, and she set her bags against the wall and sat at the table. At least the water in the kettle was still hot. Lavena fixed them both a cup of tea and sat across from her. "Now, out with it."

Betsy took a sip of tea and sighed. "I missed this."

"Well?" Lavena strummed her fingers on the table. "Are you going to tell me what's going on or not?"

"There's not really much to tell. After you left, I joined the nursing corp, and here I am. They assigned two to a cabin, and I asked to stay with you. They agreed since they've assigned me to work for the Ohio Seventh's surgeon, and he's set up near here."

"How did you know I was here?"

"I asked. Dr. Walker, she's a woman doctor. Isn't that amazing? Well anyway, she said you'd interviewed her. I asked someone to show me the way, I think it was a major. Do they have strips on their uniforms?"

Lavena tried to catch her breath. "No, that would be a sergeant or a corporal depending on how many strips."

"I start in the morning. That gives us time to catch up. So, tell me all about Captain Cage. Did you get the interview? Have you learned anything about Nate? Tell me everything."

Lavena couldn't help the grin that spread over her face. "I missed you so much."

Betsy looked around and scowled. "You would think they'd at least give us a house to stay in instead of this tiny cabin, but I suppose it can't be helped, it being wartime."

Lavena chuckled. "This is an officer's cabin."

Betsy crinkled her nose. "Really, I would have thought a private stayed here."

Lavena took a sip of tea. She'd forgotten how good it was to talk to someone who didn't wear a uniform. "You must tell me every detail of your adventure."

"I will." Betsy set her cup down. "But first, have you seen Nate? How is he? Is he all right?"

Lavena took another gulp, this time allowing it to loosen the lump in her throat. "I have seen him. He's fine."

Betsy raised an eyebrow. "I know that look. Tell me everything."

"About Nate or about…" She couldn't help the tear falling down her cheek.

Betsy handed her a yellow embroidered handkerchief and patted her hand. "Tell me about Nate first. Then I want to hear what caused you to become so weepy. If it had been anyone else, I'd swear it was a man."

Lavena wiped her face and blew her nose.

"It is a man. Okay, I want to hear about this first."

Letting out a sigh, she filled Betsy in on all that happened and how Cage had captured her heart. "I shouldn't have allowed myself to become so fond of him. What am I going to do?"

"Lavena." Betsy put her hand on hers. "You're going to do what I did with Nate. You're going to pray and trust God to make things right, and then you're going to forgive him."

Lavena bit her bottom lip. She needed to change the subject. "It's time I told you about Nate."

The cup rattled in Betsy's hand, and she set it down. "What's happened?"

Lavena took a sip of tea. "He didn't desert."

"I knew it. He would never do such a thing, but why did his captain write me that dreadful letter?"

"It was a deception. Nate is a Union Spy in the Confederate Army. He's stationed on Missionary Ridge near here."

"A spy?" Betsy groaned. "That man is determined to get himself killed and make me a widow. I want to see him."

"You can't. Only a few people in command know about it. I wrote you a letter." A lump formed in Lavena's throat. Betsy wouldn't be there to receive it. If it got in the wrong hands... She let out a calming breath. It was a federal offense to open someone else's mail. Everything would be all right. It had to be.

Chapter Forty-Seven

November 22, 1863, two days before the battle

Lavena sat quietly while General Grant briefed her about the upcoming battle. She wrote notes from time to time she could refer to later. It was late in the evening, but the general never seemed to bother with sleep.

So far, the newspaper hadn't informed anyone she was no longer working at the paper, and her replacement hadn't shown up yet. But he would be here soon, she was sure of that. Mr. O'Brady and Mr. Cowles would want to make sure he was on time to report about the upcoming battle.

Until then, all she could do was wait and do her job. When her articles were read by the other newspapers, at least a few would pick them up. Hopefully that would happen before the new correspondent arrived.

General Grant cleared his throat. "Of course, you understand none of this can be reported until the actual battle takes place."

"I give my word, General."

Captain Cage burst into the room and saluted. "I'm sorry, Sir, but this is urgent. I met with our spy. Colonel Creighton said I should tell you about it."

General Grant glanced at Lavena. "Perhaps you'd better leave."

She wanted to hear what was happening, but she needed to keep the trust she'd built with the general. She stood and headed toward the door.

Captain Cage shook his head. "If you don't mind, Sir, I'd like her to stay."

Colonel Creighton wiped a hand across his mouth. "Captain Cage, may I remind you...

"Sir, she already knows. She..." He pressed his lips together. "She came across us when we were meeting with him."

General Grant's brow furrowed. "Did you report this to your colonel?"

"No, Sir. I didn't, but I will when I leave here."

"See that you do." The general turned to Lavena. "You've shown yourself trustworthy up until now." He stroked his beard. "You can stay, but none of this gets reported.

"Of course, Sir." Lavena sat down.

Cage continued. "The mail cart that left a week ago has been apprehended by the enemy."

Her throat closed up. "What about Lieutenant Jed Jackson?"

"The men on that cart are now prisoners of the Confederate Army," Cage said.

"Jed." She blinked to keep the tears out of her eyes." Now he would never get home to his family.

"This is disturbing news." General Grant gouged the back of his neck. "At least there weren't any military communications, only letters to home from the soldiers."

Lavena swallowed hard. The letter to Betsy was in that cart. "Sir, do you think they'll read the letters?"

General Grant nodded. "They'll go through every last one of them. Hopefully the men didn't write home about anything vital."

"They know not to do that," Cage said.

There didn't seem to be enough air the room. What had she done? "Sir, there's something--."

General Grant interrupted her. "I'm sorry, Miss Falcon, Captain Jones, but I have an important meeting with my staff. I'm going to have to ask you both to leave."

The major ushered Cage and her out the door before she could think of what to say. She needed to warn somebody. Nate was in danger because of her carelessness.

All she could do was confide in Cage. He'd know what to do.

He grabbed hold of his ear. "It's late. May I escort you to your cabin?"

"Yes, but there's something I have to tell you." As they walked, she told him everything.

Cage stopped by a poplar tree, his jaw working back and forth.

"I'm so sorry." She pressed her lips together. "I didn't mean to do anything to put him in danger. I only wanted to reassure Betsy."

He looked like he might wrap his arms around her, but instead, he pulled back. "We'll talk about this later. I have to let General Grant know." He marched back toward the general's office.

*****

Nate climbed up a steep embankment and almost lost his footing. Steadying himself against an elm tree, he stopped to catch his breath. He had to keep going toward Missionary Ridge even though the sun had already set.

Cage had been late for their meeting, and Nate hadn't figured out how to explain why he took so long to deliver the message to Lookout Mountain.

Maybe he just didn't want to lie to his father again. Betraying him hadn't been easy, but the information he'd retrieved would save countless Union lives. That's what he reminded himself when the guilt gnawed at him.

Soon this would all be over. The battle for Chattanooga would begin, and Nate would join his company as soon as the first shot was fired. Jed and the mail cart driver would be with him when he did.

The meeting had been productive. Nate passed along the code the Confederate generals planned to use in battle and plans they made to attack Chattanooga within a week's time, and he informed Cage about the new prisoners and the mail Bragg's troops had captured.

Before he made it to camp, Father stepped out from behind a tree with his hand on his revolver. Nate's heart dropped to his stomach. Something was wrong.

"I hoped it wasn't true." Father strode to him with his jaw jutted and hands clenched. "That you weren't betraying me a second time," He grabbed Nate by the collar.

"Father, I was just…"

"Don't." Father let go and drew his pistol, pointing it at Nate's chest. "Shortly before you left, I read an interesting piece of mail." He held up a letter. "This is a heartfelt letter from a friend of your wife's reassuring her you didn't desert and you're still loyal to the Union."

Nate kneaded the back of his neck. "I don't know why anyone would write that. Whoever did was lying."

"You're lying now." Father spit out the words. "I followed you. I saw you meet with a bluebelly captain. My own son, a Union spy."

Nate thought about reaching for his father's gun, but even if he managed to get it away, he wouldn't shoot. He shifted his weight. "What happens now?"

"General Bragg hasn't seen this yet, but as an officer of the Confederate Army, it's my duty to turn you over to him with the letter."

Nate swallowed. "Father, please. He'll hang me."

"Most likely."

A heavy sigh escaped him. The muscles in his body felt as if they had weights tied to them. This is how he expected it to end, but now that Betsy forgave him, he wanted to live – for her.

The vein in Father's neck throbbed. "Your wife won't take you back. You did the same thing to her you did to me, running after your causes, deserting her. You never loved her."

"I've always loved Betsy."

"No, you never loved anyone, not even your mother or me. Your causes always came first."

Nate kept quiet. What could he say? He did love his father. He hadn't realized how much until this moment, but he always wanted to mend the relationship. Now it was too late.

Father's Adam's apple bulged. "Here's the thing." He holstered his gun. "You're my son even if you are a traitor and a spy. I lost you once. I won't lose you again."

"What are you saying?"

Father's voice thickened. "I'm not going to be the one who gets you hanged no matter what you've done."

It took a moment for the words to register. Nate took a step back, gasped. "But... You... You're not going to tell them?"

"Oh, I'll tell them. I believe in my cause too."

A dizziness came over Nate, and he tried to remain steady on his feet. "What are you going to do?" His voice came out shaky.

"I'll give you until sunrise to get back to your friends on the Union side."

"Just like that." Nate swallowed. "You're letting me go."

"Don't think any of the information you passed on will still be accurate. By the time you've reported what you know, we'll have everything in place. What you told your friends is worthless."

Nate blinked. "I don't know what to say."

"Don't say anything." Father reached toward him and pulled him into a bear hug. "I love you."

"I love you too, Father." His voice cracked. "I'm sorry. So sorry."

Father pulled back and kneaded the back of his neck. "Now, get going."

Nate nodded and took off running. He wouldn't be able to rescue Jed now. He needed to get to camp in time to warn Colonel Creighton. If Grant's army didn't attack right away, Bragg's army would invade Chattanooga.

And it would be his fault.

Chapter Forty-Eight

November 23rd, one day before the battle

That morning, before Betsy had gone to the hospital, Lavena had told her what she'd done, how she put Nate in danger.

Betsy had handled it well. "There's no way you could have known. You were only trying to help me. Nate will be all right, you'll see."

Lavena couldn't sit still. She tried to convince herself that was true, but it didn't work. Nate was in danger, and it was her fault.

A knock sounded at the door, and when she opened it, Cage walked in.

He didn't bother to greet her. "We need to talk."

Lavena nodded and motioned for him to sit down.

"When I told General Grant what happened, he was furious, and I can understand why." He gazed at her for a moment as if he were letting her think on that. "I tried to convince him to let me launch a rescue, but he wouldn't allow it."

She couldn't believe what she was hearing. "But what about Nate and Jed? Are you going to leave them in the hands of the enemy?"

"Do you think I want to? There's nothing I can do. I'm needed for the upcoming battles." He stood and paced. "Why did you do it? I warned you not to tell anyone."

"I'm sorry." Heat rushed to her face. "I didn't mean for this to happen." Now Nate and Jed were in danger, maybe even dead, because she thought she knew best.

This is how Cage must have felt after setting the fire. He hadn't meant to hurt anyone either. She'd been so wrong.

He sat back down. "General Grant sent a telegram to your newspaper. They know you no longer work there."

Her bottom lip quivered. She'd judged Cage for deception when she'd been just as guilty. She deserved to be booted out of camp. A lump lodged in the back of her throat. "What happens now?"

Cage stood and began pacing again. "I tried to explain that you were writing for other papers now, but General Grant and Colonel Creighton believe you deceived them by not revealing your change in status."

She stared at her hands folded in her lap. "They're right. I did."

He stopped and faced her. "I also received a dressing down for not telling them about your career change or the fact you stumbled on us and found out Nate is a spy. That will be added to the charges against me."

The lump in her throat threatened to choke her. "Oh, Cage, I'm so sorry. I didn't mean for you to get into more trouble. Do you want me to talk to him, maybe explain?"

He sat, rubbed his jaw, and stood again. "No, I'm the one who decided to keep it quiet. I should have reported it as soon as it happened."

"Why didn't you?"

"Don't you know." He touched her cheek gently with the back of his hand. "I'd do anything for you."

*****

Shots fired. Cage's men were assigned guard duty this morning, so he ran toward outside and to where the sound came from.

He soon reached the line. Soldiers stood pointing rifles toward a Confederate prisoner. The man in gray stood leaning against Private Amon, his face scrunched, his pant leg covered in blood.

"Nate!" Cage ran toward them. "What's going on?"

Sergeant Garrett saluted. "We caught the deserter, Sir. Lieutenant Teagan. And he's wearing a Confederate uniform."

"You should have aimed at his heart," Private John spewed out. He kept a rifle pointed at Nate.

Lavena had caught up with him.

Cage swallowed hard. "What happened?"

"He was running into camp," Private Amon said. "I shouted for him to stop. I didn't know it was Lieutenant Nate, Captain. Honest I didn't. All I saw was the gray uniform."

"You did good, Private Smith," Sergeant Garrett said. "The man's a deserter, maybe even a traitor. He'll face the firing squad for this."

Others voiced approval and patted Amon on the back. Rifles still pointed as Nate as blood seeped through his pant leg.

"Men, stand down." Cage got on the other side of Nate. "Private Amon, help me get him to the surgeon."

The soldiers dispersed until only Private Amon, Sergeant Garrett, and Lavena remained.

"Cage." Nate's voice sounded weak. "I need to tell you…"

Cage lifted a finger to silence him. "Sergeant Garrett, get Colonel Creighton down here."

"Yes, Sir," the sergeant said, "but he won't be happy having his sleep interrupted for a wounded deserter who'll be shot anyway."

"Get him. Now!"

Garrett saluted. "Yes, Sir." He marched toward the colonel's cabin.

Cage and Amon helped get Nate to the hospital, a two-story federalist house with a large yellow banner with a green H painted on it hanging from the porch. Cage pushed through the heavy wood door and called for help. The hospital had only a hand full of patients lying on bedrolls near the fireplace.

A nurse ran to them. "Nate."

Cage stepped back. How did she know him?

She motioned for orderlies to come to Nate's aide. They laid him on a table in the corner.

Lavena started blubbering. "Betsy, I'm so sorry."

Betsy? That explained it. Lavena had told him she was rooming with Nate's wife.

Dr. Patella came rushing over. "What happened?"

"He was shot," Cage said.

The doctor cut off Nate's pant leg and examined the wound. "What's his name?"

"Lieutenant Nathaniel Teagan." Cage's voice thickened. "He's a hero."

"I'll take good care of him."

"Cage." Nate tossed to the side and groaned. "Need to tell you."

The orderlies held him down.

"Just rest, Nate," Cage said. "You did your duty."

Nate closed his eyes.

Cage held his breath for a moment until he saw the rise and fall of Nate's chest. He turned to the surgeon. "Is he going to be all right?"

"It shattered the bone," Dr. Patella said.

Lavena swooned, and Cage caught her before she hit the floor. He sat her in a nearby chair. Betsy ran to her and put smelling salts under her nose. She coughed a few times and curled up her nose, but she recovered and sat in stunned silence.

"We're going to have to cut off the leg," the doctor said. "I'm sorry."

Nate's eyes shot open. "No." The orderlies held him down as he struggled against them.

"Nurse," Dr. Patella said to Betsy. He pulled out a wooden box of tools and opened it. "Get me the chloroform."

Cage couldn't comprehend what he was hearing and seeing. He had to be mistaken. This nurse couldn't be Mrs. Teagan. She acted too calm. She brought the doctor a cloth and a bottle.

The doctor dripped some liquid onto the cloth.

"Wait. I need to talk to the colonel." Nate tried to move his head away. "Cage, don't let them do this."

Dr. Patella held the cloth over Nate's mouth, and he stopped struggling and fell into a deep sleep. The doctor turned to Cage and Lavena. "I need to operate now. You two should leave."

They nodded, stepped outside onto the porch, and sat on the front steps. Cage grabbed hold of Lavena's hand, and she didn't pull back. He was glad because he needed her support. The thought of what they were about to do to Nate sickened him.

Colonel Creighton rushed to them. "Sergeant Garrett informed me that Lieutenant Teagan was shot trying to sneak into the camp. Is he alive?"

Cage rubbed his hand across his cheek. "Yes, for now. They're cutting off his leg as we speak."

"It's all my fault." Lavena stood and swayed a little.

Cage put his arm around her and helped her sit.

The colonel gave Lavena a disgusted look, and Cage stepped in front of her.

"Did he have any information for us? I have a meeting with General Grant this morning. Did he say anything?"

"He needed to tell you something, but he passed out before he could tell us what it was," Cage said.

Colonel Creighton ran his hand over his face. "I should've had you tell the men to be expecting the lieutenant. This tragedy could have been avoided."

Cage grabbed hold of his ear. There was enough blame to go around. "Sir, Nate knew the risk he was taking, and he knew we couldn't tell the men about him until we started into battle. These things happen."

"I suppose you're right." Creighton glanced at his watch.

Dr. Patella came outside and made his way to them. "It's done. He's resting comfortably. There's no sign of infection. He should live through this."

"How long before he wakes up?" Colonel Creighton asked.

"A day of two."

The colonel's jaw clenched. "That's not good enough, Doctor. I need to talk to Lieutenant Teagan as soon as possible."

"Sir," Dr. Patella said. "The lieutenant has just been through major surgery. When he wakes, he'll be in a great deal of pain. We need to keep him under so that his body can rest."

Creighton glanced at his watch again. "We don't have the time to wait. Can you wake him sooner?"

The doctor nodded. "The anesthesia will wear off in an hour. I can keep from giving him a dose of laudanum until you talk to him, but he'll be in a lot of pain."

"Captain Jones." Colonel Creighton said. "You stay here. As soon as he wakes, notify me. I'll be in a meeting at General Grant's headquarters."

"Yes, Sir." Cage saluted. "At some point, I'll need to inform the men that Nate isn't a traitor or a deserter."

"That can wait until he wakes up. You have your orders." Colonel Creighton glanced toward Lavena.

She looked so vulnerable and lost.

"Miss Falcon, I've heard from your newspaper, but we'll discuss that later." He walked away.

Cage turned to her. All he wanted to do was wrap his arms around her and tell her everything was going to be all right, but he couldn't.

He knew what it was like to have something tragic happen and know it was his fault. His heart went out to her, but he didn't want to make things worse by giving her comfort she didn't want from him. So, they sat there, waiting for what seemed an eternity, neither of them saying anything.

Chapter Forty-Nine

Nate woke in worse pain than he'd ever known. A blanket had been pulled up to his neck, and he lay on the floor next to the fireplace, but he still shivered from the cold.

He let out a groan, but in a way, the pain in his right leg was comforting. He was afraid they would amputate.

The doctor darted outside before Nate could call out to him, but he managed to grab the arm of the private closest to him. "Orderly."

"Yes, Sir."

A moan rose in his throat. It hurt so bad. He gritted his teeth and tried to focus. "I have vital information. Need to see Colonel Creighton."

One side of the orderly's mouth twisted. "The colonel's at headquarters in an important meeting."

"Then get me Captain Cage."

"He's outside. The doctor went for him."

Even though he tried not to, Nate let out another yell. "Get him in here quick."

The private stood and saluted. "Yes, Sir." He tripped over a trunk and ran into the operating table on the way out of the house.

Wooziness threatened to overcame Nate, but he did his best to manage to stay awake. He didn't know how long he'd been out, but he needed to warn the Cumberland Army to attack right away or the Bragg's Army might be gone. The troop positions he reported to Cage were worthless. Lives would be lost if he didn't get word to them in time.

He closed his eyes for a moment. Cage shook him, and he stirred himself to stay alert. "How long have you been here?"

"A few minutes."

Nate raised up on his elbows. "Get Colonel Creighton or General Geary, maybe even General Grant. I need to see one of them right away."

Cage put a hand on Nate's shoulder and pushed him down. "Tell me. I'll get the message to them."

"They know I'm a spy. By now, everything I told them has changed. I believe they might be getting ready to leave Chattanooga and head to Knoxville, or they might be planning an attack. I have to let them know." Nate slumped back into his cot and closed his eyes to focus on anything but the pain.

When he opened them again, Betsy was holding his hand. She looked as beautiful as the day he left her. He shook his head and looked away. It couldn't be her. She was still in Cleveland. "Am I dreaming?"

"Nate." Betsy squeezed his hand, her blue eyes shining with a glint he'd never seen before. "You can't be here. Did they give me too much morphine?"

She leaned over to kiss him. Her lips felt tender. She pulled back and took hold of his hand.

"If this is a hallucination," he said, "I don't want to wake up."

A slight smile. "You're not hallucinating."

He shook his head. "No, this is impossible."

She squeezed his hand. "I joined the Army Nursing Corp, and I insisted they send me here."

"But you… how did you get here?"

"The train, silly." She let go of his hand and smoothed out her hoop skirt. "I took the train from Cleveland to Columbus to Indiana, to Louisville to Nashville, to Dayton. Then I had to walk the rest of the way from Bridgepoint if you can imagine that. Anyway, I finally made it."

"But it's too dangerous for you to be here."

The dimple on her cheek deepened. "I go where you go. You're not going to stop me ever again."

He looked around the room. "Cage, where is he? I have to tell him...

"You already did." She touched his cheek. "He's on his way to Colonel Creighton's meeting."

Nate bit his lip as another wave of pain shot up his leg. He took a few shallow breaths before he could continue. "Why would you do something so foolish as joining the nursing corp? You could be hurt or killed."

"Horse feathers. I told you before, I'm stronger than you think I am."

He let out a heavy sigh. His wife had to be the most exasperating woman he'd ever known. He gazed upon her face. And the most beautiful. "You shouldn't have come."

"Anyone would think you aren't happy to see me." She stirred some powder in a cup of water and held it up to his lips. "Drink this. It will help with the pain. It will start to work in about fifteen minutes, but before you fall asleep again, I need to tell you something. Dr. Patella gave me permission to be the one."

He lifted an eyebrow.

She kissed him long and deep, the way he dreamed about so many times. "You're alive and you're going to be all right. That's all that matters." She paused and grabbed hold of his hand again. "They had to amputate."

"No, they couldn't have. It's still there. I feel it." He pulled his hand away from her, pushed the covers aside. A bandaged stump where his leg used to be.

His hands dropped to his side. A muted scream came from deep inside, then his whole body quaked. "You let them do this! You let them take my leg? How could you?"

"Hush now," Betsy said in a calming voice, almost like you would use with a wounded animal. "It's not the end of the world. I'll nurse you back to health in no time."

"I'm not going to get better," he said through gritted teeth. "Do you think I'm going to magically grow my leg back, and we'll live happily ever after? You need to grow up."

She looked down. "I have grown up." She said it so quiet he could barely hear.

A strange look he'd never seen crossed her features. "Looks to me like you're the one who needs to grow up. So, life didn't go as we planned. None of this took God by surprise. You're my husband and losing a leg doesn't change that. I told you in that letter, you're stuck with me no matter what."

Her gestures became more animated, even her curls bounced. "Did you think I'd stand by you when I thought you were a deserter and a traitor and make it through all that nursing training, traipsing half-way across the country, and enemy lines just to leave because you're feeling sorry for yourself?" She jabbed him in the chest. "I'm. Not. Going. Anywhere."

A knot formed in his stomach. As much as he wanted to believe she could love him now, it was only pity she felt for him. "It won't last. You didn't stay when I went to rescue slaves or when I decided to go to war."

Her chin trembled.

He couldn't let her make the sacrifice. She'd already gone through so much suffering because of him. He loved her too much to saddle her with half a man. He didn't want to lose her, but he needed to finish it no matter how much it hurt her - and him. Better she left him now then wait until things got too tough.

"Let's face it, Sweetheart. I married a rich little princess whose daddy let her do whatever she wanted." He swallowed hard. "You're not equipped to handle a man who can't even walk without crutches. Why don't you go back to your daddy where you belong? He'll take you back when he finds out I'm out of the picture."

She wiped the tears off her face, but she didn't look away. "The only way I'm leaving is if you throw me out. That will be rather difficult with only one leg."

Nate opened his mouth to say something, but no words came. Could she really still love him after what happened? Lethargy overtook him. He knew he should, but he couldn't let her go.

He turned toward the fireplace, afraid that when he woke, she wouldn't be there.

*****

Cage ran two miles toward General Grant's headquarters in center of Chattanooga. It was almost noon by the time he arrived. He only stopped a moment to hold his side and try to catch his breath. This was too important.

The two sergeants guarding the building obviously had been chosen for their large builds. "I need to see General Grant or General Geary right away. I have vital information."

The sergeant with the bald head and bulging muscles shook his head. "There's no way you're getting in there, Sir."

"At least let me talk to Colonel Creighton."

"Sir," the other sergeant said, "I'm not going to be the one to interrupt that meeting. We've been given strict orders. You can wait here 'til their done if you want."

Captain Cage stood toe to toe with the first muscle bound guard. "Sergeant, if you don't want to lose your stripes, step aside."

The second guard took a step aside, but the bald sergeant held his ground. "I can't, Sir. General Grant ordered me to not allow anyone entrance, and I'm not going against his orders."

Cage removed his cap and rubbed his finger through his hair. "I'll take full responsibility."

The sergeant twisted his mouth. "If this is because of that deserter that was shot…"

Cage grabbed the sergeant by the shirt. "If you don't step aside now, I'll relieve you of duty, and you'll be hanging by your thumbs."

A bead of sweat formed on the sergeant's forehead. "Sir, I don't care what you do to me. I'm not disobeying an order."

"At least tell him I'm here. I have vital information."

The sergeant looked unsure. He glanced to the other guard who shrugged. "I guess I could ask if he wants to see you."

"You do that and tell him I have information from Lieutenant Teagan."

The sergeant spit on the ground by his feet. "Then it is about the deserter?"

"No, Sergeant, it's about the man who risked his life to do his duty."

The guard pressed his lips together probably trying to decide which officer posed the greatest threat. "I'll be back." He stepped inside.

The other sergeant went back to his post in front of the door. He obviously wasn't going to let Cage push by until he heard otherwise.

Cage paced, glared at the guard, then paced again. This was taking too long. Maybe he should try to force his way past.

The first guard came back. He looked as if he'd shrunk a foot. "The general said to send you in."

Cage brushed past him and stepped inside. He let out a gasp. Every general and colonel in the Potomac Army was there studying a map on the wall. General Grant, General Sherman, General Hooker, General Geary, and more. It left him speechless.

"Well," General Grant said.

"I received important information from Lieutenant Teagan. They know about him being a spy, and they're planning to either leave or attack as soon as they can."

General Grant sat down.

*****

Lavena sat crumpled on the floor beside the fireplace in her cabin. She didn't know how long she'd been there, and she didn't care.

She'd been so wrong, acting as if she were the conveyer of virtue. Nobody could live up to her expectations. Not Betsy or Nate. Not her father. Not Cage. Not even herself.

Her pride and arrogance were greater sins than anything they had done. She'd condemned Cage for something he hadn't wanted to happen even though he'd done everything to save those people. Now, she was in the same situation.

She shouldn't have sent that letter to Betsy. She should have listened. Cage had told her not to tell anyone Nate wasn't a deserter, but she thought she knew better. She didn't mean for it to happen, but because of her pride and stubbornness, Nate would never be the same.

Betsy would probably never talk to her again, and she doubted Cage would ever forgive her for what she'd done and the position she'd put him in.

She let out a pathetic snort at the thought. She wouldn't forgive him, but she wanted him to forgive her.

Her career in journalism that she'd put above every single person in her life was now gone, and she deserved to lose her job. The articles she sent freelance to other publications would never arrive. Tomorrow, Colonel Creighton would ship her out of camp on as soon as he could arrange it.

Lord, I've made a mess of things.

Betsy came through the door and stopped, eyes wide, when she saw Lavena "Are you all right?"

She wiped her face and stood. "Oh, Betsy, I'm so sorry for what I've done."

Betsy embraced her. "Nonsense. This isn't your fault, at least not all of it. Things like this happen."

Lavena pulled back. "How... how is he?"

"Feeling sorry for himself, but that's to be expected. He'll make a full recovery."

"I assumed you'd stay at the hospital with him."

Betsy wet her face in the water basin. "With what we gave him, he'll sleep all day and night and maybe halfway through tomorrow. In the meantime, I need to rest. There's a battle coming soon, and they'll need me at my best."

"After what happened to Nate, you plan to continue being a nurse."

"Of course, Silly. It will be months before Nate will be released to go home. Until then, I'll do what I can to help."

Lavena's cheeks burned with shame. She should have done everything she could for Cage and the men of Ohio Seventh, but she had only been worried about her job and her foolish pride.

Not anymore.

She would write the story she'd been sent to report, but she would report the truth mixed with God's grace. And she'd report on the braveness and honor of the men who were risking their lives every day.

It didn't matter if she had a place to send the articles or if she would be booted out of camp. She would leave that to God and do what she was sent here to do.

"You take a nap," She said to Betsy. "When you wake, I'll fix us something to eat. In the meanwhile, I have some work to do."

Betsy removed her hoop skirt and lay on her bed, and Lavena got out her laptop desk. First, she'd write another letter to her father asking for his forgiveness since the first one would never get to him. Then, she would finish her story.

In the morning, she would visit Nate and tell him what she'd done. The hardest part would be asking Captain Cage for his forgiveness after the way she'd treated him.

Chapter Fifty

November 24th, The Battle of Lookout Mountain Begins

Bugles blasting outside startled Lavena out of her sleep. It was still dark, and she rubbed her eyes until they adjusted to the darkness. There had been a small battle in Chattanooga near Missionary Ridge yesterday afternoon, but that had ended within a few hours. It was little more than a skirmish.

She glanced at her pocket watch. 2:30 am.

"What's going on?" Betsy sat up and rubbed her eyes.

Bugles sounding in the middle of the night could only mean one thing. "The battle's begun," Lavena whispered, almost afraid to say it out loud.

Hurriedly, they both dressed. Betsy headed to the hospital, and Lavena rushed to the field.

A scurry of activity. Soldiers dashed to get in line. Thousands stood at attention, a field of men standing rigid in blue uniforms, as if a forest with a new kind of tree had grown during the night. Each tree carried its fruit – a rifle with a bayonet and a knapsack. Torchbearers stood in from illuminating the brigade.

A few stragglers joined the blue forest as every regiment lined up waiting for orders. Lavena searched for familiar faces from the Ohio Seventh, but there were too many of them. She couldn't find Cage. If he marched into battle and something happened to him before she made things right, she'd never forgive herself.

Colonel Creighton sat on a gray stallion in front of the men. He carried a brigade banner instead of the Ohio Seventh's blue eagle. She'd heard he'd been put in charge of the entire first brigade of the Twelfth Army Corp.

If this was the first brigade, the Ohio Seventh had to be somewhere nearby. She searched for the blue eagle flag.

Her heartbeat raced faster than the train that brought them to Tennessee. She had to find him before they marched away.

Another bugle call sounded, and the soldiers of the first brigade marched toward the mountain. She ran alongside them hoping to catch a glimpse of Cage. She saw Lieutenant-Colonel Crane up ahead. She caught up with them just as Ohio Seventh passed by. "Cage."

He glanced toward her for only a moment, pressed his lips together, then stared straight ahead.

She wanted to run toward him, but she couldn't. He needed to focus on the battle at hand and on keeping his men safe or he wouldn't make it back. She felt a little sick. If that happened, he'd never know how she felt.

Men marched past her toward the river. Sergeant Garrett marched on with a scowl on his face, the same look he often delivered her way. Corporal Jake nodded slightly as he passed. Private Amon's composure was different than the young man she knew. Somehow, he looked older, more confident.

All these men on their way to battle. She watched, stunned at the sight. She might never see some of them again. She might never see Cage again.

Regiments marched through the gap toward Lookout Mountain. The sound of shuffling feet in the mud made a slushing sound that rumbled. She wiped her tears and got in line behind the regiment. Even if she wasn't working for the newspaper, she had a job to do.

The men stopped at the train tracks, and Lavena rushed toward them to see what caused the delay. The bridge over Lookout Creek had flooded, and the men struggled to cross the creek. It delayed them for a couple of hours.

By the time they made it over, the sun was cresting over the mountains. As they trudged into the fog at the base of Lookout Mountain, Lavena trailed behind, her lap-desk in tow. No matter how her heart was breaking, she needed to observe and report on the battle.

*****

Amon climbed holding onto the trees, planting his feet on rocks and in mud. He was almost to the top of Lookout Mountain and only had to fire his rifle twice. The rebels didn't seem to have the will to stand their ground and fight. They retreated faster than he could climb.

He wished he could have received a reply from Emma before this battle started. It would be easier knowing even if she did decide to give him the mitten. All he could do was trust God. He needed to keep himself from being distracted.

Struggling to get his footing, he slid down a bank. He snatched at a branch of a maple tree to keep himself from tumbling over the edge.

*****

Lavena drew closer to get a better view, but a fog shrouded the mountain. She made her way around the base of the mountain toward Chattanooga trying to see what was happening and got there by daybreak. Barely allowing herself to breathe, she squinted through the mist.

Cannons boomed and rifles fired. A fireworks display rivalling the one she'd seen in Public Square on the Fourth of July burst in the sky. She stepped back, afraid for a moment the cannon balls might reach her, and watched the battle above the clouds.

The first blue uniform appeared above the fog, then another. Soon, half-way up the mountain, men in blue chased graybacks. A Union soldier lost his footing and grasped for a tree limb. She swallowed the knot in her throat. The man plunged to the ground below with a thud.

She ran to the soldier, Corporal Jake Edwards. He groaned. Taking hold of his hand, she stayed with him. "I'm here."

He tried to speak, but she could barely hear him, so she leaned closer. "Tell my… my wife... love her."

Tears filled her eyes. "I will. I promise." A few moments later, he was gone.

Sitting beside his dead body, she listened to the booms above her, but felt no compulsion to move. The grief she felt from this young man's death threatened to choke her. No wonder Private Amon had such a hard time seeing his friends die.

She wasn't sure where she should go. The safe place would be to go back to camp and wait for the men to return, but she hadn't come here to remain safe. These brave men were risking their lives, and she wasn't about to shirk her duty. She needed to observe and report.

But report to whom.

A thought struck, and she picked up her skirts and ran to Colonel Creighton's cabin. There was a telegraph there. She would let Mr. O'Brady and Mr. Cowles know about the battle. Since her replacement hadn't arrived yet, they might want her accounts.

She sat at the desk and tapped out the dots and dashes on the telegraph in one of the longest telegrams she'd ever sent. When she finished telling them everything she could think of, she tapped her fingers on the table. If only they'd still agree to let her tell them about the battle. Hopefully this wouldn't take too long.

A few minutes later, the telegraph started sounding. She dipped her pen in ink and wrote out the message.

Need you to report. Stop. Don't let us down. Stop. You have a job here for as long as you want it. O'Brady.

She tapped the message was received and let out a sigh of relief. Even though she had been prideful throughout this assignment, God was still allowing her to fulfill His call on her life. She rushed back to where she could see the battle and wrote notes in shorthand.

After spending the day writing notes and recording the events, she took a gulp of water from her canteen. It went down as smoothly as a cup of fine tea. She pulled out some hardtack she'd though to place in her lapdesk. It satisfied her hunger pain for now.

She continued on, observing and reporting.

*****

By midday, the rebels were on the run. Cage heard a cheer as the Star and Stripes was raised on Lookout Point. His shoulders relaxed as he checked on his soldiers. Only one dead, none wounded.

He led his men on, chasing the rebels. The thick fog grew murky as the sun went down, and he lost sight of General Geary. All he could do was trust Lieutenant-Colonel Crane was leading them the right way. Up ahead, a glimpse of Colonel Creighton on horseback inspired confidence.

Sometime after sunset, Colonel Creighton ordered them to stand down, and they made camp in a peach orchard at the base of the mountain. Cage's stomach roiled. If only there were still peaches on the trees.

He tried to sleep, but he couldn't. Even though the gun and cannon fire had stopped, his turbulent thoughts wouldn't rest. Most of the Confederate soldiers had surrendered or retreated before they could be captured or killed. The Ohio Seventh had only lost one man.

His throat grew dry. Any man killed under his command was a tragic loss, but Corporal Jake having his life snuffed out hit him especially hard. It seemed worse because he hadn't been shot or stabbed. He died from falling off the mountain.

It wasn't over yet. He would do everything in his power to make sure nobody else was lost. He groaned knowing it wasn't in his control.

All he could do was pray.

*****

Soldiers in gray were running away from the mountain. They all passed Lavena, but none of them bothered to look her way. It looked as if the Union Army had soundly defeated them. The battle for the mountain would be over by tomorrow.

Wiping mud from her face, she traipsed toward General Grant's headquarters. It would be a good location to observe the battle at Missionary Ridge, and they would have a telegraph where she could give updates. She had a lot of them.

A full moon lit the night. A few men in gray came off the mountain and darted past her, but they didn't seem to notice she was there. Even though no Union soldiers chased after them, they seemed to be in a hurry to escape.

The firing of rifles and cannons had stopped, and both sides had, in one accord had apparently, decided to get a good night's sleep. Tomorrow they could start killing each other again.

She reached General Grant's headquarters late into the night. It was a white two-story farmhouse with a porch and a balcony both held up by ornate posts. A couple of soldiers sat by a watch fire nearby, but nobody guarded the house.

She stepped to the fire. "Is there some way I could see General Grant?"

One of the soldiers, a tall man who needed a shave, answered. "He's not there. His new headquarters is at Orchard Knob."

"Orchard Knob is at the base of Missionary Ridge. Isn't it still in the hands of the rebels?"

The other man, slightly shorter with a stocky build, answered. "Not any more. General Grant and some of his men took it two days ago."

So, the skirmish the day before the battle. She made a mental note to find out about the Battle of Orchard Knob later.

"We're waiting on orders for an attack on Missionary Ridge," the taller soldier said.

Lavena crossed her arms. "Do you go around telling anyone who passes by the general's battle plans?" She realized how hypocritical she was being considering she had been the one who warned the Confederate Army Nate was a spy.

The shorter soldier flushed. "Of course not. You're Miss Falcon, the reporter, aren't you?"

Lavena nodded.

"Well, the general said to tell you anything you want to know."

She leaned against the porch post. Why would he that? Last she'd heard, Colonel Creighton wanted to meet with her, no doubt to send her packing. Only the battle delayed his orders concerning her. "Do you think it would be all right if I slept in the general's house tonight?"

"I don't see why not," the tall man said. "Since he took off, it's been deserted."

Lavena entered the house. A drowsiness tried to overtake her, but she resisted. She needed to make her reports before she lay down on the settee in the parlor to sleep. She telegraphed everything she knew about the battle above the clouds and Orchard Knob with a promise of more to come.

Finally, she allowed herself to relax, but as tired as she was, sleep alluded. She couldn't stop thinking about Corporal Jake and the others who would die before the Battle for Chattanooga ended.

Cage might be one of them. If only she could have talked to him before he left.

Chapter Fifty-One

November 25th

Lavena woke up late the next morning to the sound of gunfire. It took a moment to remember where she was before she rushed outside to see what was happening. Sights, sounds, smells. She noted them so she could describe them later when she wrote her story.

The only word that fit what was happening was pandemonium. Sparks and smoke were rising above the fog on Missionary Ridge. Above the sound of the cannon fire, trumpets were blaring and drums were pounding.

Troops surged everywhere as rivers of blue diverted to the northern and middle sections of Missionary Ridge. Another river flowed from Lookout Mountain to the south toward Rossville Gap.

As she sat and watched on the front porch of General Grant's Chattanooga Headquarters, the Battle of Missionary Ridge took place. Cage was out there somewhere. She wrote her down her impressions that she would later use for the stories she would send *The Cleveland Leader*. She could hardly believe they hired her again.

She couldn't have found a better location to watch what was going on around her. Not only was it a good vantage point, but men passing by gave her updates. When she did go inside, she would eat hardtack and fix herself a cup of tea, and telegraph updates. Then she would head back outside.

Many times, civilians thought of a battle as one group of soldiers fighting another group. She'd had the same mistaken impression, but so much more happened that it was sometimes hard to keep up with all of it.

Next door, an army hospital stood, and stretchers with wounded men kept passing by. Soon, there wasn't enough room in the hospital, and soldiers lined up on the front lawn outside waiting to be treated.

Betsy was there among the nurses treating the wounded. Somehow having her friend nearby helped even though neither of them would have time to visit.

She walked over to where Betsy stood outside bandaging a man's head. "It's good to see you. How's Nate?"

Betsy didn't look up from what she was doing. "Nate's fine. These men need me more at the moment."

"Where are all these wounded coming from?"

"The North Ridge." Betsy finished with the bandage and knelt down by the next soldier who lay there without moving. She covered his face with a blanket.

Someone pulled on her skirt. "Nurse, could I have a drink of water?"

Lavena recognized the voice and turned.

"Jed."

He squinted his eyes. "Lavena?" It came out raspy.

"Are you all right? I heard you were a prisoner."

Jed put his hand over a bloody bandage wrapped around his middle. "I escaped when the shooting started."

"What happened?"

"Just a graze," Jed said. "As long as infection doesn't set in..." He had a coughing fit and Betsy gave him a sip of water. "I'll be fine."

Thank God.

"Soldier, if you want to get better, you need to rest," Betsy said.

Jed nodded, lay back on the cold ground, and closed his eyes.

Betsy wiped her brow and stepped to the next soldier. "So many of them. We can't even fit them in the hospital."

Lavena set her hand on Betsy's shoulder and squeezed.

Betsy nodded, and Lavena walked back into the house. She sent a telegraph to expect heavy casualties from the North Ridge. She thanked God the Ohio Seventh wasn't there, but she wasn't sure where they were. She'd lost track of them.

It would have felt better if she knew what was happening to them.

*****

November 26th

A flood of soldiers passed by the house, and it looked like the battle was over. The Union Army had won, but so many casualties on both sides. She managed to get a major to stop and give her a report.

According to him, they were only supposed to go to the base of the ridge, but somehow in the confusion, the men kept climbing until they'd reached the top and thwarted Bragg's men before General Grant could figure out who'd given the order.

Although the general was angry at first, he calmed down when he saw how successful the unorganized attack had been. Some of the men were calling it a miracle.

"Have you seen the Ohio Seventh?" she asked the major.

"They were ordered to Pigeon Mountain."

Lavena's heart skipped a beat. So, it wasn't over yet. The tightness in her stomach wouldn't lessen until she could see Cage and his men safely back in camp.

As a reporter, there was nothing more she could do at this point. A casualty list would be given to her in a day or two. She walked over to the hospital and found Betsy. "How can I help?"

*****

November 27th

Amon tried not to think about what had happened the last few days. Two battles won with only one man from the Ohio Seventh being killed. Corporal Jake Edwards. Another friend.

The smoke from the burning trains and supplies made him cough. In their hurry to leave, the rebels burned everything they could, but they hadn't managed to dispose of all of it. Cannons and caissons filled with ammunition were left behind on broken wagons along the path. The tents and camp gear left behind made it seem almost like an eerie ghost town.

Since then, they'd chased the rebs here, to Ringgold Gap.

The night before, Amon hadn't been able to sleep, so he'd stayed awake looking at the stars, and praying he didn't have to say good-bye to another friend.

Now, here he was chasing the rebels into the ravine.

Bullets exploded as from either side of the gap. He dashed for cover. The enemy had set up an ambush.

Colonel Creighton let out a rooster call and led the men to the left side, away from the barrage. Amon sprinted through the gunfire into the ravine where Captain Cage was headed. Private John fell at his side. He jumped over him and kept running.

The rebs opened up with a firestorm that made the earlier barrage seem like a church picnic. Up ahead, a bullet caught Colonel Creighton. Crane let out a yell and rushed toward him. He jerked and fell on top of the colonel.

Mayhem broke out. Nobody knew where to go to get away from the onslaught of bullets.

Cage jumped up and let out the rooster crow. "Hurry, men. Don't slow down. We need to get through to the other side." He climbed on top of a rock and motioned them ahead.

Other men fell near Amon, but he kept moving. The sounds become muffled. After the blasting of cannons and rifles near him, his hearing would become numb for days.

"Keep going," the captain shouted. "You're almost…" A cannon sounded, and Cage dived onto some of the men to shield them.

Amon wanted to stop, but he couldn't. They had to get to the other side of the ravine, or they'd all suffer the same fate.

Chapter Fifty-Two

December 2nd

A bugle call sounded. Lavena startled awake. The sun hadn't risen yet, and she lit the candle on the table beside her bed. They'd made it back to their cabin at Racoon Mountain a couple of days earlier.

The bugle sounded every time more wounded came into camp. At least it gave Lavena something to concentrate on to keep her from worrying about Cage and the Ohio Seventh.

Betsy groaned from the other cot. "Not again."

"Maybe it's the Seventh this time." A surge of hope went through her even though she tried to tamp it down. She'd told herself the same thing every time. She quickly braided her hair and dashed outside before Betsy could catch up with her.

The men marched into camp with slumped shoulders. Lavena could barely make out their mud-covered features. Some of the uniforms had blood splattered on them. Her chest tightened. Many of the men carried stretchers.

She ran into the crowd and tried to skirt by a cluster of dead soldiers. Private Amon carried one of the stretchers. So, it was the Seventh.

"Wait, Private Amon." She ran to catch up with him. "Have you seen Captain Cage?"

A muscle in Amon's jaw twitched. "I lost sight of him after…"

A lump caught in Lavena's throat. "After what?"

"There was so much smoke in the air. I saw him dive into a group of men and knock them to the ground right before a cannonball exploded."

"Did it… Was he hit?"

Amon's voice barely squeaked out. "I don't know."

Lavena checked as each stretcher passed. She couldn't bring herself to check the men who were completely covered. She'd find out soon enough if he was dead. So many men wounded.

There was a pause in men arriving, but more stretchers headed their way. She couldn't wait for them to reach her, so she took off running toward them. The first few men were covered. This time she did uncover the first man's face. Her hand trembled. Colonel William Creighton.

Another stretcher passed, and a man groaned. She turned toward the sound. Cage. It was Cage. He was alive.

He groaned again. The blanket covering him was soaked with blood. She uncovered his upper body tried to squelch the panic rising inside of her. His shoulder had so much blood on it, and there was an ugly gash on his head. No. "Cage." He didn't answer. She wasn't sure if he heard her or not.

She turned to the men carrying the stretcher. "Can't you go any faster."

One of the men, a corporal, gave her a weary look. "Ma'am, we've just been through a war and then marched for two days to get here. We're doing the best we can."

She flushed. "Of course you have. I'm sorry." She stepped to the end of the stretcher. "Let me take over from here."

The corporal pressed his lips together then nodded his head.

Picking up the end of the stretcher, she headed to the hospital. "It's all right, Cage. You're going to be all right."

His only response was a groan.

She understood now why the men were going so slow. The stretcher was heavier than she expected. She repeated her soothing words over and over as they marched, but he didn't seem as if her heard. Finally, they reached the hospital. "Orderly, over here. Orderly."

She followed them into a two-story house where they'd set up to treat the wounded. There were so many of them. Dr. Patella ordered one of the men to go to the hospital in Chattanooga and bring doctors and nurses. He and Betsy went through the ranks and ordered men concerning each patient. Some were taken upstairs. Others were moved to the adjoining room. A few were covered up and taken outside.

Lavena grabbed a basin of water, tore off the edge of her skirt, and stroked Cage's head with it. Tears filled her eyes. "Everything will be all right. I'm here."

Except for an occasional groan, Cage didn't respond.

So many wounded men. It was taking too long.

They finally reached Cage. Dr. Patella examined his head and shoulder and ordered him upstairs.

"But, wait..." Lavena said. "Aren't you at least going to bandage him?"

Betsy put her hand around Lavena's waist and escorted her to the stairs. "We have others to attend to first. Those not as badly wounded are being taken upstairs. There are bandages up there. You know what to do to treat him."

Lavena followed Cage's stretcher up the stairs and got the bandages. A lump formed in her throat as she cut away his shirt. The only comfort she had was knowing the men upstairs were not in immediate danger. Both Nate and Jed were there.

Still, there was no guarantee Cage would be all right or that any of them would. Infection had killed more men then their wounds. It would be at least two weeks before they knew who would make it and who would die. She finished bandaging him.

Screams filled the air from the first floor. They'd started the amputations.

A tear rolled down Lavena's cheek. If only she hadn't been so prideful. If only she had extended the forgiveness she'd been freely given.

Cage opened his eyes. "Lavena?"

She placed her hand over her mouth. "Thank God."

"The last thing I remember was…" Cage drew his hand to his head. "What happened? How many did we lose?"

She held his hand. "All that can wait until you're better."

Cage gingerly touched the gash on his head. He rolled his shoulder around and touched the bandage then tried to rise but couldn't quite manage it. "Nothing seems to be broken. I'll be fine once I rest a little."

"I know." Lavena blinked to hold back the tears.

"Would you... Would you stay here for a little while?"

"Oh, Cage." The tears fell unabated. "I'm so sorry for the way I acted. I love you. Will you forgive me?"

"Of course, I forgive you." He tried to sit up, but after a moment, he gave up and leaned back on the stretcher. "Does this mean you forgive me?"

She nodded, tears now flowing freely.

"Could you lean down a little closer?"

Lavena moved closer to hear what he wanted.

"I love you so much." Cage turned her face toward his, placed his hand on her neck, and kissed her, gently at first, then with more passion than she'd ever known.

Everything around her disappeared, and she felt safe and loved. Overwhelmed she pulled back a little. "I love you too. More than I could ever say," she said breathlessly. She touched his cheek and slid her finger across the scar on his face, the scar from when he risked his life to save that woman and her children. Why couldn't she see it before?

Cage put his hand over hers. "Marry me."

Lavena took hold of his hand. God had brought him back to her despite her stubborn pride. "Yes, I'll marry you, but...

He leaned on his left side, grimaced, and pushed himself up to a sitting position. Perspiration beaded his forehead. "But what?"

She smiled and kissed him on the cheek. "I can't wait to marry you, but please, you need your rest."

Cage's brow furrowed. "But what?"

She gently pushed on his chest to get him to lay back down. He finally did. How could she say this without hurting him? "I'll marry you tomorrow if you want me to. I love you, and I want to spend the rest of my life with you."

He grabbed his ear. "But what?"

"It's just this romance of ours has been a whirlwind." She realized she was still holding his hand, and she squeezed it now. "We've both done some things we regret, and we still don't know what is going to come of it. We need to take our time to make sure we have a firm foundation, don't you think?"

A slow smile crept across his mouth. "Depends. How long?"

"I'll marry you the day this war ends. I love you."

"I love you too." He wrapped his good arm around her and kissed her.

She leaned into the kiss, wondering if she really could wait until the end of the war to become his wife. Did she even want to?

The kiss grew softer and then stopped. She raised up. He had his eyes closed. She stroked his head as he slept. She'd be there for him when he woke and for the rest of their lives.

*****

Amon visited Chaplain Jed in the hospital. It had been a week since the battle, but God had given him peace about the men who'd died. He still grieved for them, but it wasn't like it had been before.

Jed was awake and seemed to be recovering.

He sat by the chaplain's side. "So, when you were captured, was all of the mail lost?"

Jed rubbed his temples "I don't know." He sounded weak. "At least some of it was. If there was any left behind, the Union Army would have mailed it. Why?"

Amon shrugged. "The letters I wrote to Mr. Brown and to Emma telling them what I did were in there."

"Oh." Jed sat up and placed a hand on Amon's shoulders. "All we can do is leave it in God's hands. Our three-year enlistment is up in April. If she doesn't get the letter by then, you can tell her in person."

Amon nodded. He would trust God with it. Either way, he would tell her the truth, and he knew she would forgive him. Now that he had given himself to God, he would spend the rest of his life being the godly husband she wanted him to be.

Chapter Fifty-Three

Lavena had not left Cage's side since he'd come back. She'd brought her lap-desk to the hospital and wrote her articles while he slept.

She'd found out why it was so easy to get reports during the battles. The publisher of *The Cleveland Leader*, Mr. Cowles, had contacted General Grant shortly before the Battle for Orchard Knob had begun.

Since the newspaper had no way of getting a man down here before the battles, Mr. Cowles asked the general to overlook her transgressions. They were giving her back her job so she could send them the reports they needed from the battlefield. General Grant had agreed, and Colonel Creighton had planned to tell her when they met the next day. The battles began before he had a chance.

A twinge of guilt went through her. What she had done had cost Nate his leg. She knew God had forgiven her, but she was still having a hard time accepting the pain she'd caused. Before Nate and Betsy left for another hospital closer to Ohio a few days earlier, they'd both forgiven her. She missed Betsy so much.

Cage sat up and winced. His head was better, but his shoulder still bothered him. They had to put thirty stitches in it. "So, what are you writing about now?"

"I finished my story about you."

Cage's Adam's apple bulged. "May I see it?"

She handed it to him. He read it, his brow furrowed.

When he got to the end, he shook his head and handed it back to her. "I don't know how you did it, but you told the truth and still made me look like a hero. I'm not sure I can live up to your glowing report of me, but I'll spend the rest of my life trying."

She smiled and kissed him on the cheek. "As you said, I told the truth."

*****

Cage winced as he pulled his uniform over his injured shoulder. It had been two weeks since the battle, and he was on the mend even if he wasn't back to duty yet. There was no way he would miss the memorial service for his fallen comrades.

Almost every officer in the Ohio Seventh including his commanders, Colonel Creighton and Lieutenant-Colonel Crane had been killed at Rossville Gap, and he grieved for all of them. He was one of only a few officers who'd survived.

Almost everyone in his company was dead or wounded. Amon had gotten through it untouched, and Sergeant Garrett was still alive, but so many others weren't.

They still didn't know if Jed would make it back home to help his orphaned brothers. He'd seemed to be recovering at first, but he'd taken a turn for the worse. Dr. Patella was unsure if he'd pull through.

Cage prayed Jed's brothers wouldn't have to grieve the loss of their oldest brother as well as the rest of their family.

He stepped outside his tent and found Lavena waiting for him. She'd wanted to accompany him to the memorial General Geary would give. He didn't deserve a woman like her, but the verse Jed had preached that day in the field was true. He who confesses his sin shall find grace.

The sun shone bright on the mountains, and they had a bluish cast over them. Over the last week, the rain had stopped, and the ground had dried up. Even though winter was approaching, it felt more like Spring. He could even hear birds singing.

He took hold of Lavena's hand, and they headed to the field in Rossville Gap where the men were buried.

General Geary met them there. "Captain Cage."

Cage saluted and winced. It wasn't the first time he'd wished it had been his left shoulder that had been wounded.

"At ease, Captain."

"General Geary, I'm glad we have a chance to talk before the service. Did Colonel Creighton tell you what I informed him of before he died?"

"You mean about starting that fire and lying about it and about letting one of your soldiers off because he was blackmailing you? Or do you mean how you allowed a reporter to find out military secrets without informing your commanding officer?" The general stroked his jaw. "He told me everything."

"Yes, Sir." Cage came back to attention. "I'm ready to face whatever I have coming, but I'd like to know what you've decided. Miss Falcon has agreed to be my wife, and I don't want this hanging over us."

"You present a problem, Captain Cage." General Geary rubbed his chin. "I could mete out punishment and take your medal away, but I don't see the point when I'd have to recommend you for the same medal again for your bravery at Rossville Gap."

"I didn't do anything. Those brave men who died deserve the medal more than I do."

"Trust me, they will be honored, but most of the men in your regiment told me you're the reason they're still alive. Something about climbing on a rock and shouting orders for them to move out of the line of fire then throwing yourself on some of your men to save them from a cannonball."

Cage flushed. "They're exaggerating."

"Why don't you keep your medal," General Geary said. "It'll save me a lot of paperwork getting you another one."

"Yes, Sir."

Lavena smiled. "I always knew you were a hero."

Cage shook his head. "No, I'm not. We're all capable of doing heroic acts and of sinning greatly. I'm just grateful God was there to help me keep my men safe and to forgive me when I failed Him."

They walked hand in hand to the memorial, and Cage thanked God they would continue to walk in love and forgiveness for the rest of their lives.

The End

About the Author

Tamera Lynn Kraft has always loved adventures. She loves to write historical fiction set in the United States because there are so many stories in American history. There are strong elements of faith, romance, suspense and adventure in her stories. She has received 2nd place in the NOCW contest, 3rd place TARA writer's contest, and is a finalist in the Frasier Writing Contest.

Tamera been married for forty years to the love of her life, Rick, and has two married adult children and three grandchildren. She has been a children's pastor for over twenty years. She is the leader of a ministry called Revival Fire for Kids where she mentors other children's leaders, teaches workshops, and is a children's ministry consultant and children's evangelist and has written children's church curriculum. She is a recipient of the 2007 National Children's Leaders Association Shepherd's Cup for lifetime achievement in children's ministry.

You can contact Tamera online at her website: *http://tameralynnkraft.net*